FANG

VOLUME 10

Edited by Sparf and Kyell Gold

Bad Dog Books

2019

FANG Volume 10
First publication 2019

Edited by Sparf and Kyell Gold

Cover by Donryu

Published by Bad Dog Books
www.BadDogBooks.com

An imprint of FurPlanet Productions
www.FurPlanet.com
Dallas, TX

TABLE OF CONTENTS

FOREWORD

FOREWORD BY KYELL GOLD

I still remember Alex Vance announcing FANG back in 2004 or so, adding a market for short adult fiction to Sofawolf Press's Heat (which debuted that year). At the time, furry publications came and went; Sofawolf Press was only in its fifth year and FurPlanet's emergence onto the scene was a few years away. Certainly we all hoped that fifteen years down the line, our publications would still be going strong, but I don't think any of us at the time would have believed, outside of our dreams, how exciting and expansive the world of furry fiction would become.

In recent years, FANG's editorial control has changed paws from Alex's capable stewardship, most recently brought to you by Ashe Valisca, who oversaw FANGs 5–9. Regrettably, he had to step aside to focus on other matters, and I was delighted to volunteer to guest edit the tenth volume of FANG alongside Sparf, who will be taking the reins (or the leash, if you prefer) for future volumes. Years ago, I was thrilled to have a story of mine appear in the first volume of FANG; it is my very great pleasure to be part of the continuing tradition of FANG now on the editorial side, and to present to you this new collection of excellent furry gay male stories.

FOREWORD BY SPARF

It's never easy taking on the mantle of a long-standing institution, and at ten volumes, FANG is most certainly that. FANG wasn't my first publication, but the stories I have had within its pages are among my favorites.

As the fandom has grown, and the writing community within it has expanded, formed communities and even workshops, the quality of the tales we tell has also increased. This year's selection of stories by a most skilled set of writers is just the latest in a long tradition. The theme of this year's FANG is Transitions. A shift in editorship brings a change in style. It brings new ideas, and new methods. But what it maintains is a commitment to quality writing. I can only hope to maintain the high standard set by my predecessor, Ashe, going forward.

Many thanks to Kyell for being my partner through my first editorial position. His help was invaluable. Now, without further rambling on my part, please enjoy this volume of FANG.

WATERS

Slip-Wolf

He feels sentimental for experiences that aren't over yet, but he's not me. My pelt is the brown of a creek bed after a rain. My eyes are obsidian chips hammered from the rock of a volcano gone cold. My tail is a brush of salt and pepper, short for a shepherd but thicker. He's not me, never could be. His white muzzle curls into his white haunches when the muskrat cries, the spots dapple as the sobbing quakes him. He refuses to see why I can't stay.

Refuses to go.

For the past week I've walked through the places I've been over and over for the past ten years, feeling the dull ache of knowing I won't see them again as I leave. That wickersheened coffee place, that drab laundromat with its candy machine's gum balls pastel faded. The port now sits on taller stilts, where they prep those set to depart. Entropy works faster in some places than others.

Why won't he come with me? Oh right. He isn't me. He runs from the first rain, not towards it. Life is learning to swim, always grabbing hold after you have to let go. The selfish try to do both and fail. So, he tucks his tail and holds his sobs till he thinks I'm asleep. Peace never comes.

If he could just have the strength to let go. But he's not me.

A long road brought us here. I can't breathe when I think of what I'm losing. So I don't. A whole life sprawls between here and the city. Past loves, nickers under oak bleachers, days at the lake with the fur warming under the sun's massage. My orange coupe with its cheeseburger sheen, purring up the strip on a Saturnine night. This is all gone and only the memories will remain. He'll have to settle with only the memories too, but he's not me.

And what memories we've made.

I remember the last time his apartment AC failed. We were back

11

to nature, one panting strip of clothing at a time. Windows open at the right time catch a breeze from the East, teasing the right hairs. I watch them stir his fur, that wind from eddies as far out as the ocean a hundred miles away. They came all the way here to this eighth-floor sun-baked hovel just to tickle his balls, tease a smile through chapped lips and pull his soft grey eyes to my relentless flints.

I want it too, now as then as always.

My cock brings the blessings in, parting his warmth; my paw takes hold of him. His glee is a sigh through teeth and precious. A languid fuck threads us through the bearable part of the day when the sun finds a cloud and the television is mutely showing music videos where insta-grammable club-crawl highlife moments pass again and again unlived by anyone real.

His eyes are on them and my eyes are on him, the space between his ears, the hackles that rise on static as I fuck and stroke him. He and I are the perfect engine, soaked in lovely silence, not a scratch or mutter from the adjoining world. I bring him to fulfilment first, cock behind, paw up front. He shivers around me and that does it for me. It's over too fast but I'm heady as my breath fogs his neck, my seed roils his depths. I don't let go for an hour, long after the knot surrenders. His grip on my forearm is all the poetry I need. We're one.

For the last time.

A part of us will remember this moment when we remember the best of what we had together, ignorant in the moment that it would be our pinnacle, our summit. There are others I'm sure, the first "I love you" and the vacation to the coast we went on together, but they don't hold sense memory as well. Memories that stake the deepest are greedy, leave less room for others that could make the cut. Fair enough. All we can ask for is the chance to form new ones.

We could have had an uncertain future of stolen moments together, perhaps much more. But we'll never know now. When the time came to let go, he couldn't. Because he isn't me.

The shelf cracked in September of last year, the water came up to the ankles of many nations. Whispers became shouts that the methane is free. The bees are now gone. Islands far north became ghost towns, empty as unfinished thoughts.

Refugees from every direction to every other direction under the shadows of chain link, high walls, deepening rivers. Discarded posses-sions rot and rust in the sun. We've been told to prepare, him and I, by friends close and influencers distant. No time for recriminations now. No point anyway. Billions of feet are wet every day. Fur burns on legions of heads and shoulders.

Our coffee shops and our laundromats and our bleached strip malls of rib-white shelves. Less and less comes in or goes out. My car sells cheap to someone who thinks they can find gas. We lived in the center of the universe until we didn't.

He mutters that he's with me and I don't read the signs right as he disappears for longer and longer stints into the places where he's made his life with and before me. He should have made himself resolute, seen the writing on the wall, gotten started with all we had to finish. But he's not me.

I remember sorting through his kitchen, looking for things he could discard or sell. I ask about the long elastic I find in the pantry, one of countless items to inventory. He's quick to change jobs with me, quick to get me folding clothes instead. I don't think too much about it, already perturbed at how much he's dragging his feet.

Millions making the same arrangements can crowd the exits pretty quick. The way out is available for those who know the right people. I've family who own land and have the means to sponsor us. The means to get ourselves there are fraught with complications I've had to negotiate. Forms that will never be processed turn to maps, turn to reading up on border guard interactions.

He wants a different kind of escape, so we go for long walks that are eerily quiet, punctuated by too few sirens, too few mutters. The arcade is open and we're after the high score we gave up on when we were kids, before we had feelings for each other. Nobody held me and stroked my back while I chased 2-D invaders back then. Nobody clutched me like I might blow away. I do the same when he plays, and I know he doesn't really care about the game on the flickering cathode ray bubble in the tall colorful cabinet. He leans into my warmth and is happy at what we can both forget.

The waters make us remember, weathering us forward.

The street is a lagoon, my friends have mostly gone and the flatbeds moving by have furniture crammed like firewood, charcoal stinking barbecues, dull glass globes with faded gum balls. As dusk comes, I go to his empty apartment with my second key and gaze down at the discarded trash and broken syringes that litter the alley where we first made out when he took me home. I can't reminisce with him. He's nowhere

13

to be found.

When I see him, he's haggard, eyes glazing, white fingers clutching his tail like something burned it. He talks about the movie theatre where we had our first date. They're still showing movies now, we can go there. So, we go.

They have juniper and pine scents hanging in the auditorium, around the oversalted popcorn machine. It's to cover up the stink of the rotting first four rows of chairs that are inching under the flood. Nothing electrical exists below the second-floor projector booth. Nothing will again. They'll either seal the exits up and pump the place out, or close it down when the line reaches the screen. Will have to decide soon. In the dark nobody decides anything. We've escaped ourselves for now.

I don't watch the film, just its reflection in the water between dark chair backs beneath and count the spaces between the moments in which my lover trembles. His heartbeat is irregular and panicked. By the end so is mine and my fur is on end. We have to go, and soon. I know what's coming, but what's coming that I don't?

For hours a day several inches of our world are under wooden planks. For entire days he's under a murk of a different kind. He's done nothing to prepare, it's been all me and I catch myself looking down to the alley off his balcony, wondering why whoever was shooting up down there took the time to break every syringe.

I ask him who he sees lurking in his alley at night, in a place that is emptying of souls day by day, and he changes the subject with a kiss. He's in need. I'm no less. It's too hot but we don't care.

Clothes molt. Breath quickens. Our noses hunt out each other's scent points, his between my ears, mine down low. It's been awhile and it's time to make another memory. His cock is ripe with the night tucked away with it and his pelt slides on the slick laminate as we settle low. My tongue winds his climbing cock and the sensations settle into the familiar world. Scents upon tastes upon scents. Soda spills are seeped into his carpet next to my nose from years ago. The souring of takeout noodles trace back to the kitchen from yesterday. I've got my mouth around him, nose loading with the eddy of him only when he starts to flag. As his cock goes softer, I feel the sob before I hear it.

Up at his side quickly, I'm confused. I don't ask, I just let him find the words.

"Why do we have to leave?" There's a desperation and a plea that comes from a crack in somewhere deep. I see his eyes have gotten wet.

I ask him what he means. The sexual haze has the failure of this moment miles and miles away. I can't put what he's said together.

"Why do we have to follow everybody and run away from here?"

As bald and straightforward the question, I need a moment to fully encompass this. In answer to the only question I haven't yet mustered, he spreads his hot bare white pelted arms. "All this is all we've ever had. Our whole lives. I don't wanna go."

I blink and the sex has evaporated. It takes a minute to marshal the common sense I thought we both had. It's impossible to explain this without seeming to lecture a child. Our whole lives are here, yes. But our future can't be. The only ones staying are those who haven't the means to go.

He needs to understand that. He should have already long ago understood that. He closes his eyes and squeezes out the tears. He won't hear me, doesn't want to. Can't.

My confusion and my disappointment find themselves in the hard-edged box of disgust, the only frame that can contain everything that's hitting me now. All his quiet reticence. His acquiescence to every decision without the firmness of commitment. The preparation has been all me because it is only all me. Six months, racing towards inevitability. And a treacherous foot on the brake.

This is the next chapter we were both meant to face courageously. But he's not me.

We have to do this. There's no other way.

No, we don't, he insists. We can make it if we stay.

Supplies are dwindling because they can't make it here and there are too few places left for anything to make it to.

"I can't go," he says.

It's us or this. I can't stay. We can't have a life here.

On the cusp of another plea, I storm out to his patio. The furniture is already shoved aside. Something we can't take. Or I can't take. I stare at the abstract art of plaster crumbling from brick's bones leaving vast maps of grey and wonder how many times my muskrat has gazed at this mess of geometry and burned its changes into his mind. His life is as tied to this small place as mine is. Or was. Every street corner and lot and bodega and trodden-down garden was a font of memories. Friends and enemies, joys and regrets.

If I lean out far enough, I can just see past the alley's mouth to the park where we told each other most of our secrets, huddling and giggling in the dark, weeks before we were into each other enough to learn that I lived downtown and he lived right here.

That park is gone already, just a few hedge lines breaking a darkening mirror to the sky as dusk is taking the day away. I can't see our bench of confessions, but I can imagine just two planks left above the creeping brine.

I turn back and I see him staring out at me, crying slow but steadily, sounds buried behind glass. He's watching me watch our world, hoping I'll cave to what this loss means. He's memorizing every move I make out here, watching intently as though he's terrified for me to leave his sight. As though I can only exist while he sees me.

I'm ready to go back in, to face him with ultimatum at the ready, but my toe brushes something between the steel deck slats. In the weak bug-nested light of the patio I can see it's a plastic cap on a plunger and I lean down to pick it up. The downward facing needle on the syringe has a wicked gleam. Confused, I glance back in and see his widening gaze of shock. And shame.

Down below are the shattered remains of countless vials just like this one.

The truth settles on my heart like a vandal.

I've got the emptied vial in my fingers and curses on my lips when I come back in. The growling back and forth is accusatory and defensive and furious soon enough. He's folding his arms as he denies things, shaking his muzzle back and forth endlessly. I wonder just how close to his elbow fur I need to go to see where the tracks are, the signs that surpass the sullen disconnection, the anxious underlying fear that has colored all our interactions that I took for the same thing on everyone else's shoulders on the run.

I find out soon enough that not only has he not made any plans but his money was just about gone. And we were just about to combine accounts for the flight out of here. How long does the strung mammal string along those they love? He should be stronger than this, he should have sought my help instead of somebody else's escape.

But, well, you know, don't you.

He has no problem, I have the problem. He doesn't have to go, I have to stay. The mistakes are somebody else's. The mistakes are governments that wouldn't act and people who wouldn't change or appreciate what good they had. What fucking good is that, I have to wonder? Their graves would soon be floating away. The living were left behind to handle all the haunting.

So, the ultimatum is given.

No answer is my answer. There isn't even a hunt for words.

I take my brown pelt and obsidian accusing gaze and make my way out alone. There's a number left that may someday be called. There's a contact referred who can help with cleaning him out once he's shaken his demon. I'd stay long enough to help, but the window has been closing for too long. Time's up.

So of course, there are regrets. But at least I made the right choice. You know that, don't you? At least he's not me.

I swear to you he's not me.

I get out, find dry land, make a new life and wait for a call that may never come, but I'm sure that I'm waiting all the same. What else would I do in a place where nothing is familiar, where I don't belong? Surely, I can only gaze backward.

It's all gradually becoming lost to me in the haze that hangs forever. And I've lost him as well. I've lost his laugh, his scent. Even his name is a foreign thing I can't speak anymore. The phone number got wet, faded.

I look at a bare ceiling under a leaden sky and wrap the band tight around my white fur. A prick and a sigh and I can sit on a dry bench in the shadow of an apartment in autumn and trade a secret or two. Tell me about yourself, he says to me. The spark on the edge of that answer is a place I can wait forever.

YOUR EDGE

TJ Minde

G rab me another beer, would you, Mike?" The wolf placed four burgers on a platter. "I ain't going anywhere, so why not drink a little through the game?" His grayer muzzle curled into a smile.

I reached into the fridge and grabbed another bottle for him and removed the cap. "Gotta get through dinner first, Dad." I leaned back against the counter, heart racing. "You excited for the game?"

"We've been killing it this season. The boys'll stomp 'em into the ground." He slid a bag of buns to me and I set one on my plate.

"They set for the playoffs?" I asked as I put a patty on the bread. *Come on, I have to tell him*, I thought.

He carried his plate with two plain burgers to the dining room table. "That depends how the other two games go next week." My father took a chunk out of his burger. "You usually know where the team is in the standings. What's with that?"

My anxiety rose as I swallowed the food in my mouth. "Work's been real busy." The plain flavor of the meat settled against my tongue as I thought of what to say. *Now?*

"You catch many games this season?" Dad asked.

I shook my head. "I had shifts during most games. And we don't have TV's around the restaurant, so I have to keep up with the news myself."

My father smiled. "You know that stuff is in the papers. Has something else been keeping you busy?" Dad asked.

It's now or never. I swallowed hard and took a sip of my beer to try and steel my nerves. "I... uh. Dad? I've met someone there."

Dad's ears rose in matching interest to his grin. I looked away. "Oh? What's her name?" he asked.

My heart drummed in my ears. My paws were in my lap and my gaze was on my half-eaten burger. "Charlie."

"That's an odd name for a..." Dad's voice trailed off. "Oh. *She's a he.*"

Without looking at him, I nodded. "Well, I'm happy for you nevertheless." He took another bite. "Can't say I'm surprised."

"What?"

Dad just smiled. "How'd you two meet?"

My pulse slowed. *Holy crap, this might be okay.* I forced myself to meet his eye. A knowing smile crossed his muzzle. *He expected it.* "He's one of the cooks and he's really good."

"At that frou-frou restaurant of yours?"

I rolled my eyes with a smile. "Oh, it isn't that fancy. But yeah, we met at one of the tasting nights we had a few years ago. We've actually been dating for a while and he moved in with me last year. Charlie makes the best steaks and killer burgers."

Dad reached for his beer. "Well, any carnivore worth his salt can cook a burger." As he sipped, I broke eye contact and my ears fell. "Omnivore?" he asked, reading my body language. I shook my head. "What *is* he?" A hint of disappointment seeped into his voice.

Need to choose my words carefully here. I cleared my throat. "Charlie's a deer."

"You're dating *dinner?*" His jaw went slack in surprise.

A pregnant pause settled into the room as I glared at him. "That hasn't been a thing for millennia."

"He has hooves like cattle, doesn't he?" he said. "That's as close to food as you can get!" Throwing an arm over his chair, Dad took a heavy drink from his bottle.

Words danced across my tongue, begging to be released. Instead, I swallowed them. "I don't like you talking about him like that."

"Let me guess: he's got you eating vegetables, too?"

"I told you months ago the restaurant asked that any of the wait staff that could eat vegetables with the enzyme additive should. So you can't blame him for that."

Dad ignored me and stared at my plate. "Maybe you want some lettuce and tomatoes for that?" He pointed at my half-eaten burger. Anger and disappointment bled through his body language.

Screw it. My tail bristled. "If they were from his mother's garden, sure," I said, crossing my arms in front of me.

His eyes went wide. "Are you fucking kidding me? Have you lost your edge?" Dad slammed a paw on the table. "That fancy-ass restaurant's made you soft." He crossed his arms as his ears fell against his head.

I stared at the food on my plate again, my appetite gone. "This is getting us nowhere. Now you know." I stood up and grabbed my jacket. "I'm not hungry. And I think I'll catch the game somewhere else. Enjoy your night."

My father didn't say anything back as I left his home.

***

I slammed the door when I got home.

"Mike, is that you?"

"Yeah, Charlie," I answered as I hung my coat up. "Sorry, didn't mean to be so loud."

My buck came into the living room with a towel in his hands. "You're home earlier than I expected. I just finished the dishes."

I nodded. "I ended up grabbing a few beers at the bar and watched the game there instead. Got in an argument with Dad and I left before it started." My gaze met the concerned one on my buck's muzzle. "He didn't take too kindly to me dating you."

His's ears fell. "Oh honey." He threw the towel over his shoulder as he walked over to me, wrapping his arms around my shoulders. "I'm sorry." The buck carefully pressed his forehead to mine, making my ears flick as he surrounded them with his antlers.

I wrapped my paws around his middle, closing my eyes. "He said I was soft, but I know that's not true. It's not important, anyway." My paws traveled along his hips and settled into the edges of his rear pockets. "If he wants to be a dick about it, fine. I don't need him. Besides, I have you in my arms and other things on my mind right now." I pressed my hips forward.

"Well," he began coyly, leaning back with his hands still linked behind my neck, "it *has* been a while." Keeping one hand on my shoulder, Charlie's other traveled down my chest and stomach and pressed against my growing bulge. "Maybe a demonstration is in order for how not-soft you are."

I stepped forward and settled my paws fully on his rear. "That's funny, I was thinking the same thing."

"I guess great minds think alike. What would you like to show me first?"

With one paw still on his rump, I reached the other up and grabbed one of his antlers, making him squeal in surprise before I pressed my muzzle to his. As he registered the rough kiss, his mouth fell open and I pushed my tongue in. He let out a needy whine and groped me in earnest.

I pulled him up by his antler. "No no. You don't get that, yet." I slithered my paw from his rear, over his hip to his growing bulge. "But this, I'll take." Charlie bit his lip.

I pushed him on to the couch, dropped to my knees, and quickly pulled his jeans and underwear down. I licked my chops. "My favorite cut of meat." Sliding my tongue along his half-hard shaft, I held his gaze. "You gonna be good, buck?"

Charlie raised his hands above his head, gently grabbing hold of his antlers, and nodded. Excitement and anticipation shone bright in his eyes.

"Very good," I growled. Holding him back the couch, I angled his shaft to my muzzle. Up and down, I set a quick pace, enjoying his taste each time his tip dragged along my tongue.

The more I worked his cock, the quicker he grew to full mast, warm and thick. And the more it grew, so did my desire to be filled.

Pulling off with a slurp, I admired my work. "That's what I like to see." His shaft bobbed between his legs as he whined more.

"You want something, buck?" I reached a paw out and grasped his cock, stroking him along.

"Your muzzle was so warm. I want that back, sir." He half-opened his eyes and begged. "Please?"

With a toothy grin, I stood up and pulled off my shirt in one fluid movement. "I like hearing your needy moans." He let out another as I took off my pants. "Maybe we can get you more warmth in a moment."

His eyes went right to the bulge in my briefs. My own excitement stretched along my thigh with a bead of pre marking my tip.

"Don't worry," I said, stroking my shaft through the fabric. "We'll both get what we want." Straddling the buck, I pressed my muzzle to his again. As our tongues danced, I threw the hand towel on the couch and worked the buttons down his shirt open. When the last one came undone, I broke the kiss and pushed the fabric aside, exposing his chest. The fine, soft hairs moved like sand around my claws. With another growl, the shirt began to slide down his arms. At his wrists, I stopped and pulled a pawful of fabric together and hooked it on one of his points, securing his arms behind him.

"Keep that there," I said.

Charlie gave a submissive squeak. "Yes sir."

Spitting into my paw, I reached behind me, slickening him up more.

"What are you doing?" the buck asked.

I grinned. "Taking what I want." I lifted my hips and pulled my shaft through a leg hole of my briefs. Then I curled a digit along my inner thigh, pulling the fabric back and sliding Charlie's cock between my cheeks.

His eyes widened. "Without lube?"

"You wanted a warm place; I want cock." As his warmth pressed against my entrance, I pushed back. "It's a win-win. And I wanna try this."

As the buck's shaft forced its way in, I gasped, clenching around him. A beat later, Charlie let go of the breath he was holding. "You're so tight, sir," he whimpered.

I clenched my eyes shut.

"You okay?" he asked.

"Ah!" I grunted in pain. "Yeah, I'm taking…" I lifted myself up, "what I want." Forcing myself back, I ground more of his shaft into me. With one paw on Charlie's shoulder, I wrapped the other around my cock and started riding him faster.

"Sir!" Charlie huffed.

I lifted myself up a little before falling further down on his shaft, biting my lip, enjoying the roughness of the act. Again and again, his thickness spread me as it pushed and tugged on my insides. I pressed my hips lower, forcing more of him into me.

Charlie bucked his hips with a needful grunt.

I growled and I leaned back, setting a paw on his knee and pushing him down while taking in more of him. "None of that now. You're so thick, but I don't want to stop. Don't make me *really* tie you down."

The buck gave a whimper at the threat and relaxed. "I'll behave, sir."

"Good boy." I squeezed his leg.

Little by little, the pain subsided and I relaxed. The more the two of us connected, the smoother the ride became. When my thighs finally met his lap, we both moaned, knowing how deep he was in me. From there, we got into the act more, and the better it felt. Moment by moment, my orgasm approached.

"Sir," Charlie moaned, "I don't think I'll last much longer." Fibers of the shirt ripped as he squirmed.

I lolled my tongue out of my muzzle in pleasure. "That's the idea. Come on, buck. Come in me."

With a soft moan, my paw stroked quicker along my cock while I slid up and down the buck's shaft. Faster and faster I moved my hips, and each lovely pass of Charlie inside me drove me wild.

"Ah, fuck," the buck cried, biting his lower lip. "I'm almost there, I'm almost there!"

Hearing his needy cries urged me on. Up and down, my hips moved faster as Charlie's moans grew in pitch. With each higher note, I approached my own peak.

"Here it comes, sir," he moaned. And a beat later, his shaft swelled.

As his cock throbbed, I tried to match my thrusts to each pulse inside me. And the added pressure and the wonderful pain pushed me over the edge.

Charlie let out a yelp of surprise as my rear squeezed around him tighter, and the first shot of seed splashed across his belly. String after string of white messed into his fur. Two, three, then four slowed to a pulsing dribble.

Almost as quickly as it came, the peak high left. And once I began to come down from my orgasm, I leaned forward and kissed him. Our tongues danced for a breath before Charlie broke the kiss.

"I've still got it," I said. It was more to myself more than anything else.

Charlie's ears fell and eyes filled with worry. "Got what?"

"Nothing. Don't worry about it." I reached up and unhooked his shirt from his antlers. "I'll replace the shirt when the next paycheck hits." I grabbed the hand towel and started cleaning him up.

Charlie wrapped his arms around me with a sigh, pressing his forehead to mine. His soft ears drooped against mine. "One shirt is worth you feeling better. Don't worry about it."

"What's with that sigh? Was I too rough? Are your arms sore?" I flicked and ear in worry and started to rub his biceps. "This'll just be the start of showing my appreciation, love."

The buck shook his head. "No, it's not that. But I'll take the appreciation." After he licked my cheek, I returned to cleaning him up.

"Then you'll have more appreciation than you know what to do with," I said with a grin. When the bulk of the seed was removed or pressed into his fur, I set my arms on his shoulders. "How about a shower now?"

He nodded against my head. "That sounds good. Maybe you can rub me some more as you clean our mess up."

"I can do that." Without another word, I braced myself against the couch and slid off his lap.

***

After straightening my tie, I headed to the floor. It was another busy night at Rico's. But as popular as we were, it was this way every night. The pay's good and the customers don't suck compared to other waiting gigs I've had in the past, so that helps.

A regular couple took their seats in my section near the front of the house. They, too, were wolves, and they were always easy to talk with.

I made my way up to them. "Good evening, Mr. and Mrs. Dodson. How are you both tonight?" I asked.

Mr. Dodson smiled. "Doing well, so far."

"Friday night with a lovely woman, what's not to enjoy?" I gave her a friendly wink.

"Oh, Mike, stop." Mrs. Dodson giggled. "It feels like it's been ages since we've seen you."

With my ears happy and high, I grinned. "Still here. Just been off the past few Fridays. I'm sorry to have missed you both." I waved to the wolves before clasping my paws together in front of me. "Would you two like time to peruse the menu? Or would you care instead to maybe hear our specials? We've been getting nothing but complements all week on the new rosemary and thyme crusted beef tenderloin. It's lovely and served with fingerling potatoes."

"Oh, I'd love to try a new creation from Chef Rico." Mr. Dodson licked his chops. "For a rat, he comes up with great ways to use meat. Pretty sure he prepared our food last time we were here," he added to his wife.

My ears fell. "I'm sorry if I misled you, but Chef Rico doesn't prepare meals in the evenings. All the recipes are his, yes, but as executive chef, he oversees the kitchen. He perfected the meals and ensures they are served to his instructions."

Mr. Dodson raised an eyebrow. "Who's on the grill tonight?"

"Honey, does it really matter?" Mrs. Dodson asked, setting a paw to her husband's wrist.

He rolled his eyes in response. "Of course it does. Could you imagine if, like, a deer was cooking steak? There's no way someone like that could do it well. Or right."

My hackles rose in defense, but I bit back a snarl. *No, don't repeat last week. He's not Dad.* After a breath, I cleared my throat. "Actually, Chef Charles Johnson has been the roast chef for the past month. If you've been coming here every Friday for the last four weeks, that buck's been making your food." I forced a friendly smile across my muzzle.

"That's impossible." Mr. Dodson crossed his arms over his chest. "How could an herbivore know how to cook a decent steak? It's not like they could eat it themselves."

I stilled my tail. "You're right. Chef Charles doesn't eat what he makes. But I know for a fact that the buck is one of the best roast chefs in town. If not in the state. And I've been sampling food here and at other restaurants like it for the last two years."

Mrs. Dodson's lip curled in a playful smirk. "See honey, you don't always know what you're talking about."

He didn't seem fazed by his wife's comment. "You seem very sure of your claims."

I nodded. "Indeed I am. Every order of Chef Rico's tenderloin has only received high praise tonight. And I know there's a killer salad that pairs with it."

Mrs. Dodson spoke before her husband could. "I'll pass on the salad, but I trust your judgement. I'll have the tenderloin." She handed her menu back.

I nodded. "Would you like a moment to review the menu, sir?"

"I'm leery of it, now," he said. "But I'll have my usual prime rib."

"Excellent choice," I said as I took his menu.

"And we'll have a bottle of the 2006 Chateau de Parure," Mr. Dodson added.

I gave a small half-bow. "Certainly. It's a great cabernet sauvignon. Let me get your orders in, and I'll be back in a moment with the wine." I rounded the table and made my way back to the kitchen.

Over the next hour, I moved from couple to couple. Cashed out a group, cleared plates, poured more wine. When the Dodsons' food was ready, I brought it to them, refilled their wine glasses, and scurried away.

With the worry and trepidation Mr. Dodson had, I gave them enough time to try their meals before returning to their table.

I cleared my throat. "And how is everything?"

The two wolves looked at each other and then to me. A pregnant silence fell over the table. I stared at Mr. Dodson with an expectant smile as he looked at the cut of prime rib.

"Fine, fine. It tastes just as it did last week." Mr. Dodson looked at his paws. "Excellent as always. You were right."

"No need to look so dejected, sir." My tail wagged. *I knew it.* "And your tenderloin, ma'am?" I asked his wife.

"Perfect as usual. My complements to the chef."

I nodded with a half bow. "I will certainly let him know." Once I was back at full height, I continued. "While I'm here, can I get either of you anything else?"

They both shook their heads. "I think we're alright."

"Fantastic." I pressed my paws together. "In that case, I'll send the good word back to the kitchen and check in on you in a bit."

The couple nodded and continued their meal. I turned around and headed back to the kitchen with a spring in my step and fresh wag in my tail.

I glanced to the lobby, trying to gauge the length of the evening. The pack waiting and chatting was huge. With my quick look, my eyes locked on to the gray muzzle of my father.

My ears fell. I stopped and stared back, as his tail sank into the crowd as he walked out the door.

Why was Dad here? All my new-found energy left.

***

"No, he was at the restaurant," I said to Charlie a few days later. With one paw full of groceries, I opened the door for the buck, letting him walk inside first.

"But why would he show up on a busy night then leave?" he asked, setting the bags down in the kitchen. "Maybe to apologize?"

"Hell if I know." I said into the pantry, putting things away. "Apparently he left a note with the maître d', but I threw it away. Just seeing him there spiked my anxiety and I'm not ready to deal with all that baggage yet."

"What baggage?" Charlie set a hand on my shoulder.

I sighed. "He accused me of losing my edge."

"Your what?"

I looked to my buck as I leaned against the counter. "My edge. It's something my family said. It's that spark of masculinity. I mean, after I made Mr. Dodson eat his words, I was flying high. Then I saw Dad in the lobby, and he left… It just reminded me of last week—of the disappointment I saw in his eye." My gaze fell to the floor.

Charlie set a hand on my chin, lifting it up. "Hon, I don't care what he thinks, and neither should you."

"I know, but that's what kills me. When Mom left, Dad was all I had. I care what he thinks. About me." I placed a paw on his chest. "About you. And when he barely batted an eyelash when I told him I was dating a guy, I thought there was hope."

He put both hands on my shoulder. "Honey, if your father doesn't want to get with the times, that's his loss. You have *me* now, and I'm not going anywhere. You don't need to prove anything to me." Charlie leaned forward and kissed me. A simple, loving kiss, grounding me in the moment.

"I love you too, hon." I pressed my forehead to his. We stood there, holding each other until my stomach rumbled. My ears fell as I gave an apologetic smile. "Sorry."

The buck chuckled. "Don't be. I'm getting hungry too. I was thinking a mushroom burger. Something easy to make before the game." A knock at the door caught our attention, perking our ears. "I'll get it," Charlie said. "You keep thinking about what you want."

I turned around and began looking through the fridge. *Hmm, maybe I'll work on burgers and ask him to mix up some barbeque sauce so I can join him. Then, I can have another of his mom's meaty tomatoes too.* My tail wagged faster.

"Hey, Mike?" my buck called from the entryway.

"Yeah, hon?" I closed the freezer and poked my head around the corner. When I saw him, my ears fell. "Dad? What're you doing here?"

My father looked around Charlie and met my gaze. "I left a note at your restaurant asking you to call me. I would have tried to plan this better, but you never did. So, I had to drop by." He then looked back to the buck. "Mike says you know how to grill a mean burger."

As I walked up to Charlie, the buck crossed his arms over his chest. "And steak. Or chicken." His tone was cool and smooth.

Dad broke eye contact, ears falling as he held up a grocery bag. "I brought beef. I've never had a burger cooked by an herbivore." He lowered the bag. "I heard Mike talk you up to a pair of wolves and I wanted to try it myself." With a befuddled look, he met Charlie's gaze again. "And I heard something about mushroom burgers somewhere, so I brought some of those for you, too," he added.

I looked from my buck to Dad and back. "It's your call, Charlie."

He stood there for a moment, staring at my father. "Let me see what you brought," he finally said, holding out his hand.

He looked through the bag for a moment and handed it to me. "Could you set this on the counter, Mike?" He turned back to my father. "Please, come in."

"Are the things I brought okay?" Dad asked. I heard the nervousness in his voice. It was odd.

I poked my nose into the bag and saw about a pound of beef and a blue container of white mushrooms.

I looked back to see Charlie nod.

"I prefer to make burgers with ground chuck, but I can work with this. Besides, I can add other seasonings to enhance the flavor further." He led my father into the living room. "Please have a seat. I'll let you know when it's ready."

Charlie met me in the entryway, and after a quick exchange, I headed back and found my father's head was on a swivel as he took in our living room for the first time. He sat in an armchair by the fireplace we never used, a bookshelf rested on the opposite wall from him filled with both our collections. Beside that stood our TV, partially used for gaming or movies, mainly used on weekend for football. The smaller room was sparsely decorated, but the muted canvas work was more our style.

As I took the seat at the end of the couch by my Dad, I saw his ears fell. "I hope the mushrooms are okay," he said with a flick of his ear. "It's what the dik-dik at the store suggested."

"Do you go to that store usually?" My buck asked from the kitchen. I heard his knife fly across the cutting board.

"Yeah," Dad said, lacing his digits together.

"They probably don't expect to get that from an older wolf," I said. "I wouldn't be surprised if you scared them a little. 'Specially asking such a small person." I smiled jokingly.

Dad gave me a pity laugh that sounded more than half-hearted, then silence fell over the room. It was only broken when Charlie stepped in. "I'll be right outside if you need me." He looked to my father. "Door to the patio is back there." He pointed back where he was working. "Should only take about ten minutes on the grill to get the burgers done." His glance moved between us.

I nodded. Dad didn't respond. The buck accepted the silence as acknowledgment and made his way back to the kitchen. Instead of talking, my father took in the interior of our home more.

The minutes crawled by as an awkward tension settled into the room. I wasn't quite sure what to say. *Why are you here?* That feels too direct. *How'd the game go last week?* No, let's not bring that up.

"Why did you come to the restaurant, Dad?" I finally asked.

His ears perked at the sound of my voice, then immediately fell.

"Oh. Well, I hadn't seen where you worked. Thought it would give me a chance to. And see the place that's changed you." He winced at himself as the words left his muzzle. "Sorry. I didn't mean it that way. I'm…trying to apologize."

"Do you still blame *Rico's* for me dating Charlie? I mean, you said you heard me talk him up to the Dodsons. You heard me stand up for him."

"I don't blame that place for you being gay. All I said was you lost your edge."

"Do you realize how you sound right now?"

He started at the floor. "I have no idea what you're talking about."

As if on cue, the back door opened. "Come to the table. We can plate there."

With a scowl, I led Dad through the kitchen to our dining room. On two plates were patties slathered in barbeque sauce set atop half a bun. In the center of the table were sliced toppings—onion, pineapple, lettuce, tomatoes and cheese.

In front of Charlie sat a salad.

As I took my seat, Charlie smiled to my father. "The first restaurant I worked at was a barbeque joint; this was one of their most popular dishes." He picked up a fork and moved towards the tray of extras. "Would you like anything on your burger, sir?"

He shook his head. "No, thank you."

"Mike?"

"Yes please. Fill it up." I glared daggers at Dad.

Charlie finished making my burger and tossed some of the extra toppings into his salad. "Please eat," he said.

With a nod, Dad put the bun atop the other half and picked it up, sauce dripping from the bread. After he took a bite, his eyes went wide. "Wow, this is actually pretty good." Dad took a larger bite.

Charlie smiled. "I'm glad you like it."

My father nodded again. "The sauce is a little grainy, but that must be the spices you mentioned." As he ate, the tension eased in his body. "You see the game last night?" he asked me.

Charlie answered instead. "Yeah. Mike had to work, but I saw it. The locals might have a shot at the playoffs depending how my hometown does tonight." He took another bite of his salad.

"Wait, you watch football?" Dad asked.

I rolled my eyes and set my burger down. "Really Dad? *I* watch football. Why can't he?"

"I'm not saying he can't. It's just that it's an aggressive sport, that's all." Fire was in his eyes, daring me to challenge his logic. It was a look I knew well.

Charlie didn't flick an ear. "I'm guessing you never saw two bucks in rut back in high school." He chuckled.

"What's that?" Dad asked.

"I saw plenty of fights between guys with antlers over girls. As folks age, they tend to calm some of the more outwardly aggressive displays. But kids don't know how to keep that crap in check."

Dad took another bite as Charlie spoke. Meanwhile, the buck stood up and grabbed a plate from the island. "But yeah, I actually played some in high school. Defensive line."

"No shit?" Dad said.

"I shit you not," Charlie answered as he sat back down with his own burger. "I wasn't great, but I've accidently punctured a leg or two in my day." He dressed it like he dressed mine.

"Well, that's something I didn't expect." Dad's shoulders fell slack as he watched my buck.

Charlie took the comment in stride. "It takes all kinds. What can I say?" He shrugged, taking a bite.

Dad's jaw fell open. "You can eat meat?" My father looked down at his half-eaten burger and then to me. "I thought you said he couldn't?"

"Oh, you assumed I used what you brought," my deer answered.

Dad set the burger down and took off the bun, inspecting the patty.

"It's a portobello mushroom," I said. "Think of it like a bigger version of what you bought."

His hackles rose. "Are you trying to poison me?"

I shook my head. "Not at all—"

"Then just give me the shits for days?" Dad pressed on bearing his fangs at Charlie.

I slammed my paws on the table. "You will not act that way to him. Especially for something that was *not* his idea. He was going to make you a hamburger and *I* asked him to make this instead." My hackles were standing on end, matching my father. "We shouldn't have to change our dinner plans because you didn't call."

Dad froze. I'd never raised my voice to him.

"Don't give me that look." I glared. "You come into my home, ask to see my *partner* make *you* food like a short order cook, and then accuse us of trying to make you ill. Just because you're a prejudiced asshole doesn't mean we are."

"I am not prejudiced!" With that, the fight ran out of him and he stared at his plate. "I just grew up in a different time. And I'm still trying—unlike a real bigot, and I'll probably make more mistakes. But while I've heard of mixed couples like you two, I've never met a carnivore that eats a lot of vegetables."

Charlie took another bite as if nothing happened and dabbed his muzzle with a napkin. "On their own, no, not easily," he said with a smile. "But if you mix in a new enzymatic supplement that helps your body break it down—like in the barbeque sauce, you can still get the proper nutrients from the food for it to not bother you. Congratulations, you just ate half a mushroom burger."

He looked from my buck to his plate. "And I won't get sick?"

My ears rose and I started to calm down. "I've never had a problem. And, you still have your edge, don't you? Or have you lost it because you liked a vegetable?" I glared at him.

Dad's ears fell as he put the bun on top of his mushroom again. Charlie continued to eat, watching my father, mirroring his body language.

I kept staring for a few more seconds. The older wolf was still processing everything. When my body relaxed, I took a breath and stood up from my seat, moving to the fridge. "This porter will pair well with it," I said, nodding from his plate to a beer beside it before sipping from my own bottle. "We were actually planning to watch the game tonight, if you wanted to join us." I looked to Dad.

His gaze moved from me, then to Charlie. "You don't mind?"

The buck shook his head. "Why don't you stay and have a few with us? I think I know more stupid football trivia than he does." He nodded to me.

My father stared at his plate for a moment before taking a sip of the beer. A second later, he took another bite. "If you'll have me." He looked from Charlie to me.

I smiled. "It would be our pleasure."

***

The rest of the evening carried on. My father finished his burger without another protest, albeit slower than he would have with a regular burger. Charlie offered to make him another with beef if he wanted, but Dad declined. Beers were had and the game was fun to watch. And hearing the two men I respect most in the world argue like friends about other teams and players was a cleansing experience.

Dad left a little after the game—sober and safe to drive. And Charlie and I started cleaning up. Since my buck cooked, I cleaned the dishes while he dried them.

"I'm rather surprised how smooth everything went tonight." I handed him the last pan and started rinsing the empty beer bottles. My tail wagged continuously. "I was ready to fight when he snapped at you, though. Showed him how sharp my edge was."

Charlie huffed.

My tail stilled. "What?"

"I've been trying to keep it in, but I just can't anymore."

I tilted my head. "What do you mean?"

"Your 'edge' is bullshit."

"Huh?"

Charlie rolled his eyes. "Every time I've heard you talk about it, I feel like I'm back in high school again. It's that same crap about what makes you a 'man.' It's like asking who's the girl in our relationship."

"Who's asked you that?" My hackles started to rise again.

The buck hung the towel up with a roll of his antlers. "No one, but that's what I'm talking about. Look at you—you're ready to fight and defend honor that doesn't need defending. Hell, that's probably why you didn't use lube last week when we had sex. And as long as you were in charge, you can say you were the man in the moment, right?"

"What? No. I just didn't want to stop to get it."

"I think you're more like your father than you think." Charlie crossed his arms.

"The hell does that mean?"

"It means *you're* also a product of your generation. It's all that 'I gotta be manly' bullshit. Masc, fem; I don't care. All you *gotta* do is be yourself. Your father is trying to change with the times, but it looks like you don't care to." Without another word, Charlie stormed off.

Hearing that made me stop. *I was always told having a sharp edge means you're a leader, means you're strong. That you fight for those you love.* "Change with the times?" *What needs to change?*

I continued thinking on my buck's words until it all fell together. "Oh, shit." I followed after Charlie into the living room.

The buck sat on the couch, knees curled to his chest. "I didn't want to say anything. I was hoping we could both let it go. But since you came out to your Dad, you've been more worried about how others see you. And me."

I sat beside him. "I've heard the phrase 'toxic masculinity' and of course that's bad. Saying 'boys will be boys' *is* bullshit. But when you said it…I realized that's what the 'edge' my father always talked about was." I looked down at the floor. "I never thought about it that way because my family never said it like that. It was just expected. Ingrained in me that way."

Silence fell over the room as we sat there. After a few moments, I set a paw on Charlie's knee. "I'm sorry. I'll be more conscious of it in the future."

"Thank you." His tone was still curt.

"Is there anything I can do to make it up to you?"

The buck thought about it for a moment. "Make love to me. Right here, right now." A smile curled the corner of his lip. A smile that was contagious.

"I think I can do that." I leaned in and began to start nibbling his neck, getting him to uncurl and relax.

When his feet touched the floor, the buck pushed me away. "Just go get the lube first this time."

I couldn't help but chuckle. "Yes, sir."

THINK OF ENGLAND

Sasha P.G.

Just close your eyes and think of England. Micah pulled his legs closer to his chest. The lube was cold, but Kim was doing his thing. It would just take a moment and then—two of Kim's fingers pushed against him, slipped through the first ring in his ass. Micah forced his whole body to relax. The pressure increased as Kim shifted forward and pushed them both deeper into the bed.

"You good?" Kim asked.

"Mmm-hmm," Micah smiled. Kim was going slow enough that it didn't hurt and he just looked so happy kneeling over him like that. His thick tail swooshed back and forth over the sheets, and his golden eyes shone amid the dark patches of brown fur on his face. He wanted to fuck him so badly.

The fingers slipped further into Micah. He let out a moan. Kim liked when he did that. His cock twitched and pressed against Micah's thigh. He ducked his head down and slowly licked Micah's sheath who wasn't quite hard yet himself.

Kim pushed his fingers the rest of the way in. His knuckles felt sharp and hard, he kept pushing, flexing and curling his fingers as deep as they could go. Micah moaned again. *Ohhh… come on…* Kim licked faster. His tongue curled around Micah's protruding member. *…There we go. Almost…*

Micah closed his eyes and tried to focus on the movement below him. Kim was always good at getting a rhythm going. Micah's mouth lolled open; his hands drifted down to rub Kim's cheek ruff. *He was so freaking cute.* Even doing something like this, Kim was the cutest goddamn yote in the whole world.

"I love you."

Kim mumbled something, his mouth still preoccupied, sounded like a *love you too, kitten.* And that was all it took.

"I'm ready."

Kim pulled back, looking up as if to make sure he'd heard right, but he'd have gotten the same answer looking down. Micah was finally hard now. His cock fully extended to expose short barbs along its length. Kim liked to play with them, gently touch them like they might disappear if he pressed too hard.

"You sure?" Kim pulled out his fingers. Micah closed his eyes and shivered. "How do you want to…"

Micah reached up and locked his fingers around the back of Kim's scruff. "Pull me up."

Kim flashed his teeth in that beautiful smile he did whenever he tried to be sexy; slight curl of the lips that somehow reached all the way up to his eyes and made them glimmer. He liked this position. Must have something to do with the way he could bury his muzzle in Micah's neck or the feeling of Micah's cock pressing into his stomach. Why he liked it didn't matter much though. Thrusting into Micah, arms wrapped tight around his back, always got Kim panting.

It only took a moment for Micah to ready himself. Kim pressed up into him slowly, easing his hard member inch by inch until Micah forced out another a low moan.

"You good?"

Micah pressed himself lower in response. He squatted over Kim's lap and raised himself. Sex felt okay like this. There was a pressure, but it wasn't that bad. And it felt sort of nice whenever he reached the bottom of the motion and Kim's cock hit him in *all the right ways*. Kim's enjoyment of it helped too. He let Micah take the lead at first, but his arms tightened around Micah's back with each movement and he began thrusting up into him as well.

Micah didn't need to think about moaning now. The noises came out of him. Short, frantic squeaks between longer moans. The thrusts picked up speed. They rocked back and forth, bodies intertwined, grabbing at each other's fur to hold on, pull closer.

"Fuck me," Micah managed to take a breath. "Oh, fuck me."

Kim pushed forward. His weight knocked them over onto Micah's back. He cried out but Kim pressed his muzzle against Micah's and the noise was trapped between them.

Micah clawed at Kim's back. His fingers danced between holding onto Kim's shoulders and falling back to feel the strong muscles of his toned ass. There was too much. He couldn't—there was a pain now.

Slight at first but it built inside him. He couldn't tell Kim to stop this close to the end. His breathe came as short gasps. The hot bulge of Kim's knot pressed against him.

"Kim!" Micah shouted. The pressure erupted between them. Kim thrust forward, his knot entered with a pop, and he moaned: loud, guttural, exhausted. His cock twitched as he came, but the rest of Kim was frozen. His breathing caught in heavy gasps.

He slumped forward and rested heavily across Micah's body. "I love you."

"I love you too." Micah rubbed Kim's back.

The cum was already sticking to his fur. The warm mess seeped out in a messy splotch from his cock. This was always the gross part. But Kim was so peaceful in these moments. His whole body was relaxed and at ease like being stuck inside Micah were the best feeling in the world.

They'd be like this for another few minutes; at least until Kim's knot went down enough to pull out. Sometimes he liked to stay in longer than he needed to, until the thing was completely gone. Kim said he liked how close they felt whenever they knotted, and the grossness wasn't quite bad enough for Micah to say anything. Kim just always looked so restful in these moments.

Micah shifted and craned his neck to look down at Kim. His head laid on Micah's shoulder, but Micah could just make out the side of his face. It was relaxed. His fur looked smooth; his long nose was perfectly still, even his ears seemed at ease, as if this was his favorite moment in the world.

Micah sighed. Why wasn't it that way for him?

"Two more minutes?" Kim asked

Micah let his head drop back to the bed and tightened his arms around Kim. Maybe he was just tired, but it was always this way. Maybe it was just awkward laying around with a dick in your ass. It might be different if he tried topping, but that hadn't worked out whenever they'd tried before.

Kim nuzzled against his neck. "I love you, kitten."

Micah forced his eyes closed. This could be his favorite moment too.

***

Fridays were always interesting. They'd start off the same as any other day. Kim would kiss him, hand over his coffee, and say *have fun at school, kitten.* But by noon, there'd be at least a handful of students coming into Micah's office. Sometimes they were for legitimate concerns; other times it would be for some teen-drama thing. Somebody cheated or somebody misspelled your handle on Instagram, and it was a hundred percent definitely intentional. And sometimes it was just somebody who needed a break from the constant testing. Whatever it was that brought them into the counseling office, each day was different, that was for sure. But different days made for interesting days which would always go by quickly. Soon enough, the dismissal bell rang, and all the kids came pouring out of their classes.

Micah stood leaned-up against the door to his office and waved to the kids as they headed out. Carline would be blocking his car in for a while and somebody would probably stop by.

"Hey mister." Jackie, a senior year fox, jumped out of her classroom.

"Hey, Jackie-Jay." Micah turned and let Jackie hug his side briefly. "How are we today?"

"Mister, I'm rough." Jackie stepped out of the side-hug. "I kissed a girl last night and it was just…"

"Need to talk about it?" Micah gestured with his head back into the office. Jackie had been coming to his office since her sophomore year with all sorts of questions and problems.

"Nah, they all know. It's just… why's everybody got to be so extra?"

"What happened?"

"Nothing!"

"Oh, come on girl, you know I'm a confidential reporter."

"Nothing happened!"

Micah gave her a look. She'd say what happened. Always did.

"Nothing's the problem though. I kissed her and just… eh." She shrugged.

"Aww, well, that's okay Jackie-Jay. There'll be someone else."

"Mister, you're not getting it. I kissed like ten girls last night and nothing. Kissed a couple boys too to make sure." Jackie scrunched up her nose and pretended to wretch. "Sorry mister, but boys are nasty."

"Not all of them."

"All the straight ones."

Micah laughed. "Alright, well, it's good to explore your sexuality in safe, responsible ways, but you should try waiting for an emotional connection. That should give you the spark you're missing."

"Eh," Jackie shrugged again. She pulled at her backpack strap so the heavy bag would stop sliding down. "I think I'm just ace."

"Ace?" Micah asked. That was a new one. It could mean anything—she was cool with being alone for now or maybe it was something self-deprecating and she was saying she didn't deserve anyone.

"Asexual. You know, like snakes."

"I'm pretty sure snakes don't reproduce asexually."

"Nah, mister. Some do. Like, they decide they don't need nobody else and just pop out a little baby snake all by themselves."

"Huh, well," Micah scratched his chin. That was a new one. "Today I learned. But it's a bit early to swear off all romance. You could meet the right person someday. I know I didn't think that I'd ever find somebody like my husband."

"Yeah, but before him you'd still... you know?" Jackie clenched her hand in an open fist and made a jerking motion. Micah had to stop himself from sighing. Talking with Jackie always led to lots of CYA. She was a good kid though, even with all the extra documentation that came with their talks.

"Jackie, what have we said about obscene motions in public? And besides, you know I won't discuss my sex life with you." Micah said. Though, in all honesty even if she weren't his student there wouldn't be much to tell prior to Kim.

"But what if it's to help me figure my shit out?"

Micah stared at her. She'd change the topic to something better on her own. Something they could actually talk about.

Jackie smiled and waggled her eyebrows at him.

He kept staring blankly at her. She was a good kid—lawsuit in a handbag with her familiarity, but she'd figure this all out eventually.

"We're gonna get coffee after graduation you know." Jackie laughed. "And then you'll tell me all your gay secrets."

"You have to pass econ first." Micah said. Jackie's invitation was another thing to document. Talking on school grounds was one thing, but he wouldn't do out-of-office-visits. "You keeping up with—"

Her eyes went wide. "Bye! Mister, I can't even with you."

Jackie walked past him toward the exit. Her bag already slipping back off her shoulder.

"Happy weekend, Jackie-Jay!"

She spun around, her bag swinging off her shoulder. "I said bye!"

She grabbed the backpack and ran outside. Micah shook his head. These kids... Kim only believed half the stories he told about them. He checked his watch. 4:05. Still another ten minutes or so before carline would clear up. Might as well look into this whole *asexual* thing after documenting their talk.

He pulled out his phone and googled it.

"Huh..."

There was a lot. Handful of videos, articles, and some news stories too. So, it was definitely a thing. It even had its own version of Wikipedia: AVEN Wiki. Micah browsed through the homepage. So many blue links to click on... and, oh! A FAQ for parents.

Micah clicked on it. Technically not a parent, but... it should have some good things.

"Let's see..." Micah mumbled to himself. Asexuality is a natural lack of sexual attraction... some experience romantic feelings and/or arousal, others don't... not caused by abuse (that was good). He should still look into other sources and ask Omar about it, but from this it looked like asexuality was just like any other sexuality.

One of the questions caught his eye: *Does this mean asexuals are incapable of love?*

The short answer was no. The long answer was about half a page long and contained almost as many blue links out to other pages as the homepage had. So many terms. Most of them seemed self-explanatory like sexuality and attraction, but what the hell was a demisexual?

"A demisexual person is someone who does not experience sexual attraction to another person unless or until they have formed an emotional connection with that person." Micah kept reading. "According to one hypothetical model, a person who identifies as a demisexual does not experience primary sexual attraction but does experience secondary sexual attraction."

"The hell is that supposed to mean?" Micah squinted at the phone. Experiences secondary sexual attraction? At least there was another link to that model.

The link led to a Punnett-Square like graph. Four terms made up the square: Primary and Secondary Sexual Attraction and Primary and Secondary Sexual Desire. Luckily, there was a key to describe each of those.

Sexual attraction was basically wanting to fuck the other person with primary being an immediate case of the fuck-me-eyes and secondary requiring time to build up. Desire though was the reason behind wanting to get it on. Primary desire was wanting to fuck for personal pleasure while secondary was…

"Oh shit."

—The desire to engage in sexual activity for purposes other than personal pleasure, such as the happiness of the other person involved—

"That's me." It all made sense. He was asexual!

His tail curled around his leg. Fuck…

***

They finished doggy style that night. Micah was the little spoon now. Kim lay behind him, bit at his ears, and made him laugh whenever the coyote breathed out. There was a wet spot on the bed beside them, but they could just change out the sheets in the morning. Kim would probably want to fool around after sleeping in too. They usually fucked around a bit on Saturdays when they could take their time. Start and stop with gentle touches and kisses as the sunlight crept into the bedroom. Kim would usually want to fool around a bit in the shower too.

Micah kissed Kim's paw. He was a good coyote: loving, affectionate. It wasn't as if Kim lacked passion or wasn't good with his cock or anything like that. Sex itself wasn't bad it just wasn't good either. Given a choice between fucking around in bed all day or cuddling on the couch and watching movies, Micah would never choose the bed, but Kim would probably want to wrap a paw around his sheath on the couch too.

It wasn't his yote, it was him. He was the one with the asexual problem, and he was such a piece of shit for not being able to love Kim as much as he was loved. He'd just keep quiet about it and fuck Kim whenever it was time. That was the only way to try at making it all okay. No, Micah sighed. That wasn't true. The worst part of this all was Kim might understand. They could talk about it. And all he'd have to say was… How could he say it?

God Micah closed his eyes. *Kim didn't deserve to be slotted with a cold fish like himself.* He should be with someone who needed him too.

Micah kissed Kim's paw again and held it close to his muzzle. England would be getting a lot of attention this weekend.

Who said that anyways, "*think of England*"?

Had to be some lady—it would be a bit too rapey if a guy said it. Probably said during a war too. World War I? Maybe the second one. Who would that have been? Queen Elizabeth wasn't alive yet, was she?

"What'cha thinkin about?" Kim whispered.

"England."

"What?"

Micah stiffened. Fuck. He hadn't meant to say that out loud. Why the fuck had he said that?

"Why are you thinking about England?" Kim laughed. "That's not some stripper you've been seeing is it?"

Micah sighed. He needed to talk with Kim about this. He deserved to hear about it at least. Micah wriggled around to face his beautiful husband. He looked cute: even with that semi-amused, semi-concerned look creasing his brow.

"Wait, it's not really a stripper is it?"

"So, you know how I love you, right?"

"Fuck me, it is a stripper." But Kim smiled as he said that, so everything was going to be good. He would understand. They'd been through so much already and this—this wasn't anything.

"No," Micah laughed. Why had this felt so nerve-wracking before? "It's just... I'm demisexual."

"You're a what?"

"Demisexual. It's sort of..." How should he explain this?

"Demi like demigod? You calling me a god now, kitten?" Kim growled the last word in Micah's ears and tightened his paws around Micah's waist.

"No," Micah laughed and pushed Kim's head away. He might want a second round after all this were over. "Demi. It's sort of like half asexual."

Kim pulled back.

"One of my kids told me about it. Said they think they're asexual."

"What the hell is that?"

"That's what I said. So, I looked it up online and...and I don't know. Something about it just felt right to me. Like, I don't really have a sexual attraction."

"What?"

How did it go? "I don't want to fuck you." Micah froze. Fuck. That was surely the worst foot-in-mouth moment ever.

"What? The hell, Micah? What did we just do then?"

"No! I mean, it's...I don't know! I'm new to this crap too! I meant that I don't look at you and think 'oh fuck me you hot stud.' I mean—shit! It's more like—"

He might as well have punched Kim. His ears fell back, splayed out like little airplane wings. His mouth dropped open a little as if the air had been knocked out of him. It all made Micah's chest clench. Fuck.

"I didn't—"

"We should get ready for bed."

Kim pushed himself out of the bed. He looked fucking miserable. His shoulders slumped inward, his toned chest seemed to cave in on itself as he stood half slumped over, his long tail lay flush against his legs. Even each bristle of fur seemed deflated. He looked down at the bed—at Micah—and the whole moment seemed to freeze.

The first time they'd had sex was about a month before their wedding. They'd fooled around for a while before that, but it was almost always just Micah sucking Kim off. That night was the first time Kim saw Micah naked. He'd tossed him onto the bed and tugged off his pants and had stared down at his naked body, at his cock barely out of his sheath, and he'd smiled, shook his head, and laughed. "God, you're so... so..." And he'd laughed again, shook his head again, and jumped into the bed with Micah and shown him what his words couldn't express.

Would Kim ever look at him that same way? Or, had he just fucked over everything? Kim opened his mouth like he wanted to say something, say that it would be alright, that they should keep talking about it or ask if Micah could explain more. He took a deep breath, his fur rising and falling like a wave along his cum-matted chest, but when he spoke, all he said was, "I'm gonna go brush my teeth."

Micah clenched his jaw. God damnit. Why'd he have to fuck this all up? He should've just said England was a stripper or a weird substitute teacher at work or something. He could have even said he was thinking about the queen. Kim might have bought that.

He sighed. He really should go after Kim. Even if they didn't talk about this, they could talk about something else. Ending the night on this would be a crappy way to head off to sleep.

Micah rolled out of bed. Kim was already brushing his teeth. The hard, electric whir seeped from the bathroom and made his ears twitch back. His heart thumped in his chest. Had the toothbrush always droned so loud? Did Kim have a megaphone, or something hooked up to it? There wasn't any reason for that, but the damn brush shouldn't be this loud. It was like a bomber droning on above him.

There was nothing weird about the bathroom though. Kim stood at the sink, brushing his teeth like there wasn't anything wrong in the world, but he didn't look over when the floorboard creaked. One ear flicked over but that was it. No smile, no tail wag, no nothing except the droning toothbrush.

"Sorry I'm an idiot." Micah said. The toothbrush shut off. Silence. Fuck, this was worse.

Micah shifted his weight to one foot and curled his tail around the other. Why was this worse?

"I didn't mean what I said back there. I mean, I did, I just...I said it in a way that makes me seem like a dumbass. Can we restart?"

Kim spit and turned on the faucet.

Micah swallowed. Not the best endorsement.

"Hi! You're cute and I'm Micah." He smiled and stuck out his paw. He'd blurted something to that effect when they'd first met. Kim glanced over at him. Maybe there was a smile there. Just the smallest one. Or, no...

"Yeah, that was about as bad as the first time..." Micah sighed. "Too far back? I know. I know. I'm just. I'm trying—"

"You think you're asexual." Kim interrupted.

"Y-yeah." Micah nodded.

"So, what's that mean?"

"I don't experience sexual attraction."

"To me."

"To anyone."

"That includes me."

Micah hesitated. That wasn't what mattered. Why was Kim focusing on himself? There wasn't any attraction to other people—hell, even to himself.

"That's a yes, isn't it?"

Micah nodded. "But it's not—"

"Not what? My fault?"

"No! I mean, sort of. It's not you, it's me—that sounds dumb as hell, but I mean it here. It's me that's asexual. I haven't met anybody I'm attracted to."

"And what happens when you do?"

"What?"

"What happens when you meet that special someone who you are attracted to?"

"Jesus Christ! You're not listening. I'm not attracted to people like that!"

"What if you just haven't met the right person yet?"

"The right person?" Micah yelled. This was ridiculous. "You are the right person! You think I let just anybody fuck me? So, what if I don't cum at the mere sight of you?"

Micah's paws were clenched and his tail lashed behind him. Kim's arms hung loose at his sides they didn't move at all. His whole body was completely still, ears back, tail tucked. Only his eyes moved. They shook, small rapid movements like he were searching for something in Micah's face.

Micah looked at the ground. Fuck...

"Kim, I'm..." He was a fucking asshole. He didn't deserve Kim. "I'm sorry. I wanted to tell you how I feel, but..." He sighed. He just had to be a dumbass when it came to talking about this apparently.

"How am I supposed to feel?" Kim asked. "You think I'd want to fuck someone who doesn't want me?"

Micah opened his mouth, but no words came. What did that mean? Oh, shit fuck. What did that mean? Kim wouldn't leave him. He couldn't, not for this. But his cute yote looked miserable: like he'd been beaten up and left in the rain. Every fur and whisker on his face drooped.

Kim closed his eyes, his shoulders slumped, and he sighed. The sigh was short; not exasperated or exhausted but defeated and broken as if there wasn't anything left to say.

Micah tried to swallow, but a hard lump seemed to catch in his throat. He couldn't move, not even when Kim opened his eyes. He couldn't lift a finger when Kim moved from the sink or when he slipped through the doorway. Micah stood and stared at his reflection in the mirror.

This was his fault. He should have been more patient. He should have explained it better. He should have done a lot of things.

Micah turned around. Kim was already under the covers. He lay on the far side of the bed with his back to the bathroom. There was still time to make it better.

Micah went to the bed. "Can I be the big spoon?"

Kim nodded, just a short movement, but enough.

The bed was still warm from when they'd been in it before. The sheets smelled like sex—they'd have to be washed in the morning—but there was another scent now too. Micah ignored it. They'd deal with whatever it was in the morning. He put one arm over Kim and slipped the other one under his head so that both arms held the coyote. He buried his nose in the ruff along Kim's neck. Closing his eyes, it was just the two of them. Theirs were the only two scents in the world. They could lie like this forever. They'd never need to say anything else. Micah would never be an asshole and Kim would never feel hurt. They could just be.

Something wet dripped onto his arm. The foreign smell broke into the dream: tears.

Kim shook in his arms. Deep breaths wracked his body as he cried silently.

"Kim?" Micah pulled back his arm, but Kim grabbed hold of his hand and kept them locked together. His muzzle grazed Micah's hand, his lips kissed Micah's fingers once then pulled his hand close to his chest again.

Micah bit his tongue. God, he was such a fucking asshole. He didn't deserve Kim. This had all started so suddenly and he'd been so worried about himself that he'd forgotten about how Kim would feel. He'd fucked this up which meant it was up to him to unfuck it. If he could…

"Are we going to be okay?"

***

Kim was still in his arms when Micah woke up. The sun was barely up, but a bright light shone from Kim's side of the bed. The coyote was on his phone. Micah stretched, pulling his shoulders back, and yawned, "Morning."

"I keep thinking about what you said," Kim said.

Micah pulled his arm out from under Kim. His elbow felt stiff; it always locked up a little when he was the big spoon. God, he was an idiot.

"Yeah, I'm—well, I'm sorry about last night." Micah said. "I should have…"

He frowned. What should he have done? For as wrong as everything had gone, they were still in bed together and Kim was googling about it.

"Are you sure you're asexual? Like, really sure?"

"Yeah…" It hurt Micah's chest to say that.

"Okay." Kim sighed and craned his neck back to look at Micah and his golden eyes seemed to say everything would be alright. "Okay, this is you. And whatever this is—this whole asexuality thing—it's you."

Micah smiled. His whole body felt lighter like a hot air balloon where rising in his chest. His beautiful coyote always knew just what to say. He could take any situation and say just a few short things to make everything better. Didn't matter what was wrong. Shitty day at work or fight with the family: Kim was always there for him. Always would be.

"I woke up thinking about what things would be like if you were a girl," Kim continued.

"What?"

"Like, if you were a girl and I told you I was gay last night." Kim sat up in bed. Micah stared at him. The whole room started to spin, crash back down to earth. "What would I want you to say? I'd want you to support me, of course, right? How could I act any differently?"

"But that's different." Micah's voice sounded faint.

"You're asexual."

"But I still love you." This couldn't be happening. *Oh, fucking shit, shit fuck.* He wasn't saying this.

"I love you too." Kim turned away; the dark arch of his back a hunched silhouette in the morning light.

"Then why are you saying this?"

"I..." Kim's voice shook. "I want to be with someone who wants to be with me."

"I do!" Christ how many times did he have to say it? How could he show Kim that everything could still be fine between them? This couldn't be it. They'd been—

"Can we not talk about this now?" Kim asked. He sounded miserable as if he already knew the outcome of that inevitable conversation.

Micah swallowed. No. Fuck that. He put a paw on Kim's shoulder. "No. You can't just bring this up then act like we're not talking about it! We're not leaving this bed until you know I love you. I want to be with you and that's that. All that asexual stuff, it doesn't matter."

"But is it true?" Kim sighed. "Are you asexual?"

"Y-yeah."

"Then, fuck, Micah... what else can we say?"

Micah closed his eyes. That was the truth of it, wasn't it? He was asexual and Kim wasn't.

Kim said something about mowing the lawn before it got too hot outside and Micah just nodded.

Kim's weight left the bed and Micah sat up to hug his knees. Their sexualities were too different. It was just like Kim had said, same as a gay man and a straight woman. They just couldn't work.

"Fuck no." Micah muttered to himself. They weren't some straight couple who were gonna be torpedoed by a hiccup in bed. Their relationship had never been about sex. That had never been the most important thing.

But maybe it had been to Kim. A small voice inside him said.

"Well, fuck that," Micah grumbled. That was not it. They were solid before they started fucking and they'd be a goddamned rock after this weekend too.

He grabbed his phone. That website was awesome, but it wasn't personal. They needed somebody else to talk too. There was probably a forum or subreddit somewhere, but that may not give answers fast enough. Could always ask Omar. Omar would certainly have the personal answers. Kim had looked up Omar's reviews once and all his clients agreed that he was easy to talk to.

Micah dialed the number before he could change his mind since this was probably a bad idea. Omar shouldn't psychoanalyze their relationship. That could just end up making more problems or would just make their couple dates awkward.

"Is your house on fire?" Raphael, Omar's husband, yawned. He sounded tired; must have just woken up.

"No. Is—"

"Did Kim fall down the stairs again?"

"No, but Raphael—"

"I'm just gonna give you to Omar."

Micah rolled his eyes. "Thanks."

There was a scuffle with the phone. Their voices were faint, but Micah could still understand them.

"Why's he calling?" Omar asked.

Raphael, already falling back asleep, made some sort of half-lucid noise.

Omar chuckled and must have grabbed the phone.

"Micah, darling. What's up?"

"I'm asexual." No point in dancing around it.

"That's great to hear." Omar said. "Is this a coming out call, or…"

"I told Kim and…" His breath caught. That stupid lump came back in his throat. Why was this so hard to say?

"Do you need a place to stay?"

"No! No," Micah tried to laugh. They weren't there. Not yet.

"But I'm going to go on and guess that our strong coyote isn't taking the news well."

"He said it's like he's a girl and I'm coming out to him as gay."

"Drama queen." Omar said. Micah could almost hear his friend rolling his eyes. "Though I suppose that depends. Did you say you never wanted to have sex with him again?"

"No. Of course I'm fine sleeping with him. I just don't know how to explain it."

"You're not wrong in calling, darling. And your thoughts aren't wrong either." Omar's voice changed. It was slower, calmer as if Omar were talking to one of his patients. In a way, that wasn't too far from the truth, Micah thought.

"You need to know that there's nothing wrong with being asexual or not having sexual attraction. You can still be happy in a relationship with open, honest communication. Same as any other relationship."

Micah closed his eyes and smiled. He took a deep breath. "Thank you, Omar. That... that really means a lot. But how do I explain it?"

"Sorry, darling, I truly am. You're the first person I've known who's asexual, and I can't explain it other than the clinical terminology or by what I know it is not. Asexuality is a lack of sexual attraction. I can't say what's going on in your head when you have sex, other than that it is different than what I feel."

"But how do I get him to stay?"

"Oh, darling. Oh, sweet darling." There was a pause, a breath through the line. "You two will be fine. I've seen plenty of lost causes and you two aren't one of them. Tell him how you feel and ask him how he feels. Talk, listen, and if you both do that everything will work out."

"I've told him how I feel! I love him."

"I never meant to imply that you don't, but that's not the issue here. Sex is. Have you told him how you feel during sex?"

"Oh what? So just: *Ooo Kim. I love how your thick cock stretches me open.*" He couldn't just go back and say this whole ace thing was a lie. No, the genie was out of the bottle and they had to deal with it.

"I mean emotionally. How do you feel, in your heart, when you two sleep together? What do you feel between you two at the moment of penetration?"

"Hnnk," Micah choked out a cough. God, if this weren't the most awkward conversation.

Omar laughed and Micah cringed. Just please, God, let this conversation help.

"What if... what if I don't know how I feel? I don't think I feel anything when he umm, well you know. But I mean, how do you feel when you fuck Omar? What's it supposed to feel like to look at him and think, *oh yeah I need that.* And what do you feel afterward? Kim always..." Micah trailed off. There was something intimate about their post-fuck cuddling. Even if he didn't understand it himself, he couldn't tell Omar.

"Kim says he likes the after-sex-care."

"I want to make things work."

"I know, darling, I know. This may get graphic, just so you know."

Micah took a deep breath. Why did he feel like they were back in high school? "More graphic than moment of penetration?"

"Let's start with the initial feeling of arousal and work our way from there. It's different based on the time. Sometimes it will be slow. A hand on the thigh or a brush of the tail and I'll want more. I'll feel this need— an anticipation in my chest with only one release. Other times, it will be more sudden. Like when Raphael comes home from working out and takes off his shirt and…" Omar made a huffing noise. "Let's just say his pants come off pretty quick too. As for during sex, I like the closeness of it. Being in him is the closest we can ever get, physically. And emotionally, I feel like we're on the same page in those moments. He meets my thrusts and pushes himself further onto me—" He laughed. "God, that sounds terrible, but we have the same goal in that moment. Everything else that's going on can just fade away so that the only thing that matters is that feeling between us. That shared building pressure— and the release! It's like giving him everything I have and feeling utterly exhausted. Physically, emotionally, mentally; I've given him everything and I think there's something beautiful in that. We lay together as one, truly one being."

Micah waited for Omar to say more. But maybe that's all there was to sexual attraction. Kim always seemed eager to start fucking him and he did seem to really enjoy knotting him.

"Is it the same for bottoms?" Micah asked.

"It's the same for me regardless of what role I play."

"Is it the same for everyone?"

"I can ask Raphael if you'd like."

"Yeah… sure." Micah said. Part of what Omar had said sounded self-ish: as if Raphael were meant to be taken or used as an object to satisfy Omar, but the rest of it had sounded romantic and sweet like it were a gift. Of course, that would be just like Omar to imply his dick were a gift. It could always be a top thing, despite what Omar had said.

"What's happening?" Raphael's voice was faint on the phone. Omar must have not fully handed it to him yet.

"We're on speaker with Micah, honey," Omar said. "He's asexual."

"Mazal tov!" Raphael yawned again.

"Sorry, darling. I think Raphael's too tired to be of help right now."

"No! I can be helpful." There was a slight scuffle: ruffling sheets. "What do you need?"

"He wants to know what it's like to bottom."

"I want to know how you feel about it," Micah interrupted.

"Like if it's tumah?"

"He means emotionally, honey. How do you feel before, during, and after sex as the bottom?"

"Oh, I… I've never really thought about it." Raphael paused. "I guess it's like… it's like there's something I need. If I really think about it, that's what I call it. Desire, I guess that would be the smart word for it. Omar gets this look in his eye and I feel like something wakes up in me. I feel this stirring in my sheath like it's got a mind of its own. I feel butterflies and the like. I don't know how to describe it really except that I know I want him in those moments. I need him more and more until…" he trailed off.

There was a pause on the line. Some soft noises, whispers, maybe.

"Micah, darling?" Omar said. "Raphael's a bit embarrassed by all this—"

"It feels weird over the phone," Raphael mumbled.

"But does that help?"

"Yeah," Micah said. It really did. He could talk with Kim about it after the yardwork. "Thanks. I owe you one."

"First round, tonight?"

"For sure."

Micah smiled. Hopefully by tonight everything would be okay. They could go out with Omar and Raphael and be back to their old selves. They'd come back home and sleep in the same bed. Kim's arm would wrap around him, his breath would warm the fur between his ears as he drifted to sleep, and they'd stay like that until morning. Everything would be fine, wouldn't it?

***

Sharing the yard work always made it go by faster. Kim mowed and swept while Micah did the edging and worked around the house with the weedwhacker. Dividing the work up like this helped them finish before ten most days, but it was still hot as hell and Kim had taken off his shirt between mowing and sweeping.

Micah watched Kim finish sweeping the driveway. The coyote's back muscles shifted under the fur. Lean and taut, his back seemed to dance with the swaying motion of the broom. How would Omar or Raphael react to seeing the other shirtless like this? Kim looked good, no arguing that, but there wasn't any stirring going on in Micah's pants. His mind wasn't flooded with all the times he'd been held up against the wall by that strong back. His fingers didn't feel the memory of clutching at those broad shoulders, burying his nose into that fur, crying out...

Micah closed his eyes; what did he think of?

The cute yote looks over his shoulder, golden eyes as vibrant as the morning sun, and he smiles—a full smile that stretches all the way up to his peaked ears.

There wasn't any sex in that smile. None of that wanting, lusting feeling Omar and Raphael had talked about.

He could always fake it, Micah thought. He could go up to Kim, turn him around, and slide into his arms. Press himself against the coyote and whisper something sexy, maybe slip a paw down to trace along Kim's side or rest his pads on his sheath. Any number of scenarios would work. They'd fucked a lot before after all.

Where those times faking? They hadn't felt like it at the time. Kim had never forced himself onto him or anything like that and the sex had always been enjoyable. Maybe it wasn't as breathtakingly magnificent as Omar and Raphael had talked about it, but it wasn't bad either. He never regretted doing it or sat around in fear of the next time Kim's cock would emerge.

Micah snorted. He couldn't help himself. Kim's dick wasn't some eldritch horror waiting to devour him.

"You okay there?" Kim asked.

Micah refocused his gaze on his husband: Kim was smiling at him. *Shit, he'd heard that.* But that didn't stop Micah from smiling back. "I'm good. Just thought of something funny."

It clicked into place then. Micah opened his mouth; he knew what it was. It was stupid, simple and stupid, but it seemed right.

***

"Micah?" Kim stopped in the bathroom's doorway. Small green flecks of grass dotted his arms and chest.

Micah bit his tongue lightly. How could he start this conversation? Everything had to go right this time around.

"Micah, why are you following me around all wide-eyed?" Kim tossed his shirt into the clothes hamper.

"I don't know how to start," Micah said. Honesty seemed like the best policy here.

"Start? About last night, ri—"

Micah's tail shook, his stomach clenched. Fuck it. He stepped forward.

"—ght?"

Micah placed his hands on Kim's chest...

"What are—"

... and kissed him.

They held together; muzzle pressed up against muzzle, saliva shared between them. Kissing really was disgusting if Micah thought about it, but it didn't need to be thought of like that. Kissing, fucking, and everything else could just be about the emotion behind them. The physicalness, the weight of Kim's hands on his shoulders, that didn't mean anything compared to what those actions showed.

Kim pushed Micah's shoulders. "Wait." They broke apart. "You don't have to do this."

"I want to."

Kim looked down and away at something. "But you're asexual."

"That doesn't mean I can't want this." Micah rested his paw on Kim's cheek. He looked into Kim's eyes and took a breath. This would be it.

"I don't have the love language of sex," he started. "That's probably not the right phrase, but it works for this—for us. I understand what you're feeling when we have sex, the types of things you feel and think leading up to it too. I get it but I'm not fluent, I guess."

He paused. Kim glanced up, finally meeting his eye again, but he didn't say anything. No protest or affirmation. Just those golden eyes.

Micah swallowed. He should keep talking then.

"Sex won't be the way I say I care about you—it's never been all that important to me in a relationship—but that doesn't mean I don't listen when you share that love with me. God, that sounds corny as hell, but I mean it. I know I don't feel the same desire for you that you feel for me. Not in the same way, but that doesn't mean I don't want this." Micah placed his other paw on Kim's hip. "Because I do want this. I love that you show your love in this physical, intimate way."

Kim's eyes started to water. The knot in Micah's stomach tightened. Fuck, this was hard. If he didn't keep talking, he'd break down too.

"When we have sex, it's not you coercing me or me biting the pillow until you're done. It's...it's...I don't know how to explain it fully, but I do like having sex with you. I like how we can show each other that care for one another with nothing but our bodies. I don't get off from the physicalness of you in me, but I'm obsessed with the way your eyes light up when you lift my tail. I love how you ask me if I'm okay every couple of seconds like you're afraid of hurting me. I love how your brow knots up when you're close and how you make these heavy, squeaky noises that only I'll ever hear.

"Yeah, sex is different for me, but I want to have sex with you because of you. It's you. I suck at explaining this, but it's you and there won't ever be some other Magical-Mr.-Right because that's you."

Micah looked down now. His chest hurt; throat raw like he were about to cry. That was it, wasn't it. "Is—is that okay with you?"

Kim's arms wrapped around him and squeezed him tight. Hot breath warmed the top of his head. Something pressed against his thigh.

"Man, I really want to fuck you," Kim's voice was strained. "If that's okay?"

"Mmm-hmm," Micah shook his head. A half-choking sob stuck in his throat. God! Things were going to be alright, weren't they?

Kim grabbed Micah by the ass, tossed him over his shoulder, and carried him, laughing and yelping to the shower.

***

Micah and Kim cuddled on the bed together, fur still wet from the shower. They'd really need to change the sheets after this, but that could wait. No amount of gross and cummy sheets could get Micah to move out from the crook of Kim's arm.

"You didn't?" Kim laughed.

"I wanted advice," Kim protested.

"You didn't seriously ask Omar what it's like to fuck someone?"

"Ask him tonight. I promised him first round."

"Oh, God no. What would Raphael say?"

"Probably the same thing he told me."

Kim laughed. "Yeah, right. So, what did he say?"

"He said it was like having butterflies and just really needing Omar's dick."

"And what's it like for you?"

"Honestly, I never really had any sort of thoughts about it. I thought I was supposed to have some sort of thoughts or feelings, so I sort of just thought about England for some reason…"

"You mean like that old quote about *just close your eyes and get through sex?*"

Micah smiled, no idea how that had started. "Yeah, but I found something better to think about."

"Oh," Kim chuckled softly. "What's that, kitten?"

"You." Micah kissed Kim's cheek and smiled. It was okay if he didn't have that hot desire. Kim had enough for the both.

Kim didn't say anything to that, but he didn't need to. He shifted his shoulder and moved his hand to rest more on Micah's side. Micah closed his eyes and settled further into the quasi-hug, nuzzling against Kim's fur. This was a nice moment. There would be more questions, more talking, but they would always have moments like this.

PERFECTION

James Hudson

If I told you that I used to spend almost every day of my life driving up and down the same two hundred and forty three miles of road between the middle of nowhere and the middle of some other nowhere, you'd probably think I made some pretty bad life choices somewhere along the line. Well that may be true, but becoming a truck-driver was the second best decision I ever made. The best decision was finally leaving that life behind, but you'll hear about that later.

A year or two ago, if I'd won the lottery, I still would've turned up at the depot the next morning and climbed into the cab of my truck. You see, I was a fairly typical trucker for that particular part of the world; a seven-foot-two grizzly with a liking for check-flannel and being alone. Sure, I enjoyed the company of others when I was younger, especially when others meant cute, male and cotton-tailed, but I never met anyone who was quite what I was looking for. In the end I just gave up looking and chose a solitary life. I suppose my standards were pretty high.

Before I go any further, I want to explain that I'm not a loner, I just didn't *need* a social life at that time. When I saw the other guys at the depot, I pretended to be interested in their lives just as much as they did about mine. I got along fine with everybody, okay? It's just that I was always happier when the sound of my colleagues' voices had been drowned out by a diesel-fueled rumble that made me smile every single day because I knew the dull concrete and steel of the depot, and the equally dull conversations with the other bears and wolves who worked there, would soon be replaced by hours of pine trees as seen through a panoramic windshield from the most comfortable seat in the world. I'm not saying it's easy driving a semi-truck along winding roads in all weather conditions, but I knew those roads like the back of my paw, and that meant I could relax and enjoy the ride. You wouldn't have caught me listening to rock music or whatever on the radio like the other guys either; it was just me and the sound of burning diesel. I really thought life couldn't get any better, but that was before I saw *him* standing by the side of the road with those eyes of his.

That morning started like the thousand before it; with the hiss of compressed air venting as I let the brakes off, and the growl of the engine as I pressed a foot gently onto the well-worn throttle pedal. Eighteen wheels started rolling and I felt like a king in his own private castle. The next truck wouldn't leave for another half an hour so I knew I'd probably have the road to myself save for the few moments when I would have to pass another truck coming the other way. The roads we used were so remote that you'd see almost no cars, and only a handful of buses. That would turn out to be pretty important, but I didn't know it yet.

The exit to the yard required a tight right-hand turn at crawling speed, a tell-tale sign that lumber had been hauled from that spot since the days when transportation came in a smaller package, but I knew my way around it, even when relying on my headlights in the early morning gloom. My thick-furred paws moved effortlessly across the smooth surface of the wheel and I swung the rig around to finally make my escape to the open road once again. I didn't expect to see more than a handful of other souls until I reached the drop-off point where my cargo would start the process of becoming furniture or matchsticks or whatever it was they did with all the wood I supplied those guys.

That's not a euphemism by the way. I never slept around with any of the truckers, lumberjacks or assortment of other tough guys I was so *genuinely* friendly with. They just weren't my type.

So anyway, back to that day. I'd been driving for a few miles and knew it wouldn't be too long before the first rays of morning sunshine were scattering through the trees and sending shimmering bright and dark shapes skittering across the dark scar on the landscape that was the road I loved so much. I'm certain my short, round muzzle must have been split by a wide grin because it always was on a fine morning like that behind the wheel. It wasn't warm, nor was it cold; it was just right. That's a little bear humor for you by the way. Anyway, thick fur and comfortable clothing meant I was feeling snug in my cab. If I'd been any more content, I'd have been at risk of dozing off at the wheel; a real danger for some. Me being me though, I was more awake than ever because I was having fun, and I thought only something highly unusual like a rockslide or a tire blow-out could stop me. If you'd told me it was going to be a hitchhiker, I would have laughed in your face.

There was a rule about hitchhikers in those parts; Just don't. That wasn't just my rule; it was something all the drivers swore by, and I have to say it suited me just fine. It might sound harsh to leave someone by the side of a road in the middle of a forest the size of a small country, but you've got to ask yourself: what the hell were they doing there in the first place? The only reason to be in that wilderness was because you worked there in some capacity, and in that case a driver would probably know you. Otherwise, you were suspicious.

Back in the day a driver might have stopped for some helpless-looking rabbit-lady or something only to get a gun jammed under his muzzle. Of course, there have been drivers who've taken advantage of genuinely hapless travelers too. It's amazing what a rabbit-lady might be willing to do in return for safe passage through the wilderness, even if she ends up regretting it later. The only thing is, drivers who did that usually ended up losing their jobs. So, as I said, the rule was we didn't pick up hitchhikers in the forest. We reported their location to the authorities but picking them up just wasn't worth the risk to our safety or our reputation.

But I did stop for a hitchhiker, and I'll try to explain why.

I noticed him from a few hundred yards away. I truly thought he was an animal-deer at first. That moment when your brain first recognizes something, but you haven't had time to process the information yet; when that happened to me, I instinctively let off the gas in reaction to the threat of collision. I think it must have been his big, wide eyes that I mistook for an animal's. The first thing you notice when you see him are his big, melt-your-heart innocent eyes.

Once my brain had kicked in, I realized he was standing on two legs and was wearing denim cut-offs and a T-shirt, so probably not an animal. He still kind-of looked like a dazed young buck on the run from a hunter though; not so much scared as simply helpless. I should have stuck my paw back down on the gas pedal the moment I realized what he was, but instead I lifted it off entirely and covered the brake. Honestly if it hadn't been for those eyes, I might not have stopped. It didn't even feel like a conscious decision, but I heard the engine note fall and felt myself being pulled forward against my safety-belts a little so I knew I must have pressed on the brake pedal. I must have gone through the whole process of stopping automatically because I didn't know exactly how or why I'd stopped.

When I pulled alongside the stranger, he was completely hidden from me behind the door of the truck, giving me time to think. Not being able to see him helped to clear my head a little. I knew I could still drive off, however tough that might seem, and that I probably *should* drive off if I knew what was good for me. Usually I did know what was good for me, but…

With a sigh and a shake of my head, I stretched uncomfortably across to open the passenger-side door. I could only just reach to unlatch the door, not push it open, and for a few seconds nothing more happened. I was starting to wonder whether I'd imagined the young male, in the way sea-dogs sometimes dream up fish-ladies on lonely voyages, but then I saw the door slowly swing open to reveal two huge, gently-smiling eyes that looked up at me as if I'd saved their owner's life.

"Thank you so much," said the most beautiful creature I'd ever seen as he clambered clumsily into the cab before I'd even uttered a word; before I'd even managed to exhale. My eyes were probably nearly as wide as his by this point, but not because I was annoyed or concerned. I knew straight away that the young buck was perfectly harmless. I just hadn't realized anyone like him really existed; He was that perfect.

It wasn't just his eyes, or his short beginnings of antlers covered in fine brown fur, or his little black nose, or even the masterpiece that was his face in general. It wasn't the white spots on his chest that I hadn't meant to see below the low neckline of his worn-out T-shirt as he'd climbed into the seat next to me. It wasn't his slim, almost feminine body, his round buttocks hidden poorly by tight denim, or even the white and brown bunny-tuft of a tail that he allowed to taunt me before it was hidden from view again by faux-leather seat-covering. No, it was all of that and more. It was everything. *He* was everything. He was Perfection.

Oh fuck, oh fuck, was about all I kept thinking as I watched Perfection summon all his strength to swing shut the heavy door of the cab. He looked no more than half my age, probably less; I guessed around nineteen and hoped he was no younger. So, there I was, with probably nineteen-year-old cervine perfection sat next to me in my truck, in the middle of nowhere, looking at me like he owes me a favor. The most shameful thing was, despite knowing it was the last thing that should have been happening, I felt a guiltily pleasurable pulse of blood to my gently swelling member. I looked away from Perfection in shame and embarrassment.

"Oh!" said Perfection in sudden alarm, his voice as sweet as a honeyed peach.

My eyes wandered to my lap. I was sure he'd noticed.

"I'm sorry, I shouldn't have assumed," he said, and placed his delicate fingers on the door as if he was going to open it and leave forever. "I was just so relieved someone finally stopped that I just hopped right in, didn't I?" He laughed slightly nervously, and ever so cutely.

"No…" I said, finally speaking to him. My voice sounded something like the truck's engine, and I felt like a brute next to my passenger. I wondered if he was afraid of me but decided he didn't seem to be. I was twice his size and I could have eaten him alive out there in the woods and no-one would have known anything about it. Strangely, I think *I* was the one who was afraid.

He gingerly took his fingertips from the door.

I risked making slightly awkward eye-contact. "I stopped so you could get in, it's just…"

"You're wondering why I'm out here in the middle of nowhere?" He smiled bashfully and then put a finger to his lips like he was pondering his own question.

"Yeah, something like that," I said with the slightest hint of a smile because I was relieved that Perfection understood the situation, and simply because he lit up the cab with his presence. I felt a strange fluttering in my stomach which no man had inspired in me for over a decade.

"I was visiting my parents," he said. "They live in a house near the edge of the forest on the north side. There should be a bus once a day that takes me all the way to the south side, but it never showed up and now I can't get home. I used to live nearer home, I mean my parents' home, but I live in the city now."

I nodded my head. The buses through the forest were notoriously expensive and unreliable. So few people used them that they frequently get cancelled and I assumed that was what had happened to Perfection. "Why didn't you just go back to your parents' place then? It's not safe for a guy your age to be hitching rides with strangers," I said, suddenly feeling as though I was talking to a child and making myself feel uncomfortable about the situation again. I knew he wasn't a child, but compared to me…

"I'm not a kid," Perfection replied, and made a slightly pouty face that I was sure he must have realized made him look younger. "I'm twenty-four and I don't think you seem dangerous so…"

"I'm not," I said, feeling relieved that my passenger was not dangerously young, although that only made the situation more exciting. He was almost old enough that I could have been forgiven for trying my luck with him; not that I really thought he'd be interested in a big, old grizzly like me.

"So anyways…" he said, looking slightly bashful for some reason. "I'm just trying to get to the other end of the forest so I can get another bus home. You must be going that way…"

"I am, but I still think you're being a little naïve. What you're doing isn't safe. *I* may not be dangerous, but, well, a lot of guys might try to take advantage of a situation like this."

Thinking I'd made the implication clear, I waited for him to act shocked or maybe, just maybe, say that he'd expected such an arrangement, but instead he gave me the eyes again. I remember thinking he must have had a sheltered upbringing, living so far out in the sticks.

"You mean money?" he said with obvious confusion after a short silence. "I don't have much money, but…"

"No, I don't mean money." The truck's door had been closed long enough by this point that I was starting to think I could detect the perfect scent of Perfection's short, light-brown fur. I shuffled my bulk uncomfortably in my seat to hide the effect it was having on me. *Am I really going to say it?* I thought. I knew I would never ask him for anything like *that*; Maybe just offer to buy him a drink some time.

My eyes found his slightly glistening little lips, and I found the courage to say, "What I mean is…"

I couldn't do it.

He laughed girlishly. "You mean what? You can tell me."

I felt a little light-headed as I wondered whether he was being flirtatious or just innocently curiosity. *Is he asking me to say it? Does that mean he actually expects to make that kind of deal?* I knew I would never go through with something like that anyway, but just the idea that I *could*, with someone like him… It really got me going, and I said something stupid.

"What I mean is," I began in a low, husky voice, "some guys might ask a pretty guy like you to wrap their mouth around their cock and…"

I knew straight away that I'd made a stupid mistake. Perfection sat bolt upright and looked out into the wilderness with his pretty little mouth ajar. His paws were clenched up and he just sat there, not saying anything to the stupid old bear who should have known better.

"Oh, shit," I muttered, mortified at my behavior. "I didn't mean…

Look, I'm sorry," I blurted out, trying to repair the damage. "I wasn't saying *I'd* ask for anything like that. I just wanted you to understand what guys like me would... I mean, not guys like *me*..."

Everything I said made me sound worse, and soon I was sitting bolt upright too, staring out into the wilderness with my huge, intimidating paws clawing at my thighs nervously. I expected Perfection to get out the cab and run, but he didn't.

"*You* think *I'm*...attractive?" he said in a tiny, shocked voice.

By this point I was sure I couldn't make anything worse by being honest. "Yes, of course I do. You're *very* attractive. Isn't that obvious?"

Perfection glanced furtively at me and unclenched his paws. "But, I mean, *you* find me attractive? Sexually? I mean, you're so..."

"So...old?" I asked, and started to wonder if that was what had shocked him.

"No!" he said almost apologetically, and gently bit his lower lip as he looked at me with his devastating brown eyes. "I meant you're..."

It was a long time before I found out what he'd intended to say, but I smiled when he finally told me. Let's just say it made me feel better about my waistline and scruffy fur. Anyway, the reason he stopped talking was because something bad was about to happen, as it usually does when you think things are starting to look up.

We both saw it at the same time, but only I panicked. Perfection didn't move until I told him to.

"Oh shit," I growled as the headlights of a truck returning to the depot appeared round a distant bend. My mind ran through the list of guys who might have been driving that truck and none of them were folks I wanted to see me with Perfection in the cab next to me, especially with a look on his face like I'd just asked him to suck my dick. Maybe I sort-of *had* asked him to suck my dick; I'm not really sure.

I hadn't meant to sound so forceful, but when I said, "Get down," it sounded more like a command than a suggestion. I'm a big guy and there I was growling at Perfection to get down, right after I'd made a stupid remark about blowjobs. I was just scared of losing my job or my reputation, but the way I reacted wasn't great, I have to admit. I never could have known it was exactly what Perfection wanted.

The truck was still some way off but it's twin searchlights were getting nearer, and all I could do was hope they didn't illuminate anything I wanted kept secret.

By the time I realized I shouldn't in a million years have told my confused new friend to 'get down', he'd already started lowering himself into the footwell. I remember thinking that at least the other driver wouldn't see him now, even if I'd probably accidentally terrified a hitchhiker into submission.

The thing was, he didn't look terrified. His eyes were still those of an innocent deer in the crosshairs of a hunter, but there was something else there now that hadn't been there before. I didn't know it at the time, but Perfection's eyes had been opened to new possibilities by my admission of attraction.

"I wasn't trying to scare you," I felt the need to say. "I just don't want anyone to see you in my truck. I…"

I stopped making lame excuses when I saw Perfection begin to shuffle towards me in the confined space beneath the truck's seats. His little cotton-candy tail was wiggling from side to side as he used all four limbs to clamber nearer me, out of sight of the approaching truck. By the time his little hand-paws were on my thigh, I should have been worrying about the possibility of him catching the hand-brake with his legs, or perhaps asking him what he thought he was doing, but instead I was glancing at the road and hoping Perfection could stay out of sight. I wasn't about to stop him doing whatever it was he was doing.

By the time I had a beautiful white-speckled, brown-furred face a foot from my groin, it was already too late to pretend I wasn't turned on. My pants resembled a hastily erected tent.

I took another glance out the windshield. The truck was laboring up a moderate incline and wouldn't reach me for a few minutes.

I could tell Perfection was breathing quite heavily, but whether that was due to fear or something else I wasn't sure at that point. However, if I hadn't hoped it was something else, I could have stopped him. Maybe I *should* have stopped him, but if I'd known then what I know now, I would have felt better about doing what I actually did, which was absolutely nothing.

When his fingers reached for the bulge in my pants and began to tentatively stroke it, he was giving me a chance to stop him. He was silently asking, "Is this *really* what you want?" and when I moaned and dug my claws into the armrest, I was saying "Fuck, yes!"

There was a slight laugh-like quality to the excited sound Perfection made when he realized, I really did want what he was offering. A simple exhalation of air but it said so much.

The truck in the distance was gaining a little speed again now. I knew it would be no more than a minute before it reached us. The thought that I probably wasn't going to be discovered with a cute young buck in the passenger seat was a relief, but I knew I'd have to keep him down until the truck had passed by, and he was so sexy that I knew that was going to be a challenge. I still wasn't sure he knew what would happen to me if he was seen either.

There was something almost cat-like about Perfection's arched back and outstretched arms as he reached up a little further and pulled my sweatpants over my erection. It bounced a little as it was released, the bulbous tip already glistening with anticipation.

I heard Perfection mutter something cute in approval and I could tell he'd never seen a cock that size before. I didn't know then that he'd only fooled around with a couple of collage mates before, but I could tell he'd never seen anything like ten inches of bear-cock before, and he was practically licking his lips. I was in no doubt about his desire now.

The truck was thirty seconds away by this point, it's headlights starting to illuminate the cab and giving the scene below me an ethereal quality. If I'd thought about it, I would have realized what was going to happen when the truck reached me.

Perfection wasted no time in wrapping his hand as far around my cock as he could manage, but he didn't stroke it yet. I muttered something unintelligible as he shuffled his slim body closer, his once-in-a-lifetime face inching closer to the point of no return.

It was around this time that I started to realize what was going to happen in about thirty seconds time, but it was too late to change anything even if I'd wanted to.

It was his perfect, pink little tongue that wetly met the tip of my cock first. I'd never felt anything so soft. Then he opened as wide as he could and wrapped his moist lips round the end of my dick in a kiss that left me gagging for air. He giggled again and his grip on my shaft tightened. If I'd just let myself release in his mouth straight away it would have saved so much trouble, but instead I tightened up and controlled myself with a grimace. I couldn't let perfection last only a moment; I couldn't let go so soon.

By now I could hear the other truck's engine note falling, its headlights becoming a constant warning of impending ruin.

When Perfection moaned as he forced my cock deeper into his mouth, I couldn't resist placing a big paw on the top of his head and grabbing at his little, silkily-furred antlers. I pushed down a little, forcing my cock to meet the back of his throat. With a slurp and another moan, he started to bob up and down rapidly, spurred on by my act of control over him. In truth, I had little control left.

The other truck was now almost alongside us.

Both my hand-paws were on Perfection's head and his pretty little ears poked through my fingers. He was gagging my cock as far down his throat as he could manage, his blunt teeth posing no problems. Hot saliva was running down my shaft and over Perfection's little paw as he worked the base of my erection. I wasn't going to last much longer.

A hiss of air escaping from the other truck's brakes startled me and caused my head to jerk up and round. It was a surreal experience to see the long, grey muzzle and deep-set, yellow eyes of my Lupine Colleague, Jansen, looking back at me in concern as I sat in my truck secretly being pleasured by a buck who looked like something Jansen ought to have been hunting by moonlight.

Through two sheets of glass I saw Jansen mouth something which, despite his unfamiliar lupine mouth, I could still read as, "You okay?"

If Perfection hadn't chosen that second to start jerking my cock as fast as he could whilst desperately sucking on the head and looking up at me with eyes which begged me to cum in his mouth, I might have realized Jansen had wondered why I was sat by the side of the road such a short distance from the depot, grimacing and groaning for no apparent reason. If I hadn't felt my balls tighten in an explosion of un-imaginable pleasure, I might have been able to control my body enough to give Jansen a thumbs up or even a smile, but Perfection was moaning away and furiously milking my cock.

So, as I began to fire hot semen into the mouth of the most beautiful young male I'd ever seen, I thrashed and grimaced and looked for all the world to Jansen like I was dying of a heart attack. Thanks to the closed doors between us, Jansen couldn't see or hear what was really happening, and couldn't know that his desperate calls for help to the depot on the radio were unwanted.

All I could think about was Perfection's warm mouth sucking the last of the cum from the end of my cock and swallowing it without a care in the world. I wanted to call his name as I ran my claws through his soft fur, but I hadn't even gotten around to asking him what it was yet.

By the time he was sitting alongside me again in the cab, trying to hide the fact that he'd cum in his pants as I'd cum in his mouth, all we had time to do was smile at each other in disbelief at what had happened. The cab was now lit by the intermittent blue light atop an ambulance. How close I'd come to *actually* having a heart attack I'm not sure, but I felt as happy as I had in years. I knew I was going to lose my job, but I was surprised to realize that I didn't care all that much.

So, it took a little longer than expected to get Perfection back home, but I managed it in the end, and I've not left since. I don't mean he's locked me up or anything, I just mean I'm living with him now. Once he'd convinced the authorities that he was the age he claimed, and that I hadn't forced him or paid him to do anything, we were free to get on with our lives. Of course, I still lost my job, but I didn't care. I realized that I'd been running away from the life I thought I'd given up on years ago, and that I only liked being alone because I thought I could never find someone I wanted to be around. With Perfection by my side I feel twenty years younger, although he wouldn't like that; he's into older guys. Oh, and if you're wondering what Perfection's real name is, all I can say is, mind your own business. I've found my Perfection; you can find your own.

25 Miles East of Fate

Buck C. Turner

Fate threw me and Chad together, but not that destiny garbage. I'm not big into that kind of belief in higher power stuff; I prefer computers. It was Fate H.S., about two hours away from the last suburbs that could still be credibly called Dallas. Fate, Texas is a small town, but not quite as small as it looks if you're just judging by what you can see from the interstate. Believe it or not, there are bastions of almost but not quite civilization in the fields of Texas. Besides, two hours isn't that long of a drive.

I'm not a hundred percent sure this is real, even as I lay here listening to Chad snoring softly, smelling (and still tasting) his musk over the smell of cheap beer. The panting and overheating in the small tent we're sharing make it something less than a fantasy even though I'm not ready to trade the comforting bulk cuddling up against me for some almost cool night air. His last sleepy question, "You still gotta go back to school?" still rattles through my head and keeps me from joining him in dreamland.

Chad was a football player named Chad, and his family has money, so he gets lumped in as a bro, but that wasn't really him. Being a bear in a small Texas town nearly demands your participation in the peculiar religion of high school football, but he played along without taking it so seriously that he got pulled off to college to play. I kept up with the team in school less out of choice and more through osmosis. Even if I was a gangly wolf (or scrawny if you wanted to be mean) who preferred computers to sports, half the honors classes I took in high school were still made up of football players.

That meant I've known Chad forever. Still, we weren't close in school, not back then. My family wasn't poor—my dad was a diesel mechanic and they make pretty good money—and Chad wasn't one of the few 'oil money' kids in school, but his dad had a big ranch, and that meant

Chad could get a pickup that was only a decade old, instead of one that was two decades old. He could afford the lift kit, but he had to order it online and put it in himself, as opposed to paying someone to do the grunt work. That and the football kept him in something of a different orbit than me.

Still, you don't spend that much time with someone in the same room without getting to know each other well enough. I never would have figured to be naked in this tent with him now, surrounded by his bulk. That really just kind of happened at the start of summer. I just finished my freshman year at University of Texas at Dallas. Sounds fancy, but it's not really all that impressive. It's a pretty small branch of the big football powerhouse, where most of the students are commuters lured by the promise of in-state tuition rates. The locals mostly see it as a 'safety pick' for when you don't get in or can't afford your first (second or third) choice school. I still wound up with a big ass loan and a job in one of the computer labs on campus. It's a lot less work than actually getting a real job, but getting a campus job meant that it didn't cover summer. I had tried to get a paid internship to cover housing for the summer, but they all wanted at least two years of school.

That was a rough spot to be in, since I was still short on rent money and seasonal jobs generally didn't pay enough to cover rent and food without another loan. It was a fair bit of luck, mostly bad, that got me on Chad's dad's ranch for the summer. I hadn't even wanted to go back home, but I couldn't really justify the extra loans on top of a fast food or grocery store job.

Going back to Fate should have made it harder to pick up work, and it would have been if not for my dad. He picked up extra cash on the evenings and weekends doing maintenance and repairs for tractors and the like around the area. That meant he had an inside line for when Chad's dad busted his knee up by rolling one of the quads they used on the ranch. It was bad enough to need surgery, and that meant minimum of 8 weeks, maybe longer off it.

Chad's dad was kind of a hard ass who did a bunch of stuff around the ranch himself. With him being laid up, even temporarily, he needed to hire someone to fill in. I'm not exactly sure what favors were exchanged, but the day after I got home from school I was off to the ranch. I wouldn't be surprised if that conversation had included phrases like, "an honest day's work" and "put some meat on his bones." It wasn't my idea of great, but four-fifty a week cash under the table wasn't something I could turn down. That and free rent more or less sealed my fate for the summer. And as much as I wasn't looking forward to it, it was work I was at least familiar with. I did 4H instead of scouts growing up, at least until dad let me quit to join computer club in junior high.

I'd always been small and smarter, which meant that I knew I didn't belong in some tiny-ass town, surrounded by assholes who thought they could pick on me. It only got worse when puberty came around and I figured out that the girls clearly didn't have the same effect on me as the other boys. But knowing that you're gay is very different from acting on it, especially in a small town like Fate.

It wasn't exactly the end of the world growing up there, but there was definitely some risk involved. I just steered clear of demonstrating any kind of romantic interest in high school. Fortunately no one actually expects the nerds to have a sex life, so tiptoeing my way through high school avoiding the label of one of 'them queers' wasn't difficult. From what I could tell, avoiding relationships seemed pretty common among the kids that were bent on getting out and going to a school somewhere in a big city. I kept myself, in a word, unremarkable.

So just before the ass crack of dawn, I drove my little beater out to the Rolling T to get started on whatever work was neglected. I didn't see Chad's dad around, not that day nor most any other 'cept payday. Chad was around to let me know what to do. Most of the proper farm work was taken care of by year round professional ranch hands, so it was the unessential landscaping sort of work, or special project type stuff that I was left with. The first two days I spent on a tractor and on my paws cutting the grass in the huge ass pasture they kept facing the frontage road. I wound up looking closer to a brown wolf than my normal gray from all the dust. It especially stood out when I saw my reflection next to my dad, who had his typical oil and grease stains from a day at the shop.

After a couple of days of collecting some basic tasks in the morning and being left largely to my own devices for the day, Chad asked me to help him with some stuff he needed an extra pair of hands for around the ranch. I really didn't mind the company. Chad had more or less the complete rundown of everything that had happened to everyone in our senior class over the previous year. At first it was pretty weird, hearing these stories connected to names I hadn't even thought since gradua-tion. Chad was a bit incredulous the third time I had to stop and ask, "Wait, who was that again?" I guess I hadn't really engaged a lot there toward the end, but it did sound like most of the honors class crowd was actually doing pretty well, and a bunch of them still got together regularly, even the ones who went far away from school had been joining up on holidays.

It made for a good start to summer, and Chad made it a little nicer by seemingly never wearing a shirt. All the professional guys seemed totally immune to the heat, but usually within five to fifteen minutes of getting to whatever barn, outbuilding, or fence section we were working on that day, Chad's shirt was on the bench or hanging on the fence. I don't actually know if that made him cooler, since most of the time we were outside, and Chad's medium brown fur had to be soaking up a bunch of heat, but I wasn't about to question my good fortune.

That second week played out in a similar rhythm, though a lot of the chatter moved away from town gossip to Chad's school. I'd known he was basically getting pressed into the family business, but he was still getting a degree, just slower—some program in agricultural management administered by A&M tailored for remote students who were already working in agriculture. It was pretty interesting, and I was surprised about how many of the same classes overlapped with things I took in my comp sci plan. It wasn't just how to take care of cows and horses, but with as much automation and programming is happening, it's important to have someone around who can troubleshoot all that. And in just a few weeks, a summer on the ranch turned from kind of a nightmare to normal.

Ok, obviously that wouldn't stay true for much longer or I wouldn't be here in this tent. That part started a few weeks into summer, when we got an unusual set of summer storms that rolled through. An odd thunderstorm here and there isn't that out of the ordinary during the summer, but we had wound up with nearly four days of heavy rain in a row. That made for a pretty crappy few days at work choosing between wet and miserable or overheated in a poncho and miserable. Chad never seemed to mind much, about the only concession he'd make was adding a ball cap to keep the rain out of his eyes. The wet fur and rain-soaked jeans just seemed to emphasize that even if he wasn't working out for football anymore, the work on the ranch was still keeping him built like a powerlifter.

The weather finally broke on a Friday, and I was looking forward to a weekend. Chad had invited me to go out with the group from high school on Saturday night, but I turned him down. I had been thinking about making the drive into Dallas to catch up with some college friends, now that I'd gotten a few paychecks.

Chad altered that plan some when he asked if I wanted to go muddin' the next day. I hadn't really been expecting anything like that, since for all the time we had been spending together, I still didn't really consider us friends yet. He was just being friendly is all—something to pass the summer. He knew I was heading into the city that night, so I really should have said no so I could sleep in. The chance to hang out with that big shirtless bear on more casual terms must have clouded my judgement, because I told him that I could head out with him as long as we made it back by early afternoon. He agreed and told me to show up the next morning at 9.

Now if you're a city type, you probably don't really know what muddin' is, or why someone would get up to that on a perfectly nice Saturday morning when you could be sleeping in. Well, truth be told, I couldn't really explain the appeal myself, at least not before that particular weekend. But what it is, is kind of a freeform off-roading in a big swampy field. Out in the flats of Texas, we didn't really have the kind of trails and hills that you get out west, but we still had lots of overly built up four by fours looking for any excuse to get off road and justify the exorbitant prices of massive wheels, tires, lift kits and custom gearing. Muddin' is basically just finding a big field where you can tear through and get almost, but not quite, stuck in mud as deep as your rig can handle. It might sound a bit low-brow, but given the cost of a good truck for it, muddin' is actually kinda upscale out here.

I showed up the next morning, not exactly sure what to expect. I'd only been out muddin' once or twice in high school, and those had been larger groups, a bunch of other kids getting together to show off. Chad hadn't mentioned getting anyone else to come along, or if we were going to meet up with folks. I pulled up next to his truck, and he was already out by it, checking stuff over. Like nearly always, he was shirtless, just wearing jeans and boots. When I got out, he told me to grab a couple bungees out of the back of the cab and strap down the cooler in the bed of the truck. That was really about all the prep to be done, and the two of us were off, bombing off down the gravel road that led to the west side gate out of the ranch, away from the main roads.

Chad started off the drive with the requisite jawing about all the stuff he'd done to his truck, and what he'd be doing if he had an extra two or three or ten grand for bigger tires, more suspension, blah blah. It went over my head in terms of what any of that stuff really did, but I knew the brand names from stickers on trucks in town, and knew enough about cars from my dad to nod along in the right places without sounding like a total idiot.

It wasn't long before we got to what seemed like a relatively unassuming field, looking like pretty much any other save for the remaining puddles were maybe a little wider, a little deeper than those in most of the other fields I'd passed that morning. It looked like a likely spot to me, but we weren't slowing down. I was about to ask if we were meeting anyone else when Chad gunned it and cranked the wheel hard right. Unprepared, I damn near toppled over into his lap.

"Shit dude!" I grabbed at the door and yanked back barely in time to avoid my head landing in his crotch. Chad just grinned and focused on the field ahead as he gunned the engine again and bounced through the mud, going deeper than I expected in a few of them and sending a curtain of dirty water over the hood of the truck. He continued toward the far end of the field, cutting back and forth to hit some of the deeper pools and mud puddles, but by now I was prepared for it and rolled with the truck as it bounced and heaved. He slowed up as we got close to the far border of the field and swung around so we could clearly see that first track. He hit the windshield wipers and let out a hearty laugh.

"You should have seen yourself! Not a clue..." His laugh was tapering off, but his chest was still bouncing with suppressed chuckles.

I responded with the best glower I could manage around my grin. "That's not the first time you've done that, is it?"

"Ha! Hell no, man, always gotta bomb the first run without stopping. Keeps everyone on their toes when I show up." He leaned forward and scrutinized the first track, likely planning out another run across the field.

"Everyone? We meeting anyone else today?" When no one was with Chad at the ranch, I sort of assumed we'd be heading out to meet up with some of his other friends.

"Nah, short notice and all, was kind of a spur of the moment thing really. 'Sides, I could use a break from some of the usual crowd. It's been kinda shitty lately, all of them seem caught up in some kind of miserable relationship... I just wanted to drive, ya know?" Before I could respond he'd popped the gear selector into low and raced off again. I didn't get to say anything, but I was a little surprised, since he had told me about a bunch of his friends' relationships, and none of them seemed bad? I didn't have time to bring it up as we bounced through the paddock.

This time, it was less of a speed shot across the field, but slower and more deliberate, a line that twisted around, doubling back on itself and crossing the first trail through some of the deeper mud, spinning tires and digging the track out deeper. Cutting the wheels back and forth near the edge of the field, Chad bounced the truck over a rocky section and through a set of saplings. That was new to me. The few times I'd been out before it was a bunch of guys trying to make a bigger splash, or playing a slightly more advanced version of chicken, swerving to miss each other at the last moment. The way he was focused on hitting these invisible marks, the rolling and bouncing of the truck became much more purposeful and meaningful. It changed the experience from a kid jumping in puddles to a roller coaster off the tracks.

He pulled off his run and coasted to a stop on the more solid ground at the edge of the field and put the truck into park. "You ready?" he asked.

My eyes would have given away the surprise even if I hadn't blurted out a sharp, "Huh?"

"Well, yeah, not gonna come all the way out here and just drive by myself all day. No fun in that." There was a pause before he added, "Well, not nearly as much anyway."

"Oh, sure, I just hadn't ever actually driven before going mudding is all." I was surprised enough not to think too hard about what I was getting myself into as I unbuckled myself from the passenger seat.

"Bullshit, I've seen you out before..." Chad was furrowing his brows, thinking back to different times he'd been out with folks, trying to remember me there.

"Well, I've been out before two or three times, but it was always with someone... I don't have a truck, duh, and usually I'd be out here with Jason, and he sure as hell wasn't interested in anyone else driving his truck." I opened the door and stepped out.

"Yeah, fair enough. He would be the kind of jackass who invites someone out and then doesn't give them a turn." Chad gave a halfhearted roll of his eyes and a sympathy shrug. I imagine I was probably supposed to feel slighted, but truthfully I didn't really care. After all, I hadn't felt like I was missing out given the way things usually went at the previous meet ups I'd been at.

Chad got out and we swapped places. He gave me a few pointers and it wasn't long before I was tearing across the field myself. It was fun

I guess. I wouldn't say it was some great revelation about the pastime, and how I suddenly realized what I was missing and that I needed to go find some used 4x4 to jack up. Still, I was having a good time, blasting through the standing water, and trying to follow some of Chad's previous lines. It was harder than it looked for sure, but I was starting to get the hang of it pretty quick, at least if I was reading Chad's grunts and growls correctly.

After a while, we pulled out under some shade and grabbed some cokes out of the cooler. Chad was definitely more relaxed out here away from the ranch. I wasn't really used to him letting his guard down like this. Sure he'd chat during the days at work, but out here he was actually willing to complain some about the ranch, and admitted that he was actually at least a little jealous of me going to school in Dallas. I was a little surprised he said that given how much he seemed like he liked it here.

"Really? It's not like you couldn't have gotten into like—a half dozen different schools there. Wouldn't your dad help you out if you went to one?"

Chad sighed and looked across the field. "Naw, he can be a pain sometimes, but he's not that shitty. I think he did expect me to go somewhere for a degree. I just didn't want to leave for that long. I don't think that I could come back after that."

It was all I could do to keep my eyes from rolling. "I mean, isn't that most of the point? There's just so much out there. I always knew I wasn't really supposed to be here."

"Always?" Chad looked a little sad.

"Hell, I dunno, I just feel like there's probably somewhere that I feel like I belong, and that isn't exactly here."

When we finished up the drinks, he got back into the driver's seat and fired up the engine again. He went through the center of the field and started getting more aggressive with his turns. He was following some of his previous tracks through one of the deepest sections when we started to slow down. Chad pulsed the gas, trying to surge through mud. It wasn't working though, and we came to a stop despite the engine's high revs. Chad cursed under his breath and put the truck in reverse. A pattern of slow pulses rocked the truck some, but when Chad tried to give it more gas we didn't break out and just settled in deeper.

"Fuck!" Chad gave a halfhearted pound on the steering wheel. "Well, shit. Looks like winch time." I raised my eyebrows and Chad answered my unspoken question. "Yeah, it's in the bed, I don't have a front end mounted one." He peered around the truck at the muck we were stuck in. The word 'fuck' was muttered in many different combinations. The final version of that was, "Well, fuck it…" And that's when he unbuckled, first his seatbelt, and then his belt. He was unbuttoning his pants when it was my turn to start swearing.

"Huh? What the fuck?" I was suddenly quite unsure of what was going on. Chad had his pants down and was awkwardly reaching down to the footwell to push off his shoes.

"If we're not moving, that mud is at least two feet deep. Now, I could wade through it, get mud completely soaked into my jeans, fill up my boots, probably get my boots pulled off anyway when I try to walk, and still get my fur covered. Or I can just cut to the chase. It's easier to get the mud out of just fur." He flopped back in the seat, having freed both his paws and gotten his jeans off, now wadded up on the seat between us. "You'll want to do that, too. That winch isn't mounted to the truck, it's gotta be hauled out to a tree or something, and it's too heavy for me to get by myself."

I stared at the ceiling for a couple seconds and then finally growled, "Well shit, may as well get it done then." And I started kicking off my shoes.

"Aw, c'mon, it's no big deal. Didn't you ever play in mud puddles as a cub? Same thing." Chad seemed to be almost enjoying himself now.

"Um, not since I was like, four?" I moved on to pushing down my pants, having a bit of an easier time than Chad did since I was so much less cramped in the cab.

"It didn't stop being fun just because you got older." And with a goofy ass grin, he opened his door and jumped out into the mud. I finished taking off my own pants and gingerly headed out myself.

I immediately sank up to about my knees, holding on to the side of the truck to keep from toppling over. Chad was already back around the tailgate and had climbed up into the bed of the truck. I was now just under eye line with his crotch, and very aware of bulges accentuated by the white UnderArmour compression shorts he was wearing. I bit my tongue and slogged around to the back.

Now, contrary to what anyone might imagine in stories, casually stripping off like this isn't exactly normal just because we're in the country. I was not ready for 250 pounds of nearly naked bear grunting as he dragged a two hundred pound winch toward me. I think the only saving grace that kept me from losing my mind was that we were stuck out here unless we did the very mundane task of hooking a winch up to a vehicle and towing it out of a ditch.

Chad got the winch to the edge of the truck and hooked up the free end of the line to the hitch on the bumper. We then grunted and slogged away from the truck carrying the heavy-ass gas powered winch. It was a pain, but pretty quick it turned pretty damn funny, when you took into account all the rude squelching sounds we made as we trudged toward the neared solid ground and sturdy tree. By the time we had gotten to said tree, I'd pretty much gotten over the nudity factor—at least until he bent over the winch to get it started. Seeing that butt presenting itself—and barely covered—was definitely starting to provoke a reaction.

I avoided the situation by looking back to the truck, fixating on it as I heard the little two stroke winch finally crank over. Once set to reel in, I wandered over away from Chad just in case the cable slipped lose and recoiled back at us. Fortunately nothing so dramatic happened, and the truck lurched free of the mud and started rolling back toward us. Chad pulled it back to solid ground, then drove it back the rest of the way so we wouldn't have to carry the winch.

Once we got everything stowed, Chad tossed me a ratty old towel from the back of his truck and said, "Probably enough excitement for today, right?"

I brushed what mud I could off, but it was rapidly drying in my fur. "Yeah, I did want to get back so I could head off into the city." With a nod, Chad got back up in the driver's seat, making no moves to put back on his pants or shoes. It was largely a quiet drive back to the ranch, but a comfortable one, somehow.

When we got back, Chad pulled up to the barn by a water spigot where they kept a hose. We climbed out and went over to hose off. I grabbed the hose and started working the mud off my legs, spending a couple minutes before handing the hose over to Chad. I went over and shook out my legs in the sun, hoping to dry off at least a little before getting back into my pants. I looked back and Chad had moved on from just cleaning off his legs, running the water over his head and arms, not keeping any care to stay dry. That meant his tight white underwear had been soaked as well—turning largely translucent and even more clinging.

Don't stare... Don't stare... Don't stare, I just kept repeating to myself as I limited myself to fleeting 'casual' glances at the might-as-well be naked bear. I forced myself to go back over to the passenger side and grab my pants and shoes, forcing them on despite the inevitable pulling and discomfort of putting denim over wet fur. Once safely sequestered, I shut the door and was about to make my way back to my car and escape.

I was just turning to head to my car when I heard, "Hey!" as chad came around the front of the car, completely unconcerned by his virtual nudity. "Thanks for coming out today, sorry about the mud and all."

"Eh, don't worry about it. I had a good time. See you Monday?"

"Bright and early! Have fun in the city." And with that he came forward, paw up to fist bump. We bumped fists, and before I could turn, Chad casually reached out and slapped my ass. Not content to stop there, while I was still frozen, he leaned in and gave a big lick right up my cheek! I was speechless as he grinned and wandered back around to pick up the hose he'd dropped, and casually started to hose off his truck.

I stiffly made my way over to my own beater car and got in. I was very much on autopilot as I drove away, and not until I was at least two miles outside the gates of the ranch did I howl into the empty cabin, "What the fuck was that!" I shivered just a bit as I remembered the feeling of that tongue on my cheek. I had to keep convincing myself over and over that it really happened, the slight sting in my butt, the cowlick I suddenly had on the left side of my face... It was evidence, but every thirty seconds or so, I kept imagining that it was all in my head. At least every fifteen seconds I had convinced myself that it didn't mean anything, Chad was just overly friendly now, like maybe that was a jock thing?

I'd been surreptitiously enjoying the view Chad had been providing for the past few weeks. He had that powerful football player build, but never seemed to take it as seriously as a jock is supposed to. I never had any kind of interest in building myself up like that, but I certainly did appreciate the look. I didn't get too invested in guys that looked like that, though. It just seemed so completely out of reach that someone like that from a little town like Fate would be seriously interested in me. I was just happy to have the excuse to be in close proximity as the half-naked hunk would heft supplies, stretch, and bend over. Seeing that underwear, that ass slap, the lick! It changed the way I thought about the past few weeks, and the rest of the summer to come.

Two hours never felt so long as I burned up the miles into town with only myself and the radio for company. Not that arriving made me feel much better, but at least I could get distracted by my school friends for the evening. I did spend a lot of the evening preoccupied, and while my friends noticed, I just played off that I was tired. It wasn't like any of them had ever spent time on a ranch, and they all expressed a great deal of sympathy for my current job plight, even if most of them weren't making as much (or even any) money this summer.

After too few hours though, it was time to get back on the road. As it was, I probably wouldn't get home before 2 a.m., and that's if I made good time getting out of the city. It still boggled my mind that there could be heavy traffic in Dallas at midnight. Coffee and loud music kept me awake on the drive home, but didn't do anything to keep my mind from drifting back to Chad for those two hours.

The last year at least, I'd been out of the closet, or at least my own halting version of out... I didn't run off to the pride parade, or fly a rainbow flag or anything, but I'd been to a few of the campus LGBTQ Association meetings. I even had a few awkward first dates; a second date once. I'd used the hookup apps a couple times even, which was ok but the nerves it caused usually weren't worth the encounter.

That was all rolling around in my mind as I drove home, unexpectedly invading my summer. I assumed that the few months I'd be back home would be back to that high school undercover, furtively jerking off to whatever I found on the internet whenever I had some time I could be sure I wouldn't be interrupted. The addition of an exhibitionist bear was suddenly making everything hard. He would have to be wearing those compression shorts, too. I had only glimpsed that waistband maybe once or twice before. Another shiver as I remembered them clinging to his crotch, soaking wet and so very nearly see through...

Monday was going to be hell.

Monday was in fact hell, but for a different reason than I anticipated. All the rain that had allowed us to go mudding meant that the grass was growing faster than usual for this time of year, so I was once again spending my day alone on a tractor slowly mowing back and forth. It was worse this time, partly because I'd done it before and knew exactly how boring it was, some because the weather was way hotter, and mostly because it gave me more time alone to think about what the hell Chad had been up to on Saturday.

Roughly every 30 seconds I vacillated between a different meaning, always just coming back to him just being friendly and oblivious—at least until the next moment of disbelief. Really I couldn't conceive how he would be interested in someone like me, much less that he could be gay—or bi? He'd certainly dated in high school, always girls. Even if he did have a well-hidden fondness for guys, how could I fit that? And that he'd even risk making a pass at me? What if I talked about it with—well anyone else in town? Not actually much risk of that though, given I was still ducking the local hangouts.

I could even rationalize almost every last thing away. The underwear? He's just comfortable with his body in front of the guys... I mean, he was always in a locker room in high school, and it might not be exactly common, but it wasn't like that sort of thing was unheard of. The wet fur show just made sense, it was hot out, and he was covered in mud, so that was just him being practical. Even the ass-slap. That's a football thing, or a jock thing, right? I saw that at least a dozen times whenever I was at a football game. I ran a paw on my cheek. That lick though—that part didn't fit in.

It was just as well that I was driving back and forth through an empty field, or I'd have probably hurt myself. I actually finished up in just a day and a half instead of the two full days it took the first time I mowed, too. I caught up to Chad about halfway through Tuesday after finishing the mowing. I fell in alongside Chad as he worked on a baling machine that they'd need in a few weeks. It wasn't like *nothing* had happened this weekend, but he acted just exactly the same as he had last week, not talking a whole lot as he guided me through the process of greasing, tightening, calibrating the big hunk of machine that I was kind of hoping I wouldn't need to use.

Wednesday was just the same, back to the 'friendly enough' but reserved Chad. Thursday too, at least until I was just about to leave for the day. I was heading out to my car when Chad caught up with me.

"Hey, you doing anything this weekend? I was thinking about going out camping." He was being casual, but this was also coming pretty much out of nowhere. I don't think he'd even talked about camping that I've ever heard, and I sure as hell hadn't brought it up. Hell, I'd never even been camping. It wasn't something that 4H had done when I was a kid, that was left for the scouts.

"Camping?" I was in no way managing to hide my surprise.

"Yeah, camping. My uncle has some land a bit outside town, and it's got a lake with a dock, and not like, a cabin, but it's pretty much set up good for a weekend." I must have looked dubious because he continued, "I just wanted to get out of the house for a weekend, ya know? The old man's been starting his rehab, and he's been shittier than normal. He'd be pissy if I just ran off by myself, but if I told him I was going with someone that wanted to go..." He trailed off, and for a moment he didn't look like he was just one year out of high school, but older, and tired, and maybe just a bit vulnerable?

"Yeah sure. It's not like I don't know about wanting to get the hell out of your parents' house for a while. When did you have in mind?"

He looked relieved. "Just tomorrow after we get done here, figure be back on Sunday afternoon?"

"Ok, I can do that. What do I need to bring? I think my dad has some stuff out in the garage."

"Don't worry about it, just bring some clothes, a sleeping bag if you have one. If not, don't worry, I still have one or two older ones you can borrow. We've got the rest of the gear around here." He grabbed my shoulder, "Thanks man, this is a real lifesaver."

I said goodbye and got in my car to drive home. He had been so much friendlier and relaxed out away from the ranch. Maybe that had been what that last weekend had been about and there wasn't any ulterior motive? Was I overthinking this? Of course—but how could I stop? It wasn't like I could just walk up and ask him if he was interested in me, was it?

My dad seemed thrilled that I was going camping with Chad, taking part in those rural masculine rituals that I'd always spurned for a computer game ever since I could get away with it. Given the way things had gone with Chad last weekend, I had to wonder if he would have been as enthusiastic. Either way, he was happy to dig out a serviceable sleeping bag while I threw a couple sets of clothes and a toothbrush into a backpack.

The next day at work was disgustingly normal, though we did knock off work a little early while Chad ran around grabbing things to toss in the back of the truck. There was a tent, sleeping bags, a big ass cooler, a couple of bags of unspecified 'gear', and a couple fishing rods. Somehow, I thought there'd be more to it, but those few minutes were it. I added my backpack and sleeping bag to the pile in the bed and we headed off. Our campsite was on the other side of town, so we had a slower, longer drive away from the ranch, during which Chad did visibly relax, especially once we got past what counted as 'town.'

Still, it was pretty quick that we pulled off the Farm to Market road, onto a country road, and then on to a dirt track with a gate. In a hilarious bit of laziness, rather than get out and open the gate, Chad just drove around—there was no fence.

It was probably another two, three miles of dirt track before we got to a roundabout clearing where Chad turned off the truck. There were some shade trees and I could see the lake and dock, with a rowboat upside down on the bank. The main campsite area was also nicer than I had expected, a huge fire circle with built in seats around it, an outhouse and a big stack of firewood already gathered. I hadn't been expecting all that much, but this was nicer than I was led to believe about camping.

It was barely two or three minutes before the truck was empty and there were a bunch of bags unloaded by the fire pit. Chad's shirt, which had been on for the drive through town, was nowhere to be seen. I headed back and saw Chad dumping a pile of charcoal into the fire pit and spraying it with lighter fluid.

"You want to grab a drink while I get food started? There's stuff in the cooler." I nodded and popped the top on a massive cooler and checked out the contents. There was actually a bunch of steak, some bottled water, cokes, and what looked to be a case and a half of cheap beer. I probably shouldn't have been as surprised as I was, Chad probably had any number of ways to get his hands on beer. Still, at school it was harder to get than I expected. I went to a commuter school, not a party school. It wasn't impossible to come by, but certainly not a regular occurrence. I grabbed a beer from the cooler.

"You want anything?" I figured it was only polite.

"Yeah, grab me a beer."

I picked up a second beer and went over to the fire pit where Chad was tending a roaring ball of flaming lighter fluid. He popped open the beer I handed him and probably drank a quarter of the can in one go. Chugging probably would have left less of the taste in my mouth, but I was much more restrained in my drinking.

"We should probably get camp set up while the fire is getting ready." I followed Chad back to the truck and we grabbed the remaining camp supplies and carried them over to a flat sandy area that looked like it had been kept raked clean for the purpose of pitching tents. Having never used one, I was impressed at how fast and easy we got the tent up and situated. Just as the coals were died down and ready for cooking we had finished our setup.

Chad grilled steaks, we ate, talked, Chad had another beer. After we were finished eating, Chad grabbed a few logs from the woodpile and threw them on the fading coals to start a campfire. "It's plenty damn hot, but I just can't call it camping unless there's a fire. 'Sides, the smoke will keep most of the bugs away." Once he was sure the wood was catching, and well contained in the fire ring he sat back down on the bench around the fire pit.

"I was wondering. What is it that you want to do when you're done with school?"

"I mean—lots of stuff?" *Get a boyfriend.* "I want to travel. Obviously I've got to get a job somewhere, something that can be a home base." I scratched my neck a bit, "I haven't exactly worked out too many of the specifics I guess, it's still pretty early. I can't even get a good internship yet."

"That sucks. My program may take longer, but at least I'm making decent money in the meantime." He casually crushed his empty and tossed it into the empty steel trash barrel across the fire ring. "Maybe you should defect and become an Aggie?" He stood up and wandered off toward the dock. I didn't have any comeback to the Aggie remark, but I also didn't have anything else to do sitting by the fire on a hot night so I got up and followed.

He wandered to the edge of the dock and bent over, splashing a hand through the water. He glanced around mischievously, as if checking to see that we were really alone. "I think I'm gonna cool off." And with that he was unbuckling his pants and quickly pushing them down over his hips. He bent over to pull them the rest of the way off, revealing another pair of those clinging white compression shorts. His little round tail was wagging, would have been hitting me if it were as long as mine, and as soon as his paws were free of the denim he leapt off the end of the dock into the lake.

I glanced back toward the truck, where my backpack was still sitting, containing a perfectly good pair of swimming trunks. Chad surfaced, turning around to look at me expectantly. He didn't actually say anything, just waggled his eyebrows at my momentary paralysis. I stalled by taking off my shirt, which earned a sarcastic [I think?] whistle from Chad. By the time I dropped my shirt to the dock next to Chad's pants, I couldn't see myself walking back to the truck to fish out a pair of swim trunks, so I unbuttoned my pants and pulled them off.

Standing there in my pedestrian cotton boxer-briefs, I avoided catching Chad's eyes and quickly moved to leap into the lake. A few steps and a cannonball into the lake and I was concealed—with the side benefit of splashing Chad in the face and making him turn around. The water was cool, a break from the heat and the week of stress and overthinking. It was like getting over the first hill of the rollercoaster and surrendering to gravity. If Chad wanted to show off, and see me do the same, I may as well go along and see where it leads. The beer—well the beer might have had a little to do with that decision.

Letting go did make the swim nicer, as Chad chased me around and I chased him back. In fact it would have been quite nice if I had actually been in shape and could keep it up for more than about 10 minutes. Working on the ranch may have been slowly been turning me from 'scrawny' to 'wiry', but at the same time I was quickly reduced to hanging off the dock as Chad swam around. Chad was still swimming and splashing, laughing as he swam up next to me. He took in my panting and exhausted face and gave an exaggerated exasperated sigh at my lack of stamina. He pushed himself up onto the dock, and that ass was right in my face. Translucent white shorts framing those round cheeks, close enough to reach out and grab...

I ducked under the water to get a hold of my thoughts and not get a hold of that ass. After a few seconds my lungs started burning and I popped back up. Chad was walking off the dock back toward the campsite. By now I wasn't surprised that he was still in just his underwear, carrying a bundle of clothes with him. I climbed up onto the dock myself and shook as much water as I could out of my fur. I looked around and noticed that along with Chad's pants, my own clothes had vanished. I sighed and padded back toward the fire circle where Chad was poking around in in some of the bags he'd brought out of the truck.

The sense of calm and ease that I felt while swimming did fade a bit as I walked toward Chad in my soaking wet and clingy boxer-briefs. As I returned to the circle Chad was once again bending over and showing off his ass, this time fishing through the cooler. His tail was wagging again, and I just couldn't—didn't want to—believe it was innocent anymore. He stood up and turned around, holding a beer for each of us. He was completely unselfconscious somehow, even as his wet shorts completely showed off his package.

I took the beer and sat down by the fire. Chad sat next to me and started in on his beer, as I did likewise. And he just... talked? He told me about his dad, putting up with him in the best of times, and how that's gotten even less tolerable with his newfound lack of mobility; his frustration with living in a small town, but reluctance to actually leave; and frustration at the way his friends hadn't changed at all. When he got up to get another beer, he sat down quite a bit closer. I could smell him over the beer then, musk and smoke, the inevitable agricultural scents of hay, feed, and cow that followed around a ranch worker.

Chad finished off his beer and went to toss the can in the trash barrel that was conveniently next to the fire pit. Coming back, he sat even closer—hip to hip now. I certainly felt how much bigger than me he was in height and bulk. It should have been intimidating, but all I wanted to do was cuddle into him. The scent of his musk was stronger now, and it was definitely affecting me. My head was buzzing, from the beer and the musk, and I wasn't sure why I *wasn't* cuddling Chad. All of the downsides I'd thought about making a move over the past week were falling out of my head and I put my hand on his knee and leaned into him.

Chad stopped for a moment, not immediately reacting. For a few seconds I wondered if I had somehow misread everything, that maybe it was just wishful thinking. Chad left me hanging for only a few seconds, long enough for my heart to start pounding, but not long enough for me to pull back. I was reassured when Chad put his arm around me and pulled me tight. He put his nose down next to my neck and sniffed.

He whispered into my ear, "Mmmm, finally." And he then returned his snout to my neck and nibbled. I found that I had a spot—I couldn't help but react. I moaned and gripped his leg.

"Finally hell—how was I supposed to believe that this was happening?" He forestalled answering by planting a gentle kiss on my cheek.

"I dunno, you could have taken a hint?" He licked along my neck and I yipped.

"I'm here now." I paused, not sure if I was willing to risk the mood by asking, but I wanted to know. "But me? Really? I mean why?" I don't know what made me ask right then. I mean, I desperately wanted to know—after. I couldn't imagine anything he'd say that would stop me from going forward now.

He responded by taking a deep sniff along my neck again, and I could feel my fur reacting to his breath. "I could say a bunch of stuff—but you smell *right*..." I was floored. I took his cheeks into my paws and guided his muzzle to mine. That first kiss just seemed to last forever and ended too soon.

There are a million 'sexy' things that he could have said—he could have called me sexy, or cute, or smart—any of those things might have done it for anyone else. They certainly wouldn't have sent me off hunting for my pants; but that? It had me hard and turning my underwear into an impressive impression of the tent across the fire pit.

I couldn't say how Chad's kissing stacks up, I really didn't have much experience on that front. Speaking for myself I was thrilled to be exploring Chad's muzzle. After the first kiss broke, I planted short staccato kisses along his muzzle, before returning to his mouth proper. Chad clearly had more experience in kissing; I knew he dated a lot in high school. He largely took charge of the next few minutes, using his long bear tongue to explore my muzzle. I tried to mimic the movements, running my own tongue along his teeth and familiarizing myself with the texture of his tongue.

Chad's paws were not idle during all of this. He was holding me close, scratching me behind the ears, rubbing my sides. He ran his paw down the outside of my hip and moved it over to feel my crotch. I gasped into his muzzle and he broke the kiss, and licked my nose. "You're big…" He ran a thumb over the tip of my cloth covered penis, "And wet."

He got up from next to me and positioned himself between my legs. He kissed me again and hooked his paws into the waistband of my underwear and pulled them over my erection. I let him feel me, he was using both his paws to explore my erection. He was kneeling between my legs and I felt like I was supposed to tell him to do something, but I was still so surprised that this was happening that I just sat back and let him play with me. He squeezed my dick and I grunted. He moved his muzzle down to my crotch, sniffing my musk, pulling in the scent with deep breaths, but also rubbing it into his muzzle fur as my dick rubbed against it. His tongue darted out and licked the base of my shaft. I gasped and Chad earned a shot of wolf pre across his muzzle.

He looked up at me then, with a big dopey grin as he licked the side of his muzzle, getting a taste of me from his fur. He gave another lick from the base of my dick all the way up to the tip. Then he opened wide and took me into his muzzle, just the tip at first, but quickly taking half my dick into his mouth. I groaned, unable to form coherent enough thoughts to try to talk dirty or command him. It was well enough, as whatever it was that Chad was deciding to do was definitely getting me closer to cumming.

If the moans and grunts that Chad was making as he bobbed up and down on my dick were any indication, he was having a good time as well. I reached down and grabbed his ears, rubbing my thumbs along their inside edges, scratching behind them. It was clearly the right thing to do, Chad let out a much louder moan and redoubled his efforts. It felt like a long time, but it probably wasn't before I was moaning and crying out. I wasn't articulate enough to tell Chad how close I was to finishing, but the way he was speeding up and grunting encouragingly, I felt that he could tell.

I threw my head back and as if I was howling, except I didn't have the breath. I was pushed over the edge and started to unload into Chad's muzzle. Chad stopped moving his muzzle, as he continued to work the shaft with is paw. He had his eyes closed, and looked supremely satisfied as I continued to cum. After a few moments, my orgasm started to taper off and he let me slip from his muzzle. I still had a few weak shots left and they landed on his neck and chest.

Still on his knees he hugged me. I rubbed his shoulders as the last vestiges of my orgasm dribbled out into his chest fur. It took a bit of time, but I finally regained some self-control and pushed him away so I could get a look at his face. He was clearly embarrassed, his fur matted and spiky. He looked up and asked, "Did I do ok?"

I pushed him back, and despite being much smaller than him, he fell backward due to surprise. I pounced him, kissing his muzzle and holding him tight, heedless of the mess in his fur. I took my own turn to nuzzle at his neck, taking in his scent. It was still there, still unique beneath the fresh musky scent I had just added to him. "Fuck, that was amazing!" I didn't have any better words, so I just chewed on his neck gently, enjoying his soft bulk and the unique combination of our scents. My tail wagged lazily in satisfaction.

If I let myself, I could have fallen asleep right there. I didn't want to though, I still wasn't sure how much of a chance I would get to do this again and I wasn't going to let it go to waste. I ground my crotch against Chad's for just a moment before sliding down to explore his crotch up close. He was still fully hard and had clearly been leaking for the duration of the blowjob, the crotch of his underwear was soaked. I grabbed his dick through the slick cloth. His head shot up.

"Um, Y-you don't have to, I mean—If you don't want to…" He stammered and looked a little embarrassed. I gave a quick lick to the head of his dick through his underwear and Chad woofed loudly.

"Don't want to? Are you going to tell me I have to stop?" I gave a longer lick along the trapped penis and pressed my nose into the damp cloth, filling my senses with his unique masculine scent.

"Um, no?" I could feel his crotch trembling as he kept himself from bucking his hips.

"Good." I moved my muzzle along the bulge in his underwear, gently taking the head into my mouth, tasting the pre-soaked fabric. As sexy as

I found that tight underwear, it was getting in the way and had to go. I pulled the shorts down and off. My own briefs were still halfway down my thighs, so I pulled them off too and was about to toss them to the side with Chad's when he grabbed them from me. He held them up to his nose, huffing in my scent.

Now that I could see his dick I was pretty impressed. It was longer than I was expecting, but thinner, too. It was jutting out from a hefty sheath and above a big pair of balls. It wasn't so oversized like the bears in the porn I had become suddenly more interested in over the past few weeks, but that made it less intimidating and more inviting. I grabbed it at the base and pointed it up, taking most of it in my muzzle before it became uncomfortable. I didn't know exactly what I was doing, but I was enjoying myself, and if I learned anything from Chad's efforts minutes ago it was that enthusiasm counted for a lot.

I bobbed and licked and rubbed, listening to Chad pant as I sped up and slowed down, ran my tongue all over the different spots, finding the different noises he made as I tried each spot. I shortly found myself lapping rapidly as I listened to the panting accelerate in tempo, until it suddenly stopped and Chad cried out.

The penis on my tongue throbbed, and was suddenly cumming. To be honest, I was less into the taste that first time, but not enough to let Chad's dick slip out of my mouth before he was finished.

Once the throbbing eased, I did let the dick drop from my muzzle. It did ooze a few last dribbles of cum out, adding to the mess in his crotch. I looked over the bear in front of me and wanted to laugh at the scene. It was just so tawdry. Chad was laid out, eyes closed, crotch fur covered in various fluids, spikey fur along his chest and neck, and my underwear covering his muzzle. I laid myself down on top of him, and nuzzled his muzzle without removing my underwear.

Chad moaned, and leaned back, exposing his throat. I took the hint, and licked, nuzzled and nibbled on his neck. Eventually I couldn't resist and tossed the underwear off his face so I could give him a proper kiss. After it broke, there was probably something we could have said, but I just cuddled into his chest for a while.

Eventually Chad stirred and sat up, still holding me close. He kept an arm around my waist as he wandered over by the fire pit, kicking dirt on what was left of the embers. Twilight was just fading and the first stars were starting to become visible, and under that light we went over to the tent and crawled in. It was warm enough that we didn't bother with getting in a sleeping bag, just curling up together on top of an air mattress.

Chad wrapped me up in his arms, holding me tight from behind. He let out a yawn and licked the top of my head. "I wanna do that again." He nibbled on my ear, and added, "Well, that and other stuff—"

"Yeah, me too." I snuggled back against him, resting my head on his arm. I let out a yawn of my own.

"You could stick around you know," Chad was clearly getting sleepy and fighting a yawn at nearly each word. "Do you really have to go back to school?"

And with that he finally fell asleep. His soft snoring was soothing, even as the tent and the bear holding me grew warmer than really comfortable. I did finally have the clarity of mind to think again, wondering what would happen between us. I wondered how the morning would play out, and the day, and weeks, and rest of the summer. I could never help spinning out endless possibilities of the future.

I thought about Fate—living in the town, leaving the town, what that would mean to Chad. It was silly really; we'd barely even gotten together. As much as my mind was running, I was also running on fumes from all of excitement of the day. I fell asleep quickly after Chad.

The next morning I awoke to a tent smelling of horny bear, but the source had gone missing. All of my clothes were missing, too. Or had I never put any in the tent? Either way I was going to be heading out to face Chad in the buff. After last night it no longer seemed like much of an issue.

I heard rattling and hissing from outside the tent and figured there was no point in putting it off any longer, so I stepped out into the campsite. Chad was futzing over a small gas camp stove, and he was only wearing a jockstrap. I swear, did he somehow hack my browser history or something? I walked over to him, and the smell of our combined musk from the previous night was still in the air, though frying bacon and coffee was doing its best to mask it.

He took a nice long obvious look at my crotch—so much for any subtlety or pretense about last night—and waggled his eyebrows. "I made us breakfast."

"Thanks, it smells good." I accepted a plate. The bacon was a little burnt and the eggs were a bit runny, a gourmet chef he was not. But it was still more than edible, and after last night a little effort like this went a long way.

"So, you don't have that much left of the summer, do you?" He tried to say it without much expectation, but there was definitely a lot of meaning behind it.

"Well, yeah, classes start in three weeks? I'm already signed up for my classes, and I've got my roommate lined up." There was more than that of course, plans and expectations, years of having things figured out. But there was also something else—"But I'm thinking that it might be real nice if the two of us went camping again, say over Labor Day weekend?"

I didn't have any real answers yet, hell I didn't even know what questions were going to come up. Spinning out a life from one night—lust, affection, comfort. How long could it last? There was no telling. I may have hated fate—really, who could trust in that?—but for the first time in a very long time I was feeling at peace with the idea of Fate.

The Mountain's Heart

Miriam "Camio" Curzon

Wind sang as it swirled past the stone nook Rye had settled in for his first night within Mt. Einko's reach. The snowshoe hare tipped his ears to the mountain's song as he flicked the fire starter into some dry kindling from his pack. Mt. Einko sang of his arrival in the dance of snow across the threshold.

Sparks caught in the mix of lint and tinder, setting the kindling to a slow smolder. He scattered a pawful of coal around the growing fire. As the fire crackled into life, Rye retrieved a pan of fresh white snow. The Aurora danced in the dark twilight sky. He set the snow to melt, steam rising from the pan as the snow slipped into liquid and gaseous form.

As the fire licked out heat and a bit of light, Rye swallowed the lump rising in his chest. There was no one for miles, only him and the mountain, but he shrugged his clothes off with the self-conscious deliberateness of one observed. At the very least he could hang his clothes to dry.

Chill nipped at his nethers, the fire not quite enough to chase all the cold away, but his fur was thick. It was his first night on Mt. Einko and he had to greet the mountain with the same reverence shown to his arrival. He sat with back to stone and hind paw pads touching, practicing his breathing and watching the snow disappear.

He was never particularly good at meditation. Back home they always told him to focus on his breathing; counting his inhales and slow exhales, stuff like that. Always his mind wandered off of its own accord. Even here Einko's whisper tugged for his attention, not to mention the hare's usual distractions. He hoped his worries wouldn't follow him all the way out here beyond the bonds of his civilized world.

The last of the white disintegrated in a cloudy puddle in the skillet.

He pulled one of his packets from his pack and tore it open. Herbs and minerals cascaded into the water. As the last, most buoyant herbs sunk into the water, the air turned with the crackle of the pan and his lungs warmed. His alcove filled with the scent of clove, cinnamon, lavender, sandalwood, and hashish, pricking at his tongue as he took in a lung full of air.

Rye brushed his bare sides, taking lung filling, measured breaths. Soon his body would grow numb from the incense. He closed his eyes and started to hum. The humming helped push out everything that was outside of him. Even his epidermis vanished, leaving Rye alone with his consciousness. This was him, everything that constituted the hare known to his family, friends, and village as Rye.

It wasn't even black. The nothingness just was. The sensation of suspension, no weight. Direct connection between one existence and another. Weak. Formless. Whispers. No words. No sounds. Hints of meaning, ghosts of touch.

A trail of snow blew in, kissing the hare's white fur with pearls. Rye shivered as the trail of wind mingled with the smoke of his incense. His nipples were erect. The chill of the mountain's reach drew a soft gasp. Whiskers twitched; his body's motions controlled by instinct not consciousness. Smoke kissed and swelled around his form, lapping at his chest and thighs, down between his legs.

Rye moaned and shifted. His meditative dream persisted through the night. Einko always teasing and brushing close. The snowshoe hare receptive to the wanton mountain, remote and ageless, longing for a body's warmth. The mountain covered him like a blanket. Pushed back to the cool stone floor and caressed; finger tendrils wove around and between his thighs. Rye let out a soft huff, unconsciously curling up against the phantom touches. The hare's small tail fluttered.

When morning came, bright sun struck the small mountain nook. The smoldering fire pit kept the space cozy, intensifying what little warmth there was from the sun. Einko rumbled Rye to wakefulness. His fur was damp and still carried the blanket of herbs smoked into him. "Good morning, Einko." The rock shifted around him again. Fresh snow slid off the mouth of his alcove. "Easy," he said, "I'm here. I'm coming."

The hare brushed at his fur, pushing wayward hair back into place. The fur around his crotch required special attention. He used some of the remaining water in the pan, now infused with herbs. The water was still warm, but he felt the chill sinking in immediately after. Can't sit around all day, he thought as he gathered up his clothes. Should Einko get more insistent, climbing to the cave would become all that harder. His tribe wasn't likely to be patient either. With his pack slung over his heavy woven poncho he looked down through the sparse trees to the dense forest surrounding the base of Mt. Einko.

Aside from Einko himself, only silence surrounded Rye. It was peaceful compared to his village, which had its own brand of solemn quiet. His destination was not down at the base, nor at the summit, but halfway along the east face where a small cave entrance led to a cavern in which Einko's heart resided. The heart he had to calm, offering his soul for the mountain's hunger and his village's peace.

He closed his eyes and sighed. Bright stars burst in his eyelids. The crisp air's chill with ice and juniper filled his lungs. Stepping out onto the threshold, fine layers of ice cracked and snapped beneath him. Icicles dripped from the bright energy of the sun. Einko was beautiful even if he could be temperamental—if you could reasonably call exploding in fire, rock, and poison clouds "temperamental." Rye was not the first and wouldn't be the last suitor sent to the mountain.

The sun arched slow and low over the horizon. Rye always felt comfortably warm as the season changed, like the sunlight was concentrated through a focusing glass, especially when the distant mountains filtered bits of the sun. A far cry from his valley home down past the dense thicket of trees.

His village was made from those very trees, their wood tough as metal. They'd pulled stones from glacier deposits, smooth and patterned with the passage of time. It had its charm. That's why he was out here: it was all he had to offer them. Preserve the peace of his village. There was no part he had to play for future generations, nothing but this.

Einko rumbled in faint agreement. "Nice to know you agree, Mt. Einko." Rye brushed his poncho. "Hate to be doing this if it means nothing. Then it'd just be suicide."

He'd grown up out here in the wild where he could be alone with his thoughts—those same thoughts that made his village's prescribed meditations so difficult. Alone with his thoughts among ancient trees and fresh snow was a somber thrill the other kids never understood, too busy with their gender segregated rambunctious play. Not fitting in, not having a place...

Out here he had a place, knew where he fit, and what dangers lurked in the wilds. Avoid the streams and rivers in late spring and early summer when the melt swells the waters to dangerous rapids. Stick to the woods in fall and winter when the weather is most unpredictable. He was avoiding his own wild instincts, but this was a one-way journey. He'd severed all his other physical threads, his pack contained only necessities.

In a way, Rye felt lighter, like he could just hop his way up the mountainside. There was only a spiritual thread left binding him to his birthplace. Even with his back turned he felt the faint tug during his ascent. It was strange. He had no regrets, nothing back there he'd particularly miss. So it was hard to say what was pulling at him. His sense of duty, perhaps?

"Duty?"

Einko shook, brief but deep, enough that Rye had to brace himself against the slope.

"Don't get me started on your lack of duty." It was impulsive of Rye to chastise the mountain. Probably even a bit rude. In the end, it wouldn't really matter though. Mountains like Einko were naturally flippant and prone to their own numinous ways. They do what they want, and it was his job to make sure Einko did what his village wanted.

"But what do you want?"

A gust of wind whipped the air around him. He wasn't used to air this thin, but he was more accustomed to higher altitudes than anyone else back home. Although this was his home now, he supposed, for however long that would be. At least the mountain wasn't keeping him away. He'd seen Einko angry, surrounded by pitch colored clouds roiling with ice and snow, unapproachable to even the most experienced expedition. That's how he knew he was welcome, Einko had rarely been this approachable.

A small pine snaked her way out of the mountain, and an ice-carved boulder slept beside her trunk. Rye felt the bark and examined her small needles. The bark was a rich, rough, red-hued umber and needles deep emerald and soft. So he took a seat, pulling his legs up under him on the rock and resting against the small pine. She smelled of sweet spice. "May I?" he asked before reaching and snapping off some small needle-laden twigs. He also pulled some loose bark off her trunk. The twigs he slipped in his pack for later, while the bark he set about chewing in small pieces. Pieces of bark oozed satisfyingly saccharine sap.

It was a good resting spot. Einko was patient. Rye felt no urgent prodding pushing him to speed up his climb. Even with the unpredictability of weather and Einko himself, Rye sensed no danger. Last night had been one of his best—safe, secure, and wanted. Einko's shadow reached deep into the eastern valley. "Time to move on." He'd still have a good deal of twilight-like light to travel in, but the rest of his journey would be chillier with the sun hidden by Einko's tall peak. "Thank you." Rye patted the small pine as he stood.

Rye continued to chew on the bark as he took the winding path upward. Energy and altitude fueled his pace which increased, slowly at first, just a small burn in his thighs. As the burn grew to engulf his stomach and limbs he burst into a hopping sprint. Wind blew his whiskers and he leaned in with eyes watering. There was a roar in his ears and a rumble deeper and stronger in his chest than Einko could ever manage.

He leapt stride by stride through snow drifts and glacial rocks. He leapt until his clasped paws dripped blood and frozen fur streaked his cheeks, until his heart burst from exertion and his lungs gave up and he fell into the snow. He cried, screamed, his voice echoed across the desolate slopes of snow, Einko and the distant pine his only audience. A gust of blistering wind brushed his ears.

The snowshoe hare pushed himself. Flecks of snow fell from his nose and whiskers. Snow clung to his poncho and paws. The pain dug icy needles into his bloodied palms. His lungs rebelled against his breathing, but his heart acquiesced slowing to a measured pounding. He glanced behind him at the frantic tracks. Eyes wide, he half expected a great phantasm to lumber up from the mountain's base. Even he was shocked by the sudden surge of adrenaline. There was nothing there, of course. "What was that?" His voice was hoarse. A shiver caused his tail to quiver.

But here he was. Rye looked up at the dark cave. Einko was open wide and that was it. He was here. There was an unshakable abyss in his stomach clawing him down into a pit. Why was he now so uneasy? It was as if he'd crossed some barrier he was never meant to cross. The cave in front of him was a point of no return. While the way behind him was clear his path back seemed a labyrinth, he could never find his way through again.

"You can turn back."

A howl echoed from the mountain's throat. He couldn't leave or turn away and he shuffled forward until only damp stone was under paw. There must've been several other openings to the air, because the cave whistled and a breeze greeted him.

Inside it was cool and damp. The floor was uneven but the stone smooth. Rye expected darkness but as his eyes adjusted to the cavern's dimness, he noticed an odd, phosphorescent glow in the dark above reflected by glittering crystalline deposits. It was like a real night sky with stars and the Aurora. He found it hard to not stumble, unable to pry his eyes from the profound beauty crowning the cavern.

Rye followed the undulating lights as Einko ushered him deeper into his heart. The path constricted until his whiskers brushed rock and he had to move at an angle. He braced his paws against the walls, pulling himself along. The stones were warm, not cold as he expected. A brush of air prickled his nose with sulfurous minerals. The hare had explored a fair share of caves, but this was the first time he'd ventured into one so grand as Einko. He couldn't help but shiver at the strangeness that closed in with every shuffling step he took.

Heated rocks and air more potent than any his village alchemicals could muster. Sourceless, floating lights. All these were a show of Einko's powers. All the more reason Rye had to calm the mountain.

A luminous glow grew from the darkness at his feet like warm mist rising in the light of a full moon. His heartbeat echoed in his tall ears.

"It's unnatural."

"Turn back."

"*You are worth it.*"

His heart skipped several beats, hushing the organ's terrified calls. The bridge of his nose wrinkled as a gust smacked his nose and battered his ears with the words.

"This is sacred," his brain uttered.

The walls squeezed tighter in front of him, pulling at his poncho and back. How tight would it get, he wondered as he was pressed into a sideways shuffle. His bag snagged on a rock and he was pressed into the uneven crevice in front of him. The bag hadn't torn, at least, but if he moved much more, Rye suspected he'd get wedged between the walls worse. To go any further, he'd have to get the bag off, the gap ahead barely wider than him.

Rye rotated his shoulders the best he could manage. With the bag held in place between his back and the rocks, he was able to slide the straps down his arms. The bag landed between his feet. He started an awkward shuffle with the bag between his legs until there was enough space to kick the bag ahead. Even without the bag, the slim hare had to contort his body through the small, sharp gaps between the odd angled walls.

The glow cast ethereal shadows that grew less faint the deeper in he went. Still the earth closed tighter around him. Rye doubted that he was the smallest sacrifice to travel this way, but certainly he wasn't the largest. Did this mean Einko was rejecting him? Rye assumed that it was within the mountain's power to block access to whomever he chose. What if this passage kept getting tighter until he could no longer progress? The bit of doubt grew in his chest, driving up his pulse and breathing.

The slight awe Rye felt for the dim glow faded as the shadows grew sharper. His hind paw scraped the between the walls, catching on a jut. He tried to move, but the rock held tight to his paw. The doubt was growing into panic. With his body contorted to squeeze through the gap he couldn't rightly tell which limb was caught. He closed his eyes. "Pleasepleaseplease," he whispered, frantically tugging with his waist at the stuck paw.

The mountain rumbled in response. With a strong shift of the earth, Rye tumbled forward, his poncho catching on the rock wall, tearing as he fell forward into an opening. His knees and palms scraped against the ground, the impact reverberating through his bones. Einko had let him though—he was through, wasn't he? Pushing himself up on to his paws and knees, Rye immediately sensed the spaciousness of where he'd stumbled.

There was a roundish pool toward the opposite end of the domed cavern emitting a soft blue glow. A kind of mist billowed from the water: the source of humidity and the mineral odors he'd sensed back in the tunnel. Was that the heart? The spring seemed to breath and shudder beneath the shroud of moisture.

Rye shivered. It could be the humidity, or it could be his nerves. He fingered the frayed knitted weave along the gashes of his poncho. It was ruined and seemed to have increased in weight. Too heavy. With a sigh he pulled the poncho over his head and dumped it on the ground. For a moment, he stared at the heap on the ground. The rest of his clothes followed. They were unnecessary, earthly and repulsively tangible for what was to come. *I should burn them*, he thought, *leave nothing behind*. Anything that could despoil the hallowed ground he now trod should be disposed of.

Beside the pile of clothing he laid the contents of his pack, side by side, in a neat an ordered line with methodically. The tree bark beside the strips of pine needles. Then his small, shallow pot. That would be difficult. It would remain here and rust long after he was gone. A small bag of herbs. His striker and remaining bricks of peat coal. Was that it? All he brought? All he had left? What did it matter in the end?

The cavern thrummed as the striker sparked into the briquettes. As the peat caught the air filled with the earthy aroma of coal dirt. Sitting cross legged, Rye ripped his clothes into small strips, throwing one on the young fire absentmindedly. *Rip*. He singled his focus on destroying his clothes, making scraps small enough to burn controllably when he needed. Despite the small pool and high stone ceiling, the walls seemed to close in on him. The night before had been fine because it was merely an alcove, he'd still felt the breeze of fresh air.

Rip.

Concentrate, he told himself as he started tearing into the light weatherproof canvas sack. Rip. Pull. Stretch. Shred. Tear. Leave no trace. Einko would forgive him the striker and pot. He chewed on his remaining slice of bark. Better *here* than *there*. At least here was still in the wild even if he was secreted off in Einko's heart now.

Finishing the last of the bark, Rye stood. His knees cracked and his tail was a little kinked from sitting. He patted down his fur as he picked up his pot. The water in the pool swirled and bubbled slightly. It was clear with a slight emerald and blue hue. Slight ripples distorted his reflection. He dipped the pot in, careful to not submerge a paw before he'd purified his flesh. The heat radiated and warmed the handle. He couldn't deny the beauty of his grave. *Not yet*, he thought, eyes locked into the depthless expanse.

The hare stumbled back, pulling away from Einko's pull. Not yet. Water sloshed about, but he steadied himself. He pinched the bridge of his nose. Bright starbursts exploded in his vision as his eyes readjusted to the Euclidean space outside the pool. He placed the pot on the fire, still half blinded, and poured the needles and herbs into the pot.

The aroma seemed to fill the cavern faster. Rye sat with his nose right over the rising steam. At first his nostrils burned, and his lungs rebelled. He'd poured everything he had left, a much more potent mixture than the measured experience from last night. *Now then*. He closed his eyes and focused on his breathing. With each breath he took more of the potent concoction into his body.

His breathing slowed. Thoughts seemed to hurry from his head. He couldn't catch on to even one. In the silent mountain heart Rye swore he could hear the grinding of stone. Not the grinding of a mill or the alchemist's mortar and pestle, but as unnoticeable as the subtle curve of the planet. He, or he supposed, they, were moving as the ground beneath and around him moved at an imperceptible speed.

His body swayed of its own accord, matching the rhythm of the grinding stones and time slowed. The time between heart beats and breaths grew so long, Rye forgot them, his body keen to keep his functions going unconsciously.

Are you here of your own volition?

"Yes, I am," Rye answered.

Did your village not send you here?

"Yes, they did."

How then are you here by your own action?

"They had a lottery, but I volunteered."

Why?

"Because I had nothing but the wilderness."

But did you choose that exile? To spend your days in solitude? To hide away from your neighbors?

Rye paused. He had no answer. Thus far he'd answered on instinct, every answer already there and available. For this question he had no answer.

"No," he stammered.

Then how can you be here by choice if everything up to now was engineered by your neighbors?

"Ho—however my village treated me, I am here now. Whether or not I am here by their grand design is irrelevant. Not one of them could claim to love you as I do. Who I am now is all that matters."

A drop of water splashed down on Rye's cheek from the ceiling as if the stone itself was crying. It was a tether, a fleeting touch that joined him to Einko. But who was entering who?

Utterly engulfed, Rye's flesh tingled, hot and cold all at once. He stretched his limbs, his paws, reaching out in the infinite haze. The movements were laborious like he was controlling two bodies at once. Two bodies and one mind.

Mist coiled around Rye, wrapping around his waist, ankles, and wrists, as delicate as whispers. His body hovered now lighter than air. It started with the lightest of pressure, just above the center of his waist.

You want me?

Rye arched his back in unconscious response. "Yes."

The particles of mist congealed into a paw. It seemed to Rye it was only that light pressure that kept him from flying or dissolving. The paw trailed down to his hip, suddenly growing to reach around his thigh. A second paw grabbed him from the other hip. A soft dampness pressed against the top of his groin. Warmth slipped down between his legs, delving deep into him, filling him with heat. It was an inconspicuous touch without the formed nature gripping his sides, like a tongue that writhed about his mound.

Rye's body had contorted from his original sitting position. His limbs spread apart along the fire warmed stone. A blanket of mist covered the ground rendering the fire a full, diffused light. Behind his head the pool seemed to glow in oscillating rhythm like a heart beating out light. The silence of the cavern was broken periodically by the hare's squeaks and moans. His hips shifted, pulling and pushing against an invisible force. Tiny specks of blood dotted the white fur of his outer thighs.

It was like he was bound by air and he weighed even less. Einko's claws seemed to sink into his thighs, but without any resistance of fur or skin or sinew. Rather than pain, it was a pleasurable tickle uniting their senses. He tasted himself on his tongue like a neutral spirit burrowing down his throat. The warmth snaked up his sides and stomach until it reached his throat then lips.

Tell me to.

Mist brushed his whiskers and traced up and down his ears. Rye nodded against the phantom touch and voiceless words.

Tell. Me. Yes. No.

"Yes."

At once Einko enveloped his body. Tendrils of mist wrapped in and out and around and through him. A presence pressed against his entrance, a hard point tracing between his legs. It then reached deeper into him, parting him, opening him up for his beloved wilderness.

Rye was filled to the brim, bursting at all his seams. His hips rose as Einko hoisted him higher, mashing their bodies together. Muscles tensed. He'd wrap his legs around Einko's jabbing hips if he could. Anything that would fuse them together more. But his body was still held fast, his flesh overlapping with Einko's ethereal essence. Einko was taking him. Claiming him as the ritual allowed, as he'd allowed. He had no time to process conscious thoughts as his mind scattered like Einko's spectral tendrils. There and not there. However he tried to reach out and touch his lover, he couldn't; there was nothing there to touch. But Einko was touching him, reaching inside and churning him into a frenzy. Like a surging spring thaw everything within and without him burst forth in a wave of trembling pleasure.

Was it morning? Rye had no way of knowing. When he opened his eyes, his fire was but a smoldering pile of ash. He breathed life into it, feeding it his torn scraps of cloth. There was a powerful warmth within him and the fur around his groin was matted and crusted. The fur tugged uncomfortably at him. The hare hissed under his breath as he pulled at the fur surrounding his sore mound.

What now? The ritual was complete, Einko's seed was in him. The mountain had claimed him. Yet here he persisted.

His ears twitched. There was a heart beating that wasn't his. His whiskers twitched. There was breath that wasn't his. His nose twitched. There was a scent that wasn't his.

In the dim gloom of gray and brown stone was a curled ball of fur. At first, he thought they had four legs. Then they stretched, uncoiling from the camouflaged mass of grey fur. A lynx of uncommon slimness and sinew blinked eyes the color of fire, pupils dark and shimmering as obsidian.

"Einko," Rye whispered, eyes wide. The spirit had taken physical form and was waking up right in front of him. He stumbled through his thoughts, but what does one say?

"Good morning, Rye." Einko spoke with the smoothness of water-worn stone. "Fancy a dip?" he asked, rising to his full height he towered over the hare.

Rye followed the lynx as he strode straight into the spring. He disappeared beneath the mist and water without a splash. The hare crawled over to the rim of the pool and saw Einko floating there, suspended just at the water line so his muzzle poked out. He motioned to the hare with a paw, beckoning Rye into the pool. That was his second invitation. It would be rude to force a third and he slid his hind paws into the warm water.

Rye recognized immediately that the pool was special. Not simply its association with the lynx floating near his shins, but in the water's resistance to his weight. From the moment his body sank in he found himself floating like a branch in a river.

"Never had they ever sent a boy to me," Einko said, breaking the silence. "I'm glad."

Rye frowned, hoping from their positions Einko couldn't see it. Sure, he was happy that Einko recognized him, but that his village didn't still stung however far away he may be now.

The stone ceiling had vanished leaving them floating side by side in darkness. Paws brushed as they passed one another, unmoored in the abyss. Einko grabbed Rye, clasping their paws together.

"Thank you for coming, Rye. I am truly grateful it was you who came." The lynx pulled Rye over him, rolling them into an embrace.

It was cool, wrapped in Einko's arms. The spring's mineralized water sizzling around the mountain's touch. Rye sighed, unsure quite what had led him to deserve such grace from a mountain god. In Einko's presence he'd only known sublime pleasure in what had regularly made him uncomfortable, or confusion from the rare lovers he'd had. Provoked those looks of tolerable disdain from his neighbors. Pity from alchemists who never knew quite what he needed. Not pity, not help. Yet the night he was to serve Einko as tribute had seemed more like the mountain worshipping him.

With all the water and salt, he couldn't tell if he was crying into Einko's chest or not. Overwhelmed he nuzzled into the lynx's chest, his neck, his muzzle. Einko simply held him, stroking along the hare's slim spine.

Rye's consciousness faded as even the water surrounding them faded from notice. They were both here, no longer an intangible dance, but cold and hot and physical. His heart exuberantly pounded at the inside of his chest, underlying his continued existence.

Rye's paw drifted downward, brushing through the thick coat. He wanted to touch and hold and caress the lynx. Feel every inch of what had been inside him. Einko was still soft when his paw brushed the lynx's soft thigh. The back of his stubby claws brushed the length of Einko's delicate flesh. He brushed back up, this time gliding a single digit from covered tip to base. Einko's hips rolled and Rye wrapped his paw along the slim length. He even threw in a playful nip on the lynx's jutting out chin.

Breathing heavily, Rye pulled himself back until he straddled Einko's hip and the lynx's hardening erection rose up against his abdomen. He ground himself against Einko's slim hardness, careful to avoid squishing the tight scrotum beneath him. Einko stared up at him with those magna colored eyes. The hare had the lead and he found his heart fluttered faster at the realization.

With Einko's shaft trapped between them, Rye clutched his hips, pressing his claws into the luxurious coat. This was more or less new to him. Sure, he had done stuff before but never with the reins in his paw without expectations. Nobody was pushing his head down or pulling his tail up. Memories of their previous encounter floated through the haze of bliss. He wanted to feel that again.

Rye rotated until he felt Einko's hot breath against his slit. Then the feeling returned. It was almost too much, the lynx's tongue rougher in tangible form. The fur along his spine bristled and he held his breath as he grew accustomed to the mix of sublime pleasure and mild discomfort. Einko was gentle of course. The mountain's length leaked right in front of his nose and Rye ran his tongue down, tasting himself along the moist member.

Rather than suck, Rye ran his muzzle up and down the sides of Einko's shaft. His paws would mirror his movements on the other side, applying force rather than silken heat. Every few revolutions he'd kiss Einko's pointed tip while brushing his jewels. The lynx was also using his digits and claws to brush and tease and push into him.

Rye found his thighs were trembling. Muscle spasms ran down to his toes. While Einko was difficult to read, the hare implicitly understood that it was up to him and not the lynx. He wanted to be held once more. To have Einko's arms wrapped around him. To have their bodies dissolve together into a singular mass. He pulled from the mountain's reach and took the hard length into himself.

Rolling his hips back against Einko's prone form, Rye gasped. Without words the mountain rose and wrapped the hare in a tight embrace. Their bodies rocked together, and Rye could hear short breathy growls against his cheek. Once more the space between them vanished. *This is it.* Rye didn't mind and grunted as Einko's paw slid down his chest and stomach to the spot they joined. *The end.* He squeezed his eyes closed so hard he saw nothing but bright behind his eyelids. Teeth pricked his neck as another rush of lava exploded inside him.

When Rye reopened his eyes, he was floating on his back. His ears were clogged with salt and minerals and water. Otherwise he felt fine. Einko was gone.

He grabbed for the rock ledge and caught on with sharp claws. The cavern seemed warmer now, the spring water cooler. There was no sign of Einko in the cave. *Wait, he is the cave,* Rye corrected himself. There wasn't any trace of the lynx, not even on him, just vivid memories.

Fresh air blew through his whiskers. It lacked the bite of winter, carrying the freshness of late spring full of pollen. He followed his nose to the source, swearing the path was wider and shorter than when he came through it the first time. When he emerged from Einko's heart Rye was grateful it was early morning. Otherwise the sun may have burned his eyes.

Hours, you think?

Rye had been unconsciously clutching something to his chest. It glittered like black glass; a piece of Einko's heart, strung from an impossibly strong cord.

Much more than hours or even seasons.

Down the mountain covered in green grass and masses of purple and blue flowers was a grove of tall pines. Some unknowable amount of time had passed since he'd been inside Einko's heart.

No more sacrifices.

"What about my village?" Rye asked the mountain.

Gone. A long time ago. Now there is a city as dense as any forest.

"But what about..."

The forests and I are still here. We all change with time. Some much slower than others. You fulfilled your duty to your village and now you have a new home with no more sacrifices. You choose what you want to do, and no one else.

From a distance, Rye could hear sounds that were unnatural and alien to his wilderness. His village had always been quiet, barely a whisper beyond a few thousand feet away. It would take a while to get used to.

You have my heart and I'll be sure to visit. Keep my eye on you, my beloved.

THRESHOLDS

G.M. Rader

Wendell Jones—that is, newly promoted *Sergeant* Wendell Jones—put on his beret one-handed as he exited the building housing the Transition Assistance Office, snapping off a smart salute to an officer entering the building. Walking toward the street, spotted his boyfriend's car. Micah's sharp coyote vision had already spotted what little of Wendell's leopard rosettes were showing and was pulling the car up to the curb so he could get in.

Wendell put the folder of paperwork on the dash and buckled up. Micah glanced at it as he pulled back into traffic. "Are they still trying to convince you to reenlist?" he asked, half-chuckling.

"Nah, that's a different guy. These people are all about helping you prepare for 'The Transition To Civilian Life.'" Wendell reached for the A/C vents to turn them away. Micah had it running full blast. "How to write your resume, look for jobs, that kinda thing. How can you stand it this cold?"

Micah chortled. "You're not in the desert anymore, cat. Eighty-five is a hot day. Didn't you grow up here?"

Wendell grunted. "Yeah, yeah." His dad had been stationed at this same Army installation for about half of Wendell's teenage years, before retiring and moving back north just after Wendell himself enlisted. But after six months where mid-eighties was a cool night and the daytime was a hundred and ten in the shade..."I'll get used to it again."

Micah's ears flicked upright and he grinned. "Guess you'll just have to snuggle up to a coyote to keep warm at night." He clicked on the indicator to make a turn into a grocery store parking lot. "I need a few things for the barbecue. You should come in. I want to walk around with you."

Wendel tensed at the reminder of the upcoming party. They had been talking about moving in together since the repeal of the Don't Ask Don't Tell policy, midway through this last deployment. While Wendell was overseas, it seemed to come up at least twice in each of their almost-daily long-distance conversations. Micah had rented the place about a month before Wendell came back. Then he'd found out he made the list for promotion, and now...Micah had managed to wrap up four or five different celebrations into one event. Housewarming, sort of a formal coming out—although everyone pretty much knew about him and Micah—and Wendell's promotion, plus celebrating their return from deployment. Fortunately, it would just be a few close friends in attendance, mostly Wendell's squad.

Wendell sighed. "Yeah, I'll go in with you." He glanced at Micah as he unfastened his seatbelt, noting the coyote's look of concern. He flashed his canines in a grin, and that seemed to ease the concern as he hopped out of the car. Wendell's grin faded almost as soon as the coyote looked away. *It's just a party,* he reminded himself. *Nothing fancy, just friends. They all know. It'll be fine.*

***

"Hey Jones—I mean, *Sergeant* Jones." Rogers laughed, the old joke of forgetting his squadmate's promotion ever-hilarious to him. "You sure you don't want one?" The jaguar held up the cigar he'd just lit in one hand and the box he had taken it from in the other. Rogers had purchased them as his contribution to the festivities, but only three of the six soldiers in the squad were partaking, along with Green's date.

Wendell shook his head. "Nah, thanks. You guys enjoy them." He rattled down the ice in his glass then swirled the remnants of the cubes in the bourbon and cola. June Tennessee heat had the ice melting fast.

Beside him, Micah tapped the grill with the spatula, looking at him sidelong, as if he was about to say something, but Wendell shook his head and smiled, trying not to fidget. The sliding glass door opening interrupted them anyway. Corporal Powell and his wife, Deanna, a pair of wolves, stepped outside; Powell slid the door shut and Deanna smiled widely.

"This is a really nice place you guys have here," she said, Micah started to reply, but Rogers interrupted. "Yeah, I was expectin' shelves made of cinderblocks and sheet metal furniture, like Jonesy's room in the barracks!" He laughed at his own joke, just a little too loudly, as always. Hunter, Wendell's former barracks roommate and closest friend in the squad, had a theory that Rogers laughed at his own jokes to fill in for the silence while everyone else was rolling their eyes. But they regarded him with good-natured tolerance; he was part of the team and a pretty good technician, one of two in the squad who kept the satellite communications gear running for everyone else.

"I moved my things out of my old apartment," Micah said. "And when he—that is, when you all got back, we brought his stuff over from the barracks." He smiled and started flipping the burgers over. "Of course, some of his things were at my place, too."

Hunter, one of two cheetahs in the squad, raised his glass. He had known about their relationship since Wendell and Micah first started dating and had been to the partly-shared apartment many times. "Sure beats the B's, don't it, Jonesy?" He grinned. "'Scuse me, *Sergeant* Jonesy."

Wendell snorted and rolled his eyes. "Well, it's only been a few days…" He glanced at Micah, who was already eyeing him and lifting the spatula menacingly. He suppressed a grin. "But yeah, I'd have to say so. No more room inspections. And they were going to make me move out anyway after getting promoted."

"Yeah," Hunter said. "Rest of us single folk still suffering along while you live the good life." He winked.

"You know you can always come hang out with us here," Wendell said, feeling a little guilty. "I mean, any of you can." He looked up and scanned the rest of his squadmates.

"Just be sure to call first," said Micah. "We might be busy." He flipped one of the burgers again.

The others snickered and the conversation moved on. Wendell rubbed the back of his ear, not really listening. They'd been back only a week, just starting to adjust from being overseas, and already so many *other* changes. New responsibilities with the promotion, now Assistant Squadleader, bumping Corporal Powell out of that spot. Actually starting the process of getting out of the Army, while at the same time moving into a house with his boyfriend, whom he could now openly acknowledge, after so many years of hiding his preferences so he could *stay* in the Army. He shook his head and blew out a long breath.

Micah twitched an ear and glanced toward him but didn't say anything. The others didn't seem to notice much, and Wendell shook his head again, coming back to the conversation.

He immediately had the feeling that everyone was looking at him and he just missed something important. He looked at Micah. The coyote was looking at him expectantly.

"Huh?" Dead giveaway, but he couldn't think of anything to say to cover.

"I said," Micah said with exaggerated patience, "what do you want on your burger? They're done."

"Oh. Uh, you know, whatever. The regular."

Micah nodded, looking at him a moment longer, before he turned back to the grill. "The rest of you are going to have to make your own. Special treatment is only for my Sergeant." He said it with an exaggerated sweetness and a toothy smile.

Wendell forced a chuckle he didn't feel, while everyone else laughed more freely. He didn't like being put on the spot, and Micah knew that. He moved toward the table with the condiments. "I'll do it," he mumbled. "I don't need any 'special treatment.'"

Micah waved the spatula at him, already holding a plate with a burger patty atop a bun. "No! Bad cat! Outta my way. Promotions are rare and I want to spoil you."

Wendell flicked his tailtip, annoyance growing, but he relented and stepping back. The others queued up by the table, apparently not noticing the exchange or Wendell's tension. There was that, at least.

He took his burger with a helping of potato chips and macaroni salad and retreated to one of the patio chairs. He listened to the conversation whenever the group got loud or laughed at someone's joke, but didn't join in, quiet with his thoughts and glancing at Micah now and then. The coyote still seemed at ease, talking and laughing with the others.

Glancing around the group, though, he found Hunter watching from the other side of the patio. Their eyes met for a moment and the cheetah flicked one ear forward inquisitively. Wendell shook his head and picked up the remains of his burger, finishing it off with a scowl.

He stood up as he finished the last of it and mumbled something about throwing his plate away, then stepped inside, and closing the door behind him. Carefully.

He dropped the plate in the kitchen trash, then stood there a moment, until he heard Micah's voice behind him. "I put a trash can outside, hon. It's by the door, you went right past it." He turned, startled. He hadn't heard the door.

Wendell's annoyance spiked again. "I wanted to throw it in this one," he said lamely, trying not to snap and only partially succeeding.

Micah's looked concerned. "Hey…that's fine. I mean…" He laid his hand it on Wendell's arm. "You okay, hon?"

Wendell shook it off, taking a deep breath and turning around. "I'm fine." He growled, jerked a cupboard open, then closed it, opened another, and found a glass. Filled it with water at the sink. Why couldn't everyone just back *off* a bit?

He drank his water, then set the glass carefully on the counter, forcing himself to calm down. "I'm fine."

Micah nodded. "Okay," he said softly. "Just let me know if..." He trailed off, then finished with, "I'll just be outside."

Wendell squeezed his eyes shut and let out another quiet growl, leaning on the counter. Why the hell was...why the hell *was* everyone annoying him tonight? It's just a barbecue, he reminded himself. Just my buddies and my boyfriend. It's cool. Everything is fine.

He shook his head, breathing deeply again—and as he turned to go back outside, caught a glimpse through the window blinds half-open over the sink: Micah talking intently to Hunter, while trying to look casual. Hunter glanced toward the house.

He growled. "Same shit," he muttered, suddenly not wanting to go outside. And in a minute, Hunter would be come looking to ask if everything was all right, at his boyfriend's request, when the only thing that was wrong was that everyone kept asking him if something was wrong!

He muttered and left the kitchen, taking a route to the front door that didn't go by the sliding glass door onto the patio. He closed it quietly behind him, looked across the front yard to see if any of the neighbors were out. They weren't, so he sat down heavily on the steps, ducked his head to rub behind his ears, and sighed. It would be an escape for a few minutes, at least. However long it took Hunter to search the house.

His ears twitched up at an indistinct sound from down the street. It turned into the rumble of a lawn mower, several houses down and not very loud at this distance, but it caught his attention for some reason. He looked toward it.

Half a block away, a car pulled up to the corner and stopped. The neighborhood was pretty quiet (except for the lawn mower now), and the black SUV with tinted windows sat there longer than seemed necessary to verify there was no traffic coming. Which there wasn't.

He leaned back, narrowing his eyes and taking partial cover behind one of the bushes flanking the porch, just enough that he could still see the vehicle. It started to roll forward, no turn signal. Then it rolled out into the street and turned away from him.

He let out a breath and started to relax, chiding himself for his paranoia, when Hunter's voice startled him.

"Sup?" Hunter stepped up onto the porch and leaned on the railing, crossing one bare cheetah foot over the other. He was quiet with no shoes.

Well, at least he hadn't asked if he was all right. Wendell shook his head. "Nothing." He looked back down the street, toward the lawn mower and the now-departed car, still feeling silly. He decided not to say anything, lest he sound paranoid, crazy. What was up with that, anyway? It's cooling off, time to mow the lawn. And the car's driver was probably just checking their phone or something.

Hunter pulled a pack of cigarettes out of his shirt pocket, tapped one cigarette out and captured it in his lips, freeing it from the pack. He held the pack toward Wendell. "Mmh?"

Wendell shook his head. "Nah, thanks. I just quit. Promised Micah I would."

Hunter fished his lighter out of the same shirt pocket and lit the cigarette. He grunted and deposited pack and lighter back in the pocket. "Yeah, I should quit again, too." He looked down the street, then back at Wendell.

"Good idea," Wendell said. "Knocked half a minute off my run time already." He glanced up at the standing cheetah. "Micah send you out to ask if there's something wrong, too?"

Hunter shrugged and blew a puff of smoke. "Nah, not really. I mean, that's what he wanted, but he didn't say that. Just asked if I'd go talk to you." He examined the claws of the hand holding the cigarette. "But I was gonna anyway."

"You were, huh? 'Bout what?"

Hunter shrugged again, casually. "You seem a little stressed out since we got back. More than when we were downrange, I guess."

Wendell focused his eyes somewhere in front of him. Across the lawn, across the street. He narrowed them slightly, thinking. It was true, he was definitely feeling off today, but couldn't put his finger on exactly why—other than everyone doing things seeming specifically designed to bug him—and it had been going on for a few days, now that he thought about it.

"Yeah. Maybe. I guess." He curled his tail around his hip, rested his elbows on his knees, clasped his hands in front of him. He flexed his claws once, then stopped and flicked his ear, annoyed. Jesus, *everything* was annoying him. What's *up* with that?

Hunter took another drag on his cigarette and didn't say anything for a long moment. He seemed to be waiting for Wendell to say something else, but when he kept his muzzle shut, Hunter went on. "Was a weird deployment. It's nice to be back now. But it seems like the weirdness is lingering. I've noticed it." He stepped off the porch, stripped the ember from his cigarette, then pocketed the butt. "I'll toss it in the trash out back. You wanna come back out, feel free; it's your place, after all." He grinned, then paused. "And you know you always have my ear."

With that, he walked back around the house, leaving Wendell to his thoughts again.

***

Wendell stayed quiet for the rest of the evening, though he rejoined the others and eventually his mood improved enough to chuckle along with the jokes. And when the evening ended and everyone went their ways, he and Micah stood on the porch and waved together.

He leaned against the door after shutting and locking it, closed his eyes, and took a deep breath. Micah stood in the doorway to the living room, watching him.

Wendell sighed. "I'm sorry I snapped at you earlier." He paused, but not long enough for Micah to decide that was all he was going to say. "I don't know why. I'm just…kind of irritable lately. Too many changes all at once, maybe. Right after getting back, you know?"

Micah nodded, smiling. His face had a pleasant glow about it in the setting sunlight streaming through the window set in the top of the door. "I understand. I mean, mostly. You know what I mean?" He stepped forward and slipped his arms around the leopard's deep chest, resting his chin on Wendell's shoulder. "I'm here for you, whatever you need."

Wendell sighed. "Micah, I'm fine, really."

Micah laid the heel of his hand on Wendell's collarbone and stroked his fingers lightly down the leopard's throat fur. "Yeah, you got that right. Damned fine…" He grinned and touched his nose to Wendell's. "And everyone's gone, now." He plucked at Wendell's shirt, then reached over and clicked the lock on the door, arching a brow, still grinning.

Wendell couldn't help but grin back at the coyote. He had always been charmed by the way he could turn playful, mischievous, on a dime. "Yeah, bedtime," he said. He feigned an elaborate yawn.

"Well, I intend to keep you up a *little* longer. You don't have to work tomorrow. Or the next day." Micah hooked his fingers in Wendell's pants and turned down the hall. "C'mon, cat. I know it's cold here. Let's warm you up."

Once in the bedroom, Micah turned toward him, sitting on the bed, and tugged him closer, fingers still in his jeans. Tail wagging and a goofy smile on his muzzle, he unfastened the leopard's pants and tugged them down, while Wendell pulled his shirt off and dropped it on the floor. He started trying to work his pants off, but Micah slid his fingers in the waistband of his boxers and tugged them down, promptly wrapping his hand around Wendell's swelling sheath, tugging it back, and then wrapping his lips around the bared feline flesh.

Wendell inhaled slowly, closing his eyes and laying his hands on the coyote's head, rubbing his ears slowly. Warm tongue sliding up the bottom of his cock, lips following until they held only his tip; then a swirling lick around the head of his cock and a slow swallow…and just like that, he was rock hard.

Micah pulled back, curling his fingers around Wendell's cock, stroking as he looked up. "I've been waiting months to do that," he said, tail wagging across the bed behind him. "And to get you behind me. I wantcha, cat. Grrr!"

Wendell quashed a grin, but already he was feeling better. "Well, how'm I supposed to do that with all those clothes on you? That won't work at all."

Micah laughed and scooted back on the bed, working his pants off and kicking them aside, then pulling his shirt off. He wasn't wearing any shorts, and his own hard-on was already half out of his sheath. He laid back naked on the bed and arched a brow, drumming his fingers with a smug little smirk while Wendell finished pulling his pants off, hopping on one foot a couple of times to keep his balance, laughing softly and shaking his head.

Finally divested of his clothing, he leaned forward over the coyote, climbing onto the bed, while Micah wiggled back further to make room. Wendell brushed his fingers up under Micah's sac, lightly applying his clawtips, rolling them lightly over his fingertips with his thumb. The coyote drew a sharp breath, canting his ears back and curling his toes, spreading his knees a little wider. He raised a hand to stroke Wendell's chest, then laid back and reached across the bed to his nightstand, pulling the drawer open and rummaging for a moment, before coming up with a tube of lube.

Wendell moved his hand to cup the coyote's balls, then curling it around his shaft, stroking him casually and watching, feeling him stiffen in his grasp; a moment later, Micah pulled back, moving onto his knees and reaching for Wendell's cock, closing his fingers around it, cool gel squeezing through them as the coyote stroked him to spread it along his full length.

"Mmm. It's good to feel *you* doing that again," Wendell murmured. "My own hands get old."

"Oh, believe me, I know." Micah chuckled, still stroking him, before finally turning and lowering his shoulders, resting his head on the pillows while reaching up between his own legs to apply the lube under his tail. He shifted his knees and shimmied his hips.

Wendell growled and put a hand on the coyote's rump, squeezing firmly, with just a hint of claws again, and squirmed up behind him on his knees, his other hand angling his cock forward. He nudged forward, a little too low, and Micah reached back to help line him up, but the leopard's cock slipped out of his fingers, both still slick. He laughed, while Wendell growled, frustrated.

"It's been a while," the leopard muttered, lining up again.

"Tell me about it. It's fine just—o…oh…yeah. There…" Micah pushed back, panting and groaning softly, just as Wendell felt him spread around his cock.

"Fuck," he growled, pushing a little deeper, swallowing hard. He put both hands on the coyote's ass, thumbs tucked up under the root of his tail, and pushed forward, clenching his jaw as he tried to restrain himself, keep from going *too* fast. He was already panting.

Micah didn't help. Ears laid back from the intensity of being filled after so long, he still rocked back firmly, arching his back and propping himself on his elbows. "That's…yeah. Yes…"

Neither of them said much more, panting and growling as excitement grew. Wendell growled, finally giving up on trying to go easy, and just let the coyote push back, hilting him until his balls brushed just above the coyote's. Then he drew back, beginning to thrust in earnest.

The bed was new, unfamiliar, but it didn't rock as much as the old one, gave him better control over his motions, but Micah's body felt just the same—no, better, after all this time. Tight, hot, responsive; he'd been dreaming of this for months, too, needing it, *craving* it. He swallowed heavily and slapped his hips up against Micah's ass, hard and throbbing as he hilted again and again, harder, heart pumping faster until he could hear the blood rushing in his ears, the metallic taste of exertion on his tongue, the prickling of hackles lifting along his neck and shoulders...

He flicked an ear, panting, swallowing again, harder. He flexed his fingers on Micah's hips, nails pressing through fur, a little too far pricking skin and making the coyote squirm.

"Easy there, claws, kitty..." Micah laughed, breathy with his panting, and closed his teeth on his lower lip. "That... yeah there...ngf!"

Wendell looked down at his hands, lifting his fingers lightly. Have to be careful. The rush of his pulse in his ears turned more to a thud; his chest tightened and his head swam a little, and he slowed his pace. Mouth dry, he tried to swallow again, head buzzing. Something... something was wrong.

He paused, panting, shaking his head to clear it and catching his breath. Micah looked back at him over his shoulder, starting to say something, then tensed—Wendell could feel that around his cock, under his fingers.

"You okay?" the coyote asked.

Wendell looked up at him. Blinked. *Fuck, that? Now?!* He tried to push back the frustration. "Yeah, I'm fine. Just...gimme a second." He swallowed again, rubbed his head with one hand.

And felt himself going soft. *Fuck!*

He shut his eyes tightly, tried to focus, tried to think about how good sex with Micah was, how much he'd missed him, how much he wanted to finish...then sighed. "Damn it."

He slipped out, turned away, and sat on the edge of the bed. Micah got up and turned toward him, rubbing his shoulders. "Hey, what's wrong?" he asked, his voice soft, concerned.

"N—damn it, nothing is wrong!" Wendell cringed at the frustration in his voice.

Micah sat behind him, wrapping his arms around the leopard's body, resting his cheek on his shoulder. "Hey, it's okay. It's all right." He nuzzled the leopard's neck, holding him and swaying lightly side to side.

Wendell shook his head, laying his ears back, eyes closed. Nothing was *fine*. Could anything else go *more* wrong? The tightness in his chest returned. He squeezed his eyes shut tighter, breathed through his mouth, willed the moisture away from his eyes.

"I'm sorry."

Micah shook his head. "Shh, nothing to be sorry for. It happens sometimes." He kissed the side of his neck and squeezed him tighter.

"It's fine, really."

Wendell shook his head, then nodded. "Yeah…s'okay," he agreed. It felt like a lie.

***

Sunday went by without major incident, guilt keeping Wendell's ongoing frustration and consequent irritability mostly under control. He and Micah sat together for a while on the patio in the evening, but when they went to bed, the coyote was cautious not to press.

Wendell was, if not exactly not in the mood, still feeling some guilt over their interrupted interlude. Something else about it, or his reaction to it, bothered him as well; but he couldn't put his finger on it until he was drifting off to sleep—and that brought him wide awake again for another half hour, while Micah snored softly beside him.

Shame. He felt shame mixed with disappointment and guilt, and overarching frustration, at not being able to finish the act of sex with his boyfriend. And not even knowing why.

It still grated on him Monday morning at PT formation, fueling his push-ups and grass drills. Those at least kept his mind occupied. The three-mile run at the end did not.

He didn't like running to begin with, and liked running around the track even less. Twenty-five minutes of tedious, monotonous exertion, panting the whole time, heart rate kept up by design…the very things that had triggered his inexplicable interruption with Micah in bed, and *that* to stew over, as well. He growled, frustration and exertion turning to anger, while the underlying feeling of *wrongness* boiled. He ran faster as the physical and emotional fueled each other. Heart pounding. Chest tight.

By the end of the run, he was in a near frenzy, heart pounding hard enough to make his head buzz and swim, sweaty, tired, the sudden nausea that came with not-running.. He panted hard, gasping, pacing and trying to walk it off but never getting enough air. He stopped, bending forward far enough to brace his hands on his knees but keeping his head up lest he pass out.

The two cheetahs in his squad, Hunter and Staff Sergeant Bennett, had naturally finished the run before him, but only barely. He heard SSG Bennett say something to him about a good job improving his run time, but he ignored it, not even faking catching his breath. He was dimly aware of the two of them watching him as they waited for the others to come in. It bothered him, but he couldn't *stop* them, and he couldn't catch his breath to say anything. As if he hadn't run fast enough. *Far* enough.

Rogers came in about a minute after him, the heavier wolf panting, too. Wendell was still hunched over, panting like he couldn't breathe at all, couldn't even get a throatful of air; Rogers clapped him on the shoulder and said, admiringly, "Damn, Jonsey, leave some oxygen for the rest of us!" The wolf actually managed to bark a laugh.

Something snapped. Wendell stood up, turned to face Rogers. Stepped forward, planted both his hands in the wolf's chest, and shoved. "Shut the fuck *up*, you little *shit!*"

Rogers staggered back, surprised. His ears went back and he stepped forward, hands curled into fists at his sides. "The fuck, man?" he snarled, still panting. "Learn to take... a fuckin' joke?"

Wendell's hand came up, claws out—but before he could strike, rake his claws right across that *smartass's wolf's muzzle*, someone grabbed him from behind and two other bodies got between him and Rogers, pushing them apart.

He twisted his body to break free or turn on his new assailant, threw an elbow back, but the arms held him tight, pinning his left arm against his body. He looked down, ready to dig his claws in and pry off whoever's arms were around him, and saw spots. Cheetah spots. Hunter's scent.

"Settle the fuck down, Jones," Bennett growled. She was one of the two between him and Rogers. She turned to face him. Behind her, Rogers was turning and walking away, hands held up.

Bennett started to say something else, and a fourth voice interrupted. Authoritative. Pissed. "Exactly what the hell is going on here?" Sergeant First Class Andrews. Their platoon sergeant.

"This motherf—" Wendell snapped, shaking Hunter off and leaning to one side to point past Bennett at Rogers, not even realizing that he wasn't sure what he was going to say yet.

Andrews cut him off anyway, the fox scowling. "Shut it, Jones. I don't want to hear it. My office, zero-eight thirty. Both of you." He looked at Rogers, too.

Wendell laid his ears back, still scowling. But with raised voices of authority now in play, military bearing took back over. Andrews turned back to him. "You hear me, Jones?"

He growled. "Yes, Sar'nt."

Andrews turned away and took his place in front of the platoon, everyone watching warily. "Everybody here? Form it up! Form it up!" Wendell fell in with his squad, Bennett on one side and Corporal Powell on the other. On Powell's other side, Rogers look bewildered.

***

At 08:15, Wendell was waiting in the hallway outside SFC Andrews's office. At 8:20, Andrews walked past him, unlocked the office, and entered silently. Two minutes later, Bennett walked by and gave him a look, but didn't say anything, either. She went in after Andrews and shut the door behind her. Wendell could hear them talking, but couldn't make out what they were saying. He scowled, and then Rogers showed up, too, but also didn't say anything, just standing arm's length away in the hall at parade rest, head and eyes forward.

Wendell sighed. He turned his head slightly, not quite all the way toward Rogers. "Look, I'm sorry about this morning. I was winded from the run and I've been in a bad mood… Some stuff happened over the weekend. I know you were just joking. I shouldn't have lost my shit at you."

Rogers didn't reply. A moment later the door on Wendell's other side opened, and Bennett stepped halfway through. "Specialist Rogers."

Rogers glanced at him and gave a just-perceptible nod as he stepped past and into the office. The door closed again. More muffled voices, more time to sweat. It wasn't long though. Rogers came out, apparently dismissed, not stopping as he went down the hall.

"Sergeant Jones." Bennett put some emphasis on the rank, and Wendell's jaw tightened. Yeah, he was going to get his ass chewed.

He did a right face toward the door and marched in briskly, directly to the appointed spot in front of SFC Andrews's desk, coming to attention, head and eyes straight forward.

"Sergeant Jones reporting as ordered, Sergeant."

"At ease. You want to tell me what happened this morning?"

Wendell snapped to parade rest and worked over what he'd planned to say in his head. When he answered, his speech sounded clipped, even to himself.

"Specialist Rogers slapped me on the back while I was catching my breath and I lost my temper, sar'nt. There's no excuse for my reaction."

Andrews seemed to have been expecting exactly that response; he didn't miss a beat. "No, there's not. Especially with an NCO, a leader, dealing with his troops."

"It won't happen again, sar'nt." Wendell kept his eyes straight forward.

"See that it doesn't. That's not all I'm talking about, though. Is there something else you want to tell me about?"

Wendell looked down to meet Andrews' eyes, surprised. The fox sat with his hands clasped on his desk, watching him. He cleared his throat to cover the pause. "No, sar'nt."

"Are you sure?"

"Yes, sar'nt." Wendell set his shoulders and raised his head to eyes-forward again.

Andrews looked at Bennett and sat back in his chair. "Have a seat, Jones. Relax. This isn't an ass-chewing."

Wendell did not relax, but he did sit in the chair in front of Andrews's desk, tense, on guard. He could handle getting chewed out, he was prepared for that. Being told to relax put him on edge.

Bennett spoke up next. "Deployment is stressful no matter how many you've been on," she said. "Pretty sure everyone knows that. People don't realize that coming back can be just as stressful, sometimes even more. We just got back and we're all on edge, at least a little." She paused, choosing her words carefully. "I talked to Hunter," she went on, and Wendell tightened his jaw again. "You two have been close, and he said he's noticed you've been a bit out of sorts. For a while, but especially since we got back. I've noticed, too. And now it's affecting you more directly.

"I'm fine," Wendell growled, interrupting. "There's nothing—"

Andrews broke in just as easily. "Not saying you're not, Jones. But this morning happened, and it wasn't really a surprise. We want to deal with it before it becomes an *actual* problem. For you, for us, for the unit. You know how this works. And you're not the only one."

"I'm fine, sar'nt." Wendell repeated himself firmly, setting his jaw.

Andrews sighed, leaning forward to slide a folded sheet of paper across the desk. "Look this over. Resources. We'll talk again in a few days, and we're going to have some unit training this week. If anything comes up, you can come directly to me or Sergeant Bennett. Dismissed."

Wendell stood and took the paper. "Roger, sar'nt." He came to attention, then faced right and strode toward the door, stuffing the sheet of paper into his pocket.

"Leave the door open," Andrews said.

Wendell looked back over his shoulder and gave another "Yes, sar'nt," before stepping into the hall. Bennett followed, checking her watch.

"Motor pool, nine-fifteen," was all she said.

"Yes, Sar'nt."

He left the building, frustration simmering just beneath his carefully controlled exterior military bearing. Why couldn't people just leave him *alone?* The only thing that was *wrong* was constantly asking him if something was fucking wrong! He scowled, crossing the parking lot, flexing his claws as he reached past the paper in his pocket for his car keys.

Someone called his name.

He scowled. Hunter. Of course. The designated smoking area was just on the other side of the parking lot by the street, and they both parked there, next to each other, by old habit, even though Wendell had quit smoking.

He stepped around his car and onto the grass, laying his ears flat. Hunter froze, his own ears tipping back.

"What the fuck, man?" Best friend or not, Wendell's simmering frustration needed an outlet. "Way to throw your buddy under the fucking bus. The hell are you doing?" He stopped a couple of steps away from the cheetah, tail lashing.

Hunter's ears stayed back, but he didn't back up. He took another drag from his cigarette, looked at it, and tossed it into the bucket of sand serving as the butt can. He blew the smoke out after a moment and looked Wendell in the eyes.

"Trying to help you," he said evenly. "You're getting more and more—"

"I don't *need* any fucking help!" Wendell threw his hands up, started to turn way, then changed his mind, jabbing a finger in the air. "What I *need* is for everyone to back the fuck off and give me some goddamned space!" He turned and stalked back to his car, jerked the door open and got in. Slammed the door, started the engine, and pulled out into the parking lot without looking. He checked his mirror as he pulled into the street. Hunter was rubbing his forehead, walking toward the building.

Wendell muttered, shifted gears, and put his foot down on the gas.

***

Wendell's mood was barely improved by the time he got home, but the way Micah's expression went from cheerful to ears splayed when he saw him brought the guilt back.

"Hey," he said.

"Hey."

It seemed that was it, so Wendell went to strip off his uniform and change clothes. He took a deep breath, resolving to be less crabby, and went back to the living room and dropped heavily onto the couch.

Micah turned down the TV. "Everyth—How was your day?"

Wendell caught the shift in the question, but he was determined to let it slide. The replacement query was loaded, too.

"Well..." He shrugged. "Got into a fight at PT. Got a ticket. Got referred to the shrink. Otherwise..." He shrugged again. That about summed it up.

Micah blinked. "You got a ticket? For what?"

"Fifty in a thirty-five."

Micah blinked again. "Jesus, cat. Was that before or after the fight?"

Wendell shrugged. "M.P. let me off with a warning. 'Cause there was no traffic." He looked at the TV. "You heard, huh?"

"Yeah. Bennett called, told me about it. Asked if we're doing all right." He cringed a little at Wendell's restrained growl. "She also thanked us for having her over for the barbecue. Her husband is still deployed. That's all."

Wendell grunted. "Yeah. He gets back next month, probably."

There was a long pause. When Wendell didn't seem to intend to break it, Micah did. "I know you don't like it when people ask if you're okay, but—" he hurried on before Wendell could reply "—we all care about you, you know that. Especially me. But Hunter's been your best friend for a couple of years, and Bennett is looking after you, too. And these deployments have been coming non-stop for years. You can lean on us. Talk to us." He laid a hand on Wendell's arm.

Wendell looked down at it. "I know that," he said slowly. "But really, there's nothing wrong. I'm fine. Seriously."

"You got in a fight with Rogers. I mean, his jokes are bad, but he's harmless."

Wendell slumped further into the couch. "I was trying to catch my breath." It still wasn't a good excuse.

"You weren't the only one they're talking to, either. They have to talk to everyone in your unit. It's a policy."

Wendell looked at him sidelong. "I thought that was all."

Micah flicked one ear back, looking a little sheepish. "Well, we talked for a while. Like, half an hour. She really *does* want to help, though. Hunter does, too. And so do I."

Despite his resolution to stay calm, be cool, the frustration was simmering again. Wendell tipped his head back, closed his eyes, and took a breath. "I...hell, Micah, what the hell does everyone think is wrong with me? Everyone keeps asking, am I okay? Is everything fine? Like you're expecting that there's something terribly wrong. But what *is* it?" He turned a momentary glare toward the coyote, then sat forward and rubbed his face and muzzle.

"I don't know." Micah was quiet for a long moment. "I don't know. Maybe something happened while you were over there?"

Wendell rolled his eyes and scowled. "No, nothing happened while we were over there. Seriously, *nothing*. It was quieter than the last deployment. We literally just went to work every day and sat in air-conditioned trailers, or the air conditioned chowhall, or the air-conditioned hooches. Except for *being* there it was practically the lap of frickin' luxury." It was mostly true.

Micah turned his hands palm-up. "I'm not trying to push the issue. I mean, I am, kind of, because I want you to be happy. But I don't want to fight about it." His ears were angled back.

Wendell sighed, closed his eyes for a moment. "Look, it's fine. I'm fine." He looked back at Micah, offering a weak smile, one he certainly didn't feel. But he didn't like seeing the coyote unhappy, either. He leaned over and nuzzled the coyote's muzzle, closing his eyes a moment. "It's fine, really." He got up and stepped around the coffee table, pausing almost mid-step when he realized he had no idea where he was going. He just needed to get up, burn off some of the energy. Get some peace and quiet.

"I think I need to go for a walk." He tried to sound upbeat as he said it, glancing over his shoulder. Micah perked his ears up. "I'll be back soon."

***

He started off in the uphill direction because it was easier to burn off energy that way. The sidewalk crested the hill and then started down again before it hit the main road at the edge of town about a mile later, which wasn't quiet; but on the other side it looked like the road continued through trees, not too many houses either. He crossed at the light and, because the sidewalk ended, walked on the shoulder of the road.

It was a few minutes of walking before he came to the first building—not a house, but some kind of old store, long since boarded up, the sign taken down. A quarter mile later, as he came around a curve, an old bridge came into view.

He stopped, stared, and then grinned broadly, realizing where he was. They'd just called it "the bridge" in his teenage years; it spanned the river which, downstream, ran through the middle of town, along the scenic riverwalk. The passage of time made it smaller than he remembered, dirtier, the pavement cracked and patched, but never repaved. He walked down the sidewalk on one side to the middle of the span, leaned against the concrete railing, and looked down.

Back in the day, he and his buddies…John? John and Richard, and that other kid—hell, he couldn't even remember his name now. They'd walked or ridden their bikes into town along this road, and they'd always stopped at the bridge, tossing rocks or, he remembered with a touch of guilt, soda bottles, down into the river below to sink to the bottom or be carried off. Inevitably, there were dares to climb over the railing and jump into the water below.

That looked like a shorter distance, too, he thought, leaning over the railing. Maybe twenty or thirty feet, where memory would have sworn it was at least fifty. The river was only a couple of hundred feet wide, muddy water that didn't move too fast. That much hadn't changed. Back then, he had gone as far as climbing over the railing and clinging to the outside, but he had never jumped. Some of the others had, of course. He heard about one kid, someone he didn't know, who broke his shoulder or something trying it. All their parents had given them strict warnings to *stay off that damned bridge*, which, of course, they'd ignored. Nothing like that would ever happen to *them*. Ah…the immortality of youth.

He didn't feel immortal anymore. Partly because growing up did that, and partly, he thought somberly, because of the people he'd seen, people he'd known, people he'd heard of, coming back from deployments with life-changing injuries. Some from combat, some just from accidents. And of course, some never came home at all.

He was lucky, he thought. His first deployment, there were a few mortar attacks, and they'd had to take shelter in the bunkers, but never anything nearby. The second one, the one they'd just returned from, nothing "exciting" really happened at all. Some helicopters had come back with battle damage, but everyone had been okay as far as he knew. There was some gunfire, but it was always way outside the wire, sounded like it was miles away. Eventually, you even learn to sleep through it.

He put his palms on the rail and pushed himself up, feet leaving the ground a few inches, balanced on the inside, so he could bend forward and look over, down into the water. Here, it was peaceful. Quiet, no traffic, no people. Serene, even, the river's surface rippling and opaque. No kids throwing trash into it just to make waves or free their hands for horsing around on the walk home.

Roger, that was the name of the kid who'd jumped and messed up his shoulder. He chortled at the fact that he could see Rogers, from his squad, probably talking about doing something like that, but never *actually* doing it, even though it was only twenty feet or so, maybe twenty-five. How that kid had hurt himself jumping off, he couldn't imagine. Hell, he could lean forward a little further, and probably manage a full somersault before he hit the water. Shoot right through the surface, disappear into that silty, opaque water, maybe all the way to the bottom. It was probably quieter there.

He was almost tempted. He might be a cat, but he knew how to swim, and the drop to the surface wasn't nearly as intimidating as he remembered.

The sound of running feet interrupted his reverie. His ear swiveled before he looked, hearing a familiar voice calling his name. Micah. He let himself back down to the walkway, dusting his palms on his pants.

Micah came to a stop two or three paces from him, panting, looking a little wild. *"What are you doing?"* There was a frantic edge in his voice. "What? I'm...looking at the river. Used to come here as a kid." Wendell tilted his head, puzzled. "What are you doing here?"

Micah swallowed and his shoulders relaxed, but the coyote still looked tense. "I thought it would be nice to go on a walk together, so I figured I'd join you. By the time I got my shoes on... It took me this long to catch up with you. You walk too fast, cat." He spoke in bursts, still catching his breath, and offered a smile, but it looked forced. He hesitated, but his tension seemed to ease. "You used to come here as a kid? I didn't know that."

Wendell shrugged and started walking back the way they had come, slower so Micah could keep up more easily. "Neither did I, until I saw it. I didn't recognize anything out here until I saw the bridge. I didn't realize we were in the area. Me and some friends used to walk this way into town. Or ride our bikes. There was a convenience store up the road... actually, that's the boarded-up place I passed. I didn't recognize that, either. It was kind of an odd place for one, out in the middle of nowhere. At least at the time. Maybe that's why it closed up."

While they walked, he went on about living near the base when his father was stationed there, and how he hadn't really thought about any of it in years, how it was actually kind of nice to see it again. He told him about John and Richard and the other kid whose name he couldn't remember, and about Roger.

But by the time they reached the edge of the road, traffic noise was loud enough to halt conversation until they got into the quieter neighborhood. It was strange how finding the bridge and thinking back, looking down at the placidly running water, made so much of the tension fall away. He felt more of it coming from Micah, now, than himself.

Once back at the house, he flopped down on the couch, the TV off this time, and Micah sat beside him, leaning against his side. Wendell draped his arm over the coyote's shoulders. "That was a nice walk. We should do that more often."

Micah relaxed and let out a breath. Wendell felt him shudder, and looked down. "Hey, you okay?" He flicked an ear wryly, realizing that after feeling like he was being asked that non-stop, he was the one asking now.

Micah nodded. "Yeah... I'm fine. I'd like that. It was nice."

There was a long moment, then Micah sat up a little. "Actually, no I'm not. I mean, not really fine." He looked at Wendell, but held his muzzle low.

Wendell felt his ears shift back, lifted his hand to brush his knuckles through Micah's cheek ruff. "What's wrong?"

Micah didn't answer immediately. He cleared his throat, looked down at his hands in his lap. "When I saw you on the bridge I was worried." He paused. "I thought you were thinking about jumping." He looked up. "You looked like you were going to. And you've been acting really out of it lately."

Wendell leaned back, laid his ears back. "Huh? What would give you *that* idea?"

Micah looked at him levelly. "You were hanging out over the railing. Looking down. Just staring down." He waited a moment; Wendell just stared at him, at a loss for words. Micah asked quietly, "Were you?"

"Was I what? Thinking about jumping?" Wendell laid his ears back, then got up off the couch. "No! Don't be ridiculous. I was just looking down at the water, and the railing is too high. I was less than three inches off the walk."

Micah splayed his ears back, but didn't look down. "I don't want to live without you, Wendell."

Wendell turned to face him, his voice firm. "I'm not going anywhere. I'm not going to jump off a bridge. That's not what I was doing."

Micah nodded and slumped back on the couch. Wendell rubbed his face. "I need a drink."

He walked into the kitchen, got down a glass, filled it from the tap. *Ridiculous*, he thought. *Not going to jump off a damned bridge. And that one ain't even that far.*

But…He had been thinking about *exactly* that. He'd never understood, through all the Army-mandated suicide awareness and prevention classes, how anyone could get to *that* point and not realize they needed help. How people around them couldn't notice, say something, *do* something. It always seemed like the most obvious thing in the world.

But Micah had done that, said something, just now. Obvious…?

The fur on the back of his neck prickled, and his ears laid back of their own accord. *Is that how it starts? Just a few quiet thoughts in a peaceful moment, not even realizing what you're thinking about?*

His tail lashed low by his ankles. He wanted to ignore this whole line of reasoning, but now that it had come up, now that Micah had said something and he started questioning it himself, he couldn't. If he did nothing, or did… something, the coyote would be devastated. And now Hunter, and Sergeant Bennett, and Sergeant Andrews, everyone he was close to and respected was worried about him. If he were headed down the road of malaise and depression by himself, he might "suck it up and drive on," as they say in the Army. But they were all doing what they could to offer him a way out if it came to that. And he did not want to let them down. Especially not Micah. He tightened his grip on the glass of water and exhaled deeply, staring down into the bottom of the cup. He could decide to get help, too. Maybe he should.

Maybe he should. Either way, he could worry about it tomorrow. He drank the water, set the glass down, and went back out to the living room, joined Micah on the couch again. The TV was on this time. They sat, each with their own thoughts. Micah curled up against him halfway through the first commercial break.

***

"Hey. You awake?"

Micah opened his eyes slowly and yawned. "Mmyeah…"

Wendell chuckled. "Show's over."

"Yeah. I know. You can turn it off."

Wendell turned off the TV with the remote, then touched his nose to the coyote's forehead. "I love you, you know."

Micah nuzzled up under his chin, grinning. "I know." Then, "Love you, too, cat."

Wendell paused, then grinned. "I want you, too," he added, lashing his tail. He leaned over to slide both his arms under the coyote, one under his knees and one behind his shoulders, then slid forward off the couch and stood up, staggering once before planting his feet wide and regaining his balance. Micah laughed and threw his arms around the leopard's neck to hang on.

"I haven't carried you across the threshold here yet," Wendell said, still grinning.

"There's plenty of time if you want to." Micah put on a thoughtful expression. "You could do it now. The front door is right there."

"I think the bedroom door will do for now," Wendell growled. He grinned wider, showing his teeth, and carried the coyote down the hall, stepping dramatically though the bedroom door, and then tossed Micah onto the bed.

Micah laughed as he bounced. "Feeling better, I take it?"

Wendell lashed his tail, unbuttoning his pants, a low, rumbling purr in his throat and a sly look in his eyes. "Are you...?"

"Yeah."

Their clothes came off, faster as more fur came into view; by the time Wendell climbed onto the bed, crawling up between Micah's lifted knees, he didn't need the coyote's hands to unsheath him. He pushed into the exploring fingers, rocking forward as Micah slipped one hand down to cup his sac, exhaling a heavy breath as he stroked the leopard's stiffening length. Wendell looked down, propped himself on one hand's knuckles, and curled his fingers around the coyote's cock. Stroking him in turn, grip sliding over the the stiff warmth of his flesh. He squeezed the swelling knot, pleased with the way Micah arched under him, fingers tightening around the Wendell's own cock, a panting groan as he slipped his grip back up, angling the coyote's hard-on to lay next to his own and squeezing them together. His own breath came quicker, shallower.

Micah looked up at him, stopped stroking his cock to reach for the nightstand, where the bottle of lube still sat. Wendell watched, lashing his tail, listening to the snap of the cap opening, watching the coyote's dexterous use of the fingers and thumb of one just one hand to squeeze a dollop of the gel into the same palm, before dropping the tube beside him.

He groaned, arching and panting faster, feeling his lover's fingers close around his cock again, swiveling, smearing the cool gel first at the tip of his cock, then gliding down and up, down and up to smear the length of his rigid shaft. He looked down when Micah let go again, finding the coyote grinning up at him as he slipped his hand down between them to spread some under his tail, too, his tail wagging enough to brush against the backs of Wendell's thighs and calves.

He gave the coyote's knot another squeeze, then propped himself up on both hands, moving back just a little, while Micah gave his cock one more slow stroke, then angled it down, brushing past the coyote's balls, lining him up…

The first push was maybe too quick. Micah gasped, and his tail stopped wagging, tucked up against Wendell's ass… he swallowed, lowered his head to bump his nose with Micah's, and pushed again, slower.

Both of them held their breath a moment, muzzles touching, Wendell because of the tight warmth wrapping around his aching erection, the tickle of Micah's tail brushing against his own. Micah because of the aching fullness of Wendell's cock pressing, gliding, pulsing deeper, his belly pressing against his cock, and the scent of hot, wanton arousal flooding his nose. It was as much Micah's legs wrapping around Wendell's hips that hilt the leopard's cock as it was the urgent thrust the leopard's put into them. They lay pressed together a moment, Micah rubbing his muzzle against the leopard's throat and squeezing him tight, inside and out; Wendell panting hot, quick breaths against the coyote's shoulder, cheek pressed against his ear.

Micah was the first to move. Holding Wendell in with the grip around his hips, he pushed with one arm, rolling them both over until Wendell was on his back. Then he sat up, straddling the leopard, and began to ride him.

Wendell arched, clawing at the bed before moving one hand to the coyote's hip, following him up and down, the other wrapping around the coyote's cock. He grinned up at him as his fingers found the stiff length already slick; he hadn't even noticed the coyote smearing the lube on his own cock. Micah somehow looked a little smug even with his tongue hanging out, panting, but he never missed a beat.

Wendell laid his head back, narrowing his eyes, but not quite closing them, trying to remember not to press his claws too hard on Micah's hip, letting the coyote's pace guide how he stroked him, faster and faster…trying to focus just enough that he wouldn't finish too quickly. It must have shown on his expression; Micah leaned down with a sly smile of his own, the squeeze of his ass gliding up almost to the leopard's tip, and breathed in his ear, "Here, kitty, kitty…" His little code phrase telling him, *Come.*

Wendell groaned and thrust up hard, his cock sinking deep, hips slapping the coyote's ass. Faster, harder, tension mounting, the rushing buzz of blood in his ears louder as he laid them back, clenched his eyes shut, clapped both his hands to the coyote's hips and hilted again…

A strangled yowl broke from his throat as the pressure broke, pulsing waves of pleasure radiating through his body. His breath caught, he swallowed, and his arms slid up from Micah's hips to wrap him in a tight hug hard against his body as his climax peaked, the coyote tense and trembling with him, shallow, shuddering breaths against his cheek, before he began to relax, the peak subsiding.

He planted a hand against Micah's chest, pushed him back upright, and curled his hand around the coyote's cock again. He stroked quickly, wanting to feel Micah coming, too, clenching tight before the bliss began to subside. He rocked his hips lightly, still hilted deep, and with his other hand, dragged his nails lightly over the coyote's balls, then up to curl and squeeze around the swollen base, still stroking. Micah liked that, he knew: the dangerous feeling of claws, of a tight grip, while knowing he was never safer than with his leopard. He held his breath, writhed slowly back and forth, and then exhaled explosively, his cock pulsing hard and fast in Wendell's hands, streaks of his cum painting his mate's belly clear to his chest.

They collapsed together on the bed, laughing softly, needing no words. Wendell slipped free but pressed closer, spooning up to the coyote's back, holding him tight, muzzle resting between his shoulder and neck.

***

PT the following day was uneventful, and Wendell made sure he didn't run too hard. He changed at home, but Micah was already gone to work. He still felt unsettled, frustrated, but for the moment, had some motivation to do something about it. For his coyote, at least, he would try.

He dried off after finishing his shower, took down a fresh uniform, and got dressed. He paused, then, before leaning down to open the hamper. His pants from the day before were still on top. He reached in, pulled out the paper Sergeant Andrews had given him, and read it: a list of resources for soldiers returning from overseas. People to talk to, to assist with readjusting, for those who needed it.

He tucked it into his pocket and picked up his car keys and cell phone. Just a quick message, sent to Micah.

I'll *be* fine, promise. Thank you for asking. Love, Cat.

A Friend in Winter

Mikasi Wolf

Everyone in Twotown University loved the Christmas holidays, whether they celebrated them or not. Those who did went home to family or their SOs, while those who didn't also went home to family or their SOs. Except for a select few, including Tsang Hai Jun.

As is the case with many Asian naming systems, Tsang's first name was actually Hai Jun, though everyone in school called him Tsang. It was Tsang's first year studying World Economics, and in normal times, he would be looking forward to seeing his family back in Taipei. This didn't include his older brother Hai Seng, but younger and older brothers never do get along, even less when they were felid. With his head marked with white and dark stripes, accompanied by a spotted pelt, many recognized him as a leopard cat, which, as Tsang had to constantly remind others; was neither leopard nor common cat.

Tsang and his family were Buddhists, so they didn't celebrate Christmas like some Taiwanese did. But like most traditional Chinese, they did observe *Dongzhi*, the Winter Solstice Festival. Falling during winter—22 December to be exact—some have made comparisons of it to Christmas, with its importance second only to the Lunar New Year, which heralds the coming of spring. In both these festivals, conversations at family gatherings tended towards the side of whose son and daughter got into university or compulsory military service, along with the dreaded "When're you getting married?"

Since his admission as a freshman in September, Tsang made regular calls back home. All through spotty Skype and Whatsapp calls, of course—long distance calls cost more than his student loans combined. Aside from having to deal with his dismissive brother, it gave a sense of normalcy despite being so far from his hometown. Ma and Pa had encouraged him to pursue his studies in the states for the reason that he would have "more opportunities", but they also seemed to have the preconception that he would also have more opportunities to get hitched. Every other weekly call had them asking about his well-being, and even whether he remembered to use protection or not. That, despite the fact he had yet to meet anyone outside of lectures. The fact that he wasn't all that suave and confident in speaking to others didn't exactly help that fact. By the time December drew near, Tsang had had enough of parental interference, well-meant or not.

"Ma, Pa, I'm never getting married, if that's what you're asking." Tsang snapped on the phone. His parents always listened to his calls on speakerphone; all the better to talk over each other with. Sometimes his asshole brother even joined in, all part of being one big happy family.

"Son, everyone has to go through the process. It's part of the full cycle of life! Just like all your ancestors that came before."

"Well, here's some news for you, Ma. I like men, not women."

Taipei has a progressive LGBT movement, though many traditionalists still frown upon it. Tsang immediately learned Ma and Pa weren't any different. Their stunned silence was quickly punctuated by Hai Seng's declaration that he'd be damned by the Eighteen Courts of Hell, and that he'd sooner kill him than have a fag for a brother. Tsang cut the call, and it took 15 minutes for his breathing to get back to normal.

He could no longer return home, that's for sure. His parents tried calling back, but he chose to ignore their calls, knowing ignorance was better than hearing whatever they deigned to say. And what was there to hear, anyway? "Son, you better do right by your ancestors, or the Gods help me, I'll matchmake you faster than you can say 'gay'!" Two nights later, when the phone rang and he forgot to check the caller ID, he heard the beginnings of a roar from what sounded like his dad and dropped the phone. The parents had sent him countless text messages, but Tsang couldn't bring himself to read them. He'd grown up with his family for close to 21 years, if he included his time in military service, and he couldn't bear to see the words of ridicule and denunciation from the only people he could have counted on. They hadn't yet cancelled his university education, though it would probably be a matter of time before the admin office contacted him. It felt better pretending that he still had a family who would accept him for who he was, rather than waiting at the airport with cleavers. Needing all the cash he could have on paw, Tsang cancelled his flight back home, to receive 50% of the ticket's value.

None of Tsang's dormmates knew about his sexuality. They'd likely assumed he was just another loner who spent most of his day studying or more likely jacking off to whatever porn he called up on his computer, as if anyone could jack off more than an hour straight. He didn't have anyone he could call friends, unless he counted Mike Zhang, a yellow-throated marten who studied the same economics program Tsang did.

Mike was born and raised in the states, his parents having come over thirty years back, and though he didn't speak much mandarin, he and Tsang got along fine. He always seemed so laid back in lectures, yet always had an answer for the lecturer's questions, and had a joke ready for everyone. Mike was on the debate club and had no shortage of friends, and Tsang had so far failed to talk him into going out for a movie or lunch, with others having beaten him to the punch. And as the Christmas break neared, all the students new and old packed their stuff and returned to their hometowns or birthplaces, till school resumed in January.

December 20th came. Being alone in the dorm was a most surreal and unfamiliar experience. Whenever the other dormmates were around, Tsang could never summon the courage to tell them to change the TV channel to something he's a little more familiar with, even if it was in Cantonese with English subtitles. They left him pretty much alone, but as Tsang saw it, all it would take was one dispute for everyone to hate him for the next three years they were to room together. Now that they weren't around, Tsang felt slightly liberated having the dorm and TV to himself, yet felt something was missing. For lack of anything to do, the leopard cat headed to the mall to do some grocery shopping.

The university campus was devoid of any soul, save for a few work staff and the university's security officer. The university's LGBT association had some of their lights on, however, suggesting they had an event on for those who hadn't yet returned home. Or perhaps couldn't return home for reasons just like Tsang's. A knot made itself known in his stomach, and Tsang fought back the tears that threatened to come. He'd considered dropping in on a LGBT meeting to see what they had to offer; perhaps even see if there's someone he could relate to. But the fear of cultural differences and the potential of someone he knew spotting him headed there caused Tsang to give it a miss. Even now, with the building more deserted than during the school terms, he didn't think a great idea to pay a visit like he was desperate for company or something.

The leopard cat made his way to the city center, where the roads were busier, and the sidewalks crowded. He huddled into his jacket, wondering once again if he should buy a thicker one, or wait for his winter coat to grow out, which it never seemed to do. Perhaps his body was too used to coming home to a warm house. His home in Taipei never lacked for heat, that's for sure. And because of that, he now had to shiver in half-assed dorm heating.

Last-minute shoppers thronged the corridors of the malls, looking for that special something for that special someone. Tsang wondered how many of them were there looking for something meant for their significant other, yet not being able to tell their family about them. He wished he had an SO to call his own, and not have to tell his family about them, but the truth was, he didn't even have anyone remotely close. Mike was straight, and he wouldn't be paying attention to Tsang even if he wasn't. There were lots more choices for him in and outside of university, and the marten didn't have to worry about an ocean separating him from the other.

Tsang trawled the shelves of the supermarket, figuring that if he couldn't celebrate *Dongzhi* at home, he could at least celebrate on his own. Instead of hitting the liquor shelves in a bid to spend his night drinking, he looked in the confectionary section for *tangyuan*, glutinous rice balls filled with sesame seeds and sugar. They were an integral part of every *Dongzhi* gathering, and symbolized unity on aspect of their roundness. Despite the relatively international offerings on the shelves, no *tangyuan* could be found. The fact that few if any people here celebrated it probably helped make that fact, and Tsang settled for getting some microwavable *mochi* instead, his tail lashing a wild storm. He rarely drank, but grabbed some ramen fish noodles, fish chips and two cans of Tsingtao fermented milk beer anyway, figuring it would be a pain to rewalk the cold streets to get anything he felt peckish for.

Tsang's phone vibrated as he joined the snaking queue to the fast check-out lane. He always kept his mobile data connection on, and figured it was his parents doing their best to get him back in the fold again. Two expletive-laden messages had made their way to his phone recently, but the manner of phrasing had him wonder if Hai Seng was the one who sent messages through his parents' phone. The older leopard cat was never creative enough to vary his sentencing and words, and one could pretty tell it was him who wrote any message. Figuring he had nothing better to do with his time, and the queue wouldn't move faster anyway, Tsang thumbed the screen with a pad, his unsheathed claw slipping twice against the tempered glass screen protector.

How's your holiday so far? Tsang stared at the Telegram message, be-

fore registering that it had come from **Uni: Mike Zhang Economics.**
Mike had asked him to join the guys for meals before, but aside from
that project on Informal Economies in 3rd World Countries, never contacted him on the phone before. But then, this was also the first holiday break they had at the same time, so perhaps he'd just been flipping
through his contact list in his spare time. Wondering if he should text
back or save face with silence, Tsang hitched his groceries under his arm
and settled for the former.

Boring as Hell, he typed. Back home, words in the equivalent of "Hell"
or "Death" were avoided, as it's believed to bring bad luck or misfortune.
Even the number 4 was avoided where possible, as it sounded like the
mandarin word for "die". But Tsang figured the rules didn't apply if he
wasn't actually home. *Shopping for some snacks and beer X0.* Mike's gotta
love all these emoticons.

Some call it "booze". Where you at? Still at your dorm? :P Mike's reply
came fast enough that he was likely chilling on the couch or something.

Yes. Tsang figured there wasn't any need to lie about that.

For the next 30 minutes he was in the queue, followed by the long
walk back to what looked to be his new home for a while, Mike didn't
reply. Tsang had never felt more lonely.

***

Tangyuan is traditionally served after being boiled, but it seems that
this wasn't to be the case with microwavable mochi. Tsang stuck his
tongue out as he scraped it down with a plastic tongue cleaner, wondering what possessed him to try getting a taste of home when mochi were
most definitely *not* from home. The mochi had disintegrated as it was
boiled, turning the water brown with its red bean filling, and Tsang had
sampled one before deciding he'd pass. He cracked open a can of milk
beer to wash the taste out of his mouth, and headed over to the common room couch, turning the TV on to see what's planned. Plenty of
Christmas-themed shows were on different channels, including *Home
Alone,* a movie about a young dormouse forced to defend his under-
ground country home against two psychotic cats when his family forgot
about him. Just as he settled on that, the bell to the dormitory rang.

Tsang's ears stood as he wondered who could be visiting. Definitely
not the housing staff; they had their own access cards and didn't need
to ring. Once they even entered when he was trying his hand at cooking pasta at the stove, and meekly offered them some. The thoughts of

an armed gunman outside entered his mind as he thought back to all those online news stories he'd read before coming to this country. His parents had even insisted he buy a gun as soon as he enrolled. Tsang had refused, given he'd no idea how to go about this. Besides it would look strange that a foreigner was trying to get one for whatever reason. And anyway, his university didn't allow students to carry on campus. They'd insisted he get pepper spray at least, but given that his nose couldn't stand even the emissions of pepper from curry Tsang never thought it a good idea to incapacitate himself at the start of a fight. The leopard cat got up from the couch and pressed the intercom button.

"Yo, who is it?" He added the "yo" so that the newcomer wouldn't guess he was a foreign student on his lonesome.

There was no response, and Tsang briefly wondered what to do. He then remembered the intercom system on their end had been broken since the semester started, though Maintenance had insisted they'll fix it in due time. A month had already passed since the last request, and Tsang had no doubt yet another month would on account of the Christmas break. So this was what $30,000 a year got them.

"Hang in there," he said ineffectually to the intercom, and walked to the main door. Through the glass in the door, Tsang couldn't see anyone. He decided that he'd open the door quickly, stick his head out and shut it if anyone tried anything.

He opened the door and looked both ways. Seeing no one save bushes, he made to shut it, only for a resistance to make itself known on the door.

"Surprise!" A flash of bright yellow and brown appeared before him, and Tsang jerked backwards, falling onto his tail. He cursed in mandarin, springing upright with his claws unsheathed.

"Mike?" He asked uncertainly. The intruder held his arms out, a grin across his muzzle. The yellow fur on his shoulders stood out even in the dim light of the hallway, and in one of his paws was a six-pack of beer.

"In the fur!" The marten proudly declared. Tsang's mix of surprise and confusion had him slowly retract his claws as Mike helped him up. Tsang's fur was all bushed out, and he tried his best to flatten it with both paws, licking his arm fur as Mike laughed.

"You really should ask who's at the door with the intercom," Mike commented. "I could always be some nutter with a gun."

"Intercom's down since the semester started. Who knows? Maybe for the last three years." Tsang waved the marten to follow him through the hallway.

"I doubt it. The seniors say this building got a makeover just last year." Mike confirmed.

"A piece of shit renovation it turned out to be, then." Tsang opened his dorm's door with his access card.

"I was wondering when you'd get into the lingo," Mike laughed as they entered the lounge. He stared at the remains of Tsang's meal. "What, you were drinking alone?"

"I don't have much of a choice. Everyone else is gone." Tsang shrugged, picking up the beer can where he'd left it.

"Nice choice of movie, this." Mike indicated the movie on screen. The movie had progressed to the psycho cats sharpening their claws with a hand file right after they'd considered the dormouse's home perfectly ripe pickings.

"It's what's on. I saw the mandarin dub back when I was a kit," Tsang looked carefully at Mike. "Didn't you say that you're returning home for Christmas?"

"Last I checked, Christmas Eve's on the night of the 24th. Ma doesn't mind as long as I turn up a little before then," Mike chuckled. "My ticket for the Greyhound is booked for tomorrow, so I only have to wait till then." The marten flopped down into the couch. "Speaking of which, I heard you saying you were flying home to be with the family."

"Not anymore. I cancelled my flight weeks back." Tsang sat on the opposite couch.

"Shiiiit…your family okay?" Mike's muzzle creased in worry, his ears flat.

He looked so cute whenever he did that, but Tsang wasn't in any mood to think about such things. "They're fine. So's my jerk of a brother." The leopard cat picked up his beer where he'd left it and sipped, but the familiar taste now tasted bad. The first time he'd drunk was back when he was 16, in one of the food streets that dotted Taipei. He and his brother Hai Seng got along better then, and Hai Seng wanted to celebrate his becoming 18 with two cans. Though Tsang was underage then, his bro had bought another two cans on his behalf, which they'd drunk till they were absolutely wasted. Hai Seng had checked whether Ma and Pa were asleep first before letting Tsang enter the house. It was the first time he awoke at noontime.

Then Hai Seng had trouble finding work after high school. He was exempted from military service because of some health condition or other, but this also meant even blue-collar jobs weren't eager to hire him. Tsang, on the other paw, did relatively well in school, and this made Hai Seng jealous. When he got accepted into an overseas university, the two brothers' relationship took a turn for the worse. Hai Seng blamed his lack of opportunities to that of it all being given it to all the "uni scum" and was always ready to say it was not so much his skills as Tsang having gotten lucky in school. Tsang was more than glad to be rid of his brother ever since he left for the States, hoping he would return to Taipei next time to find Hai Seng had moved out.

And here Tsang was, far from home, wondering whether or not his parents still accepted him. Hai Seng was now an even bigger asshole, but could he really blame him for that? The little brother he knew had bested him, and to top it all off had turned out gay. Back when the brothers had gotten along, Hai Seng had been pretty vocal about not wanting to have anything to do with homosexuals, especially after seeing one of the local LGBT representatives hand out flyers. If Pa wasn't around, Hai Seng might have started a fight with them, outnumbered in public or not.

"Then why are you still here? Family's where the heart is." Mike popped a can from his six-pack but didn't make to open it.

Tsang opened his mouth to explain, but wondered whether he should be sharing personal matters with the marten. After all, how well did they know each other, really? Here in the States, everyone referred to anyone they knew, classmates included, as "friends", even though they might not go out to the movies together, or even be on talking terms to begin with. To Tsang, friends are people whom you felt comfortable with, people you could count on not to not sell you out to others. Sure, he'd spoken to Mike a couple of times, both about schoolwork and personal stuff, but that hardly counted as being friends, as much as one could call their coworkers friends. Even now, when Mike was telling him how family is so important and all that, wasn't he just saying what any random stranger would say? Everyone says family is the most important thing in public, but the truth was, they probably had their own issues with them to begin with, shitty siblings included. Why were he and Mike even shooting the breeze to begin with? Because Mike was bored, and had no one else to talk to?

"You know what, Mike? I don't want to talk about them. Hell, all I want to do right now is watch Home Alone and think happy thoughts opposite of the movie's theme," Tsang turned pointedly to the screen.

"Hopefully, no psychotic canine comes along to ruin my fun. You can stay if you like," the leopard cat added as an afterthought.

Mike opened his muzzle, whether in shock or in the middle of an unspoken question. "Come on, Hai Jun. I'm just trying to help. No one should ever have to bear the burden of their problems alone," Tsang flicked his ears at Mike's usage of his first name. "Just tell me what it is, and we can work it out, alright?"

"It's a personal matter, and I intend it to stay that way," Tsang snapped. "Look, why are you even here? Because there isn't anyone else in your dorm you could talk or drink with? You think I don't know how things work here, just because I'm a foreigner who doesn't know any better?"

"God above, Tsang." The marten's neck fur was starting to bristle, but Tsang had enough by now. Enough of people who wouldn't think twice about ostracizing a homosexual coming to terms with his emotions, enough of asshole family members who wouldn't accept their son for who he was rather than who he preferred to fuck. And last of all, Tsang had enough of a certain entitled marten who thought they could gate-crash his own melancholic self-reflection just so that they had someone to help while away their time before catching their own ride back home.

"I'm gay, and I really don't care what you think about that!" snarled Tsang. "And neither do I care what my family thinks!" He sprang up from the sofa, and Mike fell off the side of his sofa in shock. Tsang stalked towards the dorm door, yanking it open. "I think you'd better leave."

Mike stood slowly up from where he fell, his fur all bushed up. His expression looked uncertain as he walked slowly towards Tsang. "Tsang, I get that this must be all…"

"Leave. Now." Tsang's voice took on an edge that had Mike stride out with his ears down. Tsang slammed the door harder than he ever had, his breaths coming in hard and fast.

Now that Mike wasn't in front of him asking difficult-to-answer questions about why he wasn't going back to the family, Tsang wondered if he had overreacted to the whole thing. He didn't have to tell Mike he was gay, and he certainly didn't have to tell him to get the fuck out, although spending the afternoon in an uncomfortable silence with someone else holds very little appeal. But Mike hadn't been a jerk to him in any way, and could always have found some other way to spend his time, such as pay-per-view television or something. Everyone seemed to have a subscription to Netflix these days. The marten had no lack of friends he could have called or messaged through any combination of messaging apps, let alone some foreign leopard cat he'd only spoken to a couple of times.

Tsang put his face in his paws, wondering just how deep his problems had gotten. He'd been disowned by his family, no question about that; but he'd also ostracized one of the few people that would ever consider talking to him, friend or not. Damn, Tsang didn't even have any childhood friends in Taipei he spoke to after High School came and went. He'd been alone most of his life, and now he would stay alone now, doomed to spend *Dongzhi* and Christmas and the rest of the holidays alone, subsisting on ramen and what passed off as shitty *tangyuan* over here.

The leopard cat spied the remaining cans in the six-pack Mike had left behind. He really probably should return those cans to Mike, at least as a common courtesy, but Tsang couldn't bring himself to speak to the marten at this moment. The last thing he needed was for a full-blown argument to make itself known right now and make the situation far worse. Besides, if Mike had brought the six-pack down all the way here, he must have been willing to share. Tsang would need something to take his mind off his troubles anyway.

He prised a can of Budweiser away from the cardboard packaging, opening it with a satisfying hiss. The smell of hops and alcohol emanating was far more noticeable than that from the milk beer Tsang was drinking, and at least didn't remind him of his brother. And as he poured the golden fluid down his tongue, the sting of the mix of fermented grains enlivened him somewhat, reminding him that for everything that happened, he was still alive and kicking. He drew his eyes back to the movie before him, Kevin the dormouse's jury-rigged traps having wounded the psychopaths. Despite that, the two burglars remained determined to pursue the mouse who'd caused them so much bloody grief.

This drew Tsang to an interesting observation. Like Kevin, Tsang was alone and vulnerable to the cold cruel world. A world that really didn't give a shit about their fates mainly because they had no one to care about them. Despite the difficulties faced by the cat intruders, and being the lowliest of scumbags to say the least, at least they had each other to count on, to understand their trials and tribulations, even if it was a common enemy three-quarters their height. The leopard cat felt that having someone to count on, be they friend or lover would make

137

life so much bearable, so much less harsh. He, Tsang Hai Jun had not a soul to count on, but that doesn't mean it had to be this way. A warmth spread itself from the pit of the leopard cat's stomach, and he sat up straighter in the couch, reaching for his phone.

The modern world had its advantages, and Tsang knew how he could make use of that. He had a Fuzzbook account, though its settings were always set to private so no one else could add him unless they were friends of someone else who actually knew him. And in the US, that was nobody. Tsang unchecked all those restrictive settings and applied them, right before realizing this wouldn't help him, at least in the short term. It's not like people he knew from classes would be queuing up to add him on Fuzzbook, especially when they already tried and failed almost a semester ago.

Tsang knew he needed something more immediate to find someone he can relate to. He knew about dating websites and apps; they were popular in Taiwan where one's success in life was also counted in whether you had a girlfriend or boyfriend. But those required time to build up a conversation and trust with someone before meeting them, assuming things even got that far. The leopard cat doubted anyone would be online or even be checking their accounts with Christmas so close.

Tsang flipped through the other apps he had installed in his phone but never used. These included Tinder, Grindr and Knaughty. He remembered from his search months ago that Tinder seemed more oriented towards a straight audience, and Knaughty seemed more targeted more towards canines, what with emphasis on the more canid details such as tongue length and knot size. He'd liked Grindr the most, because of the good-looking male models he'd seen, but had yet to install it because he didn't have the confidence to talk to anyone there. Tsang figured that it was time for him to set up an account after all, something that was long overdue.

There were several sections regarding his personal details that he filled up, including "Pelt Makings" and "Sheath/Shaft Appearance", of which he took a selfie of his own dick he stroked to feline perfection. Thrice Tsang had to retake the photo so that his barbs were shown in full view, though he hoped that wouldn't put anyone off. But better to be rejected beforehand than right at their door, right?

He checked the location map of other nearby Grindr users, noting that most of them were situated in the City Center. There were at least three others on campus, however, or at least those who didn't turn their location finder off. One was in the staff block, probably a TA or lecturer. Tsang figured it might be better to speak to someone of his own age, so that they had some common ground to begin with. It'd be a real joke speaking to someone who could be grading him on this semester's finals and have a shit grade come back to bite him in the ass. Looking at the map once more, Tsang saw an account by the name of H4ppyLife located somewhere in a dorm building.

The name looked promising. And he was a jaguar, so there would at least be some species familiarity. Tsang took a minute to gather the courage to type a message out to the guy.

Yo, you hanging out in the dorm or something? Tsang typed. Despite not having done anything like this, Tsang didn't think he had time to watch a Youtube video or read an article on the best conversation opening lines he could use. Especially when the few people who would understand his situation could already be getting ready to leave for home.

It was several tense minutes as Tsang stared at the form, praying to the Heavenly Deities that H4ppy would reply with something, anything, so that he could go through another avenue of recourse already. Then H4ppy's status changed from "Away" to "Online", followed by <*Typing...*>

H4ppyLife: *Yep, nowhere else to hang around! Family is and will always be a pain xP*, came the reply.

Well, they definitely have a common point to relate on. In this case, a shitty family. Tsang's tail quit lashing in anxiety, an involuntary purr building up in his throat. The use of emoticons would also mean this guy would express his emotions overtly. Tsang always had difficulties reading other people's emotions, even if they were of a similar species, but this could have been from being on his lonesome much of the time.

H4ppyLife: *What's up? You don't seem in a rush to get back home either.* ×.× A confident guy the jaguar seems to be.

Lonelyheart: *It's complicated. You don't want to hear about it.* Tsang kicked himself right after he sent the message. If he sounded troubled, practically any sane person wouldn't want to touch or whack him with a barge pole, or whatever the idioms around here was.

H4ppyLife: *Hey, lighten up already. That's what this app's for :D. Look, how about you come up and let me take care of it for you? My dorm's in Elden's Gate, level 2. Just ask for me at the intercom?*

Gods of the Heavenly Palace, was this guy a professional counsellor or what? Not wanting H4ppy to think him ungrateful, Tsang thumbed out a quick reply.

Lonelyheart: *Thanks! See you there :)*

***

Elden's Gate was an older dorm block that seemed even further behind in its renovation plans. The landscaping on the exterior looked recently redone but the building itself was still of the old brick that came with the university back when it was built in the 1950s. Tsang figured not every student could afford the costs of living in a more modern building, and what mattered was the character of the people who lived inside. He got buzzed in by H4ppy at the intercom and made his way up the creaky wooden steps to the second floor. The door opened as soon as the leopard cat reached it.

"Hey man, come on in!" A huge jaguar with an accent greeted him at the door, silhouetted by the light from the common room. He moved aside as Tsang entered, his eyes blinking at the change in lighting. The common room had the makings of a place that saw extensive use, with sofas that looked to have their cushions unchanged since the last decade. Even the TV was one of those older boxy CRT models that had crap resolution and took up all the space on the table. Someone managed to connect an old PS2 to it, at least.

The leopard cat turned to regard his host, only to stare at the fact he wasn't clad in anything at all, save his own pelt.

"I…um…" Tsang stuttered.

"Like what you see? Don't be too shy to say so." The jaguar chuckled. A faint scent of beer came from his breath as he walked towards the common room's fridge. Tsang knew it was wrong to stare, but he couldn't quite resist looking at that well-toned ass, rosetted pelt meandering into cream fur where the jaguar's balls met.

"What can I get you? Beer? Coke? Pepsi?" The jaguar's balls swung away from view as he turned with a smile. "Not sure why the roommate buys both; Coke and Pepsi's basically the same thing."

"Umm," Tsang tried and failed to think of anything else other than the felid's bare balls. "No thanks, I already had some milk beer before coming."

"Direct and straight to the point. Good." The jaguar strode over to Tsang and stroked his cheek ruff. Tsang was far too surprised to react. "Look, you're a cute one, and playing the hard to get angle, I get it. But I showed you mine, so how about you show me yours, hmm?"

"But I..." this wasn't how Tsang expected things to go. No one he'd met was ever this direct and upfront about something so unspoken as sex, not even the dorm or class talk about who'd fucked whom, and whether they did oral or missionary or whatever. "I thought we could talk first. I'm Tsang from Economics."

"And I'm Fabian from Civil Engineering." The jaguar rolled his eyes. "Look, kit, I get you're new to this. When you meet someone out there in the wild, you make small talk and shoot the breeze about whatever the hell you manage to come up with. But when you arrange a meetup through Grindr, it means less talk, more play." The jaguar placed both paws upon Tsang's smaller shoulders. "So let's play."

Tsang wanted to say something, anything to get out of this. The leopard cat had figured that apps like Grindr were similar to social media apps, except catered towards gays like him. He'd thought he'd finally found a listening ear for his problems, but instead this guy wanted something else entirely. And he'd been so sincere about it online! But then, there was something nice about this guy's scent, something about the way his rosettes moved in the light that had Tsang wonder if it's such a bad idea after all. Maybe if he gave this guy what he wanted, he'd be more amenable to talking about his problems, and maybe more. It wasn't like Tsang was in any particular hurry, given his current situation.

"Y-yeah, let's," Tsang replied. He'd watched a lot of porn back in Taiwan and most especially in the States, so he decided to tap on some of that experience. He gave a few experimental licks on Fabian's neck, his raspy tongue scratching across the pelt of the larger felid's neck, detecting a faint taste of musky sweat in it. The jaguar gasped at the sudden sensation, a low purr emanating from his throat. Tsang figured he'd done something right, so he proceeded to nuzzle beneath the jaw of the larger felid, his tongue rasping his neck as he did.

"Alright, enough of this foreplay bullshit," Fabian said, and Tsang stopped in mid-nuzzle. "Get your clothes off already!" His claws snagged upon the bottom of Tsang's sweater as he pulled, and for a moment the leopard cat couldn't see a thing, his arms tangled in a flurry of fabric. He swore he could hear some ripping in the thick fabric, but figured the guy was one of those "dom" types he'd heard about on some of the gay sites, always acting like everything should go their way. Suits him fine for now. Before Tsang could get free of his confounded sweater, Fabian had already yanked his pants forcefully down, belt be damned. Being a little hard by now, Tsang yowled as the waistband of his jeans caught upon the tip of his shaft, leaving it smarting.

"Aw, did I hurt little puddy cat? Here's to making it better." Fabian purred as he knelt. With no warning to speak of, his mouth engulfed Tsang's member in one gulp, the leopard cat gasping at the sudden warmth across his shaft. Never in his wildest dreams had he expected to feel something so wonderful, so right. He knew oral was supposed to be enjoyable, as attested by those in class who'd supposedly done it, but he had neither the flexibility nor outgoingness to ever have tried it before. Tsang moaned as the warm slick maw slid over his own similarly warm slick shaft, collapsing back onto the sofa as Fabian nuzzled forward, his tongue and muzzle coaxing every pent-up emotion, every hidden wish and dream the leopard cat had or could ever have dreamt.

Tsang wished he could relish this forever, but Fabian was really good at what he did. The leopard cat yowled, his body exploding in a flurry of emotions clear and intangible, sparks of light dancing before his eyes as column after column of cum passed through his cock, spurts of ecstasy making itself known in Fabian's enthusiastic muzzle, his throat gulping as he made room for more. And as Tsang thought he was done with the first barrage of long-overdue release, Fabian's tongue got him cumming once more, a two-hit combo of carnal satisfaction.

Tsang's chest rose and heaved as he panted, and the leopard cat was vaguely aware of Fabian cleaning the remaining drops of cum from his rapidly-waning shaft. He wondered why he was so stupid to wait so long before this moment, when he would have been far happier and more confident of himself should he have done all this earlier. He knew men also had sex in other ways, but couldn't imagine himself having the energy to have a go at that just yet, at least for the next hour or so.

"Little kitty like that very much?" asked Fabian with a chuckle, to which Tsang nodded. "Well, it's my turn now."

"Er, yeah, I guess that's fair." Tsang made to get up, but a hard yank on both his legs made him fall back on the couch with a meow. He made to scrabble upright to better see what Fabian was doing, but a firm push on his chest made him lie back down. Tilting his head slightly, he could see Fabian lathering his sizable cock with lots of lube from a bottle, his barbs out in full storm.

"I like to fuck twinks when they just came. Makes them real nice and tight," grunted Fabian as he got the lube on. Tsang shivered as the jaguar slid several cold lubricated fingers into him, turning them round to get it all slick. He then proceeded to hold Tsang's legs apart, his shaft prodding his entrance.

"Wait, can you please put on a condom first or something?" Tsang asked, suddenly remembering what's wrong in his mind. He shuffled backwards quickly with his paws. Fabian growled and flipped him over, such that the leopard cat's belly was now on the couch. Tsang tried to twist and wriggle back, but Fabian lay his entire weight upon Tsang's back, his huge paws pinning Tsang's arms by his side. Try as he might, Tsang could never hope to break free from the stronger jaguar, even as his wriggles tried and failed to do so. As he did so, however, he could hear the ripping of a plastic wrapper, followed by the sound of rubber rubbing over flesh, followed by another lathering of lube.

"If you say so, puddy cat." came Fabian's growl next to his ear. "I'm really big, by the way. Don't say I didn't warn you." And with that, Fabian pushed himself slowly into Tsang's clenched pucker, millimeter by millimeter.

Tsang had never felt such an intense pain in his life and yelled, his pucker barely conditioned to accommodate someone of Fabian's girth. Even with dedicated feline condoms, he could still feel the rubbing of the barbs. He knew from online self-help guides that he should be relaxing, not clenching, but how could he relax when he finally had someone mounting him after all these months of only imagining how that would feel like?

Fabian seemed to understand, however, quickly withdrawing as Tsang groaned. He slid his lubed fingers into Tsang once more, easing him for what was to come.

"You ready for more?" Fabian asked. Not being in much state to answer, Tsang merely nodded. Fabian slid back into him with a slick slurp. Strangely enough, the jabbing in Tsang's asshole felt far less painful now, pleasant even after he'd been loosened up. He could feel his own dick reawakening from its limp slumber, bouncing along as Fabian gave thrust after thrust, stretching Tsang's confines wider and better. Tsang hadn't had sex with anyone before, and already he could feel the aching and soreness on his chest from being pressed on the sofa for so. Fabian's breaths started coming low and ragged, however, and Tsang could feel a certain urgency to the jaguar's tempo.

"Oh, fuck, yes." Fabian huffed. And then he roared, Tsang jerking in surprise. Fabian's cock pulsed and throbbed inside Tsang's asshole, and were it not for the condom, he would probably have felt a warmth spreading inside him. Fabian huffed, holding Tsang to him as he climaxed, turning such that they both lay on their sides on the sofa. The leopard cat felt hard, but hadn't yet came, so he stroked himself off with a paw, grunting as a rope of cum erupted off his tip.

"That's it, little cat," Fabian sighed as Tsang's asshole clenched on his shaft. He held the leopard cat closer to him, the smaller felid feeling the breath squeezed out of him, yet relishing being held so close like this, the chest of the jaguar warm against his back. The two of them lay there for a few minutes in silence. Only the wind outside blowing across the building could be heard, along with the almost inaudible clank of the ventilation system.

"So…what do you want to do now?" Tsang asked, for need of something to say, and to be released from Fabian's tight grip. "Want to… erm…grab a drink at the city center?"

"I've got what I need on the table and fridge. Besides, it's damn cold out." Fabian mumbled. "That's what I've got my kitty here for." He gave a pat on Tsang's belly.

"Okay." Tsang kept silent for a while longer. "So, how's your family back home?"

Fabian got back upright, his wrapped shaft flopping against Tsang's thigh. "Fuck, kit. Do you have to ruin the mood like that? I don't want to talk about them. Not now, not ever."

"Yeah, I get it, it's fine." Tsang sought for something else to talk about. "Well, the reason why I'm still in campus is because I'm afraid what my family thinks about me. They found out I'm gay a few weeks back, you see—"

"Yeah, well. Your family can go hang for that." Fabian got up, peeling his condom off as he did. Tsang stared in shock at his vehemence. "Look kit, you're fun as a fuck toy and all, but I got myself some stuff to do in my room. But if you ever want to get together like this again, that's fine. Just add me on Grindr and you're all set." The jaguar stood at the door to the dorm, and it took Tsang several moments to realize Fabian was telling him to leave.

"Erm, alright. Let me just get my clothes on." Tsang quickly got dressed, trying his best to ignore Fabian's hard stare. As he made his way past the leopard, the door shut behind him, followed by the beep of the electronic lock. Tsang made his way slowly down the wooden staircase, his mind processing everything that had happened. Even as he walked through the cold to his own dorm building, Tsang couldn't believe that his efforts to find a listening ear had been met with dismissal. The cold of the air outside didn't exactly make him feel any better as he thought about all this. And when he finally got inside his cold and silent dorm, turning on all the lights, the leopard cat fell into the sofa and cried.

Fuck. *Ma-de.* Some attempt at finding a friend that turned out to be. Now that the leopard cat wasn't pent up any longer, he could already feel that what he'd done had been nothing more than a mistake, that all Fabian had wanted was for a twink to fuck. The jaguar practically admitted he only saw him as a sex object, a "fuck toy", no less. How could he have been so stupid to think hooking up is the same think as finding a friend? Tsang felt he should have seen that mistake, but he was so desperate for someone, anyone to talk to him, when there was no one else.

Well, not no one. Mike had tried to help him. Dear Mike whom he'd not two hours back told to get out of his dorm, all because he had the heart to ask Tsang what was troubling him so much. Tsang felt like shit, not because he'd been a complete asshole to what might have been his only friend in the world, but perhaps because he was self-centered enough to believe no one other than he would understand his problems to begin with. And despite Mike trying to do what any good friend would, Tsang had accused him of using the leopard cat as a means to pass the time before heading back home to a family that cared about him. Tsang had no idea what to do now, and he didn't look forward to meeting the marten in classes after the holidays. Assuming his education wasn't cancelled by then.

Tsang's phone rang, and he jerked so hard that his head slammed on the sofa backrest. Wondering whether his parents or brother were trying to add further insult to injury by chosing to call now, Tsang reached slowly for the phone, turning it screen-up. He stared worriedly as the Caller ID showed the caller as Mike, then decided it was best to get this over with. He swiped the blinking green icon with a sheathed thumb, and listened to the earpiece.

"Hi, Tsang. Look, I'm sorry I asked you what's going on with your family. It's just, you know, I don't think anyone should have to bear this alone," the marten took a breath. "Can I come up and we just, erm, talk? I'm at the front door. You mentioned the intercom wasn't working?"

For a moment, Tsang couldn't believe it. Despite treating him like shit, Mike still came round to ask how he's doing? Who else would do such a thing?

"You still there?" Mike's voice came through the earpiece.

"Yes, hang on a minute." Tsang went down the stairs two at a time, not wanting Mike to wait any longer than necessary in the cold. The marten stood in plain view at the glass set in the door, his muzzle looking worried.

"Hey, I'm sorry about earlier, Tsang," Mike began as the door opened, but Tsang threw his arms around him with a sob. The marten stiffened in surprise, but Tsang didn't care, the words coming hard and fast as he sobbed into the marten's shoulder, wishing the marten didn't think him weird and creepy and needy.

"Mike, I'm sorry! I shouldn't have asked you to leave! I was just so fucking pissed for the last two weeks that I told my parents I'm gay and I don't know whether they hate me so much that I cancelled my flight back home, and I was so lonely and depressed that I decided to try finding a friend on Grindr, and instead all he wanted to do was fuck but not even talk—"

"Whoa, settle down, my friend. Settle down, alright?" soothed Mike uncertainly as he stroked Tsang across the back. Tsang would have purred if he wasn't breathing hard and fast from all the things he wanted to say. "Could we talk inside? I'm getting a little sick of the cold. They say this winter's one of the coldest yet." Mike gave an involuntary shiver.

"Oh, yes, right." Tsang said hastily. He led Mike up to the common room and set the kettle to boil some water. "You want tea or coffee?"

"Hot chocolate, if you have it," Mike managed a chuckle. When Tsang had gotten some cocoa powder another dormmate had bought in a cup, Mike came up to him. "Tsang, you told me you're gay, I get that. I might even get why you don't think it's a great idea to go back to see the family. But can you tell me what you're going on about earlier? It seems I'm missing something here."

"Yes, I understand, Mike." Tsang's ears flattened as he heard that. So he told Mike about what he did after the marten left, desperate to find someone who would understand the problems he faced, someone he could relate to by the sole fact that the person was also gay and horny like him. Only that it'd proven not to be the case, and now Tsang was all alone again. The incident with Fabian happened so fast, Tsang wondered if he had imagined it all, but the rip on his sweater and soreness of his asshole was as plain as can be.

**

"But you aren't alone, Tsang. I'm here for you. That's why I called." Mike's ears flattened. "I'm sorry if I didn't seem like much of a friend before, but

I do care. It's just; well, I was pretty surprised at what you said."

The kettle whistled, and Tsang poured its contents into the mug, a homely aroma filling the room. The leopard cat decided that perhaps he should get a mug for himself too. Mike uncrossed his arms as he accepted the cup from Tsang, taking a deep breath of the still-hot contents. The two of them went to the sofa to sit across one another.

"Listen, Tsang. Whatever problems we may have, sometimes we need help from others to get through it. Even if you don't have anyone you consider a friend, you could always talk to the school counsellor. They have really strict laws on confidentiality here. Keeping problems to yourself just make things worse. I've been there." said Mike. Tsang couldn't quite imagine what problems the affable marten could have had, but perhaps that was the nature of problems themselves. They were often embarrassing enough that people kept silent about them, so that others didn't think poorly of them. "As for hookups; well, they're just that. A chance for people to satisfy whatever desire or urge they have at the time; not a listening ear for your problems. Whatever trouble you may face, know that I'm here for you. Do you understand that?"

"I do now. Thanks, Mike." Tsang sniffed. And for a moment, there was silence between the two, punctuated only by Mike slurping the cup, and for Tsang, that was enough. No one was criticizing or ostracizing him for what he believed in or who he fucked, and that was pretty great considering there wasn't anyone else Tsang could imagine him having this conversation with. Not his dormmates. Not the school counsellor, certainly, because even with all the student confidentiality crap, he didn't know whether it would get back to affect enrollment in the university in some way, or whether the counsellor would know what a big deal it was to be gay back home in the first place. For now, Mike cared, and that was enough.

"You know, Tsang. I was thinking that you shouldn't spend Christmas—I mean *Dongzhi* alone. Be on one's lonesome isn't exactly a good feeling." Mike said.

"I get that, but I don't have anywhere else to go. I might not even have a university to come back to, should my family get round to cancelling my tuition." Tsang replied, averting his eyes. "I want to enjoy whatever time I've left in the States, even if it's not for long."

"Well, that's why I'm asking if you want to spend the holidays at my place. You know, with the family. Mum and Dad won't mind." Mike look Tsang right in the eyes as he said it.

Spend the holidays with Mike? Tsang felt the beginnings of a blush creeping into his face. "Mike, I don't know what to say."

"You can say yes. Can't think of a good reason not to." Mike took a sip from his mug.

"Mike, just wondering, are you...?" Tsang frowned.

"Sorry to disappoint, Tsang, but being gay isn't the reason for my wanting to spend time with you," Mike chuckled. "I'm straight as an arrow, there's really no denying it, but that doesn't mean I don't count you among those I call friend. Friend enough that I'll see if I can get my parents to try to make things right with yours, and a place to stay if not. Our parents are both of the same generation, so they'll at least see some things eye-to-eye. But it's hard for my parents to speak up for you if they haven't met you, and for that, they're more than happy to welcome you at our home. We can even do a *Dongzhi* celebration at our place. My family does that every year, though not always with me around. So how about you say yes?" The marten reached his mug forward.

Mike's eyes were so bright, so earnest, and Tsang dared to say, cute, and it was impossible for him to turn down the marten's invitation. He no longer had to spend *Dongzhi* or Christmas break alone, but more importantly, what Mike was suggesting held some hope for the future. A future that no longer looked uncertain and bleak. And with that, the leopard cat smiled for the first time in many long months, and tapped his mug against Mike's, toasting to a better future soon to come. For now, nothing else mattered as long as he had someone who accepted him for who he was.

Night's Dawn

Jaden Drackus

The red fox dropped to one knee and leaned forward, bringing his nose almost to the ground. The high mountain wind tugged at his hood, pulling it back and exposing his ears to the black jaguar crouched behind him. Shadow smiled as Korwyn sniffed the trail, the jaguar's long tail flicking behind him as he watched the fox.

"Someone's been this way," the ranger said as he stood and adjusted the longbow and quiver on his back. "Several people. Scents are weak though."

"More bandits, Kor?" the assassin asked, keeping his paws stayed away from his twin swords. They had encountered a group working the mountain passes that morning, but no group would waste time working a trail that led to a solitary lodge—even if Shadow considered it the most important one in the Empire.

He and Korwyn were heading to the place the jaguar considered home. For the first time in the three months since they had met, the jaguar had decided that the Nightguard could survive a few weeks without its Master Assassin and newest member. The Grandmaster and the Emperor agreed, with the Emperor going so far as to suggest an Imperial wedding between a count and a neighboring princess as an opportunity to get way. With the Imperial City in full celebration, the Emperor was content to allow his favorite shadow agents to rest. Those who had taken advantage of the lull in the Nightguard's activates would be dealt with after. And so, here they were, despite Shadow's reluctance to come to back to the lodge. For the first time since…

Since scattering Raj'arr's ashes from the roof.

"Bandits don't clear snow," Korwyn replied, breaking the jaguar out of his thoughts. The ranger stood again and pointed. "That's just drifts."

Shadow didn't reply to that. His own gaze was down the trail, which ran for about a hundred yards before disappearing around a bend. Once they rounded that turn, the lodge would be in view, and the jaguar wasn't sure he was ready for that sight. Lost in his thoughts, it was some time before he realized that Korwyn was studying him. The fox's ears were down and there was a worried look in his eyes.

"We don't have to do this," he said as he closed the distance between them. "If you're not ready, we can be back to town by nightfall."

Shadow met Korwyn's gaze. The red fox's tail and ears were still, but his whiskers twitched in the sign of deep thought in foxes. Kor was so excited to get out of the Imperial City—his tail a blur, his ears up and his nose twitching as they wandered through the woods and mountains. This wasn't the first time he'd suggested to Shadow they could go elsewhere.

Shadow shook his head. "No. We do need to do this. If we're a couple, then I owe it to you to share what I shared with him."

As he started moving again, his mind cast back ten years, to the when he'd last brought someone up here for the first time.

***

"Com'on!" Shadow called back over his shoulder as he paused at the turn in the trail.

Behind him, the caracal laughed, hurrying to catch up. "I don't see why your family couldn't have built this place on a trail that didn't run by a bandit lair."

"Can you think of a better way to keep it safe?" Shadow asked, deadpan.

Raj'arr sighed and adjusted his cloak. The caracal shook his head as he studied the younger jaguar. "I just want to see what's got you all excited. Last time you were this worked up…"

He trailed off, but the smile on his muzzle made it clear what he was referring to. Recognizing the memory—of the first time they'd said "I love you"—Shadow's tail became a blur as he smiled as well. They would have plenty of time to make more of those memories—if they ever got to the house. And with Raj'arr stopping every half hour to sketch, that was very much an "if" to the jaguar.

"I've been waiting for you to finish so I can show you."

"Alright, alright," the caracal said with an exaggerated sigh and flick of his tail. "It was a nice countryside is all."

"You haven't seen anything yet," Shadow grinned and, with a slight hesitation, took hold of Raj'arr's paw. The twinge of fear that his lover was mad at him returned.

The caracal laughed as the slender jaguar dragged him down the trail. Shadow's tail flicked against his lover's legs as they moved, almost in time with his hammering heart. He was sure Raj'arr would like the place, but would he like it as much as Shadow thought he would? He knew when Raj'arr cleared the last turn by the gasp that escaped the caracal.

Shadow grinned as he looked back to see the expression on Raj'arr's face. He found his lover's muzzle hanging open, ears forward, tail whipping in excitement. And his paw reaching into his pack for his sketchbook.

"There'll be time later!" Shadow said, laughing as he pounced on the smaller cat. Taking hold of Raj'arr's wrist, he started dragging his lover up the trail. "You haven't even seen the best part yet!"

***

An elbow in his side brought Shadow back to the present. Korwyn was staring at him as they approached the door. The jaguar shook away the visions and took a deep breath. Silently, he cursed himself for missing the fox's reaction to seeing the house for the first time.

The lodge was set on a cliff, the three story building forming a block against the sky framed by pine trees. The house itself had a stone first story, with natural logs for the upper floors, giving the impression that it was partially carved out of the mountain. Golden light spilled out of several windows, showing that the servants on loan from the Imperial yacht had arrived safely to warm the house.

Kor's green eyes took on a hint of worry under his natural inquisitiveness. "I asked how long you've had this place."

"Been in the family a long time," Shadow replied. "A few generations, at least. The first member of my family to be the Master Assassin of the Nightguard built it for when he needed to get away from everything. He found this place chasing some damn fool who'd murdered a duke. Decided he liked it."

"Can't get much further away from everything than this," the fox agreed with a swish of his tail. "But, if you're not up to it, we can go somewhere else. I know some places."

"We're here," Shadow said as he stepped up on to the flagstones.

"That's not the same and you know it," Kor snapped. "You're nervous about coming up here, and for you to be nervous about something says a lot."

Shadow's whiskers twitched as he pondered a response to that. He shook his head and stared up at the house. He felt a paw on his chest, pressing his locket—his most prized possession—into his fur.

"I can guess what this is about," the fox said, his tone softened to a comforting level. "If you're not ready, we don't have to do this now."

Shadow hesitated for a moment before reaching up to touch Korwyn's wrist. He guided the paw away from the pendent, pulling the fox in closer to nuzzle his ear. "We're here."

Kor's muzzle twitched, and a defiant gleam appeared in his eyes before vanishing as quickly. His ears drooped and he shook his head as he stepped back from Shadow. "We are. And remember that it is *we*, you're not facing memories alone."

"I will," the jaguar assured him as he opened the door.

The otters from the Emperor's yacht greeted them, but the couple thanked them and sent most of them back to town. Only the cook, who'd known Shadow for years, and a pair of cabin boys stayed to keep the house in order. They said they'd stay out of the couple's way, even with how Kor was racing to explore the place in typical Kor fashion.

The fox made his way from room to room, his tail a blur behind him, looking at every painting, piece of furniture, and trophy in the lodge. Shadow trailed behind him after passing their packs and equipment to the otters. While his partner's obvious excitement made him smile, everything he looked at reminded him of Raj'arr. Even over a year later, the pain of the caracal's death continued to leave a hole in the jaguar's chest.

He stopped in front of a panting that showed the view from the top of the house. On a clear day, the cliff afforded a panorama of almost the entire Imperial Province. Raj'arr had spent a fortnight on the roof sketching and choosing colors for the piece during a summer stay. Shadow felt the numbness in his heart spread throughout him, leaving him cold. The jaguar's eyes fell to the ground, and he padded to catch up with Kor.

"I'm sorry it's not furnished and drafty. It's been empty since my parents died."

"It's alright," Raj'arr replied with a laugh. *"Just means we can make it our own. I would have asked for a transport mage if I'd known we'd be shopping."*

"Yeah," Shadow agreed. *"I didn't think about it."*

"*Don't worry,*" *the caracal said as he pulled the taller cat into a hug.* "*All it will take is time. But for now, let's get to sleep—it's getting cold already.*"

The slender young jaguar didn't have the heart to tell him that even with the chill of worry he felt, the house already felt warm to him.

"I can't believe you didn't bring me here sooner!"

Shadow snapped back to the present, and his eyes came up to meet those of a smiling fox. A momentary frown crossed his muzzle but vanished as he took the jaguar's paw. Shadow laughed as Kor began dragging him deeper into the house. The questions came fast and thick as the ranger pointed to various objects: where did that chair that looked like a carved tree come from? Was that a real landscape? Did you pose for that painting of the gladiators in the arena? He wanted to know the history of everything, but was content that he was exploring with his lover. Finally, he wrapped Shadow in a hug that almost drove the chill away from the jaguar.

"I like this place," Kor said, resting his head against Shadow's chest. "Thank you for bringing me."

"Of course, Swishes," Shadow replied before licking the point of the ear that tickled his muzzle. "Now it's getting cold, so why don't I show you the bedroom?"

"It's not that cold," the fox snorted. "And I'm more hungry than tired."

"Well, let's get out of our armor at least," the jaguar said. "Though with how hard you're swishing against me, I may still need mine."

Kor laughed, the sound echoing down the corridor. He squeezed Shadow even tighter before breaking the embrace and standing on the tips of his claws to lick the taller jaguar's cheek. "Com'on. Show me the bedroom. We can change and then see what the otters set up to eat. Hope they brought poultry. It's been a while since I had good chicken. I wonder if there are pheasants up here we can hunt?"

***

The next morning, Shadow jerked awake out of a dream made worse by the warmth next to him in the bed. For a moment, the shape laying there was the slender, tawny colored body of a caracal—crisscrossed with dozens of open wounds marring the fur. Exactly the way the way he'd look the last time Shadow had seen him alive. The remembered stench of blood and pitch filled his nostrils.

Shadow hissed, causing the sleeper to roll over and stare at him with vacant eye sockets. The jaguar gasped and jerked away from the figure, tumbling to the floor pulling the blankets with him.

"Moons?" The nickname shattered the vision—leaving only a concerned fox looking down at him.

Shadow shook his head and blinked away tears. "I'm sorry."

"Don't be," Kor said, sliding to the floor next to him and freeing him from the tangle of blankets. The fox wrapped his arms around the larger jaguar. "Nightmare?"

"Yes," the assassin replied, feeling his ear warm in embarrassment of the admission. He gripped the fox's tail and held it close. The thick fluff was so different from then Raj'arr's thin tail.

"It's okay," Kor said, freeing himself from the jaguar's grip and moving to kneel in front of him. He reached out and put his paw on the locket hanging from Shadow's neck. "It was about him, wasn't it?"

"Yes," the jaguar admitted, staring at the floor. The ranger was the only other person in the world that knew the full story of Raj'arr's death. Not even the Emperor knew every detail.

Kor leaned in and held the assassin close. Shadow returned the hug and pressed his head against the fox's thick chest fur. He tried to hold back the tears, but his chest jerked with the effort. Kor said nothing, just ran his claws through the jaguar's shoulder fur.

Shadow took a deep breath full of the earthy, woody scent of fox—so different from the warm grassy scent of caracal. The jaguar nuzzled Kor's thick chest fur—he had an idea that might help him calm down. He reached down, tracing the divide between cream belly and orange-brown flank until his paw arrived between Kor's legs. The fox moaned as Shadow caressed his sheath and sack. The jaguar's thumb encountered the warm flesh of fox shaft before he moved his paw under Kor's balls.

Kor knew what to do. He stood, bringing his crotch level with the jaguar's muzzle. Shadow brought his nose up to the plump sheath, getting a yip and a moan as his breath washed over the fox's bits. His tongue ran over the emerging shaft, drawing an even louder moan from Kor.

Shadow breathed in the fox's scent, trying to drown out the grassy smell of aroused caracal that was no less present, even if only a memory. He took the pointed, barbless shaft into his muzzle and began to suck, hoping that this time the differences would keep the memories at bay. He set a rapid pace, barely aware of the sounds of pleasure coming from above him, lost in the desire not to feel the presence of a different cock in his muzzle. Yet even as the blunt canine claws dug into his fur and the yips became pants, he could feel barbs brushing against his rough tongue. The woody scent of fox was gone, his world filled with the grassy, sandy smell of caracal approaching climax. The yaps changed to chirps as paws grasped the back the jaguar's head and pressed him up against the hips.

When the climax came, it was preceded by a throaty feline growl of pleasure. Warm spurts of seed splashed against the roof of Shadow's mouth. He sucked it down, licking the shaft as the chirps of feline pleasure became the throaty huffs of a satisfied fox. The illusion shattered, and the shame and loss filled his ears with fire. He focused on making sure Kor was completely finished and clean before releasing the cock from his muzzle.

"Gods, Moons," the fox moaned. "You're so good at that."

"I try," Shadow replied, running his tongue over his nose. The scents were all fox now, the ghost of Ra'jarr had departed.

"Your turn?"

The jaguar looked up, golden eyes meeting Kor's green ones. There was a desire to return the favor in those eyes, but no judgement or pressure. Shadow looked down to find his own shaft still sheathed—usually he'd be wondering if he'd get off just from pleasuring his partner. But since Ra'j died...

"I'm good for now," he whispered. "Why don't we see about breakfast?"

Korwyn's ears drooped and tail went still. "Okay," he said before turning away and collecting his robe from the floor. He threw it on and pulled the sash tight before headed to the door. As he went out into the sitting room, he looked up to his left and muttered something. Then he was gone, leaving Shadow on the floor with the sting of tears in his eyes. The jaguar knew what he heard.

"How," the fox asked the painting of Ra'jarr seated on a couch in his favorite court outfit that hung there. "Am I supposed to make him happy if you won't let go?"

***

They'd been at the cabin a week, fitting out the place with furniture and stocking the pantry and cold storage. Then the task of setting areas for them to work began, with Ra'jarr taking what was technically the attic as his studio while Shadow set up training dummies and sparring equipment in the cellar. It had been a busy week—so busy that they hadn't found time for sex.

That fact was at the forefront of Shadow's mind as he worked his way through a routine with his twin swords. He'd made a few attempts to get Ra'jarr into bed, but the caracal had only done so to sleep, not for sex. As he worked through a series strikes on the training dummy, Shadow began to worry that his mate was genuinely mad at him for what had happened on Shadow's most recent—and first solo—assignment.

While the Nightguard's primary task was to eliminate the Empire's enemies with a maximum amount of plausible deniability, they used less lethal versions of neutralizing threats as well. For this mission, Shadow had ensured the loyalty of a minor lord in the Imperial Province by exploiting the noble's love for lean male felines. But since that time, Shadow had wondered if he had done the right thing, and what Ra'jarr would think about what he'd done. As the jaguar spun to the other dummy to begin the next segment of his routine, he still wasn't sure.

The caracal never said anything beyond thanking Shadow for being honest with him. He'd said that sometimes missions asked you to do things like that—it was part of the life they lived. Shadow wasn't so sure. He'd been on the lookout for signs that Ra'jarr was upset, but aside from the lack of sex—he hadn't seen any. And saying they hadn't had sex was somewhat inaccurate—there had been blow jobs and paw jobs, but Shadow hadn't had a caracal under his tail since that mission three weeks ago. It was starting to get to the jaguar. He could feel the desire, an itch that was there constantly now.

He growled, his ears pinned to his head as he stabbed a sword in each dummy and let go of them with a huff. His heart hammered his chest, and his muscles burned with exhaustion. Shadow blinked and wondered how long he had been going. Why hadn't Ra'jarr come to check on him? That wasn't like the caracal. Was this another sign that despite his claims, he was upset that Shadow had slept with the bear? He sighed and left the basement without bothering to collect his shirt, his tail flicking behind him.

An hour later, he slunk out of the bath, shaking the last of the water out of his black fur. He'd made a decision in the tub, and he was going to carry it out. Now. Before his resolve could waiver. One way or another, he needed to know what was up with Ra'jarr. Even if it meant an end to their relationship. Shadow retrieved his robe and searched the house from top to bottom.

The caracal was nowhere to be found.

***

Shadow awoke shivering the next morning. His mind raced to figure out why, and his eyes drifted to the empty half of the bed beside him. The realization brought him fully awake, and he flung the blankets off and leapt to the floor. Kor usually slept deeper and longer than Shadow did. How had he missed the fox getting up?

He sniffed the air. Kor's scent was weak; it had been over an hour since the fox left. Shadow's tail slapped the floorboards. Without bothering to grab his robe, he set off in search of his fox. The first stop was the library, to see if the amateur historian was doing research. When that turned out to not be the case, he padded to the kitchen, where the otter cook took the jaguar's nudity as a sign of urgency and called for one of the cabin boys to search the house while they made Shadow a tea. He politely refused, but the otter insisted.

"You both been out of sorts since you got here," they said as they set the mug in front of the assassin. "I can tell. And you ain't exactly the easiest person to read, Mister Master Assassin. Might wanna think about that for a bit."

Shadow stared into his tea, trying to think up a good retort. But the otter was right, meaning nothing came to mind. Instead he just sipped his tea and stared at the table. Out of the corner of his eye, he swore he saw a figure. A tan figure, too light to be an otter. His head swung to look at it, but there was nothing.

The otter chirped in confusion as the jaguar looked up at them and scratched behind his ears. Shadow sighed. "Have you ever seen or heard anything in this house that you couldn't explain?"

It was the wrong thing to say. The otter grinned, their muzzle split in a way Shadow had seen many times on Kor's when the fox was being snarky. The black jaguar's eyes rolled and his ears folded flat against his head. The otter slapped both paws on the table.

"Seen the Emperor's favorite problem solver jumping at nothing like a damn cub and get so bent outta shape he can't even find his own fox. That what you mean?"

For a long moment, the jaguar stared back at the otter, giving serious thought to if he should summon the dagger magically bound to him and kill the smug chef. If it had been anyone else, he might have. But the otter had known him long enough to know what they could get away with. They'd earned Shadow's respect. Besides, they were right. He should have already known that Kor had left, and have a pretty good idea where he had gone. Nor should he be jumping at shadows—even if they were Ra'jarr. In the end, he simply stared at the otter, his eyes going distant as his thoughts turned inward.

"Guessing that's not what you're asking, though." The otter turned back to the small cooking fire and threw some rashers of bacon into a pan heating on it. "Emperor said there might be ghosts up here, but I ain't seen none, and neither have the boys."

"So, I'm just crazy," Shadow muttered, his claws digging into the wood of the table.

"Didn't say that," the otter called over their shoulder. "Momma always told me two things when it came to ghosts: they can't cross runnin' water, so bathe in streams if you think you're near one; and they can get on just one person. So maybe you got one attached to ya. We found some good streams, but they're gonna be mighty cold as the leaves fall."

"And if I don't want the ghost gone?" Shadow asked after another long silence.

"We all got choices we need to make, boss." The otter turned back to face him. Their eyes were full of understanding, worry, and pity. "But I don't think you're liking the river this one's leading you down. And if it's in yer head…"

Shadow's fingers drummed on the table. They were right of course. If he was truly haunted, then the ghost was leading him down a path that could lead him to lose Kor. And if there wasn't actually a ghost beyond his own inability to deal with Ra'jarr's death, that would be even worse. The otter finished cooking, set a plate of bacon and toast in front of the jaguar, topped off and sweetened his tea, then moved to clean up without saying another word. In the silence, the ghost of Ra'jarr pressed close again, but offered the assassin no direction in his musings.

Finally, a growl escaped the black jaguar's muzzle. The otter was right—it wasn't like him to wait for confrontations to come to him, to cower in fear of what might happen when they arrived. No. He needed to face this head on, since waiting was clearly doing no good. And worse, it might cost him everything—especially Korwyn.

But did he really want to banish this "ghost?" Would giving up Ra'jarr make him happy? The caracal was important to him and the person he'd become. Would he be the same if he turned his back on that past just to keep Kor in his life?

The debate raged in his head for what felt like hours, and his frustration at his indecision grew along with it. A memory drifted up—a memory from a decade ago, when a twenty-three-year-old Shadow had brought his mate up to the cabin while trying to work through his feelings towards them. The situation was almost identical. Except he wasn't a kid trying to figure out the difference between "love" and "sex" anymore. He had no excuses.

"Damn fool," he sighed into his tepid tea.

A cough caught his attention, and Shadow's ears folded as he realized the otter was still there. He met their eyes, shook his head, and tossed the tea back like liquor before shoving himself up from the table. It was well past time he dealt with this problem.

Shadow shivered as the basement door closed behind him fifteen minutes later. Naturally cooler than the rest of the house unless a fire was lit, the basement had an extra bite to the chill with the approach of winter. The jaguar, who had never quite managed to overcome his ancestors' lack of resistance to cold, was glad he'd stopped to grab a tunic and pants. But the clothes couldn't protect him from the ghosts that pressed close to the assassin. He paused and looked around. The glow from under the door gave enough light for the feline to see. Not that there was much to look at: crates lay everywhere, furniture was piled in corners, and the frames of paintings leaned against the walls.

Even with his resolve, the assassin hesitated on the threshold. Here, the memories most closely linked to Ra'jarr were buried. It was here that Shadow would have to face the past. He took a deep breath and stepped into the room. The past closed in around him, threatening to smother him as he padded to the first torch on the wall. *I will not back down,* he told the urge to bolt back upstairs. *I need to face this.*

He could, and probably should, have waited for Kor. It would be easier to stand up to the ghosts of the past with the present at his side. But Kor was still gone, and Shadow would be more ready to find and face the fox once he'd laid his ghosts to rest. So the jaguar was here, alone, to face whatever waited. He reached the torch and pulled the enchanted striker from his pocket. Two flicks and the torch caught, causing the others to ignite, spreading a warm glow around the room. Shadow stood fully upright and looked around. Nothing was visible save for the crates and furniture stored in the basement, but Shadow knew what else lurked between them. He picked up the first painting that leaned against the wall near him. With a deep breath, he braced himself and flipped it to face him.

Ra'jarr looked out at him, a seductive smile on his muzzle as he reclined on a couch that Shadow was sure was farther back in another room. The scene itself was a villa in one of the southern provinces, hence why the caracal was wearing only a translucent silk loin cloth that did absolutely nothing to hide the erection peeking out from his sheath as he lounged on a patio. Shadow studied the painting, trying to remember if he had posed for this one or not. If he had, this was one of Ra'jarr's later pieces, where his lover had learned to better cover that he'd put a caracal build over the taller, bulkier form of a jaguar.

Shadow stared at the painting, feeling his heart beat faster and his breaths threatening to become sobs as he gazed at it. His paws shook as the feelings came to him: the anger, the sadness, the bitterness, and most of all the numb feeling of loss. It had been over a year since that horrible night, but as he met Ra'jarr's painted eyes he knew the wounds were still open as if they were fresh. He set the painting down and reached under his tunic for the locket he never removed. He thumbed the release on the circular pendant, revealing another portrait of Ra'jarr smiling and opposite it the inscription: *So I am always with you.*

Shadow squeezed the locket tight, pressing it against his chest as the memories returned. He closed his eyes and instantly he was back in that castle, padding down the stairs to the hidden dungeon. The smoky scent from the torches filled his nostrils, along with the cold odor of stone. He moved forward, dreading what he might find. The glow at the bottom of the stairs grew stronger, and his ear swiveled desperate to catch any sound. Nothing—save his own breathing and the hammering of his heart in his chest. His paw touched the final step and a new scent joined the burning torches—the copper scent of blood. The jaguar bit back a sob, knowing how this would end, willing himself not to turn the corner, but his past-self refused to listen. The memory played on, and revealed a wooden table, covered in fresh blood and char marks. And lying on top of it was a mound of tan fur.

The pain of his knees hitting stone snapped Shadow fully back to the present. Tears burned his eyes as he went down on all fours. When he'd first seen Ra'jarr on the table, he'd feared the caracal was dead. When he'd seen what had been done to his mate, he'd hoped Ra'jarr was dead. The jaguar had been wrong. Shadow crawled forward, tears flowing freely and reached out to caress the frame of the painting. *Why? Why did you ask that of me?*

The painting simply smiled back. Shadow closed his eyes against the tears and heard it again—the sound he would never forget: a dagger slicing flesh, and the contented sigh Ra'jarr always made after sex. The jaguar—an assassin for his entire adult life—who'd taken more lives than he cared to remember, who'd stared down ancient spirits and demons without flinching, collapsed to the floor sobbing as he held himself close.

He lay there, curled up and crying, until he ached from the cold, hard stone floor. The tears slowed, and he looked out back at the painting. He felt the pressure against his body, and a little of the basement's chill faded. The assassin looked over his shoulder. Nothing. But the presence remained, the feeling of a caracal pressed against him in a comforting embrace. The jaguar could almost smell the grassy, sandy scent of his dead love.

"How am I supposed to be good to Kor if I can't let go of you?"

Remember your promise.

Whether the words were actually spoken, or came from his memory, Shadow couldn't tell. It didn't matter—he heard them as clearly as if they'd been whispered in his ear. He knew which promise, it was unforgettable—no matter how hard he tried. You didn't forget a promise made just before you ended your mate's suffering.

Promise me this. I don't want to see you again for a long time. Find another to make you happy. Live a long life. Live for both of us.

Even now, a year later, the jaguar's heart stopped as he remembered. His mind went blank, and the words became his entire world. Shadow stared at nothing until finally a new thought broke the spell: *I can't break my word.*

Instantly, the world snapped back into focus—an electric sensation as if he'd been hit by a shock spell. If he gave up, if he gave into his despair he would be betraying his love for Ra'jarr. He blinked away the last of his tears, and locked eyes with the painting.

"I have to try."

***

Ra'jarr closed the door behind him, shifting his easel under his arm as he threw the latch. He turned to find Shadow seated in the middle of the floor, legs crossed and staring at him. The jaguar's tail slapped the floor boards, echoing in the silence as they looked at each other. Shadow broke the silence.

"I looked everywhere for you."

"Not everywhere," the caracal said with a frown. "I was just up the trail, painting."

"You didn't say anything."

"You were training. I didn't want to disturb you." Ra'jarr's whiskers twitched and his tail flicked behind him.

Shadow took a deep breath and let it out, forcing his ears to remain still. The conversation would become a fight if it kept going this way, and that was the last thing he wanted right now. At least, he didn't want to fight over something so petty. The jaguar closed his eyes to find his focus, then met the caracal's gaze.

"Are you angry with me?"

"Why would I be angry with you, Spots?"

Shadow sighed and looked at the floor. "I think you're angry with me. You've been caught up in painting and haven't wanted to be intimate since I got back from Garwhal."

"You think I'm mad about the bear?" Ra'jarr asked with a laugh. His whole body shook, and his ears went flat as he chortled.

Shadow's ears caught fire as the caracal set his supplies down to wipe tears from his eyes. The jaguar whiskers twitched, suddenly uncertain about everything. He had been convinced that Ra'jarr was upset about him sleeping with the noble, but here was the caracal laughing like it was nothing. With an effort, he willed his muzzle to move. "But…"

Ra'jarr crossed the room and knelt next to the puzzled younger feline. He reached out and put a paw on the jaguar's shoulder before looking him directly in the eye. "I'm not upset with you. I've been waiting for you to stop being upset with yourself."

"What?"

"Shadow," he said, pulling the jaguar into a hug. "You have been bent out of shape since you got back. I was pretty sure I could guess what was bothering you, but it's just something you have to work through yourself."

"What do you mean?"

"I mean, Spots, you have to come to terms with what being the Nightguard will ask of you. Let me ask you something: did you love him?"

"What?! No!"

"Then it doesn't count. It was part of the job. I'm sure he won't be the last mark you sleep with to get information from. That's not love, it's work. So why should I be mad at you for doing the job you're supposed to?"

"I didn't think about it like that."

"I know you didn't. I didn't for a while either. It's just something you have to learn." He stood and pulled Shadow up. "And it's not something I expect you to fully understand right this minute."

"I think I understand, a little."

"Good. Now, shall we test that understanding?"

"How?"

Ra'jarr's smile told the jaguar all he needed to know.

***

A decade later, little had changed. Shadow was again sitting in the entry way waiting for a lover he feared had abandoned him. The jaguar's tail flicked as he waited for the fox and pondered the situation. At least this time he knew what he had to do, which made him feel a little better despite feeling like a fool over how similar the situation was.

His ears flicked as they caught the sound of blunt claws on stone a moment before the latch turned. The door swung open to admit Korwyn, in his hunting gear. The fox's eyes shone from the shadows of his hood as he realized the jaguar was there. He didn't say anything, just turned and locked the door before setting his bow and quiver against the wall. If he'd been successful, he gave no indication. Shadow guessed he'd mostly been exploring, looking for signs of the history of the area.

"You've been gone a long time," Shadow finally said.

"It's a hunting lodge. I went hunting," Kor replied as he turned back to the jaguar and dropped his hood. His ears were up, his posture was stiff, and there was a look of determined resolve in his eyes. The fox had made a decision, and was prepared to fight about it.

"You didn't say anything. I could have come with you," Shadow said with a sigh. He tensed—how the fox responded would determine everything.

"No," Kor said firmly as he padded over and settled into the chair across from Shadow, wrapping his tail around himself. He looked so vulnerable, and the fact that his gaze was on the floor did little to help. "I had a lot to think about. I needed time alone. We both did."

"Yes," Shadow replied, skipping over the fox's different attitude when they had arrived at the cabin. "We did."

Kor said nothing, just watching the jaguar. Shadow let the silence linger until the fox began to twitch. Then he rose and crossed the sitting area to kneel in front of his confused lover. The jaguar reached out and took Kor's paw in his. The fox sniffed, his ears rotating in confusion.

Shadow looked up at him. "What did you decide?"

The ranger sighed and wiggled his paw until the black jaguar released it. He reached up and undid the clasp of his cloak and let it fall to the chair. Then he reached down and clasped Shadow's paws. "After a lot of thought, I realized that you're worth waiting for."

"And I," Shadow replied, giving the black paws a squeeze. "Don't want to make you wait any more. I've been unfair to you and I am sorry."

"Don't be. I can't even begin to imagine what it's been like for you."

"That doesn't make it right," the assassin said as he stood and pulled the fox upright. "I made a promise. I need to live up to it. And I start now."

Korwyn didn't get to reply before Shadow leaned down and kissed him full on the muzzle. The fox went stiff in surprise as the bigger jaguar wrapped him in a warm embrace, but after the initial shock wore off, Kor threw his own arms around Shadow's neck and returned the kiss. They leaned into each other, parting muzzles only long enough to get air before returning to the kiss with the urgency of lovers who'd been apart for years instead of hours. It was Kor that finally pulled back.

"I. Uh. Didn't really have a chance to get ready."

"Didn't think so," Shadow whispered as he licked the fox's pointed ear. His fingers began undoing the straps of the canine's arm guards. "But I did."

Kor's eyes went wide and his tail, which had been beating a steady rhythm against the jaguar's leg, went still. His ears flicked forward, then folded back. His whiskers twitched as he studied the floor at Shadow's paws. "Oh. But. I thought you…"

"*But, I thought…*"

"*Shadow,*" Ra'jarr purred. "*I was just waiting for a special occasion.*"

"*Oh.*"

"*You're adorable when you're confused.*"

Kor's armor was strewn over the sitting area. Shadow's tunic didn't make it up the first flight of stairs. A thud resounded through the lodge as the two collapsed on the landing, still urgently kissing and running paws over each other's fur. Kor's pants slid down the second flight of stairs, as the throaty growls of a jaguar with a muzzle full of fur and the breathy moans of a pleasured fox echoed down the corridor.

The door to the bedroom flew open, admitting the nude caracal and black jaguar in his pants. Their muzzles were locked again as they made their way across the room. Shadow pulled back to gasp for air, only to be jerked towards the bed by his belt. Ra'jarr purred hungrily, his shaft already out of his sheath. The jaguar reached down to fondle the smaller feline's cream furred balls, drawing a satisfied growl from the caracal that grew louder as Shadow's pants fell to the ground.

For a long moment, Ra'jarr and Shadow stood there, their arousals rubbing against each other as they embraced again. Ra'j was the slightly leaner of the two, but one would never know it from his aggressive assault on Shadow's ear—even though he had to stretch to reach it. Shadow was reduced to moans and a growling imitation of his lover's purr under the other male's attentions. The assassin breathed deeply, letting the grassy scent of aroused caracal mixed with the woodier scent of jaguar fill his nose. His paws traced the caracal's lean flanks while the smaller feline took a firm grasp of the jaguar's rear before shoving him to the bed.

Shadow stepped into the bedroom with Korwyn nude and giggling in his arms. He paused in the center of the room and set the fox down and pressed his blunt muzzle into Kor's ear. The ranger moaned as the assassin pressed his tongue along the divide between the white of the inner ear and the black of the outer ear. The fox moaned, drawing a seductive growl from the jaguar. Shadow switched his attention to the other ear, even as he felt fingers fumbling with his belt. He eased back, letting Kor concentrate enough to undo fastenings and drop the jaguar's pants. As they fell in a puddle on the floor, Shadow lifted the fox off his paws and buried his muzzle in Kor's neck, nipping at his fur. The fox huffed, wrapping his arms around the jaguar as his tail beat a staccato rhythm against the feline's hip. Shadow got a firm grip on Kor's scruff and took the remaining four strides to the bed. He leaned forward gently depositing the fox on the mattress.

Shadow leaned back, instinctively spreading his legs to give his partner access to his rear. His thick cord tail flicked back and forth as Ra'jarr took hold of the jaguar's shaft. The woody, earthy scent of fox filled the air as the jaguar began to stroke his shaft. As he stroked, the caracal knelt between the jaguar's legs. His warm breath flowed over Shadow's balls, drawing a sigh of pleasure from the younger feline. The sound changed to a gasp and then a moan as the rough tongue ran up his sack to his exposed sheath.

Kor moaned and squirmed as Shadow licked his shaft, catching the dribble of salty pre as he went. The fox chattered, his tail hammering the jaguar's shoulder as his shaft slipped into Shadow's muzzle. He took the fox's entire length in his first motion, and held his nose against the white fur of Kor's crotch as blunt claws scratched behind his ears. His own claws kneaded through the orange-red fur of the fox's thighs. The sounds of pleasure only grew louder as he began to bob on the warm thickness filling his muzzle. He growl/purred as the yips and moans continued above him.

"I think that's enough," Ra'jarr said with a chuckle as he released the jaguar's cock from the warm confines of his mouth. "Much more, and you'll go off in the wrong end."

"Sorry," Shadow replied, crossing his legs in embarrassment.

"Don't be," the caracal soothed. He stood and motioned for Shadow to pull himself on the bed. "Just get the oil."

The jaguar nodded and crawled to the bag next to the head of the bed and pulled out the vial. He passed it to Ra'jarr, who took it and playfully pushed the jaguar over. Shadow laughed as he landed on his back, but went quiet as his lover straddled him. Ra'jarr got in position, and let their pink shafts rest against each other, both felines twitching as the sensitive barbs rubbed those on the other's cock. The caracal purred as he gave both of them playful strokes. Shadow looked down, and for the first time he could remember was aware of the difference in their sizes. The caracal wasn't lacking—and on the smaller feline body it looked much bigger, but the jaguar had a noticeable advantage in that department.

"Are you sure you want to do this?"

Shadow smiled up at the ranger. "Swishes. You're not the first fox I've been with. I'll be okay."

"Spots, you're not the biggest guy I've been with. I'll be fine. You just lie back and enjoy. But tell me if something's wrong."

"If you say so," Kor replied, his tone somewhat nervous. "How did you want to do this?"

"The best way for you," Shadow answered, rubbing his cheek against the fox's erection.

"Okay. Uh. Only done one way as top. You on your back on the bed, me on the floor."

"Missionary it is." The jaguar stood and moved to the side table. "Let me get you the oil."

Shadow did as he'd been told, and lay back with his cock throbbing as Ra'jarr prepared himself, with two fingers slipped inside his rump. As the caracal purred and pulled his fingers from his tail hole, the jaguar poured a measure of oil into his paw and slickened his own shaft.

He had just finished when Ra'jarr crawled atop him. The smaller feline pressed his nose against Shadow's before they kissed again. The jaguar shud-

dered as a paw took hold of his cock and stroked it firmly. The caracal broke the kiss and sat up, sliding Shadow's shaft between his cheeks.

"You like?"

"Yes," the jaguar whimpered playfully. He thrust his hips forward, showing that he was ready.

Ra'jarr chuckled and lowered his weight on to the jaguar, putting a stop to that. He licked his lips and placed a paw in the center of Shadow's chest. "Good. Remember, I always want you to be happy…"

"Ready?"

"I'm ready Swishes."

Kor nodded and adjusted the jaguar's legs to get between them. Shadow smiled at him, savoring the slightly awkward motions of the fox as he lined up his cock with his lover's hole. Kor looked almost as intense about this as he did with a bow in his paws and a target in his sights. The jaguar shuddered as the fox's tip came to rest just against his ring. His claws dug into the sheets in anticipation as the fox hesitated. If Shadow wrapped his tail around Kor as best he would have pulled him forward if he could. For the first time in over a year, he had the itch under his tail again. He wanted one thing—that cock inside him, and if the fox wasn't going to give it, he'd take it.

Kor must have sensed his mate's need, as he gently pushed forward. Shadow gasped as his ring spread to admit the fox's shaft, the sensation warm but not terribly painful. Kor took his time, letting the jaguar adjust to the feeling of fox filling him. Shadow shivered as each motion set shocks of pleasure down his spine.

Ra'jarr had been correct, with the warmth of his lover's rear enveloping his shaft, Shadow could already feel the pressure of orgasm building inside him. He squirmed as the caracal bounced up and down, his rear thumping against the jaguar's hips each time he reached the bottom of Shadow's shaft. The assassin could only moan and knead at the sheets as his lover rode him. The doubts melted away. With the bear had been nothing like this. This was different. This was special.

"Remember, I always want you to be this happy…"

Shadow breathed in the warm grassy, woody scent of his fox as Kor's hips smacked against his rear. The jaguar moaned and looked past his leaking shaft at the ranger. The fox's eyes were closed, his face intense, his breath coming in huffs as he focused on working Shadow's rear. His heart swelled with love for Kor as he felt the shocks of pleasure surge through him each time the fox's cock touched those sensitive places inside him. His own cock throbbed and leaked each time Kor filled him.

Shadow's claws kneaded the sheet as he relished the feeling of his rear being filled. He'd missed this feeling. There was a warm sensation—not quite burn—that reminded him how long it had been since he'd experienced this pleasure. The sting faded as they continued until Kor slipped out, cursing. The jaguar asked for more lube, which the fox obliged.

"Getting knotty," Kor said as he slid back in. "Sure you want it?"

"Yes," Shadow groaned as he felt the warm thickness spreading his ring. "Please."

Kor nodded and got back to work, setting an ever-increasing pace that reduced Shadow to half growls and moans. The fox let out yips and breathy chitters as he went, his blunt claws digging into the jaguar's hips. Shadow jerked as what felt like a wall bumped against his ring. It took his mind a moment to recognize his lover's knot, and another heartbeat for it to remind him what that would feel like. His body tensed at the thought.

But the rest of him didn't care. Deep in his loins, the pressure was building to an inevitable peak. He took hold of his shaft, forming a ring with his fingers so that Kor's motions had him stroking himself. He willed himself to relax and savor the sensations of having a lover under his tail. He should have done this long ago, he thought to himself as he began to pant.

Kor growled at the jaguar's recalcitrant rear and redoubled his efforts. Shadow's whole body shook as the fox slammed into him again and again. The jaguar shuddered and moaned as the fox huffed and chittered. Shadow purred and grunted, urging the fox on. Kor took the hint, and shoved one final time.

Shadow's rear yielded with a *pop* that might have been audible if it hadn't driven all the air out of the jaguar in a loud gasp. The jaguar's cock throbbed in his paw and gave such a spurt of pre that he almost thought he'd finished. Firmly tied in his love, Kor's pace became frantic, until it seemed that he was moving in time with Shadow's racing heart. The jaguar was reduced to burbling groans as the pressure inside him built and built until it hovered on the edge of eruption.

Kor reached the peak first. He shoved himself hard against Shadow's rear one final time, throwing his head back and letting out a breathy, chattering moan. The thickness inside the jaguar's rear throbbed, and he swore he felt a swelling as the fox released. Another throb, and another.

A few more strokes were all it took to push the jaguar over the top, and Shadow let out a growling moan as his own shaft throbbed and spurted again and again. Judging from the noises Kor made, it was an impressive eruption—which was confirmed when the warmth of his seed splashed against Shadow's face.

The jaguar opened his eyes and looked down to see a trail of white down his neck all the way to his rapidly retreating pink shaft. He looked up and met the green eyes of a very contented fox. It took him a moment to realize that there was only a fox with him—he couldn't sense a caracal at all.

Kor dropped to the mattress on his paws and knees with a contended sigh. For a long time, there was no other sound but the panting of worn out lovers.

Shadow blinked as what happened fully dawned on him. "He's gone," the jaguar whimpered.

"Hmm?"

"He's gone… I. He was there like always. But at the end it wasn't him. It was just you…'"

"Oh. That. But that's a good thing, isn't it?"

"What? How did you—"

"Moons," the fox cut in with a sigh. A claw ran through the jaguar's fur, tracing the semi crescent shape of a rosette. "It took me a while, but after so many times of you looking surprised to see me, or jumping when you felt my knot, it was pretty easy to figure out you had someone else in your head. Wasn't a challenge to guess who."

Shadow met Kor's sleepy gaze and felt the heat of embarrassment rush into his ears as they pulled flat against his head. He closed his eyes against the burn of tears. "I'm sorry," he whispered as his paws reached behind his neck to undo his pendant. "It won't happen again."

He was still fumbling with the catch when a black-furred paw landed on his chest. He opened his eyes to find Kor looking down at him, his green eyes full of determination, the locket clutched tight in his paw.

"Don't you dare," the fox growled, exposing his teeth.

Shadow froze. For a heartbeat, he was actually frightened of the smaller predator. His ears stayed flat and he slowly let go of the chain.

Kor's expression relaxed, changing to a knowing and comforting smile. He let go of the locket and ran his paw though the jaguar's matted, sticky chest fur. "Moons. He's not gone. He's just giving us our space. Does always thinking of him when you're with someone else make you happy?"

"No," Shadow admitted, choking back tears.

"And Ra'jarr knows that. But you had to give him that space too. He'll be there when you need him."

Shadow sniffed away the tears, suddenly in awe of the fox. "How are you okay with this?"

"Because I love you, dumbass," Korwyn said with that sardonic smile foxes did so well plastered on his muzzle. "I don't know how you had the strength to make it through what you did. And like I said, you're worth waiting for."

Shadow took a deep breath and wrapped the fox in a warm embrace. "I love you too, Korwyn. As much as I loved Ra'jarr. And I hope you can forgive me for taking so long to show you."

"We should clean up," the fox said sleepily. He pushed himself up and worked his hips, tugging his knot free, provoking a startled chirp from the jaguar.

"Or," Shadow said with a grin of his own. He yanked Kor down next him. "We can stay like this till we wake up."

"Fine," Kor replied with a yawn. He draped his arm over the jaguar's chest. "But if we get stuck, you're carrying me to the bath. It'll be a great story someday."

Shadow chuckled but didn't reply. The jaguar felt his own eyelids getting heavier as he squeezed the fox up against him. From the window, still open in the mid-autumn evening, a breeze stirred the curtains, heavy with the cool scents of stone and pine. As his eyes closed, the breeze drifted over them, and for the briefest of seconds Shadow thought he smelled warm, sand and sun baked grass. He heard Kor sniff—as if he could smell it too. As quickly as it came it was gone, and the jaguar and the fox drifted off to sleep.

Ghosts of Cinnamon and Lavender

Thurston Howl

CW: Implications of self-harm

Past: October 1985

Two foxes walked into a club, and neither knew the other existed, not at first.

It was around ten at night when one of the foxes came in. Despite the rain and the cold that had settled over the Los Angeles streets, he was dressed in short shorts and a crop top. He knew what he was wanting from the club tonight, and he planned to get it, rain be damned.

A knock on the door later, and a slot moved at the top of the iron door. A burly wolf glared out from the slot. "Password?" the gruff voice said.

The fox hooked his thumbs in the waistband of his shorts and gave the wolf a wink. "Oh, come on, Marv. You know who it is."

"Password?"

Rolling his eyes, the fox replied, "Milk makes your bones strong." While he understood the phrase was mostly a call to the late Harvey Milk, an openly gay politician, he was more than aware of the double entendre, with the nature of the club in mind.

The door creaked open to reveal a bearish wolf, his rotund stomach hanging over the lip of tight leather jeans, leaving very little to the imagination. But even more than the sight, what hit Rhett the most were the smells: he inhaled wafts of sweat, leather, and, of course, cum. He walked in and wrapped his arms around the wolf's hips and pecked a kiss on the wolf's cheek. "Thanks, babe."

"Hey," the wolf started, closing the door, "be careful tonight."

Still walking toward the flashing lights down the hall, the fox looked over his shoulder and said, "Hm? Is there supposed to be a raid tonight?"

The wolf grunted. "Not to my knowledge. But with the gay dog cancer going around, just be careful who you're fucking, yeah?"

The fox laughed and saluted the guard. "You got it."

The club itself comprised mostly private rooms in dark corners. A few central areas had flashing strobe lights with loud music—Beardonna—and slings already occupied. It was a mass of bodies in the center of the Club Muskrat, yet they appeared as a blob amid the flickering lights. Rhett could recognize no faces, even though he had been here countless times and had probably been fucked by a third of these guys already.

With a grin and a flick of his ears, he pulled his shirt over his head and threw it and his shorts into a pile in the corner. Now he was naked before the masses. While he had cleaned out under his tail, he hadn't showered since this morning, and his natural musk wafted throughout the space, adding to the other smells. As he made his way to the back where there was a vacant sling, he noticed guys turning his direction. It could have been the way he was unashamedly naked here. It could have been that natural musk of his. Or it could have just been the way he swished his tail slowly behind him, inviting any and all to come play.

By the time he was situated in the sling, his ankles resting on straps along the chains and his paws gripping the chains near his head, guys had started to form a circle around him. There was very little foreplay at the Club Muskrat. Very little. The night became a blur of cocks, poppers, cum, and even fists.

The world only sharpened to reality when the second fox appeared. It had been a couple hours already, and the circle had diminished. While a stallion was pounding Rhett's tailhole, this other fox came up and planted a kiss on Rhett's snout. There were new scents suddenly: lavender and cinnamon. Rhett's eyes opened wider as the older fox kissed him, and he felt himself melt into that kiss, oblivious to the stallion breeding his ass.

"Hey, stranger," Rhett said, rubbing a paw through the fox's white belly fur.

The other fox smirked. "Hey there, cutie. Got any plans after this? Or tomorrow?"

"Just you."

Laughing, the fox pulled out a marker. "Would you mind?" He gestured toward Rhett's stomach.

"Not at all," Rhett replied, just admiring the fox's body. While the older fox wrote down his phone number in large, black digits on Rhett's stomach, the raised fox leaned forward and pressed his nose into the standing fox's balls, inhaling deeply and licking at the orbs. Even when the fox finished writing the numbers, he just let Rhett enjoy himself.

And Rhett was already madly in love. He couldn't wait to tell his boyfriend back home about this guy.

***

Present – August 2019

Galan was not as spry as he used to be. He was what was now being called a graymuzzle. Usual for his morning jog, he was reminiscing about past times. He thought often, especially recently—with that special day today—of the Club Muskrat, in all its grungy splendor before it was shut down. He remembered all the men he'd meet there and how glorious it felt. It was a different time. People rarely saw and internalized faces there. Nowadays, you open Knott-e, and there's either face pics or dick pics, in bold clarity, too. Back then, back in the 80s, those spaces were a kind of celebration of sex positivity and freedom. Now, it takes months to set up a basic threeway. And of course there was the tracker dog disease epidemic.

Huffing, the fox picked up speed down the road. His legs felt great, but over the years he had started losing his breath more. Getting old sucks. The morning mist washed over the road, and the sunlight danced through the trees on his left. His backpack bounced against his shirtless back, and his belly bounced with each step, too. He didn't jog to lose weight; he felt proud in his body. But it just felt good to move, to *run*. He had been doing marathons recently, and he had all the newest gadgets to track his speed, heart rate, and steps taken. He always finished a jog feeling accomplished.

But today…today might be different.

He looked deeper into the woods. Up ahead on the road, he was about to come up on his house for the end, but he wasn't ready for that. Maybe not ever again.

He took a sharp turn and jogged into the woods and down memory lane, chasing the ghosts of the past, of foxes, lavender, and cinnamon, of when he used to go by a different name.

***

Past – December 1985

"Marcus, this is the cutie I've been telling you about. Meet Blaine," Rhett said, holding Marcus' hand while gesturing to the fox across the table.

"Wow! Nice to meet you finally. Rhett's talked a lot about you."

Blaine blushed. "Aw, well he shouldn't have. I'm glad to meet you too." He scratched the back of one ear absently and looked away. "So, uh…are you both sure about this? Like, really?"

The two foxes squeezed each other's paws before saying in unison, "Fuck yes."

Rhett smiled. While he knew other poly partners, it was technically his first time as much as it was Blaine's. He was usually a sexual slut, not a romantic one. But he loved both of his foxes, and he wanted to show them that. And in a gay space like this one, the Fleecewood Diner, they wouldn't even get second looks holding hands in the open like this.

Then, Rhett had a foxy idea, which is to say, an evil idea.

He lifted his foot and pressed it between Blaine's legs, brushing against the crotch of his pants. The fox let out a yip and then clamped a paw over his snout in embarrassment.

Marcus laughed. "Oh, what's the matter, Blaine? You're getting all blushy." Rhett knew that Marcus knew what he was doing. Marcus had done it to Rhett countless times.

Blaine just whined in a low voice and looked out the window.

When the waiter came with their drinks, Blaine's fur stood on end as he jumped.

Rhett and Marcus laughed, and Rhett just kept stroking Blaine's boner with his foot. "Say," Rhett started, "after drinks, would you feel comfortable coming to our place?"

Blaine's eyes widened. "A-Are you sure?"

Marcus reached a paw across to hold Blaine's. "Look, I know you and Rhett are close as fuck already. From what I'm seeing so far, I like you too. We can chat some more over coffee, and, if you're still ok with it, we would love to have you over. But there's just one condition."

Blaine looked between the two foxes, his nose twitching with anxiety. "What?"

Marcus leaned forward. "I call bottom!"

"Hey!" Rhett punched his arm with a laugh. "Always so vulgar!"

Blaine laughed. "Alright, I guess I'll call top."

"Fuck. Guess I get middle then." Rhett turned to his boyfriend and gave him a kiss. Then before Blaine could feel uncomfortable, Rhett leaned across the table, pulled Blaine forward by the collar of his shirt and kissed him, too. He could taste the cinnamon. That fox was always chewing his cinnamon gum. Blaine leaned back and blushed, stroking his tail and looking out the window. "Heh, always my gallant fox," Rhett said of Blaine, leaning back and wrapping an arm over Marcus' shoulder.

"So," Marcus started. "Rhett said you guys met fucking at the Club Muskrat? You a regular there?"

"Nah," Blaine said, waving a paw. "I might go a couple times a year. But besides, they're tearing it down anyway. Since the feds got their way regarding this gay dog cancer, all the clubs are gonna shut down for a while."

Marcus nodded. "Yeah, that's what I heard too. Since it's on the edge of a damn residential area though, they are thinking of making the area a park or little woodsy area. It's great the owner gets a say in what the land will be used for. Otherwise, it'd just be a parking lot or supermall. Won't catch me complaining, for sure. But it's cool you weren't a super frequent regular. I hadn't recalled meeting you before either. Part of me was a bit nervous to meet you, for fuck's sake. Thought you might be some guy I rejected in the past or something."

Blaine's jaw dropped for a second, and then they both started laughing.

"While you two are bonding," Rhett said, shaking his head with a grin, "I'm gonna go use the bathroom. I'll be right back, cuties." As Rhett walked to the back restroom, he made sure to swish his tail nice and slow for the boys to look at, teasing the waistband of his shorts down an inch while he did so.

***

Present

The woods swallowed Galan. After a few minutes and a few hills, he could no longer see the road. He had taken an old trail that was mostly faded, but it was there nonetheless, and it was a trail he had taken many times, especially around this time of year. But somehow, the woods seemed different now. There was more mist than sunlight, and the air was cold. The trees towered above him and around him, and the soil and leaves crunched beneath his bare paws. As his jog slowed to a stroll, he noticed how old all the trees had become. There had once stood a sex club here, the Club Muskrat. It all used to be right here. The place had become a verdant forest, thanks to the previous owner of the Club, commemorating those who were lost to TDD, but to Galan it would always just be that: a monument of death. Each singular tree looked like a silent sentinel over the memories it guarded; each tree, to Galan, stood for a life lost.

His paws sore, he stopped at a tree and rested his back against it. Each puff of breath crystallized in front of him, and his tongue lapped at the air as he panted. The woods were so quiet. Not even the leaves above him rattled in the wind. No early morning birds chirped. It was silent. Too quiet.

Until he heard a twig snap.

He whipped his head around to see the source of the sound, but he was alone. There was no one there. He sighed and let his knees fold until he was resting on his ass on the pine needle-laden ground. Then, he pulled off his backpack and opened it. The sack rattled. He looked inside and saw two pill bottles. One was for his tracker dog disease, which had once upon a time been called the gay dog cancer. The advances of medicine had made it so he could live as long and as healthy a life as literally anyone else as long as he took a pill a day. Things weren't like they were thirty-five years ago. It just wasn't a death sentence. But his paw moved past that pill bottle and grabbed the other instead. He popped five into his mouth. He paused before swallowing, as if to reconsider, but then he swallowed anyway. The more he thought about it, the more likely he would be to back out.

He leaned his head back against the tree and stared up at the canopy. At first, he felt nothing. Then, coldness enveloped him. His heart started pounding in his ears. It was like taking a hit of poppers, just much more intense...and scary. Gradually, the colors of his vision started to blur together. Then, he heard another twig snap. This time, when he looked, he saw forms appear through his blurred vision. All kinds of people were around him: lions, tigers, and bears, oh murr. Horses, wolves, and, of course, foxes. He smiled. He thought he recognized the wolf night guard from the Club Muskrat thirty-five years ago in the group. "What the fuck, man? You're here? I thought you died years ago," Galan said. He staggered forward, only to realize the ensemble around were all naked among the trees. He collapsed to his hands and knees. No, this could not be real. There was no way. But when he looked up, there was a red cock in his face. The wolf guard looked down at him expectantly with a sneer and, snapping his fingers like one does when commanding a dog to sit, pointed down to his dick.

Galan shivered with—

***

Past–May 1989

When Rhett heard a knock at the door, he tried to raise his voice. "Come in!"

Both of his foxes opened the door. Marcus had a bouquet of flowers in his paw, and Blaine had a small box with red ribbon wrapped around it. "Surprise!"

Rhett laughed weakly and gestured for them to come in. "Hurry up before the nurse finds out you both got in here without being family."

"Ah, fuck her," Marcus said.

Blaine sneered and squeezed Marcus close. "You would, too."

"Fuck yeah, I would. She was nice as hell. You know she'd be a nurturing lover."

"Alright, alright, you two," Rhett said with a cough. "To what do I owe this surprise?"

The two standing foxes looked at each other with concern and then came to sit beside Rhett's hospital bed. Blaine was the one who started, "Well, we have a…proposition for you."

Rhett arched a brow.

"Yeah," Marcus said, ears flat but his tail still wagging. "We brought you flowers or a box."

"*Or?*" Rhett said, checking to make sure he had heard right, and that the tracker dog disease wasn't starting to affect his hearing too.

Blaine nodded. "Yeah. We have a question for you. If you say yes, you get the box. If you say no, you get the flowers."

"Ok…" Rhett looked away as if in thought before coughing. The coughs became violent but subsided after a few seconds. "I guess… what's the question?"

Marcus opened the box. A red-stoned ring. It was clearly too big for a finger. It took Rhett only the duration of one cough to realize it was a cock ring. He laughed weakly. In unison, Marcus and Blaine said, "Will you marry us?"

Tears started welling up in Rhett's eyes, but a mischievous look filled them. "Well… um… what kind of flowers are those?"

Blaine just about died from the remark, much to Marcus and Rhett's amusement. Amid the laughter, Rhett smiled and said, "Of course I will marry you. Of course. Yes, yes, and fucking yes."

Marcus squeezed both Blaine's and Rhett's paws. "Good. Once you get the fuck out of here, we'll start planning the wedding."

Rhett didn't have the heart to tell them what the doctors had said, not today.

"Would you like to do the honors?" Marcus said, handing the box to Blaine.

"Me?" Blaine blushed. "Alright." Reaching a paw under the sheet, he slowly worked Rhett up. While the fox looked like he was enjoying himself, he looked strained too. His whole body was emaciated and shivering. He looked like roadkill that was still moving. But Blaine and Marcus still loved him, with all their hearts. Once Rhett's cock was hard, Blaine worked the cock ring over the fox's member and squeezed his balls through. Then, Blaine and Marcus switched places. Blaine pressed a thumb under Rhett's tail and worked his tailhole, while Marcus stroked the sickly fox's cock.

Rhett came, thinking about what he would look like in a white gown at a wedding with his two gentlefoxes.

***

Present

Galan did not know what to believe. If what he was seeing was a drug-induced hallucination, he didn't want it to end. He wanted, more than anything, for this to be real. It had been over half a century since he had seen these faces, and his longing for all of his friends back was such a visceral feeling, something that had been locked away. Most people today, even gay people, don't know what it was like to lose most of your friends in just a couple of years.

Eagerly, he lapped at the wolf's cock, just focusing on flicking his tongue across the tip, before the wolf wagged a finger at some of the other ghosts, urging them to join in the fun. Galan saw them all in full detail, like he was seeing them all in HD for the first time. These were no invisible ghosts; they were full incarnations of the past. He smelled it all: the sweat, the cum, the leather, the lube, and, of course, somewhere in there, lavender and cinnamon. He felt like he was lost in that euphoria again. As a feline's barbed cock pressed against his tail, he spread his legs on the cold ground and invited that embrace. The wolf grabbed him by the ears and pushed his cock in further, the tip pressing against Galan's throat. All of it didn't just feel real; it felt *intense*, like when you're sleep-deprived but you just drank three cups of coffee. Everything is vivid, even while you feel far away.

He wasn't used to being the center of attention like this, but here he was, in the midst of a pack of hungry ghosts, and they craved flesh.

Their paws explored his body, caressing the muscles in his legs, working through the fur on his chest, sliding their trimmed claws over his nipples, fondling and pulling lightly on his balls, letting their fingers wander into his mouth while he sucked on the climaxing wolf.

When the cum hit the back of his throat, Galan swallowed eagerly, milking the wolf for every last drop. Then, the wolf pulled out and patted the fox on the head before walking away.

The headspace shattered around Galan. The wolf began to fade, back into memory, a past about thirty years old, as he walked, and Galan felt tears running down his cheeks. Ignoring the other ghosts exploring his body, he crawled forward, trying to chase after the wolf, after the memory, but he was gone. Galan turned back around, and all he caught were the forms dissolving, back into the trees.

"No, no, no…" Galan muttered, making his way back to his satchel. He noticed belatedly that his shorts and underwear had ended up being discarded by a tree, and his cock was leaking a long tendril of pre, but he didn't care. He wanted to go back into the dream. He didn't care how far he went.

He pulled out the pill bottle and opened it. There were still quite a few pills left. He could do it. He could end it all, and it would all end in bliss. He could have it all back: the memories, the club, his lover, the past. He could have it all back. All he had to do…was take the dive.

His paw was shaking, and he started crying harder, muttering over and over again, "I want it all back…I want it all back…" As the colorful figures faded into the trees, he recalled the lists of names, the eulogies in the papers he would check every week. He recalled how the lists became similar to a Friends list on Facebook: everyone you know is right there on that list. But when he saw that friend's name, it meant he'd never see them again. Most days, he still felt that loneliness deep down. It was over twenty years ago by this point, but losing almost everyone you know over the course of a few years wears on you. It tears. It keeps tearing until you feel like you're one of the last ones still standing.

"No," he said. "I won't let you go." He kept taking pills. "Just a few more…won't hurt." He wanted the ghosts to stay with him.

***

Past– August 1989

When Rhett woke up, he saw Blaine standing there. He smiled, but he had already lost the ability to speak. He just smiled up at the handsome fox and flexed his fingers. Blaine saw and reached out to grab his paw. It felt so warm, Rhett thought. Then, he frowned. Where was Marcus? His ears flicked once as he looked at the door then at Blaine.

Blaine's ears flattened and shook his head. "Hey babe…they tested Marc. He's…he's got it, too."

Rhett felt a gasp rattle up his throat. He tried to shake his head. He couldn't imagine his Marc, *his Marc*, going through the same thing he was going through. He felt like hell and wouldn't wish it upon anyone, especially not either of the tods in his life.

"I'm sorry," Blaine said, squeezing Rhett's paw softly.

But Rhett just shook his head more, looking up into Blaine's tear-soaked eyes. He refused to let Blaine apologize for all of this. Blaine was one half of what kept Rhett going through all of this. "N-no…" he managed finally.

Blaine's ears flicked. "Don't try to talk, babe. You'll hurt your throat. I'm so sorry about this…about everything. I…" Blaine sat down and wiped his eyes with his free paw. "I'm sorry I wasn't strong enough. I couldn't stop you from getting sick, and now I couldn't stop Marcus either. What did we do wrong?"

Rhett shook his head.

"Babe, why do you keep doing that? What is it?"

The tears in Rhett's eyes changed. They were not of sorrow, or pity, or desperation. They were of admiration. The sick fox reached his shaking paw up and caressed Blaine's cheek. "Y-y-you're plenty s-strong. My g-g-g—"

"Babe?"

"G-Gallan—g-gallant f-fox, I l-love y—"

A low, flatlining beep sounded from the machine Rhett was hooked up to, and Blaine jumped up. The nurse, a young stoat, forced him out of the room, and Blaine watched as he and a doctor pulled the white sheet over the fox's blank face, Blaine knew two things at that moment: one was that what Rhett had called him would be his name from then on, always his fox's Galan, and two was that Rhett had gotten his wish—even in death, he looked beautiful in that white gown.

***

Present

A paw swatted at his, knocking the pills to the frozen topsoil. Galan leaned forward and wept without control. His face contorted with the sheer sorrow he felt at the wave of memories, and tears streamed down his face. The paw patted his back and rubbed him. He felt the figure kneel down beside him and hold him in a close embrace. No words were spoken, just the embrace. Eventually, Galan turned and pressed his face into the fox's chest, sobbing still.

Finally, the other fox, Marcus, said, "It's ok, love. I miss him, too."

"It's not fair, Marc. It's not fair."

Marcus looked out between the trees and saw the gravestone they had erected for Rhett. It was indeed twenty years to the day since their fox had died. He felt sorrow spasm across his spine, too. "I know, love. But hey…" He pulled the older fox's snout up, so they were eye to eye. "But I already lost one of my foxes. I don't want to lose both of you."

"I'm sorry…I'm so sorry. I wasn't being…as careful as I should have. When I took the pills, I could see them. I could *see* them, Marc." He nuzzled Marcus' shoulder. "I'm sorry. I don't want to lose you either."

Galan nodded. The day Marcus got better, thanks to the meds, was such a relief for him. He had worried he would have been forever alone. When Marcus got out, they helped each other get through Rhett's passing. True to their word, they still married, and they did it by Rhett's grave when Marcus got his full strength back. When Galan was diagnosed years later, he thought it was the end for him, but it wasn't. When people told Galan to kill himself for being open about his diagnosis, he didn't. But all the same, all of it wore down on him. It tore. And some days were better than others. This was not one of his better days.

"C'mon, I'll help walk you back to the house." Marcus grabbed Galan's clothes, helped him get dressed, and started to guide him out of the woods. When they reached the top of the hill, Galan heard something, something that sounded like an old dance song. He turned to look over his shoulder, even as Marcus kept guiding him.

Just past the trees where he had cried, just past the gravestone, he thought he saw it, just the slightest swish of a red tail among the pines.

THE HONEST THING

Ethan Burrow

Audrey Parker, the effortless beauty, prankster incarnate, bane of teachers, dispenser of wit, breaker of hearts, crusher of dreams, general blasphemer, and pretty much coolest possum in Stonewall Michigan, was now officially, *not* my girlfriend.

I know it's not newsworthy material or anything groundbreaking really. Audrey's well known for her disinterest in the stuff she calls 'samey'. You know, routine. Commitment. Wanting to obey the law. All the usual stuff. So it's no surprise that we only dated for about a month, which in Audrey-time, is comparable to a life sentence. It doesn't bother me so much thinking about it—the breakup part of it, I mean. I'm just confused about the why.

"Charlie."

When Audrey's bandit-like eyes cut into me, my teeth clenched hard against the Nutrigrain Bar I had half-shoved down my muzzle. Audrey only ever looked at anyone, and I mean really looked, when she was in the mood to lecture about lines from her favorite songs, poetry, or whatever else had her fancy that week. She had this way with talking, where even if you knew it was mostly bullshit, you still wanted to see where she was going with it. I just had this feeling I wouldn't be hearing more about Whitman or the Smiths today, especially when she crawled down onto the floor with me in her usual subtly seductive fashion.

"Do you know how I really feel about you?"

"I don't know. That you like me?"

"Sort of. I think I love you, Charlie."

I choked a little. You can't just shuffle these sorts of things off to a guy with his pants down, at least metaphorically speaking. When I think about confessions of love, my mind wanders to movie perfect moments or meaningful nights out. This was just my mom's basement. The only thing really going on was the soft hiss of the radio, currently advertising penis pills that would "change your life forever." That, and the washing machine, diligently fighting stains from my briefs. It was about as romantic as it gets.

What I'm trying to say is that when Audrey dropped the L bomb, it felt wrong. Here I was, this shaggy, wiry joke of a collie who skipped gym back in high-school, and Audrey-fucking-Parker was face-to-face with me, with her lucious hips and crooked tail, picking a few crumbs from the carpet with her pointed, pink fingers. I could make out these blotchy black patches of fur that sat between the mess of whiskers littering her snout.

"That's why I think we should see other people."

"Uh."

"I'm sorry. It's just this whole thing. It's inconvenient. For me."

"Yeah?"

"Look, it's complicated, Charlie. I just don't want this anymore. Okay?"

"Okay."

She was touching my shoulder now. I suppose it was for comfort or support, but it felt cheap. Condescending even. I just wanted some clarity, literally anything to help me understand whatever the heck just happened. But when I went to talk, the way you expect adults to, my words came out all cracked and full of holes. It's not that I was even really that sad, I was just what my parents called "a very sensitive boy." I could tell she felt bad too, since she sat there watching me with her ears cupped back and brows all wormy and confused. Despite being a master in the art of break-ups, I don't think Audrey ever anticipated seeing me on the verge of tears.

Fortunately, when my mom came down to ask if she was staying for dinner, Audrey practically flew out the back door of my basement, breaking the metric ton of silence she'd managed to create. I swear she almost slammed the door on her scraggly tail on the way out. I think my mom knew.

But before she got the chance to ask me what happened, I'd bolted for the door, sneakers half-on, accompanied only by some track pants and my last clean shirt—definitely not the kind of stuff I should've been wearing this late into the year. I want to clarify that I wasn't looking to catch up with Audrey. It sounds like it. I know. But she could've been anywhere on earth by that point and it wouldn't have mattered to me. I just needed to get out. To get away from whatever the hell just happened.

***

When I made it to Paxton Lake, my lungs choked on the cold air and I practically tumbled into the water.

The surrounding thicket of golds and browns acted like a barrier from all the things that made Stonewall bad. All the new neighborhoods. All the convenience stores and shopping centers we didn't need. It isolated itself from whatever my town was becoming, for better or for worse, and in that moment, I knew why. I'd kicked my feet over the concrete drain that jutted from the lake. It was this crude ugly thing that'd only been installed about a few months back, but as much as it sucked, it was usually dry, and definitely a great place to sit.

I was down to my last cigarette, battling all the obnoxious and heavy remnants of whatever just happened. I wasn't crying. Honest. It's just that every time I went to inhale, I made this pathetic wheezing sound, barely grasping onto the air around me. I was trying to understand where it all went wrong, so I went back to where we first met: Professor Steinman's class, "Science for the working man." She'd perked up when Steinman caught me mid-lecture, eyes tightly shut.

"A sleeping man makes not an educated one, Mister Stokes." I swear behind all the wrinkles and faded fur, he was hiding the faintest of smiles. I hated him.

I argued that "Mister Stokes" pulled an eight-hour shift at CVS three nights in a row, but I guess minimum wage isn't a job you can really apply science to. Steinman demanded I leave his classroom at once, and to not come back until I've made sure I gave his lectures as much attention as my part-time job. I don't think he understood how little I actually cared for either, but Audrey did. She shot out of her seat mouthing off to this poor old raccoon, who mind you, was barely able to lift his shaky dark paw up to the chalkboard to write down both our names. When we dipped from that catastrophe, I was surprised, since she just kept on talking to me. She said how much "college academic elective requirements suck," and how we're just going to forget most of this junk anyways. I kept agreeing, without really saying much. Somehow we ended up at the new McDonalds they built off campus, destroying fries and shooting the shit. All the while Audrey just kept talking and talking and talking. Thankfully, the talking ceased when it turned to kissing and the kissing became way more than just kissing pretty. Eventually, it was just the two of us stowed away in the trunk of my station-wagon, fucking over this mix-tape I had stuck in my dashboard. I think the Pixies were playing.

"Uh. Hey man, you alright?"

I must've looked like a nervous mess, since this fuzzy little shepherd reeled back when I whipped around to meet his gaze. An oversized auburn flannel hung loosely over his compact frame, pooling beautiful blue and burgundy fur from every opening. I didn't know the guy, but I wasn't trying to be rude, so I cleared the snot out of my throat and wiped my eyes as if I had a cold.

"Oh. Yeah. I caught something bad. I'm just airing my lungs out."

"With cigarettes?"

I coughed hard, lowering my ears and disproportionate muzzle. To him I must've been another after-school special martyr, ready to ruin my life, which made me feel pretty lousy about my excuse. That's when he procured his own cigarette from a badly bent package he'd fished from his pocket. As he lit up with the lighter I passed him, he gave me the warmest smile.

"My name's Charlie." I offered.

"Olive. And Charlie?"

"Yeah?"

"You're sitting in my spot."

His eyes dotted to where I was sitting, before rolling up to mine.

Apparently, Olive had been coming here since he'd moved in right down the street about a month ago. He said he was from New York, and that he was here because he had family in Stonewall that would take him in. That's where he left it. I told him about how I'd lived here my whole life, and how I'd always wanted to see New York—at least the upstate parts—because of all the great poets and artists that came out of there. He said it wasn't so bad, but that the people there were distant and the weather was always terrible. I decided to hold my tongue about how awful Michigan actually was. I didn't think he needed that.

Olive had these tired, green eyes that complemented this big toothy smile. He also had a way of looking at you that made you feel like you mattered. It's kind of hard to explain. Maybe it was the lake and the trees. Maybe it was just the way he was put together, with his tattered skater clothes and ridiculously short tail. But being there with him felt pretty great, even if my stomach was tied in knots and all my words came out like I had stage-four lymphoma. The nice part about sitting there, with him, was that he didn't throw around tacky jokes or try to impress me with bogus stories from his time in New York. Nothing like that. He just asked me questions while he chain smoked, as if I had something interesting to say.

"What are you doing out here, Charlie?"

"Just trying to stay warm, I guess."

"You sure you don't want to go inside?"

"I'm pretty sure."

"Then why don't you have a coat?"

"Because I didn't think I'd be out here so long. You're not helping that."

That made him laugh. He told me all about his friends back home, and how they used to get into all sorts of trouble. His parents thought he was in with "the wrong crowd," which to their credit, Olive didn't really deny. He said they used to camp out in old hospitals and broken-down houses whenever they needed to lay low. They did that a lot, apparently.

For a while, we just sat there all quiet-like. We watched the lake, the trees, I talked about how much I hated the ducks here. It was pretty great. It started to get dark, so I ended up walking with him back to his place, which was only about a mileish up from Paxton. Eventually we made it to this older-looking house that smelled of burnt coffee, mothballs and oakwood. We were at his porch when he told me to smile more, since that was "one of the best things" about me. If I'm gonna be honest, it felt good hearing that.

"Thanks Charlie," he said, going in for a hug.

"For what?"

"Just this. I needed this."

So I hugged him back.

It wasn't long before this old, exasperated voice croned from behind the front door, "Oliver, is that you out there?" It sounded real close. He told me that was his uncle, and that he needed to go, so he dusted himself off and said he'd catch me around. I'd only made it halfway off his lawn before I'd turned back. He was already gone. All that was left was me, his porch, and a few Halloween decorations that didn't have much of an excuse to be out this late.

When the sun went down I was already back in my room working on another mixtape. It was originally for Audrey, since it had a lot of her favorite bands. Stuff like the Smiths, Ride, the Cure, U2. You know, the good stuff. I just wasn't sure if I should really be enjoying these things, since we weren't together anymore. They were mine now too, obviously, but they'd always have a part of Audrey in them. Maybe I was over-thinking it. Either way she was back on my mind, so I put down my tapes and tried my hardest to sleep.

***

"Well. At least that's over with."

Spencer eyed me over his homework, ears flat and unsurprised. He was this nosy white fox who relished in all things drama. Strangers, friends, celebrities, it didn't matter. If there was dating involved, Spencer definitely knew about it. His homework was unfinished and due in ten minutes, but he'd already closed his math book.

"So what was her excuse?"

"What do you mean?"

"Was there another boy? Did she say she was bored of you?"

"She said she loved me. Almost. I still don't get it."

"Hmm…"

We had a unique kind of relationship. Spencer helped me not suck at trigonometry, since we had math together on Wednesdays, and I'd give him opinions on all the boys I knew from Stonewall Community College. He really loved talking about boys.

"That's not like her," he said, deep in thought. "Excuses are her strong suit, and believe me, that girl can lie."

I actually was aware of both Audrey and Spencer way before I got to personally know either of them. But I guess everyone back in high school did, considering they were the infamous *Terrible Two* of Welvern Creek. Spencer would always brag about how nothing got by them—how they were nowhere and everywhere at once. I know it's a little ridiculous say-ing that, but honestly, you'd be hard-pressed finding any kid willing to debate the authenticity of their status. Principal Folderman had his eyes practically glued to the two, especially after they'd put up a local list-ing for his house, thousands of dollars under the actual market value. Folderman had to take the week off to defend his estate from frenzied house hunters, which led to pure unbridled anarchy in the many halls and classrooms of Welvern. Most kids still refer to it in hushed tones as the "Schoolpocalypse," even the ones that weren't there for it.

Spencer said she never talked to boys like that. She'd told him love was a weakness. The kind of thing that'd keep her from all the things she loved doing herself. So whenever she got bored of a boy, he'd help her forge an army of escape plans, and they'd move onto their next big heist. It was just the kind of thing they'd do when they weren't terrifying the rest of Welvern Creek. But that was well over a year ago, before they'd stopped talking.

I could see the scuffle of our classmates heading towards another agonizing hour of cosines and tangents, so I started to pack my things. I already wasn't that keen on math—we had a very rocky relationship since high school—so I spent most of class scribbling in my notebook and tapping my claws, trying to understand the words Spencer perforated into my consciousness. People lie all the time, of course. There were always speeding tickets to hide, affairs being had, leftover pizza in the fridge that technically wasn't yours. It was the why that left me feeling the way I did—the bellysick of a Sunday when the sun goes down. Why would she have lied about loving me, when she had every other excuse to break things off? Despite being mostly collie, I was far from elegant. My brown fur covered itself in awkward speckles of grey and marbled blue thanks to my dad, and my snout was honestly so long that kids likened it to a jumbo jet back in grade-school. I wasn't a sports guy or in a band. I wasn't even cool. I was just Charlie. Quiet, unassuming, and practically drowning in anxiety.

I could tell Spencer must've been thinking about it just as much, since he barely spoke a word during lecture, only eyeing me every-so-often the way my dad would after seeing one of my report cards. Very serious.

After class, we cut through the gaggle of students escaping campus, making our way towards Stonewall CC's comically oversized parking lot. Spencer was a bit over six feet even without his ears, so he'd often part the crowds for me while I struggled to keep up. He was without a doubt, an awkward shock of white lightning amongst the crowd.

"Lars Olsen." He pronounced, not even looking at me

"I don't know…a seven and a half?"

"Seven and a…" he trailed off. "Charlie, that's not even remarkably close. Lars Olsen has the chest of a rippling stallion, not some twinkish art student. Eight and three-quarters without a doubt."

"I'm sorry, I'm just not really trying to think about 'Lars Olsen' and his clearly immaculate pecs right now." I huffed in frustration, nostrils flaring just the tiniest bit.

"Don't tell me you're still on that."

"But what if it's different this time?"

"Charlie," he stopped dead in his tracks and turned right at me, leaning in close "that road goes nowhere. Trust me. We're talking about the girl that decided to fill the school's ventilation unit with confetti in ninth grade, because 'it was something to help pass the time.' She wants a challenge. Not a tether."

"A tether?"

"Right. Something that won't keep her back from acting like a wild animal. She wants stuff that'll give her purpose, and people just don't do that for her. She's incapable of sticking around, especially when you need her the most. I had to learn that the hard way."

Hearing that shot pangs of guilt into my gut. Here I was complaining to Spencer about Audrey, someone I'd just barely scratched the surface with and Spencer had literally lost years of his life to her. She wouldn't even look at the guy anymore. I wanted to ask about what happened to them, what tore something so genuine to shreds. But this silky black lab stopped us. I recognized her as one of Spencer's coworkers.

"Jesus. Here we go again..." Spencer rolled his eyes towards me and worked himself up, acting as if he was excited to see her. "Oh, Charlotte honey."

She was sobbing heavily behind these thick framed glasses. "Crocodile tears" is what Spencer called them afterwards. She was on about how she was running behind on all her assignments, and how her little brother was so sick, and oh, just how awful of a time everything else had been. Spencer was eating every bit of it up too. You could always tell when that was happening, because his tongue would dip out of the slight overbite he had, and he'd look away as if something else had his attention. Today, it was the custodian trying to pry a rosebush loose from his mower. Point is, she wanted Spencer to take her four-hour shift, like, right then. So he did.

"Look. I know it's hard. Relationships are awful. But you have to focus on the people in front of you, the people who aren't kicking in your teeth and taking your money." Spencer was grooming the loose bits of fur from his bushy tail, clearly caught in thought.

"But she never took my money."

"It's a figure of speech, Charlie. Jesus."

***

I didn't see Olive again until the end of the week. The sun was setting and the air was already so much colder. I'd gone through half a pack before I heard his scratchy little voice call out. It was a bit of a relief seeing him, honestly, with his wild fur tucked every which way between his tight jeans and oversized sweater.

"Yo, my man actually brought a coat!" His excitement was infectious.

He sat real close to me this time, dangling his short legs over the side of the drain. When he accidentally dropped his speckled paw over mine, I let it stay there for a little longer than I should have before pulling away to grab for another cigarette. I told him I'd been working the last couple of nights at CVS, and how I was really starting to hate it. Olive said the only part time jobs he'd ever worked were office spots, jobs his family had gotten him. He said he didn't mind those so much, he just wasn't fond of sitting around for hours at a time like that, that it made him all twitchy and nervous. It was a shepherd thing, apparently.

When we'd started walking around my neighborhood, we stopped to look in on some of the houses we were passing, and he asked me if I knew any of my neighbors. I told him how I only really used to hang with this one kid, Reese, who'd lived right down the street from me. We'd go out into the woods a lot, pretending we were the Ghostbusters, Jedi Knights and all the other totally uncool stuff we were into. That made Olive snort. We'd spent most of my childhood together, so when Reese ended up moving right before the beginning of high school, it wasn't easy. All the other kids I knew had left. Off in new friend groups, venturing to different places, or just being awful to me. I ended up spending a lot of time alone after Reese moved out, since there weren't a lot of kids who liked me that much.

He got real quiet when I finished talking.

"...How did you deal with that?"

"With what?"

"Being alone."

"Poorly." I'd snuffed out my cigarette. We were a few blocks down from my place and I didn't want my mom seeing that I was still smoking. She could smell the odor from miles away, without a doubt, but that didn't stop me from spinning all sorts of excuses. Currently it was my coworkers and their habitual pounding of cartons whenever they weren't behind the counter.

"For a while, I just felt miserable." I was patting down the tufts of fur that shot from my collar, trying to look like less of a mess. "At least until I met another Reese."

"Isn't Reese like an incredibly uncommon name?"

"No, no. I mean like, I met another metaphorical Reese."

"So, you replaced him… metaphorically?" He was biting his lip.

"No!" I paused. "Wait … Maybe."

"But what about the actual Reese?"

"Still just as Reesey, I guess.." I was really bad at this. "All I'm saying is I found someone—who wasn't actually Reese—but functioned similarly and filled that empty feeling."

"So, a new best-friend."

"… Yes." That made him laugh this awful fractured lawnmower-esque laugh. I loved it.

"But actual Reese. You don't miss him?"

"Honestly, I don't know. I just hope he's happy, I guess." I laughed nervously, longing to change the subject. "Did you want to come inside?"

We'd only made it past the foyer before my mom stopped us. She had this sixth sense for company, which is probably why she spent so much time cleaning. I always got an ear-full if my room wasn't spotless and my bed was left unmade. She must've seen my tail wagging, because her muzzle wore this soft confident smile, even if she was wrinkling her nose in disgust at the smoke that clung tightly to my cardigan. I think she was just happy to see me with someone other than Audrey.

"Who's your little friend, Charlie?"

"Hey Mom. His name's Olive."

"Oliver too. But that's the one for people who don't like me." He grinned.

"That's a shame. Oliver's such a pretty name."

"Mom."

"Honestly, Charlie. You could be bringing the entire Russian embassy through here, and you'd still expect me to look the other way. Is your friend staying for dinner?"

It wasn't long before we'd all sat down at the table: Me, Olive, my sisters, mom and dad, and some pork chops. Dad must've left the TV on, because I could hear it casting play-by-plays in the other room. You could tell my mom wasn't too happy about it by the way she kept glancing towards the den. Honestly, I'd hoped they'd already eaten dinner without me. It's not that I didn't want my family to meet Olive. I just didn't want Olive to meet my family. They still treated me like a kid even though I was nineteen. I had a driver's license. I filed my own taxes. I could literally have a chiseled body and a million-dollar mansion, and they'd still call me stuff like "Sport" and "Champ". The last thing I wanted Olive to think, was that I was just another kid.

After doing the grace thing, my older sister chimed in.

"So Olive. You gonna make out with Charlie in the basement?"

"Kris!" My mom said, restrained as always.

"Debatable. Why ask?" said Olive, through-chewed pork chop.

"Charlie always does that. I literally had to stop going down there because of it."

"Kris." There was much less control in my mom's voice this time around. Thankfully, my father stepped in.

"So, Oliver. Where you from?"

"New York. Way upstate."

"You're a fan of the Giants, then. Close call last year."

"I don't actually watch that much football, sir."

That pretty much lost my Dad's interest.

"Fair warning, you might also see Charlie cry. He's an expert at it." My sister smiled.

"Eat shit and live, Kris."

"Charlie! Kris!" The whole table went quiet. My Dad held the kind of authority no one else was willing to question. Only my little sister June decided to speak up.

"Why would someone eat shit?"

***

I was setting the old Nintendo back up in my room when Olive told me I looked a lot like my mom. I think he'd meant it as a compliment, because my mom used to be real pretty when she was my age. Not that she wasn't now. It's just in all the old photos of her, she was radiant, like her fur was made of living sunlight. My dad liked to exaggerate that he fought hordes of boys to finally make a first date, but I could understand why. She had a beautiful muzzle with an elegant length to it, and these gorgeous sunken eyes that held so much sadness and warmth and kindness and depth. I don't know why he'd draw that kind of a comparison, but secretly, It was giving me a bit of a headrush.

"No fucking way. I totally knew it." Olive was standing on the other side of my room, huddling over my desk. "You make mix-tapes!"

I froze. In his paws was *Stonewall and the Many B-Sides of Disappointment*, the one I'd finally been able to pry out of my car. I tended to leave these sorts of things hanging out, since I was always fiddling with them, never really expecting prying eyes. He was turning it over, looking at the hand-colored cover and song list on the back. It had some boozed up skater kids on it, caked in colored pencil and ballpoint pen—pretty much everything I wish Olive never would have seen. I'd gotten up from wrestling cables out of my dresser, ready to snatch it from him. That's when he'd asked if we could put it on.

I spared no time hooking the player up to my new speakers, the one's I'd gotten for my birthday, and there was the first track, *Never Tear Us Apart* by INXS. I lived for these kinds of moments, the ones where I could share the things I loved with the people that mattered to me. Not that I really knew Olive that well, but in that moment, it all felt right. Not a lot of people cared about my taste in music, let alone asked to listen in.

We'd gotten onto the floor with this old shag carpet my dad gifted me. It was real comfy and had these crazy patterns and colors on it, all blocked-in, kind of like Olive's coat. I can't really tell you how striking his face looked, which was practically littered with countless Australian blots that reminded me an awful lot of a tornado filled with birds. I didn't really like birds all that much—I had terrible run-in with a goose when I was much smaller—but it didn't stop me from getting sucked into whatever the hell was going on with his fur. I really wanted to tell him just how nice he looked with the unpressed dress shirt he had tucked over his black jeans. How it complemented his slender physique and oversized paws, but I don't think that's the kind of thing boys really say to each other. He'd turned over to me with his paw tucked into his chest. Something was up.

"Hey Charlie."

"Yeah?"

"You ever want something you know you shouldn't?"

"Sometimes. Not really. What do you mean?"

He reached out and squeezed his fingers around my wrist.

This was the second time this week felt still. A kind of quiet that pulled from every direction. Everything around Olive became dead space to me, and it wasn't long before his eyes were really the only things left to see. So, there I was, stuck knowing that the chances of my mom busting in to break me out were slim to none. I let his fingers slide over my palm. And just like that, we were holding hands.

I'd barely gotten used to that before he pulled the whole thing close to his chest, and I could feel his heart beating heavily through his clothes. Three layers between me and his fur. He didn't say anything. He didn't move closer. He only looked at me, the kind of way I used to look at my friends unfinished cookies during lunch. That's when I got up the courage to move over and slide between his legs, trying my best to hide how awkward I actually was with these sorts of things. I can't tell you why that was my first reaction. There was, without a doubt, a dozen other things I could've said or done. But I didn't care. I had this burning feeling in the pit of my stomach. So I conceded to it.

I pinned Olive under me, getting close enough for our breathes to scrap. He smelled of dirt, pine, leaves and all the other things left scattered outdoors. Like Paxton. Like the good parts of Stonewall. And while he barely dared to breathe, I felt so incredibly connected to him, knowing full-well what I just started.

He'd tensed up when I began to run my fingers through the tufted white fur that lined his cheek. It felt soft, the way they make clouds look in mattress commercials, and the whole time he just kept leaning into it. I felt wanted. Like I mattered. So I continued down the coarse fabric of his sweatshirt, taking my time, only to run my paw right back under it. I caressed every curve eager to meet my fingers, exploring all the parts of him that I'd hadn't seen yet, imagining what was hidden underneath his black hoodie, button-down, and what felt like an old ratty band shirt. He'd started to squirm when I ran my paws upward, feeling his delicate chest. I'd found something that was cold to the touch. He was pierced. He'd been biting his lip the second I started toying with it, letting out a low whimper when I found the bravado to give it a good tug. Olive didn't say anything, he'd only shifted under me, giving me this anxious look. He was clearly sensitive. So I slid my paw back down to his stomach and hips, smoothing out the fur I'd displaced earlier. I didn't want to overwhelm him.

He'd closed his eyes and relaxed again, easing his hips back into the subtle motions of me petting him. Eventually I rested my paw against his belt buckle, tapping it slowly as I listened to each the little moans he kept trying to stifle. It was driving me nuts.

"Charlie."

"Yeah?"

"You know you don't have to do this. Right?"

I'd pushed into his muzzle for a kiss. Partly to shut him up, but mostly because I wanted to kiss him. He tasted of the menthols I'd lent him earlier. It was crazy how normal it felt too. Everyone I knew made kissing guys out to be a big deal, but here I was, doing it. No permits required. It left me with his funny feeling in my gut, thinking just how natural it all continued to feel. Great even. There was something under it with Olive, something insatiable. It was the way he kissed, how it felt so much like talking to him. That's when he grabbed my dick.

Honestly, I would've been okay with just the stuff we'd been doing. Just him being there with me. Soft, gentle, definitely wanting, and way too occupied with my muzzle and paws to do much else. But if he was going for it... I mean why would I stop him? The guy stuff definitely wasn't bothering me by this point. I didn't care that we'd only met earlier this week. Every bit of this felt right, and it wasn't a guilty kind of right. So I let him touch me. I even helped when he went to unzip my jeans.

He started kissing and nipping at my neck, stuff that made it difficult to stay focused. His fingers dug deeply into the elastic of my briefs, toying with the flattened fur barely an inch away from the danger zone. He snapped it back against my waist, eyes wide and curious.

"Hey."

"Hey."

"...Can we do the honest thing with each other for a second?" his paw was skating over the mound building in my briefs. I felt caught.

"I don't see why not."

"Are you gay?"

"I don't know. I really don't."

"Then what's this?" His paw gave it a tug. It was getting really hard to think.

"Confusing. Great. All over the place." I was panting. "Can we talk about this after?"

"After what?" He puffed his cheeks out behind this big, toothy grin.

"You know *exactly* what I mean."

"I don't know Charlie. I *really* don't."

And that time, he kissed me. But it wasn't the kind of kissing we'd been doing. It was the kind of kiss that made a pretty huge deal in itself. The kind that make you know it's going to be alright.

When I woke up, it was way too dark to be morning. I'd heard the scuffling of clothes and sneakers scraping against my floor. I could see Olive in the middle of my room, half-dressed and struggling to find the rest of his stuff in the dark. Our eyes met, and for a moment, he just stood there. Silent.

"What's going on?" I'd said, throat scratchy and eyes barely open.

"Go back to bed, Charlie."

"Are you leaving? It's like…three in the morning." 3:43 a.m. actually.

"… I just can't be here. Not right now."

I propped myself up, ready to get out of bed, but he told me to stop.

"What do you mean? What's going on?"

"I broke a promise." He was talking a mile a minute, through torn, distressed eyes—something I'd never expected to see inside of his unassuming demeanor. "I broke a fucking promise and it's all my fault."

"Can we just talk about this?"

"Stop Charlie. Just. Stop." He was getting real choked up. "You care about me, right?"

I nodded.

"Then you'll let me go."

I couldn't think of much else to say. Nothing would stop him. I was close to crying, but he was already hobbling to the door, hoodie half over his shoulders, determined. He only slowed down to open the bedroom door. That's when he looked right at me.

"I'm sorry."

And just like that, he was gone.

***

A few weeks passed, a few agonizing, awful weeks.

I'd started skipping class, something I'd never done before, and barely left my room for anything besides work and smoking. And boy, I'd never smoked so much in my life. They say it really helps with stress, but every time I'd go out to do it, I'd just see the dying trees and paling sky and all the leaves mashed into the pavement like a depressing pulp. It was awful.

For a while I just kept going back to the spot me and Olive shared in Paxton. I'd wait there for hours, partly because it was still a great place to smoke, but mostly because I wanted to see him again. To try and finish whatever conversation failed to happen weeks before. But he never showed, so I stopped going altogether. Just like I had with Trigonometry and "Science for the Working Man" and all the other bullshit electives I'd been taking at SCC. None of it felt worth the effort anymore. The only reason I didn't quit my job, which I hated even more, was because I still had to pay for my car and all the cigarettes I kept cramming down my lungs. I sound melodramatic. I know I do. But I wasn't happy in Stonewall. I hadn't been for a long time. It just doesn't help when you've been overlooking the things that've been staring you in the face for years. The things that really matter.

I was smoking in the open trunk of my hatchback on a cold Friday afternoon, it was after I'd talked to my counselor about possibly dropping out. He'd said I was just being irrational, but I didn't want to hear it. I could make these sorts of choices for myself. I'd been watching some anti-evolution picketers from across campus when I felt a hard smack against the back of my head.

"What the hell, Charlie!" Spencer got real close to me. He looked pissed. "Where have you been? I've been asking around all week and no one's seen you anywhere. You better have a good excuse."

"I don't. I'm sorry."

"That's right you're sorry! I thought you were...Jesus, Charlie, you look fucking terrible." He sat down on the other end of my trunk, eyes unwavering. "Did something happen to you? Was it Audrey?"

I shook my head. I didn't feel much like talking.

"Good. I swear to god if she hurt you. I can't even begin to think of the things I'd do."

I never really considered Spencer close, but there he was, teeth bared and ready to kill for me. I figured since all the smoking and not talking to anyone wasn't really working out, I might as well finally open up. I didn't stop smoking though. That was out of the question.

"Hey Spencer."

"Yeah?"

"How do you know you're gay?"

"Excuse me?"

"I'm sorry. I just mean like...what made you realize it? How did you know?"

He exhaled heavily. I was about to get into another apology before he spoke up.

"Well. It was my junior year at Welvern. Right? And me and Audrey were busy stealing the keys to the boy's locker room. Don't ask why."

"Sure." As much as I was upset, I smiled just a bit after hearing that.

"So, while she was in the coach's office, I was sneaking around, seeing what all the football players kept in their lockers. Mostly unwashed clothes and skin mags. That's when I saw Ryan Hollister from track, butt-ass naked in the shower. He'd stay behind to take these long showers after practice. He was just weird like that."

I smiled, since Spencer was still really good at telling stories. I could see him relaxing too, because his paws were folded neatly over his leg, in a very Spencer-like way.

"So anyways, there's this amazingly handsome stag in front of me, naked as a babe. And he's a solid eight on the Charlie-Spencer scale. You'd probably even say a nine, because you're too soft. So I'm just staring at his body and his junk and his muscles and everything. All the stuff I'd casually looked at in my dad's sport mags. And he sees me there, frozen solid. But he just smiles."

"Was it a sincere kind of smile?"

"About as genuine as a fuck-me smile gets Charlie."

Spencer told me he ended up ditching Audrey and blew the guy right there. He said Ryan definitely took his sweet time with it too. Spencer's jaw was messed up for practically a week. They'd started seeing each other like this in secret over the next few months, for late nights out and unnecessary after-school showers. There was a rhythm and consistency to it that started to form, the kind of expectation you'd get from seeing someone. That's when Spencer started to really like Ryan, I guess. But Ryan never talked to him outside of those moments. Not even during. They'd just hook up and move on like nothing happened. Spencer cleared his throat, taking his time with what he said next.

"For his birthday, I made this card. It had all these cute things on it, track shoes, race cars, space men, all the dumb stuff I knew Ryan liked, and in the middle of it all it held four simple words. 'I love you, Ryan.' And you know what he did when he saw it?"

I didn't answer.

"He ripped the thing up right there and told me to leave him the fuck alone."

"Spencer …"

"That's when I knew, Charlie. When I felt my heart tear open like that. That's how I knew."

I watched him. Spencer hadn't lost his composure. He didn't sound upset. He was just there, sitting at the lip of my trunk. Strong, willful, and open. It took me a long while to say what I said next.

"… I think I know what you're going through."

He paused. I think maybe he thought I'd also fucked Ryan, but eventually it clicked. He shimmied over to me, pulling me in close to his chest. Not in an Olive kind of way. Not a Ryan one either. He just wanted to be there for me.

Because that's what good friends do.

***

I was raking the leaves off my lawn early in the afternoon, thinking about all the things Spencer had said to me. He told me that real love—and he made sure to emphasize the 'real' part—was never easy to understand.

He said he was incredibly proud of me. That I went for something so big and scary, despite it being just that. I guess a lot of people don't find these things out about themselves until it's too late. At least that's how he made it sound. It sort of worries me, because I think of all the Charlies and Spencers out there who hadn't, or never will. How I just wanted to reach out and let them know it was okay to get hurt. But I guess you can't help everyone, even if you really want to. What a world, right?

It took me a minute to recognize her, but I could see Audrey walking down the block, headed towards me. She was slouched over with her arms tucked into her long plaid coat. It wasn't exactly out of the ordinary since we lived in the same neighborhood. So I just kept raking, pretending like she was some sort of haunting guile amidst the breeze.

"Hey Charlie."

"Uh. Hey."

"Do you think we could…"

"Talk?" I was panting, since I'd been out there for a while. "Uh. Sure, I guess."

I threw my rake aside and sat there right on the grass, right by the big pile of leaves I'd made. She'd gotten down too. It'd been about three weeks since she'd really said anything to me, so it was definitely awkward. Of course we still had Steinman's class together. But she'd left her spot beside me to sit at the other end of the classroom. She never bothered to look at me in passing either, at least not until now.

"I really meant what I said Charlie."

I didn't say anything.

"That I love you." She was toying with this broken leaf she'd picked up.

"Then why did you leave?"

"For a lot of reasons." She touched one of her rounded ears. "I'm sorry. I really am."

It was weird hearing her like this, with her voice all brittle. No finesse or filler, just Audrey and the few words that actually seemed to matter.

"Okay," I swallowed, "but what happened earlier, felt fucking awful Audrey."

"I know. I think about it a lot."

"Then why didn't you talk to me?"

"Because I'm *not* good at these things, I never have been."

Behind her narrow eyes and angular snout lived a microcosm of expressions that I could only describe as Audrey wearing sadness. This was a side of herself that I don't think she let people see. A medusaesque angle that shed the kind of weight and pain that I didn't think Audrey was capable of sharing. Was she expecting me to feel sorry for her? To forgive her? I felt guilty, honestly. Not because I was in the wrong. I definitely wasn't. I didn't feel like any of this was my fault. I just wanted answers.

"You could start by trying."

"Okay." She paused, closing her eyes for a little while.

That's when she mentioned Spencer.

She said it was an early Sunday morning when she found him at her front door, all bruised and shaken up. He told her it was Ryan, that they'd gotten into a big fight. I guess this was all before they'd officially broken-up, something Spencer was either too proud to tell me, or worried would ruin whatever message he'd left me with earlier this week. She'd said she spent the next few hours cleaning him up, just listening. Being there for him. Apparently Spencer told Ryan he wasn't going to be just another fuck-buddy. That he wanted to be with someone who could admit they were gay. That's when Ryan hit him. The whole time he kept talking to Audrey that morning, all Spencer could do was blame himself and the things he could've done differently, and how much it was that he really, truly loved Ryan. Audrey begged him not to go back, but it wasn't long before they were talking again. Before they pretended like nothing ever happened. She said he never came back with swollen eyes or bruised ribs or anything else, not that she noticed, but that he wasn't the person she'd known. He wasn't Spencer. So they stopped talking, and Audrey swore to never love again.

"I don't understand. Do you think I'd do that to you?"

"Not anymore." She couldn't look at me. "But I did. And I'm sorry for that."

I could hear the squelching of tires hitting my driveway before I saw my mom pull in. She'd about half-stepped out of the driver-side when she'd spoken up.

"Oh, Audrey." Her voice was layered with careful disappointment.

"Hey Misses S."

"Are you two?"

"No." I'd stepped in, forcing a weak smile. "She was actually just on her way."

"Yeah. I just wanted to drop some stuff off. You know."

"Oh. Well that's very nice of you."

The relief in my Mom's voice was so tangible that I could almost feel Audrey getting underhandedly punched off my lawn. She was already grabbing some shopping bags from the back of the family van when she said how very mature it was of Audrey to do that. How her parents would be so proud. As condescending as it was, I actually had to agree. I knew we'd be talking about this later, my mom loved knowing this sort stuff of almost as much as her soaps. I just wasn't looking forward to it. It wasn't long she wandered back inside with bags in tow, wishing Audrey a good day.

"So, I guess this is it then?" She was getting up, brushing the leaf crumbs from her coat.

"I guess so." I'd gotten up as well. "I don't know if I can forgive you. But thanks."

"Don't mention it. It was good while it lasted, you know?"

"That's up for debate."

There was an exchange of awkward laughs. That's how I knew it was okay.

Despite it still hurting, whatever happened here was good. Relieving even. She'd about made it off my lawn before I'd called out to her.

"Audrey."

"Yeah?" Her crooked tail seized up.

"Talk to Spencer for me. If anyone deserves an apology, it's him."

"Baby steps first Charlie. I'm not trying to die."

And just like that, I was on my own again. Alone and okay. And the leaves were piled, and the breeze carried through my hair, and things felt a little bit better. At least just a little.

***

It was about four in the afternoon when this old shepherd answered the door when I'd rung the bell at Olive's place. He looked a little bit like him, but his face was drained and he was stiff as a board. No bird tornadoes either, which was kind of a shame. He was easily a foot taller than me and wore this annoyed look on his face, like I'd just interrupted him.

"We're not buying it."

"...I'm not selling anything sir. Is Olive home?"

"Oliver!" He shouted, after briefly staring me down.

The door was slammed, and there I was again, alone on his porch.

There was something really sad about this place, about the way the paint was fading and how the bench by the door looked unused. I don't think anyone else lived here besides Olive and his uncle. I was reading one of those shitty 'Lord's Prayers' pillows that was left out by the window when the door opened back up. Olive was peering out behind the corner of the frame.

"Why did you come here, Charlie?"

"A few reasons" I scratched the back of my head, nervously. "Hear me out?"

He looked me over with his sad, soft eyes before pushing the screen door out. He stepped onto the porch in only a Joy Division shirt and some baggy pajamas, closing the door behind. I don't think he'd left bed all day, from the look of his ruffled unkempt fur. He seemed tired.

"I'm listening."

"So I don't think this needs being said. But I like you Olive. Like, a stupid amount."

He huffed through his closed muzzle, blowing pockets of air into his dotted cheeks.

"You're funny. You're interesting. You actually care about the stuff I have to say. You're..." I stopped myself, almost unable to commit. "You're incredibly fucking handsome."

He was fidgeting with his fingers, sinking into the porch.

"I don't know if I'm gay or anything. Honest. But you make it hard not to think that."

"...Charlie," he looked right at me, "you were balls deep in my ass."

"That I was."

He was running one of his big paws through the wild fur covering his head, wearing a small smile behind everything. At least we were both smiling at his painfully accurate comment, so I knew he wasn't mad. I started to fish through the pocket of my jacket, providing a simple mixtape titled *Olive; One of the Most Confusing People I know.* He laughed his ugly laugh even harder seeing that. That shit was like music to me. I told him I usually make these sorts of things whenever I had a strong feeling I couldn't get rid of. Never for people. He was the exception.

"You know you didn't have to do this."

"Well, it's out of my hands now." I flexed my fingers nonchalantly.

"Can I tell you something Charlie?"

"I don't know why else I'd be here."

He clenched his paws on the tape, turning it over every-which-way.

"So...I left a lot of things back in New York. Things that really mattered to me. But there was this one boy, Walter. He was an awful lot like you."

"A nervous, unfashionable mess?"

"Sort of. Walter was special. Someone I spent an awful lot of time with. Someone I could talk to, and relate with over a lot of different stuff. Someone who thought I was funny, and sweet, and didn't hate my laugh. What I'm trying to say is Walter was a pretty big deal." His words were becoming more spaced out. "Problem is, Walter's not here anymore."

"You mean like..."

"Yeah."

"Oh man, I'm so sorry."

"It's not your fault Charlie. It's not anyone's." He wiped a tear from his eye. "It just sucks, because no matter how much I tell myself that, I still don't believe it. I left New York, because everywhere we'd been, I saw him. In the school, at the construction sites, the arcade. Christ. Even in my bed. I left New York, because I had nowhere else to go. I thought that would be enough. I thought that's when everything would start to feel alright again. But it never did."

I'd reached my arm out to touch his shoulder, but before I knew it, he was sobbing face-first into my new sweater. After crying so much my whole life, I can't tell you how raw it really feels to do that in front of someone. All I could think was just how glad I was that I could be there to talk. To hold him and just listen. I started combing through the fur on his head with my claws.

"I feel like an asshole Charlie. I mean, what the hell do you do when someone goes like that? You can't just move on. That feels cheap. It feels fucking wrong."

"...You can't just live your life exclusively for someone else Olive. That's not fair."

"What's not fair, is having to live with this guilt every day. It's fucking terrible. I wake up wondering when it's all going to stop. If it's right for me to even move on. I don't know what to do."

"I don't think anyone does. Not Reese. Not Walter. Not nobody. It's okay not to."

"You sound like a fucking self-help book." I could hear him laugh into my chest.

"Look man. It's been a rough month. I've been through a lot of pamphlets."

He got up from my chest, wiping the snot from his big, wet nose.

"You're really something, Charlie. Did you know that?"

"Not really. No. But if it makes you feel better, I'll pretend it."

For a minute we just sat there. Him wiping his eyes and me still unsure of myself. Him reaching out his big paw and me sliding mine over it. We sat there all silent-like. Just looking out over the cul de sac, watching some dumb kid learning to ride his bike. He'd fallen over a few times but kept going at it, knee-scrapes-and-all, and while the kid wasn't looking, I ended up going in to kiss Olive. And he kissed me back. And somehow just then, I knew things would be fine. Even if they didn't seem like it. Even if they wouldn't always be.

Ambrose's Duty

Skunkbomb

S ister Portia glared at me. I'd never known a rabbit to be so inclined to hand out withering looks like hot chestnuts at the Winter Solstice Celebration. "I thought I asked you to coordinate the changing of the fall tapestries to the winter ones," she said.

My mouse tail wrapped around my leg. "Today? There's still three days left in Autumn."

The rabbit walked through the hallway, stopping briefly to jot the occasional note regarding the progress of the snowy decorations: dangling crystal snowflakes that caught the light just right, white and red candles for the evenings, and the spaces on the walls where those winter-themed tapestries would hang. Her handwriting was aggressively neat and sharp. "They're enormous. It'll take a day alone to get them out of the attics and even longer to perform and necessary cleaning and stitching. Fail me again and I'll have no choice but to bring Father Oswald into this. I would hate to tell him he's wrong about you."

I bowed. "Forgive me, Sister Portia."

"Apologize to me through action, not words," the rabbit said. "Now, we'll need to finalize the dinner menu for the celebration and coordinate with Father Oswald on which verses from the Collected Texts to read at the Winter Solstice Mass. I will not sit through another recitation of Father Reginald's contributions. Nothing of great value can be learned from his mushroom-addled rambling, and mushrooms are completely out of season for winter."

I bit back any disagreement bubbling in my throat. Sure, Father Reginald may have partaken in the kinds of mushrooms later in life that would eventually kill him. Still, his contributions to the Collected Texts, the notes passed down from previous Abbots and Abbesses, were still valid and entertaining.

My big ears flopped as I shook my head. There I went getting distracted again, but I couldn't help it. I can never focus when winter's just around the corner.

Because he was too.

"Perhaps I can dig around in the archives for a hidden gem," I said, taking a couple steps back toward the stairs. "And I promise, nothing from Father Reginald."

"You set foot in that archival room and I'll never get you out," Sister Portia said. "Those aren't your duties anymore. Now, I expect you to gather a team to help you swap out the tapestries. I want this all done by tomorrow night."

"Tomorrow?"

"The halls of St. Andrena's echo enough on their own," the rabbit said. "They don't need your help." She walked away, her ears swiveling to pick up the sound of anything remotely undutiful.

I sighed and walked toward the stairs. Who was even in charge of tapestries? Was it better to take the old tapestries down first or bring down the winter ones? I missed my days in the archives, jotting down the history of abbots, abbesses, and other abbey dwellers from the past. I was a quick reader and had meticulous handwriting.

My feet stopped at the hoof of a statue. Lord Asger stared ahead, his holy lance raised. I knelt.

Why wasn't my duty to the archives? Why did Father Oswald make me one of his apprentices? I shivered. Perhaps I was close enough to the stone wall for a tiny draft to seep through a crack. I bowed my head. "Lord Asger, please, I beg you to help me fulfill my duty."

"Ambrose! Brother Ambrose!"

Mac, a stout squirrel, skidded to a halt on the carpet. He leaned against his standard-issue watchman's spear, which couldn't poke a hole in wet parchment.

I stood and brushed by gray habit off. "What's wrong?"

"He's here!"

I bolted down the hallway. The tapestries could wait a little while longer.

As I sped down the hallway, Sister Portia piped up. "Where are you off to?"

"The kitchens," I replied over my shoulder. "You said we needed to finalize the dinner menu, right?"

"Yes, well, just slow down!" she called after me.

Not a chance. Silas was waiting for me.

By the time I scampered down three flights of winding stairs, I was out of breath. A lifetime of sitting in a dark room for hours on end did nothing for my athletic abilities. I burst into the kitchens and nearly collided with Eloise, specifically the sharp knife she was holding.

The skunk scowled and held the knife away from me. "Watch it! I don't have time to accidentally murder you. We're behind enough as it is with the soup for dinner and—"

"He's here!"

Eloise smiled and turned to the rest of the kitchen. "Everybody, behind!" The chefs all leaned against their work stations, clearing a path. She winked at me. "Go get him."

I cut through the kitchens past the cooks and out into the northeast section of the gardens toward the northern gate. A shiver shot through me. I should have brought my tail wrap, but I could bear the cold for him.

The towering doorway was already shut. A watchman walked and chatted alongside a rat who plucked at a lyre.

"Silas!"

The rat turned. His smile was too warm for the chilly weather to penetrate. "Ambrose, how—?"

I wrapped the large rodent in a hug. Outside and with my mouth against the rat's chest, my words were whisper quiet. "Welcome back."

Silas ran his hand through my head fur. "It really has been too long."

The guard cleared his throat. "Perhaps you'd like to take this indoors?"

I let go, straightened my habit, and looked at the ground. "Yes, of course." Even if the guard had a point, the warmth didn't leave my face.

As Silas and I followed the guard, I bounced from toe to toe. "I'm sure I've gotten all of your letters, but just in case, please, tell me everything about your travels. Did you meet any new species? Did you write any new songs? What food did you eat?"

Silas chuckled. "What is it with you abbey folk and your food?"

"Food's an important part of a culture's identity."

The rat's tail briefly brushed against mine, and the cold disappeared again. "I'll tell you at dinner. I'm about to be given the ol' St. Andrena welcome, so who knows where I'll end up."

As we walked through the north entrance of the abbey, at least a dozen different abbey dwellers greeted the rat. Heading the group was Father Oswald, a hunched beaver grasping a cane with various nibble marks.

"Silas, we welcome you back to our humble abbey," Father Oswald said. "As always, you're welcome to stay as long as you wish so long as you assist the abbey with day to day duties." He furrowed his brow, his two bushy eyebrows coming together like colliding logs. "You will show up for them, won't you?"

"Forgive a poor musician for needing his beauty sleep," the rat said, bowing to the old beaver while holding his colorful cap. "Good looks are half the battle of drawing a crowd."

"And you won't need to earn coin so long as you stay here," Father Oswald said. "We'll have someone bring your belongings to an open room. Dinner will be ready shortly. You must be frozen and dirty from your travels. Can we draw you a bath?"

An otter plucked Silas's bag and lyre from him, and before he could protest, Sister Rosaline and Sister Bertha each grabbed one of the rat's arms.

"Allow me, Father Oswald," Sister Rosaline, a chipmunk, said. "I want to make sure our guest is treated warmly."

Sister Bertha, a groundhog, tugged harder on Silas. "I wash clothes all day. If anyone is qualified to bathe our guest, it's me!"

Silas's smile strained and his ears folded back. "Thank you, but I'm perfectly capable of bathing myself."

Both Sisters hauled away the rat, who was still arguing his case with them, and the small crowd dispersed.

As I turned toward the staircase, the wooden cane tapped the floor.

"Brother Ambrose," Father Oswald said. "A word?"

I dipped my head and fell in step with the beaver. "Yes, Father." I had to slow my pace to a crawl to walk side by side with the gray-furred beaver.

"As hard as it is to believe, I was young once too," Father Oswald said, a hint of a smile pushing through his thick goatee.

I slowed just a touch so I was walking behind Father Oswald. Even with his ancient eyes, I wouldn't be surprised if the old beaver could see me blushing underneath my fur.

"I would never bar you from seeing Silas," Father Oswald continued. "But you have a duty here in St. Andrena's just like everyone else."

He paused at one of the tapestries hung on the stone wall. It depicted a grassy field with lady bugs, beetles, caterpillars, and every sort of insect under the sun eating, crawling, and flying through the air. I wasn't short for someone of my species, but I was a mouse nonetheless. The tapestry only enforced how small I was.

Father Oswald brushed his hand across the bee on the tapestry. "A single bee must work tirelessly to provide so little in its lifetime, but its work is vital to the hive."

Ever since the leaves began to change colors and Father Oswald brought me on to assist Sister Portia, I felt like an ant in a beehive. No matter how hard I worked, I could never do the job right. "Why me, Father?"

He tilted his head so his good ear was pointed at me. "Why you what now?"

"Why take me away from the archives? I was happy there, I knew the work, and my absence would surely save Sister Portia a few future headaches."

"Sister Portia may rub some fur the wrong way, but she only wants what's best for the abbey just like everyone else," the beaver said. "As for why I picked you, well, it wasn't entirely my choice."

My whiskers drooped. "So you didn't have faith in my abilities."

"On the contrary," Father Oswald said. "You may get distracted every now and then, but you've got a good head on your shoulders and a strong heart in your chest. I brought you to work more closely with me on behalf of our Lord Asger."

I did my best to keep my face neutral. Of course I believe in Lord Asger and the teachings passed down to saints throughout the ages, but did The Lord really talk to people? It seemed more like an expression, or perhaps the result of one of those mushrooms Father Reginald enjoyed.

Eyes buried deep under gray fur and bushy eyebrows seemed to read my mind. "Lord Asger didn't so much tell me with words. It was more of a feeling. I believe whatever your duty may be, it shall be revealed soon. Until then, I wish to keep you close by so I may guide you when you need it."

"Are you sure my duty lies with getting glared at by Sister Portia?"

The old beaver chuckled. "We can reevaluate that after the Winter Solstice Celebration. Until then, do everything you can to help her. It may not seem like it, but Sister Portia appreciates your help."

"Pardon me, Father." Eloise approached us. "Sorry to interrupt, but I was hoping I could borrow Ambrose to help chop some vegetables."

I caught the "we need to talk" look, and I added, "I can always continue my work with Sister Portia after dinner, and one's duty is more than just their occupation. Right, Father?"

The beaver nodded. "Yes, of course. I'll see you both at dinner."

Eloise and I walked briskly around the corner, and then the skunk practically dragged me into the kitchens.

The skunk placed me in the corner of the room and shoved a knife and a plump onion into my hands.

"Oh, did you actually need help?" I asked.

"No, but I need to pretend like I'm giving you work instead of listening to gossip," the skunk said. Her tail swished. "You'll come visit me still now that Silas is here, right?"

I slowly placed my knife over the onion. "Of course. Why wouldn't I?"

"You tend to be his shadow all winter long," Eloise said. "I feel like I only see you when Silas comes to sneak a snack before meals. And after them too. And perhaps you should peel that onion first."

I placed the knife on the counter and sighed. "I really do get distracted this time of year, don't I?"

Eloise plucked the onion out of my hand and peeled back the skin. "You have plenty of time to catch up with your rat."

I shook my head. Winter was never enough time with Silas.

The rat had first visited the abbey at the beginning of winter two years ago. Like most travelers, he needed someplace warm to stay, and St. Andrena's accepted anyone as long as they agreed to help out around the abbey. The rat was assigned to the archives next to me. He entertained me and the other archivists with stories of his travels. In return, I showed Silas transcriptions of sordid affairs and bawdy love letters from abbots and abbesses past. It was never warmer in the archival room than when Silas leaned close to me, our whiskers touching, as he said, "Read that line again. Your voice has a nice cadence."

And when the first flowers sprouted in spring, the rat would leave on another adventure, plucking his lyre the whole way. Winter was never enough time with Silas. I wasn't going to let this winter go to waste.

"I'm going to ask Silas to my bedroom."

Eloise's tail shot up. "When?"

I smiled, my heart and face warmer than any fire in the kitchen. "Tonight."

The skunk wrapped me in a big hug, and her strong scent enveloped me. With all the smells in the kitchen, I had barely noticed her smell. "I'm sure it'll be wonderful! Maybe quick, but that's how it is for most males their first time. Remember to always make your boundaries clear, and listen to what Silas has to say, and give yourself a good washing down below, oh, and wear your best undergarments."

"But all my undergarments are the same," I said, though it was muffled from my face against her apron.

"Well, I guess it's too late to change them." Eloise broke the hug. "I need to help bring out the dishes. Go find a spot before they're all taken. I'll find you when I'm done."

I quickly chopped the onion she had given me, and she gave me a smile a mother would give to a toddler's first attempt to draw.

By the time I left the kitchen, it looked as if the whole abbey was in the great dining hall. Rows upon rows of long wooden benches held abbey dwellers close enough to touch shoulders. The last two years since Silas and I entered a relationship with each other, I could never spit out my request for us to become intimate. Sure, we've traded kisses while walking past the beautiful stain glass windows, and in the evenings, our hands have roamed over one another. If I had a bit of alcohol in me, sometimes my hands would dip beneath his clothes and below the belt.

It wasn't that I had taken a vow of celibacy. Such a vow wasn't a requirement for the followers of Lord Asger. When I informed Silas of this information on the day we became a couple, it was the only time I've managed to render him speechless.

In my readings in the archives, Lord Asger's teachings seemed to imply while two men cannot procreate, in matters of the bedroom, both should be passionate, vigorous, and thorough. Even though I had little practical knowledge in that area, I planned on following the teachings of my faith to the letter. I took a deep breath. All I had to do was find Silas—

An arm hooked around mine. It might have been the lighting, but Silas's black fur looked a shade lighter than when I saw him earlier. He was still no less dashing in his colorful tunic and cap.

"I bribed some small children with the promise of teaching them swear words," the rat said. "They should have our seats saved for us."

I nodded. The darn words had retreated down my throat again. Maybe it was best to tell him after dinner when there weren't so many people around. I'd tell him the moment we left the great dining hall.

"There you are." Sister Portia marched over to us. "I couldn't help but notice there's been no progress made on the swapping of the tapestries."

I bowed my head to the rabbit. "I promise to work on that as soon as I can, but couldn't this wait until after dinner?"

The rabbit looked over at the rat and then back at me. "You seem more than happy to hold off eating for him. Sit with me. You can see your rat all you want at the Winter Solstice Celebration."

"Please," I said. "It's been months since I've seen him."

"Then what's another day or two?"

Agony. An eternity. Too much for me to handle. But words can't knock down a stone wall.

Silas smiled thinly. "Sister Portia, how I've missed those piercing looks of yours."

"And I your restless mouth."

"I'm sure you expect Ambrose here to be alert so he can hear your every order," the rat said. "But if I know anything about dinner at St. Andrena's, everyone's going to be either snoring or drunk within the next couple hours. What quality work can get done in that state?"

She fixed me with a glare. "Meet me at the north entrance after dinner so we may at least discuss the plan for first thing tomorrow." Sister Portia turned sharply and walked off.

"Thank you," I whispered to the rat as I followed him to our seats.

"No problem," Silas whispered back. His whiskers brushed against mine.

Four trumpeters, each at one end of the great dining hall, played a short, blast of a tune. No meal at St. Andrena's was complete without a bit of ceremony.

A battalion of kitchen workers rolled out carts loaded with vast bowls of salad. Every bowl was like a sunset with the red apples, orange squash, and purple eggplant resting on a dark sky of arugula. Next to those bowls sat deep cauldrons of soup. I helped myself to the French onion soup with the piece of bread floating in the middle, soaking up the broth, all underneath a tarp of melted cheese.

Speaking of cheese, carts with wheels of cheese bigger than my head came by next, along with no fewer than half a dozen different loaves of bread. I cut myself a thick slab of sourdough with a slice of cheddar on top. For the carnivorous species, there were plates of grilled fish with hunks of lemon, and marinated chicken. Another cart held nests of pasta filled with cheese and a creamy sauce. A dozen towering cakes with different icing on each tier followed.

Before we could eat any of it, Father Oswald led us in a long rambling prayer, which I'm sure would be more appreciated if such delicious food were not sitting right in front of us. The moment Father Oswald said "amen," everyone pounced on their dinner, myself included. The sooner

I finished and had that conversation with Sister Portia, the sooner I could find Silas and ask him to my bedroom.

Musicians from the abbey got up during the dinner and played their instruments between bites and sips. Kids and adults alike came up to Silas during dinner to ask him about his travels. I got to hear a couple of tidbits he hadn't mentioned in his letters, and I chimed in with parts of the stories I knew. I was drunker off the conversation than the ale.

Silas scooped up more cake. "I can honestly say the food is even better than I remembered. I could write romantic ballads just about the soup. Makes me wonder what else I'm missing spring through fall."

"Oh, you'd love it," I said. "Sometimes when the weather's agreeable, we'll have lunch or dinner outside in the gardens. There's games like croquet and lawn bowls, and you can pick fresh herbs right out of the gardens and sprinkle them on your food. Oh, and the strawberries in the summer! So refreshing and sweet!"

My rat gave me a quick kiss on the lips. "Sweeter than you? I have to say, it's tempting to find out."

Then the old hedgehog who works in the cellars came over to ask us our opinion on the new ale he'd made. He and Silas got to talking about different alcohols, but I was still stuck on my rat's words. Would he stay longer? Another few months maybe? Could he stay here with me forever?"

The great dining hall was only half full at this point. Parents carried their children off to bed and a couple of the heavier drinkers had to be dragged back to their rooms.

Silas patted his stomach. "I should quit now while I'm comfortably full, though I wouldn't say the night's done yet. We can keep this little reunion party of ours going, if you'd like."

I shot up and was about to agree, but then my eyes strayed toward the north entrance of the great dining hall. "Sister Portia's still expecting me."

"Well, we'll just have to fix that." The rat stood up and began a jaunty jig. He did so not on the floor like a normal person, but on top of the table, nearly upsetting a dish of vinaigrette in the process.

I shook my head. "Are you drunk?"

"If I was, I would have fallen off the table by now," Silas said. He held out his hand. "But just in case, I could use a steady dance partner."

The musicians upped the tempo of the song. The crowd clapping to the beat drowned a few shouts from folks telling the rat to get down out.

I grabbed his hand and he pulled me up. "I have two left feet."

"I'm sure you'll be all right." He winked at me.

I attempted to mirror his dance, and my foot knocked a plate onto the floor. "All right feet, perhaps."

He took both my hands in his. "Now we can steady each other."

There wasn't much room to maneuver on a full table, but we made it work. The crowd whistled as the rat spun and dipped me low enough to almost get the hood of my habit in the cake. Was I drunk? I was a bit of a lightweight, but one glass of ale with dinner wasn't enough to make me feel so dizzy and full of cheer.

"On three," Silas said.

"On three what?"

"One, two—"

"Silas!"

"Three!"

The rat leapt off the table, and I half hopped, half dragged myself with him. As we landed, we spun like a top through the crowd. The whole world spun even as Silas released me and I braced myself against the wall.

It took me a moment to gain back my balance, but the rat and I stood around the corner of the southern entrance of the great dining hall.

"Let's put a bit of distance between us and Sister Portia, shall we?" Silas said. "The night's far too gone for work, wouldn't you say? And yet still too young to end. Where to?"

I planted a kiss on his warm, soft mouth. When I pulled away, the words weren't stuck in my throat any longer. "My room."

***

I prided myself on my vocabulary, and Silas had learned many words through songs and various countries he'd visited, but at the moment, we only knew three words. When Silas's kisses trailed down my chin and neck or he buried my face against his chest, we said the words as if they were still brand new: I love you. I love you, I love you, I love you.

Silas's hand trailed down my chest to my stomach and followed the tenting of my habit to the tip of my erection. Little lightning bolts shot through me.

***

He sat up on his knees, tossed his colorful cap aside, and slowly raised his tunic over his head. I wanted to sink my face into his inky black chest fur.

Silas climbed off the bed. He swung his hips back and forth as he undid his belt.

The rhythm was hypnotic. Perhaps if my heart wasn't about to burst out of my chest, this would have been calming. "Is that how I'm supposed to take off my clothes?"

"I'm a performer," Silas said as he dropped his belt on the floor. "You take your clothes off however you like."

"Quickly then, so I can go back to touching you."

Silas's smile was warm and devious all in one. "Very well. Then you can handle these." He slid his pants and undergarments down to his ankles. His musk filled the room, and his pink length contrasted his dark fur. His testicles were large and plump. Were all rats like that or had he taken a vow of chastity? "I don't know how you can walk with those between your legs."

I reached for his fat balls, but he grabbed my wrist. "I want to see what's under those robes."

"Very well." Despite my trembling hands, I went about it as swiftly as possible. I untied the cord belt around my waist, placed the prayer necklace with the raised lance on the front gently on the nightstand, and then lifted my robe over my head.

I brushed the fur on my arm that was sticking up. It was the color of dead grass and was just as soft. My muscles were built as well as one would expect for someone who until recently spent most of his time sitting indoors. I didn't have anything to compare it to, but my length was probably within the average for most mice. Nothing special, but I loved my rat. It was my duty to give all of what I had to offer.

He rolled over the bed onto my side and knelt like a stage actor. "With fur the color of the desert sands."

"I'm desolate?"

"You tease infinite possibilities on the horizon." He yanked down my undergarments. The head of my cock pointed at his face. "Beautiful."

I looked around the room as if the answer was written on the wall. "So do I just…?" I climbed onto the bed, lied on my back, and spread my legs.

"Is this your—I thought there wasn't a vow of celibacy in your faith," the rat said.

I turned away from him and curled my tail around myself. "You've fallen in love with someone who was practically a hermit. There are gaps in my knowledge."

Silas rolled me back over. "I'll gladly fill your gaps. You've played with yourself before, right?"

I nodded. On more than one occasion, I'd found a rather saucy love note from an abbot or abbess addressed to a lover. Perhaps they were meant to be private, but I had taken some of them back to my room in the past to gain a full appreciation of them, so to speak.

The rat guided my hand to his crotch. "Show me how you touch yourself."

I tentatively reached up and rubbed his fat balls. There was certainly more room to maneuver with his, and he sighed as I fondled them. Then I reached for his length. I always started at the head, the most sensitive part. It was always a nice jolt, a way of confirming that yes, this was happening. I was going to pleasure myself.

I jerked him vigorously, and he placed his hand on mine. "A bit slower, please."

"Wasn't I supposed to do it like I did it?"

"Never rush touching yourself if you can help it," the rat said. "I'll be sure to give you plenty of lessons on it later."

When I slowed my pace, his smile widened. My nose twitched as I took in more of his scent. He certainly didn't smell unwashed, but Silas's crotch had a strong masculine scent to it. I thought about touching myself while I masturbated my rat, but it was probably better to do one thing well than two things just fine.

To keep things fresh, every time I ran my loose fist up my rat's manhood, I paused at the head and gave it a light squeeze. Silas squeaked, growing higher pitched each time. Soon, he grabbed my wrist and chuckled.

"It'll be an early end to the night if you keep that up," Silas said. "I think it's time I grab something important." The rat picked up his trousers and pulled out a little vial from his pocket.

When he uncorked the vial, I sniffed. "Olive oil?"

"I'll need you to bend over for this part."

My heart raced. I bent over my bed and lifted my tail for him. I tried to distract myself by thinking about the cheekiness of the situation. Silas had asked for this, but I was essentially mooning him, and I hadn't mooned someone since I was a child, and the punishment for that was being spanked and then I thought about Silas spanking me and somehow this had cycled back to the fact to sex. And for the first time.

Silas grabbed the base of my tail and lifted it a bit higher. "Are you ready?"

"Yes," I squeaked.

Then he plunged into me. It was a bit uncomfortable, but I imagined the olive oil he used must have helped with slicking it up. Whatever anal muscles I had seemed to be relaxing. I could do this.

Then he drew back, and what entered me felt twice as thick. I bit back a wince.

"It's important to loosen up beforehand with a finger or two, if you can," Silas said. "Luckily, I keep my claws short so I can play my lyre."

"That's not your penis?"

"Oh, no. You are pretty tight back there, so it may be a bit rough at first, but I promise to go slow. Think you can handle it?"

I nodded. "I certainly want to."

"Good." He drew out of me again and slapped my rear.

I squeaked and clapped a hand over my mouth.

That got a laugh out of him. "Shall we then?"

"Actually," I said. "Can we do it like this?" I turned over onto my back and looked up at him while he was slicking his length with oil.

He knelt down and kissed me. "Aye, of course." He lined himself up against me. "If anything is wrong, you tell me, okay? Then I'll stop."

"And if it's going well?"

"Always good to be appreciated, but keep it quiet for the sake of our neighbors."

I took a deep breath and nodded.

Silas did the same and pushed forward.

The ring of my anus burned as he filled me, but I bit my lip. If anything, he went past the part where if fingers reached until it bumped up against a rather pleasurable wall. At that point, his groin and waist were pressed up against me too.

"Everything okay?" Silas asked. "No pain?"

"Some, but I think it'll go away."

His dancing prowess came in handy. The rat was able to keep a steady rhythm as he bucked against me. The sting of my anus soon gave away to an ache in my rear, but a pleasurable one. It was like starving, but knowing a delicious meal was just around the corner. I pressed my butt back against him as he thrust into me. I'd be sated soon enough.

There was a strange overlap in the caring and the erotic. Silas's fat ball smacked against my rear with a steady beat. At the same time, he took my hand in his and stared down at me lovingly (though a bit more fixed and with more panting). It was a beautiful mix. I could only hope I was looking so beautiful.

The rat slowed his pace. "You look silly when you're being taken by a lover."

I covered my face. "I don't exactly know how to look good in this situation."

"Only ones who do are in the world's oldest profession." Silas pried my hands off of my face. "Your silly face is gorgeous." He bent down and kissed me again.

"Your every face is gorgeous," I said when he drew away.

He shuddered. "See where flattery will get you." His bucking increased in strength and tempo. Every thrust pressed that lovely button inside of me, and my manhood twitched. I saw the cliff coming, but soon it was like that cliff never existed. My seed shot forth, striking my chin and chest as I squeaked.

Silas grunted as he thrust even harder. "Messy mouse."

"Should have said something," I panted.

"S'okay. Want it in you?"

For a second, I was confused because he was definitely inside me, but then I brushed the seed on my chin and caught his meaning. "In."

He got only a few more thrusts in before my rear felt much more warm than before.

Silas drew out of me and collapsed next to me on the bed. I was faintly aware something was leaking out of me, but my head was too foggy to care. That was a problem for later. "I feel like a fool for not doing this sooner."

The rat kissed the back of my head. "You weren't ready until now. Besides, I found plenty of opportunities to relieve that tension on my own while traveling."

My crotch stirred, though I was feeling too listless to give it any attention. "You should have written about that in your letters."

"And here I thought I was talking to a mouse of culture." He tickled my side and I kicked against him weakly. "Though now that we're here together, we can do more than just masturbate."

I was silent for a bit before replying. "Until spring, that is."

The rat turned me over. His smile was full of mischief, but his eyes were bright with something underneath the exhaustion of sex. "Come see the world with me."

I squeezed his hand and looked away. "You know I can't. My duty is here at the abbey."

"What? Taking orders from a disgruntled rabbit?" Silas said, his smile faltering. "Would you ever be happy with that life?"

"Father Oswald said as long as I stick near him, my duty will become clear."

"I thought your duty was with the archives learning stories of times past," the rat said. "If you come with me, you'll learn countless stories from people all over the world."

I crawled away from the rat toward the headboard. "Not everyone can just pull out their roots and go where they please."

"And no one should set their roots down where they're bound to shrivel up," Silas said as he followed me.

"You don't understand duty."

"I understand devotion." He grabbed my hand and held it to his chest. The rat's heart beat the way mine did when he flirted with me. "And I'm devoted to you. Why do you think I've come back every year for three years now?"

I sat up straighter. "Will you stay? Or are you going to leave me behind again the moment the weather turns warm?"

His silence spoke volumes.

Silas's grip on my arm loosened, and I pulled it away. "Leave."

"Ambrose."

"Get out!"

The rat yanked his pants on and balled up his tunic and cap. I kept my back to him. The door hung open so long that I thought Silas had left it ajar to spite me, but it finally closed. I took grim satisfaction that he wouldn't see my tears.

***

No light poured in past the curtain when someone knocked.

"Ambrose, are you up?" Eloise said through the door. "Can I come in? I brought you some breakfast."

"Please just leave me be," I said as I pulled the blanket further over my head. It was still too soon to talk about last night. That, and I hadn't bathed since then. Eloise was my friend, but I didn't need her smelling what transpired with Silas.

"I'll leave your food outside the door then," the skunk said. "And don't worry about Sister Portia. I told her you were ill. Mac and I have been gathering up some other folks from the abbey to help with the tapestries."

I curled myself tighter. I had forgotten all about Sister Portia's tasks. This was a failure of duty on multiple counts and I couldn't even get out of bed to do anything about it. Still, it would be much worse without the help of my friends. "Thank you. I want to make this up to you, but please, I just need some time."

"Do you remember we had that nice troop of acrobats come stay at the abbey a couple summers ago?" the skunk said. "The ferret had a marvelous tongue—"

"It's too early for this conversation."

"—and as he was down on me, I accidently passed wind," Eloise continued. "He flew back because in the heat of the moment, he thought I sprayed him, and he knocked his head against the headboard and concussed himself. The whole troop had to stay an extra month. I was ready to die of shame, but after a week, it was okay. So if you embarrassed yourself in the bedroom, don't worry. I'm sure it'll all pass in a week."

I stared at the wall. "The sex wasn't the problem."

"Ah, so you *did* have sex. I knew it!"

"Please keep it down," I held my face in my hands. "What happened between me and Silas can't be forgiven in a week."

There was a brief bit of silence. "Did he hurt you?"

I shook my head. "Not in the way you're thinking."

"It's freezing out there, but if you lure him outside, I'm not against spraying him."

I tugged the blanket tightly around me. While I could argue there was an extra nip in the air due to Silas's absence, it really was chilly. I pulled back the curtain just a fraction. Snow sailed by in an onslaught of white.

"Are those footsteps?" Eloise said. "Guess there's nothing like revenge to motivate the heartbroken."

"Save your musk. Just give me some time, please."

"I'll get you an ale tonight."

"Make it two?"

"I want you drunk, not over a privy puking your guts out."

For the first time since my argument with Silas, a slight smile played on my lips. "I'm not that much of a lightweight. You should go before Sister Portia comes looking for you."

"Fine, but I'm coming back with lunch, and I want to see empty breakfast plates when I get back."

I touched a stain Silas had left on me. "And if you have time, maybe send up some clean sheets? And some bath water too."

"Of course. Now eat something, okay?"

I waited for her footsteps to fade away before opening the door and grabbing the tray. Before I opened the lid, I could already smell the butter and cinnamon covering the toast. Oats and diced apples sat in a bowl next to a mug of tea to wash it all down. The drink warmed me, and the food filled a hole, but there was still an emptiness inside me.

***

The bath water and the clean sheets arrived a little bit later. I scrubbed myself clean, threw on the fresh sheets, and tossed the dirty ones in the corner. I'd put them in the laundry room later, perhaps once everyone had gone to sleep, or I'd just get more water and clean the stains myself. I was weighing that decision when someone tapped at my door.

"Ambrose, may I come in?" Father Oswald said. "I heard you weren't feeling well, so I'll try to be brief."

If this were anyone else, I'd have asked him or her to leave me alone or at least ask me through the door. Instead, I opened my door for the old beaver.

Father Oswald hobbled over to my bed and sat down, and I was thankful I'd asked for clean sheets. "Sorry for not asking first. The stairs are rough on my old knees."

"It's all right, Father," I said, sitting next to him.

"Have you spoken to Silas today?"

I curled my tail more tightly around me. "No. I haven't seen him since last night."

The beaver nodded. "He mentioned you two fought. Silas came to speak with me this morning. He was under the impression you were forbidden from ever leaving the abbey."

"Well, that's not true."

Father Oswald's bushy eyebrows rose. "But do you believe that? Members of our religious order go on pilgrimages. Many even travel for pleasure."

I shook my head. "But my duty, my life, is here at St. Andrena's. I'm supposed to stick by you until I've found my duty."

"I believe I was wrong," Father Oswald said. "I could sense Silas's devotion to you. When Silas asked for my help, I told him he was asking a lot from you to just drop everything else in your life and travel with him. There needed to be a compromise, and he had to show he was committed. That's when he got that devilish look in his eye and ran off. According to Mac, he left through the north gate after breakfast and he hasn't come back since."

Outside, the snowstorm blew on. The bottom half of the window was completely blocked out with white.

I sprang up and paced. "Where could he have gone? And in all this? Why?"

"He intended to go to Oakhaven," the beaver said. "There's a jeweler there who sells rings."

I froze.

Father Oswald smiled. "Not that you need it, but you have my blessing."

I bolted to my closet, pulled out my warmest cloak, protective wrappings for my feet, and snowshoes, and threw the cloak on.

"You have my blessing to wed, that is," the beaver said. "Your rat's an experienced traveler. Perhaps he took shelter for the day at Oakhaven."

I wrapped my hands with cloth, pausing briefly over my ring finger. "Do you expect me to wait here patiently for him while that storm's going on? It's almost time for dinner, so he'd be back by now. I know it. Something has to be wrong."

Before Father Oswald could say another word, I raced out of the room.

It was slow going trying to run to the north gate while wrapping my feet up in protective cloth and putting on snowshoes, but I eventually made it to the door to the north gate. When I opened it, the chill hit me deep into my bones. I should have turned back and gotten more warm clothing, but I couldn't wait. Silas needed help somewhere.

The guard looked at me like I had two heads, but he opened the gate for me to rush out of the abbey. The snow was already halfway to my knees. My toes stung with every step, but I bit my lip and tried to ignore it. If I wanted to go to Oakhaven, I just had to follow the path that led from the north gate.

The path that was currently buried under a sea of snow.

I took a deep breath to calm my nerves, and the cold shocked my lungs. I'd come to the abbey as a small child, young enough that I remembered little of the outside world. Still, from books and word of mouth, I knew the general direction where Oakhaven stood. I took off straight to the thick woods ahead.

Oakhaven was formed around the same time as St. Andrena's Abbey, and the townspeople would travel from there to the abbey for services and commerce. As timed passed, Oakhaven's population introduced a multitude of Gods with no defining religion, and travel between Oakhaven and the abbey was now mostly for the sake of goods. There must still be a fairly direct path between the town and the abbey.

My teeth were chattering by the time I came to a fork in the road. I anticipated it, but I didn't know which way was toward Oakhaven. The thick trees blocked any view of a town ahead. It also blocked out what little light the snowy evening had. In my haste, I'd forgotten to bring a lantern with me.

I closed my eyes and tried to think. There had to be something in the archives about how to get to Oakhaven. When was the last time I heard about that town? Was it the Winter Solstice Celebration last year? But why?

Then it came to me. A letter written by Abbot Reginald.

Distracted by the wonders of a beautiful spring day, I'd take a wrong turn at the fork. I ended up horribly lost, and without food, I resorted to eating a pack of mushrooms by the road. I had never stared so fully in the face of our equine Lord as I did the day I went left instead of right at the fork in the road.

Sister Portia was wrong. There was value in Abbot Reginald's letters. I continued onward down the right path.

And I continued onward and onward and onward. It felt like an hour had gone by and there seemed to be no change in the path. All around me stood trees, snow, and darkness, but no sign of my rat. The wind fought its way through my cloak and dried out my eyes. I folded back my ears as the wind strummed.

Wait, strummed?

I unfolded my ears and held them up against the winter storm. It was subtle, but underneath the howling was the soft strings of a lyre.

"Silas!" I yelled. "Silas, are you here? Say something! Play louder if you can!"

I followed my ears. I could barely make out the rhythm of the song played. It was the upbeat tempo of the song we'd danced to the night before. It grew louder and louder as I walked along the trees on the left sides of the woods, but it was too dark to see anything.

"Silas, please say some—" I tripped over something and fell face first into the snow. When I picked myself up, someone sucked in a breath.

"Happy to see you, but did you have to trip over the injured leg?"

I could barely make out the silhouette of my rat lying against one of the trees with frost lining his whiskers. He was holding one of his legs.

I hugged him, equally happy to see my rat alive and to feel something resembling warmth. "Is it broken?"

Silas nodded. "Must have slipped on some ice. Perhaps if I wait a bit longer, it'll be completely numb from the cold and I could walk on it."

"That's a terrible idea." I sized up my rat and sighed. "I'm going to have to carry you."

"My dear mouse," Silas chuckled, his eyes half lidded. "I love you, but you're tiny."

"I'm of average size for a mouse!" I squatted in front of him and held out my hands behind me. "Climb on. If anything, the heat from our bodies will keep us from freezing."

When Silas climbed on top of me, I nearly feel face first into the snow again. Progress was already slow because of the snow. With my rat on my back, my pace was glacial. "This might be easier if we chat. If you're talking, I know you're okay." Even saying words took several breaths.

"Almost fell asleep until you tripped over me," the rat said. "I can barely keep my eyes open."

"Don't make me scold you, Silas!"

"At this point, I'd love to hear you say anything," my rat said, his voice low and thick. "Yelling, terrible jokes, prayer. Maybe not prayers. That'd put me right to sleep."

I shook my head. Tears froze to my cheeks. "You just had to buy a ring during a snowstorm, didn't you? All this so I'd leave the abbey forever and travel the world with you?"

For a second, I thought Silas hadn't heard me or he'd passed out, but when he spoke, it was quiet. "I don't want to keep you from the abbey forever, or to have us travel for that long. I just want my forever to be with you."

Something cold and smooth grazed my cheek. My rat held a silver ring with Lord Asger's lance etched onto the outside. My heart leapt. I couldn't tell if the ring was the most beautiful thing in the world or the most useless piece of junk.

"Ambrose?" Silas slurred. "Say something. Anything. Even your rejection would have a nice cadence to it."

I grabbed the ring. "If this is the trouble you get into on the road, you obviously need someone to watch over you."

"And perhaps we should head back to the abbey more frequently," Silas said. "So you can tell your friends all about our travels. And maybe have soup. I wish we had some now."

I slipped the ring onto my finger. "How does it look? Silas?"

I shook the rat, but he made no noise.

"Silas? Please, say something!" I said. I couldn't wipe the tears freezing around my eyes. "I want to travel the world with you. Do you hear me? Please! I can't lose you! You're my duty!"

I trudged ahead as fast as I could. If my muscles weren't frozen, they would burn from the exertion. My head was already bowed.

"Lord Asger," I prayed. "Please help me perform my duty." I took a deep, icy breath and carried on. No matter how much I slipped or how numb my feet became, I pushed through the snow. It felt like a whole day had passed before black crept into the sides of my vision.

Both legs gave out from under me, and I toppled into the snow. Lights burned in the distance. I dragged my arm behind me until I felt the familiar softness of Silas's face. Tiny puffs of breath warmed my hand. There were three silhouettes, a rabbit, a skunk, and a squirrel, and then the darkness took me.

***

The sun outside bathed the budding flowers of spring, soaking up the early morning dew. The coming of spring used to make me so melancholic, but my smile wouldn't leave my face. I wasn't well traveled, but this looked like an excellent morning to begin a journey to a new land.

Father Oswald chuckled and fingered my tunic. "I'm still not used to seeing you out of your robes."

I held up my ring. "Just because I no longer wear the robe doesn't mean I'll stray from my faith."

The old beaver nodded. "And never stray from your duty."

"Oh, Father, I'd never be unfaithful to Silas."

"I mean never let the rat out of your sight," Father Oswald said. "He has a nose for trouble."

"I've talked up the summer strawberries enough to keep him alive until we return for the Summer Solstice Celebration."

The old beaver chuckled and patted my shoulder. "I think we both know it's time."

I wrapped Father Oswald in a tight hug. "Thank you. You were more than just a Father to me."

"Then I'm honored to have you as a son."

It was slow going walking with the elderly beaver, but it gave me a chance to see everyone on the way out.

Eloise jammed snack after snack into the travel pack over my back. "I made sure to pack extra cheese. Don't eat it all in one day, okay?"

I chuckled. "What, and risk passing wind in Silas's face and having him jump back and concuss himself?"

She punched me in the arm and then wrapped me in a hug. Her scent was reassuringly strong. "You'll be back this summer, right? To visit?"

"Always."

Sister Portia cleared her throat as she approached. She thrust a tome into my hands. "Some light reading for the road. It wouldn't be proper for you to forget your faith while traveling to some godless lands. Your friends in the archives have been working on this copy all winter."

The cover was the color of the stone walls of the abbey, and in fancy script, the title read, *The Notes of Abbot Reginald*.

"I'll read it every day," I told her. "Thank you."

"Right." She cleared her throat. "Now, remain faithful to your rat or Lord Asger will impale your organs for eternity. Have a splendid trip." She hustled away and brushed at her face.

Dancing at the door to the north gate was my rat. I could barely tell his leg had been injured, though he couldn't dance as long as he used to. I treasured that time nonetheless. He plucked away at his lyre and sang a little goodbye ditty to the children and the many adult admirers he still had. I think the ring I got him made him even more desirable.

Silas planted a kiss on my lips, to the delight of the crowd.

Mac unlocked the door and pushed it open. A gentle spring breeze rustled our fur. "You two ready?"

I nuzzled my husband's whiskers and then nodded to the squirrel. "Ready as we'll ever be." Together, my rat and I took our first step into the world together.

Unknown Stains

NightEyes DaySpring

Go to work. Go home. Go to sleep so you can get up in the morning and do the whole thing over again. Life is supposed to be fun. Life is supposed to be experienced. Life is supposed to be lived! Yes, I care about my job and my apartment and all the responsibilities in my life, but at the end of the day, there are only two things in this world I really care about. One of them I like to put in my mouth and ass. The other is the person attached to that object. Some might say my real priorities are questionable, but I just call them uncomplicated. It's at least the one thing in life that's easy to deal with.

Of course, in a moment like this, when I'm covered in dried mud, being dragged through the desert by the second thing, I kind of wish I had just the first to contend with right now.

"I thought the point of this trip was to enjoy ourselves," I snip, carefully walking through the arroyo we're crossing, and the small amount of water at the bottom of it.

"Hey, you picked this trail," he calls from the top of the gully. "You shouldn't have fallen in on the way out to the mesa."

"I said we should plan a trip through the desert! Not through a lake!" I throw my hands up in the air.

He laughs. "It does occasionally still rain out here."

"You could have warned me, Leister!"

The painted dog gives a squeaky, high pitched laugh. "I figured when I jumped over the water, you would have shown some caution, Muri. But we'll get you cleaned up. I'm an expert at doing that."

I growl back in response as I reach the top of the gully and we keep hiking across the scrub desert. "You're just jealous the stream got me and not you."

He chuckles. "Just don't sit on anything of value when we get back to the van."

"Yeah, yeah. The hyena is the dirty, unclean one. Like you never dribble."

He glances back at me, his black muzzle and tan face amused. "I'm not the one who decided to play connect the dots with his fur."

I just grumble and keep following his white-tipped tail down the trail. I'll get him back later, but at least the view of his butt is really good right now.

***

There is something fun about road trips. You get to see a lot of places you've never been, and it's a great chance to relax. I have a very stressful job, but I can put that behind me at times like this. I can focus on just being me, not the me I have to be at work. I really enjoy these experiences, especially trips through the desert. Out here, you're free of some of the restrictions of daily life. There is just the sun, the sky, the feeling of freedom, and oh yeah, the gas station hose down.

"Would you stop fidgeting!" he yells at me.

The wind is blowing gently, across the open land. There are bushes nearby, but they don't offer much of a wind break. "It's cold," I whine. Since its spring, the desert heat hasn't settled in yet.

He splashes the water onto my face. "Oh, come on, it's not that bad," he says with a snicker.

I growl. "I'm wet, I'm cold, and I'm standing in a gas station parking lot in my shorts."

He smiles. "If you don't let me hose all this mud off you, your fur is going to be sticky. Plus, the instruction manual says you should wash your hyena at least once a week."

I roll my eyes. I look ridiculous. "I will get you back for this."

He chirps amused and hangs the hose back up on the air and water kiosk. "Go change, yena," he says, pointing to the van, as he heads over to the convenience store.

I climb into the vehicle and close the sliding door behind me. Outside of the windows in the front, the Transit has a window in both rear doors and one in the sliding door. The ones in the back of the vehicle have special insulated covers I can pull down. I could close them, but they're tinted, and its bright outside. I do pull the curtain closed that separates the rear of the van from the cabin in the front to give myself some privacy. If someone comes to the back, they might notice I'm changing, but I don't care. You really shouldn't be looking into someone's vehicle anyway.

Leister bought the Transit used with low mileage and has adapted it into a camper van. The van has two seats in the front, then behind that is a small kitchenette across from the sliding door. You're not going to be cooking a big meal in it, but the kitchen is functional and has a fridge. The rest of the space is taken up by a queen-sized futon mattress in the back. The bed has some storage underneath it, and you can open the rear doors for a breathtaking view. The entire living space is paneled in wood to make it feel like a home. I helped him with some of the work, but most of this he did himself. The caper van is intimate, and that's what I like about it.

I have to be careful not to get any water or residual mud on the floor while I'm changing and tossing my clothing into a laundry bag. After peeling off my wet clothes off, I towel down before I fish out some fresh clothes from the long, narrow built-in cabinet over the bed that has my clothing. I only have a t-shirt on when Leister comes back and gets into the driver's seat of the van.

He pushes aside the curtain to glance back toward me. "How you doing back there?"

"Hey, some privacy you know!"

"Not like I haven't seen that before," he remarks, letting the curtain fall back. "I got you some coffee," he adds, and I can hear him putting something into one of the cup holders.

My ears perk at this. "Is it good?"

"It smells a little old, I'm afraid. It's all they had though."

I pull on a pair of boxers and walk over to push the curtain aside. I crawl into my chair, and pick up the cup of coffee. "In moments like this, I'm reminded of how well you know me. There is nothing like a bad cup of stale, gas station coffee to get me moving and warm a yena's heart."

Leister turns on the van. "Two things. First, you're welcome. Second, have you thought about pants?"

I take a sip of the coffee. It is indeed stale, but it's sweetened and has creamer just the way I like it. "I have indeed thought about pants. They're in my clothing cubby."

He backs the van out of its parking space. "Are we giving the truckers a show now?"

"Maybe once we get off a two-lane road," I say.

"Oh, so this is an invitation?" he asks, as he pulls out of the gas station. The van bumps down the road out across the gently rolling hills.

I pull down my underwear to expose my sheath, which flops out. "Ready, willing, and able."

He glances over at me. "Ready, willing, and able to get arrested by the highway patrol."

"Hey, it's a new meaning to the term jail bait," I say.

He laughs. "Jerk."

My ears fall a little. "You don't want to get arrested?"

He glances at me. "What bad porno have you been watching that ever gave you the idea that is a good experience?"

I blush. "It wasn't—okay it was really bad."

He giggles and we fall silent as he drives down the road. When we're together like this, we're close. But when we're apart, we lose this closeness. Maybe it's us, or maybe it's just life getting in the way. My work can suck up a lot of my life. Maybe now is the time to finally ask him the question that's floating around in the back of my mind.

***

I appreciate nice things. They're pretty, and I like pretty, but I also like it when things are simple and uncomplicated; so while the mattress in the back of the van isn't super thick, I don't mind that we're sleeping on it. I'm at home in this vehicle a way that surprises me. Leister's been working on this camper van conversion for a while, and I'm glad I got to help him. In this vehicle, we're free in a way I never experienced before. I still have my life and my apartment, but for a week, it's just us and the open road.

We decide to camp tonight off a dirt road that connects to a remote highway. It's a quiet spot next to small spring, and we leave the back door of the van open so we can see the water. Grass and brush grow right along the small pool's edge that gives way to scrub desert. We build a small fire from dead brush we collected so we can make our little campsite homey. We're not the first people to do this either; there's a small circle of stones with ashes in it we use. I also run out a temporary clothesline so I can dry my clothing.

Now watching the sky darken and the stars come out, I feel at peace with the world. I like being with the painted dog, out here alone in the desert. Lying on the bed in the van, I would be remiss to say I don't have expectations of what will happen tonight either. I never did put on any pants, so the night air is cool against my fur. Leister took his shirt off a while ago.

"It's so peaceful out here," Leister remarks, taking a sip of a beer he fished out of the fridge earlier.

"Yeah, it is. I'm glad we could plan this trip."

"Yeah. It was a great idea of yours."

I chuckle and wag my tail, watching the fire. "Thanks."

"I'm a little surprised you didn't want to invite anyone else," he says.

"And waste this moment?"

He laughs, trailing a paw through the fur on my arm. "Is that what this is? I mean you still have your underwear on and all."

My ears flatten. "No need to rush it."

"I guess not." He finishes his beer and tosses the can onto the ground outside.

"Really, littering?"

"Really, turning me down for sex?" he retorts.

"I didn't turn you down!"

"Well, I didn't litter either. It's only litter if I don't pick it up before we leave. Plus, do you want to roll over in the middle of fucking and get a can in your back?" He smiles at me, his amber eyes shining when they catch the light of the fire.

"You'll still forget."

"I may be an asshole, but I'm not that kind of asshole."

I chuckle. "You aren't an asshole, Leister."

"Okay how about uncouth, blunt jerk?"

I prop myself up on one arm. "Maybe."

"Oh come on. You don't need to be kind on my account."

"Fine. Uncouth asshole?"

He slaps me on the shoulder, and his tail wags. "Yup." He lies down on the futon.

I roll my eyes. We do this dance all the time. He's told me before I should find someone better, but I don't want to. I want Leister, and that's what I'm working to get.

"Hey, why do you always put yourself down like this? You're not a bad guy."

He shrugs. "Dunno. I just do."

"You say you're an uncouth asshole, but you'd be the first to offer his seat on a bus to someone who needs it."

He gives me a squeaky laugh. "There is a difference between being impolite and being uncouth."

"Yes, but… I love you."

An arm wraps around my shoulder. "I love you too."

I whine. He's not getting it, and I'm up against his emotional defenses I don't feel I ever can quite break through. Now would be the time to try. "I love you, a lot. Like, I was thinking about asking if you wanted to move in."

He turns to look at me, ears up in surprise. "Move in?"

"Yeah, move in. We're obviously compatible. If we can live out of a van for a week, we can live together."

"I guess? I'm kind of a slob you know. I'm not sure I really quantify as roommate material."

"I think you do. You're not pretentious, and you're very grounded. I love that about you. Plus, we've been together long enough haven't we? Why not move in."

He sighs. "I dunno, Muri. I thought this was more a thing of convenience. You told me when we started you wanted to keep it open."

"You know I'm not playing around on the side anymore."

His ears lower and he looks away. "Yeah, I know."

"Are you?"

He sighs. "Occasionally, but it's not anyone new though. It's been a few months since the last time I did. I know it bothers you if I do."

I sit up. "I have to ask this, and I'm serious about this. Do you want to keep it open?"

Leister frowns. "It's not a simple yes or no answer. It's less about sexual needs and more like, why me?"

"You're a great guy."

He sighs, and his ears fall. "I worry I'm not though."

"Dude, remember last year when I went skiing last minute by myself?" I say.

"Yeah. You fell."

"Breaking your leg is bit more than falling." Leister also has the decency not to remind me that I didn't fall on the ski slope but I slipped on ice in the parking lot of a restaurant after a great day of skiing.

He grins. "Okay, a bit more than falling."

"Yeah, but you took the bus to South Lake Tahoe and drove me home in my car after I got out of the hospital. You didn't have to do that for me. Hell, no one else was going to come get me, but you, you did that. Jerks don't do that for someone else. Good guys do that for people."

He doesn't say anything at first. "I guess, but I thought we just agreed on 'uncouth asshole' instead of 'good guy.'"

I look at him, searching his face. "I mean that jokingly. You're too nice to be a real asshole."

He gets up and moves over to the edge of the van door, so he can hang his feet off the end of the bed. "I'm not sure if this makes sense, but I don't want to disappoint you, Muri."

"Disappoint me? How would you disappoint me?"

The painted back shrugs. "Don't know."

"Leister, who else knows you better than me?"

He tilts his head to glance back. "Not sure anyone else does."

"Then if I think you're a great guy, why can't you accept that?"

"Because I worry you can find someone else."

I push myself over to the edge of the bed so I can wrap my arms around him. "What if I don't want to?"

He lets his shoulders slump and he kicks his feet. The bed sits on top of a raised platform in the back of the van. It's too high for Leister's feet to reach the ground, so they swing back and forth. "I try and hold down the fears I have inside about myself."

"That you'll hurt me?"

"Maybe that. Maybe I'm holding you back. When we started I didn't want to get serious. I enjoyed having someone who was just into me. Now…now I know it's not just that."

I lick one of his ears and shift my hand through his chest fur. "The possibility of us having more sex is not why I want you to move in. I think we've reached that stage. The last three years have been great. It's had its ups and downs, but I think we're good together."

"Has it been three years?"

"Yup," I remark, reaching down toward his belly button. "Three wonderful years."

He murmurs an agreement and then leans back against me. I play with his stomach fur for a while, before I go further, gently teasing him through the fabric. He lets out that squeaky, high pitched, chirping bark he does when he's happy.

I press myself a little further, teasing him through his jeans while I snuggle up against him. When I break off and lie back on the futon, I don't have to tell him what I want. He naturally comes over to me after stripping his pants off.

His musk in moments like this is pleasant, but it isn't as strong as mine. The van already smells of us since this is the second day of our weeklong trip, but I know after tonight, it's going to be marked by us.

My tail thumps against the mattress as he straddles me. Only the soft sounds of night and the sound of our breathing fills the air. In the firelight coming in from outside, he is a series of shadows, with bits of amber on top of his whites and tans. Leister is beautiful, and I love tracing my fingers along his complex fur variations. But right now, the red shaft in front of me is my focus.

I taste him carefully, enjoying the feeling of how he twitches at my touch. His musk is stronger than normal; we've both been out in the heat today, so I imagine mine is too. The sensation is still pleasant and warm, the flesh supple as I wash my tongue across it.

He lets out another squeaky bark, this time with need on top of it as I suckle at his cock. I can feel his black and white digits wrapping around my own shaft once he pulls back my underwear.

Getting me to attention also doesn't take any significant effort. We continue for a while with him sitting on top of me before he pulls back. Wordlessly we shift positions so we can sixty-nine, me on the bottom and him on the top.

The feeling of his wet nose against my sensitive flesh is beautiful. I'm between his legs, and I can only see the outline of his body as I take him back into my mouth. He also doesn't waste any time licking my cock, as he holds it between his fingers. His long tongue paints me in wet, warm drool, coaxing me on. The sensation is blissful, and I am happy. This is my world right now, and this is the only world I wish existed.

I have my nose buried into his balls when I get that telltale twitch, and he has to break off to pant. With a shudder he cums, and I taste him, salty and familiar.

He gives me some breathing room by pulling out, but the painted dog doesn't stop. He licks teasingly and jerks me off, and I quickly reach my own climax. There is something about a job well done that I find really hot, and he feels the same way. He's a giving lover, not someone who stops once they've gotten off themselves.

I splatter cum all over me, him, and the bed. When we're done, he rolls over to lie next to me, my head at one end of the mattress, his at the other.

Being in this van with Leister that is nice. My life and work don't intrude. I can barely get a cell phone signal out here anyway. Instead, we're just together, experiencing the open road. Being with him is more satisfying than anyone else I've been with. I don't know why. Sex always puts me in a good mood, but just being around Leister, I feel complete.

Perhaps tomorrow, if I can find where I put the lube I swear I packed, we can do some anal.

"Hey, Muri, can I ask you a question?"

"Yeah?"

"Do we have a cum rag?"

"Uh, not really."

"I've got some of you on the side of my face and chest."

"Hey, you can never say I didn't give you anything nice. If you give me a bit, I can even gave you a proper pearl necklace tonight." I giggle amused.

Even after Leister punches me in the side, I am still laughing.

***

There is something about dawn that wakes me up early when I'm camping. The night air with its cool breeze begins to warm a little, and the subtle shift in air temperature rouses me as the rosy fingers of dawn are spreading across the desert.

At first the sun will brighten the sky, and deep shadows cover the ground. Then the sun breaks over the horizon, bathing what it touches with golden light, making the sand shimmer as it rises. Pockets of shadow can run for miles in the nooks and crannies of the hills until finally the sun climbs high enough to illuminate everything.

Even though we have the back doors of the van open, the space is still cloaked in shadow. I glance toward Leister, watching his back of splotched fur as he breathes steadily next to me, still oblivious to the coming morning. He's curled against the wall opposite from me wrapped around a pillow, but his tail is draped across my stomach. We're naked except for the sheet that covers us.

I prop my head up by putting one of my arms under it and sigh. I can't believe I finally asked if he wanted to move in. I've been wanting to, but it's been tough to reach this point. He didn't say yes though, and he let it drop when I let my emotions and needs run high. I guess that went as well as I could expect. I stare up at the wooden ceiling. What was I thinking?

"Stupid, just stupid," I mutter, dropping my other hand as a balled fist into the futon mattress. "Just stupid."

"Hey, don't pick on the mattress now. What did that mattress ever do to you?"

I yelp. "I thought you were asleep."

He rolls over and yawns, washing my face in hot breath. "I've been awake thinking." He opens his eyes to look at me.

"About what?" I ask.

"Just general stuff, like where my life is and where it's going."

"That's pretty serious for this time of day."

He yawns again and lets his tongue roll out. "It happens. I've got a lot on my mind."

"I'm sorry," I blurt out.

"For what?"

I lower my voice. "Last night."

"Oh, that."

"Yeah, that."

"It's no biggie," he says.

Maybe not to him, but it is a big deal to me. "You never said if you wanted to move in or not."

"I'd have to think about it."

"That's what you were really thinking about, isn't it?"

He reaches out to rest a paw on my nearest arm. "It's only the second full day of our trip. Can we perhaps deal with the heavy stuff a little later?"

I blink. "I mean, I guess, but I don't want it hanging over our heads."

"Then you shouldn't have asked. What were you expecting me to say?"

I huff at him. "Obviously more than you did."

"Muri, come on. You can't just expect me to move in with you. We've got separate lives."

"We have separate lives because you want us to. It doesn't have to be like this. We could be a couple. A real couple, Leister. One with a real life together."

He sighs. "And what about what I want? All I'm hearing is what you want."

I draw back. "You don't want this?"

He sits up. "Muri, you are a great guy. You deserve better."

My ears splay. "So you've told me."

"Look at yourself. You've got a good thing going with your job. You've got money in the bank and a nice place to yourself. Me? I live in a studio in a drafty industrial loft. My landlord keeps raising my rent to the point I'm going to have to look somewhere else to live. Part of why I've kept working on the van is because I may have to live in it someday."

"You want to live in this permanently?"

"No, but it would save me some money. Now that the sink and burner setup are installed, I can even cook in here. Plus, if I move into it, I can travel more. I don't have to stay in California."

"Leister, that's cool and all, but…"

"But what about us?"

"Yeah."

"I figure you'll find someone better."

I slam my fist against the bed. "Leister, you dense, stupid idiot! This isn't about finding someone better. This is about making what we have work better for us. What the hell am I going to do, turn on Paw Mingle or Barked and bam, instant long-term lover? It doesn't fucking work that way!"

The dog's ears go down. "If you tried—"

"Tried? Tried! Why the hell would I want to try?" I snarl. "You know what, forget this. Forget I asked." I push myself up and crawl off the bed and snag my discarded underwear. "I'm going for a walk, and when I come back, I'll pretend this doesn't bother me so we can enjoy our little trip."

"Muri—"

"Shove it, Leister!" I yell, jumping out the side of the van. My paws connect with dirt and I storm off leaving, the dog alone.

***

The desert is a harsh place, and fifteen minutes later, I realize just how stupid what I have done is. I stop to catch my breath in the shade of a scrub bush and after kicking the dirt a few times, I look around to get my bearings. In every direction is desert vegetation cut through with small rises. I didn't take a bearing or try to keep track of the vegetation I passed. I just stormed out here. I can see the distant mountains, but in which direction is the van? Even more concerning, will Leister still be there when I return?

He wouldn't just leave me out here, would he? I don't think so, but if I can storm off, why can't he? I look around to try and find my trail, but I kicked up enough dirt I can't be sure exactly from which direction I came.

"Shit." Unlike yesterday's hike, I don't even have any water. Even though it is still spring, once the sun reaches high into the sky, this could quickly turn dangerous.

"Okay, think, Muri. Your ancestors hunted on the savanna for their meals. You don't even have to chase anything down; you just have to return to where you came from. I just need my superior instincts to kick in."

I took a deep breath and look around on the ground carefully, but everything looks the same. The ground is too hard and doesn't take paw-prints easily. I'm in the middle of the desert with no water and my only article of clothing is a pair of boxers.

"I'm going to die out here," I say to the ground, as I fall to my knees. Nothing responds to me, and the insects that sing about the heat of the day don't respond to my sobbing. I'm completely alone right now, and I've taken some of the best time I've had with Leister and ruined it. I had to press him on moving in. I couldn't let it be. My desire to ask him has been eating at me for a while. I thought we were ready to take this step, but I apparently want more than he's ready to give.

Crying into the dust is probably not the best way to try and conserve water, but I do it anyway. I have so much emotion inside it just all comes tumbling out. I look absolutely ridiculous, a full-grown hyena crying in the middle of nowhere, wearing only a pair of underwear, with my head pressed against the ground.

If I don't know where I came from, does Leister know how to find me?

Big wet tears sink into the dirt, and eventually I run out of them. I am just dry heaving. I'd fucked up my vacation with Leister, maybe even our relationship, and now I'm lost in the desert. If I don't come back, what is he going to think? What is he going to do?

That last question I know the answer to. He'll look for me. He isn't going to leave me out here. He knows how dangerous that would be, and he would never do that to me, no matter how mad he is at me.

I look up at the blue sky. We turned off on a side road to get to our camping spot south of the main road. The sun is still low in the east. If I start off north and use the distant mountains to keep me on a straight line, I should intersect the main road. From there, I might be able to walk back to the van, or at least hitch a ride with a passing vehicle. I might even be able to borrow someone's cell phone, although I don't know if Leister has service out here.

Or I could head toward that distant plume of smoke in the distance. I blink. Wait, if there is a campfire, that means someone is out here. That might even be Leister. We didn't use all the brush we collected last night.

I take a bearing so I know which way north is, and then I take off in a trot. Whoever it is, they can't be that far away. I hope they like mostly naked hyena. Nothing looks familiar, but in my anger, I saw without seeing.

A quick ten minutes later, I emerge out into the clearing we camped at. The van is still there and Leister is crouched over a fire. His ears are down, and he's focusing on his cast iron skillet that sits on top of a small metal grate propped up on the rocks around the fire.

"Leister!"

The wild dog startles and his ears shoot up. "Muri!" He stands up, a metal spatula clutched in one hand. "I started making breakfast. I thought you might want to eat."

I've noticed when he gets stressed out Leister cooks. It gives him something to do, and it's one of the tells he has. "You weren't going to come look for me, were you?"

"I figured you wanted your space." He looks down at the food sizzling in the pan. "You've got good timing though. The bacon is almost done."

"I uh, got lost," I say sheepishly.

He startles. "What?"

"Yeah," I say, tail between my legs. With nothing else to say for my-self, I walk over to the van. I look ridiculous out here in my underwear. I should at least put some pants on finally.

As I walk past him, he reaches over and puts a hand on my shoulder to stop me. The spatula is clutched in his other hand. "I'm sorry. I didn't mean to upset you. I certainly didn't want you to go storming off like that."

"Well you did."

Leister's ears twitch and lower. "Sorry. I get nervous about stuff like this."

That's something, I guess. "Yeah, it's a big change."

He steps forward and pulls me into a hug. "And please don't do that again. I don't want to have to call the police combing through the desert looking for a hyena in a pair of boxers."

I chuckle. "It would be quite a story."

"Yeah, but not a good one," he says. He holds me for a minute and then breaks off the hug. He walks back over to the fire and pokes at the bacon in the cast iron skillet with the spatula. "How do you want your eggs?"

"Uh, scrambled, and wait, where did you get this food from?"

"From the fridge. Remember, I said I packed food? I wanted to surprise you with breakfast." He motions to a camp chair near the fire. "Give me a few minutes and it will be ready."

"Maybe I should get some shorts."

"Up to you. You be as naked or not as you want to be."

"I'm sorry about running off."

He pulls the bacon off the fire and puts it on a plate. He then wipes out some of the grease. "You have a right to be upset." He puts the pan back on the fire and starts to crack eggs into it.

"Yeah, but I have no right to force you into a relationship."

"We're already in a relationship."

I wring my hands. "Right, but something more serious."

He nods and keep cooking, ears focused on the sizzling grease and eggs. "If it helps put your mind at ease right now," he offers after a minute, looking up, "I wouldn't want to be out here with anyone else I know."

"Thanks."

"I mean really, I've got the best view out here."

"The spring is pretty nice."

"That's the second best view out here. I'm talking about you."

I smile. "Leister, that's kind of sweet."

"Now if only there wasn't underwear blocking it."

"Hey!"

He grins and gives me a squeaky laugh.

I chuckled and push my boxers down. "Better?"

The dog wags his tail. "Yeah," he says, going back to tend the eggs. "I'm looking forward to a morning swim after breakfast with that view, but first, can you get the plates out?"

"Sure," I respond, and walk over to the van to pull things out of the cupboard.

***

If there is one thing I have learned in my life, it's to let go of as many of the burdens holding you back as you can. The reason we took this trip is to live in the moment. To just be us. Yet here I've ruined that. Leister's cooking is good, but I've killed the lighthearted banter we normally have. We talk, but he seems pensive. I can tell he's thinking. Afterward, while I'm still poking at my food, Leister goes to make the bed.

"The two people who slept here are a real mess," says the dog, looking over the sheets.

"Sorry," I mumble, chewing on my last piece of bacon.

"I mean look at this," he says motioning me over.

"We weren't that messy, were we?" I walk over and look at the sheets. There is a dried milk white stain in the middle of the light green sheets. There are also some reddish-brown stains on the far end of the bed.

"Do you know how hard it is to clean cum out of a futon mattress?" the painted dog asks me, looking over the product of last night's love making. "And what are those?"

"If you can clean a hyena up at a gas station, I'm pretty sure you can hose down a mattress at one too."

"It wouldn't dry," he says. "Plus, I hosed you down yesterday and we still have weird mud stains on the bed. Maybe we can find a laundromat in the next town and do some washing over lunch."

The red stains do suspiciously look like mud from yesterday's dip in the arroyo. "Look, I don't know how they got there."

He glances at me. "Can you go inside and help me take this off?

"Sure," I say, going around to the side door and getting in. Leister passes me the pillows and I toss them into the seats up front. We pull off the sheets, which I toss in our shared laundry bag while he pulls out a spare set from storage area under the bed. Together we put the clean sheets on the mattress. While I'm putting the pillows back, he comes inside and sits down on the bed. There is a serious look in his face.

"Now you want to talk?" I ask him.

"Yeah."

I sigh and sit down next to him. He rests one of his paws on top of mine and we intertwine fingers.

"Muri?"

"Yeah?"

"What do you want for us?" he asks me.

"Something more serious than we have now. It's why I asked if you wanted to move in."

"You deserve better."

I roll my eyes.

"No, I mean from me. I've been thinking we could just continue as it is, but you want more. And if I want you, I have to realize that."

I nod. "I keep hoping you will, but I realize commitment isn't for everyone."

"I know and you're right. It's time to make that go."

"You aren't saying this just to make me feel better, are you?"

"No. I've known for a while you wanted to get more serious. Change isn't easy though. You keep a tight ship in your house, and me? Well I'm just kind of free spirit who doesn't want to think too hard about where they're going in life. The future scares me, and a lot of time, I'm just trying to get through the day."

I squeeze his hand since I'm still holding it. "That's one of the things about you I appreciate though. You aren't pretentious about stuff. You just live. Me? I've got things always going on. I have to organize myself in order to be able to function."

"Yeah, I understand that. I wish I could be more like you sometimes, but I always liked to play it loose. Sadly, the world seems to want more you's than me's."

"Being me is tiring sometimes," I say. "It's what I love about these trips. Out here, we aren't playing our roles in society. Everything else just falls away. We're just living."

He sighs. "The right answer is probably somewhere in the middle."

"Yeah." I lean over and give him a kiss. "I'm glad you're willing to give living together a try."

His ears shoot up and his black muzzle beams, "It will take some getting used to, but I'm excited for it."

We fall silent, and he leans over so he can rest his head on my shoulder. He tilts his head up so he can give the side of my muzzle a lick.

After a minute, his tail starts thumping against the bed, and he gives me a squeaky bark. "Hey, I have an idea."

"What's that?" I ask.

"How about we just live out of the van?"

"Hell no! Do you see how hard it is to keep this futon clean?"

"Okay, your place is fine, but I mean really, what more could you want out of your life than what is in this van right now?"

Even though I know he's not serious about living in the van full-time, he makes a good point. As long as the two most important things in my life are here, I'll be fine. Yeah, we don't have a TV or anything like that, but my priorities are simple. At least the ones I want to focus on are simple. I mean really, what's not to love about this setup? Plus, what the hell else are we going to do at night besides fuck, if we lived in the van?

Okay, we can't do that all the time, but it's nice to think we could. Yeah, I have other friends, a job with deadlines and commitments, and bills that need to get paid, but the basics of my life, the life I want to have, are here.

"With you in this van? Nothing."

ELECTROCHEMISTRY

Faora Meridian

Two elderly otters all but raced around the apartment, fingers pointing and voices raised to catch attention. The couple seemed absolutely incapable of realizing that half of what they said was lost on their audience. For one thing, their words drowned each other out and they spoke with too much urgency to be even close to coherent.

For another, their son did his best to tune them out.

And, of course, partly because their son did his best to tune them out.

He stood in the middle of the apartment's living room as his parents bustled about. Every now and then words would actually reach him, like, "—cooker unit's fully stocked," or, "I thought you were seeing that nice guy from work," or, "—no wild parties," or, "you should look into a class three of your own," or, "—so how about that nice girl you mentioned?" It was all he could do to smile and nod along for the most part. It was fine. They'd be gone soon.

"Oh, and one more thing!" his father said as they made for the front door at long last. "There's gonna be a delivery in a couple hours. Our new class three. You wouldn't mind setting that up for us, would you, Luke?"

The younger otter stifled a sigh and forced a smile to his muzzle. Of course. No wonder they'd asked him to house-sit. "Oh, sure," he replied as the smile turned into a coy smirk. "After all, you'd just blow the poor thing up if you tried, wouldn't you?"

"Be nice to your father, Luke," his mother said in that patronizingly patient tone of voice common to mothers everywhere. "That only happened twice. Now, are you sure you're going to be alright? I know it's just two weeks, but—"

"I *do* know how to take care of myself, mom," Luke protested as he shook his head. "You've been looking forward to this vacation all year. I'll take care of the simulant. You two just have a good time, alright? You've earned it."

His mother's expression softened as she leaned in to wrap Luke up in a tight hug. He returned it as his father moved in to join them. "See that, Sarah? We did a good job with him. Alright Lukey, you take care, alright? Don't blow up the apartment."

"Or the class three," his mother interjected as she pulled back. She stepped back until she nestled right up against her husband's side. "Don't forget, he's your father. Maybe his skills are genetic."

Luke rolled his eyes as he stepped back and folded his arms. "Yeah, I'll keep that in mind. Love you."

"Love you too, kid. Have fun." His father tapped twice at the band on his wrist and raised it to his muzzle. "Orbital Control, read two to displace, please."

A quiet hum filled the air in the apartment for a moment, and then his parents vanished in a flash of bluish light and a *pop* of shunted air. Luke wrinkled his nose at the scent of ozone as it washed over him. He shook his head as he heard the apartment's life support systems kick on and begin to vent the gas out of the building. "Core world tech at its finest," he muttered to himself as he looked around.

There were worse places to be holed up for a couple of weeks, the otter had to admit. He'd not been back home in a while, so getting out and seeing how the city had changed in the last two years would definitely keep him busy for a couple days. The holonet connection his parents had wasn't exactly as extensive as he'd like, but it would do.

Luke's expression soured as he frowned at the apartment's front door. That was... pretty much it. Nothing else to do. Set up the class three, explore outside for a bit... binge the holonet. *For two weeks.*

"... shit."

***

Five hours passed with agonizing slowness as Luke waited for the class three to be delivered. Two documentaries and twelve cartoons filled the time before the front door panel buzzed for attention. "Alert," came a mechanically female voice from the panel as Luke disengaged the holonet. "A delivery has arrived from BSS Transit. Confirm receipt and clear the delivery zone for displacement."

"About damn time," Luke muttered as he sat up and turned to drape himself over the back of the couch. "Confirm receipt and check delivery zone."

"Receipt confirmed," replied the panel, and it fell silent for a moment before it chimed. "Delivery zone clear. Displacing delivery in three, two, one—"

Pop!

Luke winced and shied away from the flash of displacement light for a second before it faded away. A figure stood tall in front of the apartment's front door, chrome from the top of its head to the tips of its toes. The otter frowned as he looked the ambiguously humanoid-canid form up and down. "Wow. When they send a blank slate, they really mean *blank*." With a sigh he clapped his webbed paws together and clambered over the couch fully. "Alright, simulant. Let's get you started up, eh?"

No sooner than the words were out of his muzzle than the eyes of the machine snapped open. A dull yellow light issued from them as it turned its head this way and that. "Please stand by," the droid said, even though its muzzle didn't move with the emotionless, gender-neutral words. "Your Biomech Service Solutions class three service simulant is scanning the environment in search of its proud new owner. Please say hello now."

Brows knit themselves close together as Luke stared at the automaton. *This* was new. "Hello now," he said after a second as he smirked.

That smirk vanished as the simulant's head turned quickly to face him. Those glowing eyes raked over Luke's body as he took a quick step back. "Sarcasm detected. Incorporating. Would you like to receive standard startup information now, or would you prefer to test the unit's capacity to understand organic speech patterns further?"

Luke's tail twitched as he smiled despite himself. At least the BSS engineers had a sense of humor when they programmed these things. "Yeah, go ahead. Give me the startup rundown. What could it hurt?"

The eyes of the simulant began to flicker as he settled itself into a more natural stance. "Thank you. Welcome to your very own, brand new Biomech Service Solutions class three service simulant. If the unit appears to be staring at you, do not be alarmed or unnerved. Your brain's electrochemical impulses are being read in order to facilitate a smoother startup process."

At that Luke's eyes widened. "Wait, you're reading my mind?" he asked. "That's not a good idea. It's a mess in there."

"This unit is programmed not to record any mind-state imprints beyond the setup process," the simulant continued, and its mechanical voice took on a reassuring tone. "The process is designed only to help this unit attend to your needs in a most comfortable manner."

The words didn't wipe the frown from Luke's face. "Yeah, that makes it much better, thank you."

"Your sarcasm is once again noted," the simulant replied, and the lights in its eyes solidified again. "This unit would now ask that you calm your mind as it scans your brain in order to find an appropriate form to wear."

Luke complied, for a given value of calm. The knowledge that his mind was being sifted by the machine so that it could build itself a pleasing body was somewhat unnerving, but this was what he'd been asked to handle for his parents. Maybe they'd known. Maybe they just wanted him to suffer through the weird parts.

The knowledge that his mind was being scanned was weird enough, but it was weirder still to watch as the shape of the simulant began to shift and warp. The chrome was the first thing to change, as it faded to a darker tone. The machine began to hum quietly as fur began to sprout in browns and blacks and whites. It shrunk down slightly from a head shorter than Luke to just a couple of inches taller, its body slender and elongated. The pointy canine ears flattened and rounded as the muzzle melted into a new configuration, and Luke stared in wonder as the simulant took on the form of a ferret that seemed almost familiar to him.

The eyes were the last to change, and they retained their yellow glow for a moment longer before they shimmered and shifted to a deep, ocean blue. A shudder ran through the unit before it straightened up again, and it sucked in a quick breath of air before it released it again with a sigh. "Configuration complete," it said, its voice distinctly masculine but light and airy. "Good afternoon, master, and thank you for activating me."

Luke frowned as he looked down briefly, and his eyes shot back up to lock on the ferret-droid's face again. "Hoo, yeah. You're very active. And, uh… very equipped."

"I can see you're uneasy with this state of undress," the simulant said, though its tone was amused as it reached to its back with both paws. "Interesting. Conscious/subconscious paradox noted. Not to worry. I'm equipped—pun certainly intended—for this circumstance."

"Oh, stars. It *puns*," Luke groaned as he turned away from the simulant. "What are you even doing with… bits, anyway? I thought you were a service unit."

Behind him, the ferret-droid chuckled. "I am, and this would be a great time for a 'full-service' joke if I detected you were open to such a thing."

The otter groaned again and rubbed over his face. The ads had claimed the class three possessed the most advanced organic emulation technology in the cluster, but this went far beyond anything Luke had expected. "You know, that *does* qualify for the very joke you decided not to tell."

"Which is precisely why I told it; you're a little slow on the uptake, master." The simulant laughed again. "Alright, you can turn around now. Nothing out of place. Promise."

Luke turned slowly and he kept his eyes raised for as long as he dared, but eventually curiosity got the better of him. The simulant's chest was still bare, but his—its—lower half was clad in a pristine pair of brown slacks that accented the ferret fur pattern it wore. As he watched the ferret-droid spread its arms out and gave a self-sure grin. "You see? Nothing out of place. Is this better?"

"Uh, yeah. Much. Thanks." Luke coughed as he looked the simulant over again. If not for the slightest hint of a glow behind those blue eyes, he could be forgiven for thinking he was looking at a flesh and blood ferret. Even as he stared, he realized he could be forgiven for thinking that maybe it was just a ferret with cybernetic eyes. Familiarity nagged at him again. "Damn. That's incredible. You're...you look amazingly lifelike."

"You're not so bad yourself," the ferret replied, and it laughed again as Luke began to frown. "Oh, please. I've seen inside your head. You're trying not to smile right now."

The urge to smile *had* been there, but the reminder that the machine had scanned his mind once again set Luke ill at ease. "Yeah. Well...let's just move on. What more do I need to do to finish your setup?"

At those words the simulant all but beamed. "Oh, I'm already taking care of that," it replied. "I've interfaced with your apartment's network, introduced myself to the AI—moody little thing, isn't it?—and I'm registering myself with Biomech Service Solutions as we speak." The ferret paused for a moment as it tilted its head to the side. "This isn't your apartment."

"No, it's my parents' place," Luke said as he glanced at the wall panel by the door. Moody? He didn't even know his parents' home AI *had* a mood. "You're meant to be for them, not for me."

For a few seconds, the simulant actually looked disappointed. "Oh, that's a shame," it said at last. "All of this configuration will ultimately have to be reset and started over. That's never fun."

Confusion touched Luke as he took a step toward the simulant. What an odd choice of words. "You can be disappointed?" he asked.

The ferret's eyes fixed on Luke as it began to smile again. "After a fashion. My programming is open-ended and designed to stimulate portions of my neural network in ways that replicate the emotional states of organics. I have scanned all available information on the apartment occupants—Robert and Sarah Dillinger, yes?—and nothing that I have found so far indicates that I would find them nearly as interesting as you. I'd certainly prefer to remain in your company."

Luke blinked at that. "What would make me different? I mean, my needs are just the same as theirs. What are you, uh…*for*, anyway?"

"Oh, as I said. I am a full-service class three simulant. I cook, I clean, I repair and maintain, and so much more." The ferret winked. "I could give you the sales pitch, but I know how much you hate hearing simulants drone on about their feature lists and the like. Those class twos really didn't have the best emulation software, did they?"

As Luke shook his head, the simulant spread its arms out. "So, let's make the pitch short and sweet. My neural network is, at its core, a great big learning machine. I take on the duties that I detect that you need. I read your mind-state and body language and apply advanced psychology subroutines to attend to your needs before you even know you need them." It lowered its arms again as it looked around the living room. "However, it appears that your parents keep an immaculate home and I calculate only a twelve percent chance you would be interested in food. Well, that's a shame too. I would have loved to test out my cooking subroutines."

"Well, uh… sorry to disappoint you, I guess?" Luke shrugged as he glanced around the apartment. "Is there anything that you need? Or want?"

But the ferret just waved a paw and smiled again, and once more Luke was struck with the feeling that he knew the person that the simulant had taken the appearance of. "It's for the best. I need to complete my setup procedure and then enter low-power mode for an hour or so while I calibrate my energy stores. Think you can do without a sassy robot that you like more than you want to let on for a little while?"

Despite that lingering sense of unease, Luke felt a genuine smile touch his muzzle. The simulant was right; he definitely did like how it had presented itself. It was so much more *real* than his parents' old class two. "If it keeps you from snarking at me for a couple hours, I might call it a blessing."

"That's the spirit, master!" The ferret chuckled as it made its way over to the front door panel and leaned against the wall. "You go make yourself at mom and dad's home. Raid the cookie jar and such. I'll be back before you know it."

***

The simulant had remained in low-power mode for just over an hour—more cartoons on the holonet had kept Luke busy during that time—before it woke up again. It did so in such a quiet fashion that Luke was startled when he heard a sound from the kitchen rather than by the door. A glance back at where the simulant had been showed it gone; he'd not even noticed as the ferret-droid slipped around the apartment. "Damn, that's gonna take some getting used to."

"Yeah, I'm a regular ninja-janitor," the simulant called from the kitchen, followed by a laugh. "A ninjanitor! Heh heh, sorry if I surprised you, master."

Confusion was replaced with amusement as Luke made his way into the kitchen. "You know, I didn't think a simulant could be intentionally funny."

The ferret smirked over its shoulder at him. "That's interesting. I didn't think an organic would be so easy to amuse. You know what they say about small minds, master."

Luke chuckled as he glanced at the cooker unit. The machine was in manual mode; usually the otter would just leave it on automatic. "Well, you and your neural net's probably capable of out-processing me any day of the week, so I'll have to try harder for you." His eyes flicked back to the simulant again. "You know, you don't need to call me master. It's not like I own you or anything."

The simulant's tail kinked and unkinked itself as it huckled again. "No, but your parents do," it pointed out. "And in their stead, I take your commands and serve at your whims. What would you prefer I call you, if not that?"

"Trust me, just 'Luke' is more than fine, thanks," he replied. The simulant nodded and turned its attention back to the cooker unit. "And you need a name, don't you?"

"I'm in the middle of making you dinner and *now* you want to know my name?" The words had just the right mixture of hurt and amusement. "I mean, it's less a name and more a mechanical designation, but I don't think you want to spend half a minute rattling off my serial number."

Even the thought of memorizing that turned Luke's stomach. "No, no. I just don't know what to call you. Mom and dad didn't leave any preferences, and I don't know that it's gonna matter if you're just going to be reset when they get back anyway."

The simulant paused for a second in its work before it gave a quick nod. "Ah, I see. Naming me would personalize me further, and you don't want to run the risk of attachment. I understand." Its tail slowed its manic twitching and drooped to the floor.

It hadn't turned around as it spoke and there was no trace of sadness or disappointment in the ferret-droid's voice, but Luke still felt a twinge of regret in his heart. How could he have hurt the machine's feelings? All its feelings were simulated anyway. "Well, you're still going to need a designation. Something I can call you, just for... you know. Ease of use."

While the simulant still didn't turn around, its tail began to twitch again. "I'm pretty sure 'simulant' or 'droid' or 'hey you, in the bushes!' would work just as well." Luke began to frown as unease crept up his spine. There was that familiarity again... "Maybe a name wouldn't be such a bad idea after all, attachment or not. Maybe... how would you feel about calling me Kurt?"

Hey, you! In the bushes!

Luke's eyes widened as he stumbled backward. His vision blurred and began to tunnel. Memories long buried rushed to the surface; the image of the grinning face of a young ferret boy... "What in the—"

The simulant reached out to steady Luke, his expression full of concern and its voice soothing. "Breathe, master," it cooed to him as he backed away quickly from the machine. "Just breathe. My sensors indicate you're suffering a mild anxiety attack."

Just breathe, Luke. It's gonna be okay! It's gonna be okay!

"No shit," he panted as he backed himself against the wall. Luke allowed himself to slide down it as he covered his face with his arms and gasped for breath.

As he tried to gain control of his breathing, the simulant quickly turned back to the kitchen. The food recombinator beside the cooker pinged quietly as it received the droid's command. A small cup slid into position beneath a receptacle as a brown liquid began to spill down into it.

Luke, meanwhile, was left to rock back and forth against the wall as he tried to force himself to breathe. He felt his head and his heart both pounding out of time as he squeezed his eyes shut against the flood of memories.

You can call me Kurt. Nice to meetcha!

"Here, master."

Luke's head jerked up, the otter's eyes still wide as saucers as the simulant knelt down in front of him. It held the cup in its paw, extended toward Luke. "Tea," it said as it gently shook the cup from side to side. "Also a light chemical cocktail that should help calm you down."

Panic and confusion gave way to a sudden flash of anger. Luke's paw swept out to knock the cup aside, but the simulant pulled it back with unnatural reflexes. Not a single drop was spilled as it moved the tea out of arm's reach and waddled back from the otter. "Kurt?" he growled.

"Yes?" the simulant replied as its head tilted to the side.

"No!" the otter snapped back. He sprang up out of his crouch and straightened up against the wall again. "No, you're... you are *not* him. You..." His words trailed off as realization hit. "You scanned my mind. You went through my memories when you made yourself look like that." His glare sharpened as new anger flooded through him. "What the *fuck*? What the fuck is this? You think this is *good*?"

The simulant lifted its empty paw in a non-threatening gesture. "I have placed you in distress, and I am truly sorry," it said.

It even sounded perfectly apologetic as it spoke, but that didn't matter one bit to Luke in that moment. All he knew was a burst of anger and pain he'd never expected to feel, and the otter shook his head hard as he thrust a finger at the simulant. "You need to shut down *right now*."

The request seemed to surprise the ferret-droid, but it gave a quick nod as it turned and made for the front door. It stopped by the panel as Luke watched and entered a couple of commands there. "My sensors will remain active should you require me," it said, and once again its voice carried a hint of hurt. A *perfect* hint of hurt. A mechanically precise hint of hurt. "I'm very sorry that I—"

"Shut down, simulant," he told it again, as his own voice wavered with raw, organic fury. "Right now."

A moment later it did so. The ferret's eyes fell closed as it slumped down somewhat limply, though it remained upright with impeccable balance.

Luke, for his part, surrendered to gravity. He slid back down the wall, curled himself into a ball, and cried like he hadn't cried in years.

Twelve years, three months, seventeen days, two hours, forty-two minutes, to be precise.

***

The class three breed of service simulant was a remarkable thing from an engineering and programming standpoint. Its interaction protocols were the most advanced on the market, and its emotional emulation software was practically revolutionary. They were capable of passing any test designed to root out a synthetic save for invasive examination, and even in a shut-down state they retained enough processing power to interface with other nearby AI systems and coordinate them from its own unconscious substrate.

This latter point only came to Luke's attention when the kitchen pinged for his attention a few hours later. He'd not moved from the spot he'd laid down in the entirety of those hours, content to stay on the floor and in the dark as he struggled to process something he thought he'd been thoroughly over. Concerned that the command he'd issued the simulant to shut down had compromised the house's AI—it had suggested that it had integrated itself, after all—he went to the kitchen to check.

There he found that the food recombinator had not only produced for him another mug of tea, but also a relatively healthy synthesized meal. There was no note or message attached to it even though there could have been, but there was only one possibility. The simulant had prepared it for him, even though he'd closed it down.

He considered ordering the food recombinator to recycle the foodstuffs back into storage for a moment, but his stomach gurgled for attention. Biology won out over spite, and Luke sat himself down on the couch with a plate of food in one paw and a mug of tea in the other. The former wasn't exactly tasty; synthfood from a recombinator always lacked something compared to what someone could do with a cooker. It satisfied however, and that was the main thing.

Luke continued to sit in the dark for at least another hour before the occasional blinks of blue light from the corner of his vision finally caused him to sigh and sit up. "Are you seriously just listening in and waiting for me to ask for your apology?"

A brief hum sounded from the front door before it cut off and was replaced with a quiet, almost timid voice. "Why, is it working?"

The corners of Luke's muzzle wanted on some level to curl into a smile, but his heart just wasn't in it. He sat himself back up a little higher as he looked over to where the simulant continued to stand, silent again in the dark. Only the barest hint of its eye glow lit the base of its muzzle as it stared over at Luke. "I thought you had advanced psychology subroutines. I don't think guilting me into conversation is going to help your case any."

"That's definitely not my intent," the machine replied. Its voice remained quiet as it kept its distance. "I'm here to help. My function is to be of assistance. Part of that function is being aware of my master's distress and attempting to address it."

"Well first of all, I'm not your master." Luke sighed as he buried his face in his paws. "Bloody simulants… look. I don't know what's going on here. I don't get what you're trying to do. You've… dug way too deep into my mind, so if there's any distress here it's because you ripped it to the surface."

The simulant made a quiet hmm-ing sound and Luke watched its eyes bob in the darkness as it nodded. "I can see this now. I'm truly sorry. During the preliminary setup scan of your mind, the electrochemical processes of your brain were also recorded. My programming encountered a paradox it was unprepared for, and…well, it obviously chose the wrong outcome. I'm sorry, but I'll need your help to fix it."

Luke sighed again as he closed his eyes and leaned his head back against the wall. "Yeah, I bet you do. What was this paradox, then? What'd you see that made you do *this*?"

There was a pause as the simulant cocked its head. "I detect a seventy-two percent probability that you are not emotionally ready to discuss this matter," it warned him. When Luke lowered his head to glare at the machine's glowing eyes, it nodded. "Very well. I will attempt to explain in as delicate a manner as I can.

"A form is required for any class three simulant to operate in optimal fashion. Can't very well interact with people if we don't have much of a face, can we?" It tried a little smile, but Luke's expression didn't change and so the smile faded. "And so, the master's conscious and subconscious are investigated in order to find a form that would bring maximum comfort. Unfortunately, in this case, the familiarity of the form chosen was…corrupted."

"It wasn't corrupted," Luke muttered to himself. He watched the simulant tilt its head in confusion for a second. "There's no one in my life I've ever been more comfortable around, but you already know that, don't you?"

Again, the simulant paused. "Yes," it admitted at last. "Please understand. One of my protocols is caretaking. Class three simulants are not just designed to be housekeepers and butlers. We have nursery subroutines. Palliative care subroutines. Therapy subroutines."

The otter snorted. "Maybe your therapy protocols need updating." Maybe the rest of it, too. With each passing moment, the simulant seemed to become more robotic.

Around Luke, the apartment's lights began to slowly brighten. They ramped up slowly, but they never moved beyond a dim illumination. It was enough to see, but it wasn't enough to blind Luke's dark-adjusted eyes. "Maybe they do. They detected the strength of the memories tied to your friend. Extrapolated an age-appropriate version to serve as my avatar for you. My programming detected that there was associated trauma, but your affinity for the form was deemed to be of a higher priority than the pain."

"And how'd that work out for us?" Luke asked, his tone bitter.

The simulant lowered its head in an affectation of shame and guilt. "This was the paradox my programming was unprepared for. No matter how advanced the emotional engine, I am still only a machine. I can only take solace in that I caused no deliberate harm in my attempt to ingratiate myself. It is small comfort to me and no comfort at all to you. That is why I stand ready to reset my personality matrix and form, the better to accommodate this new information."

Luke sighed as he looked the simulant up and down. It was uncanny, to be sure. It did look just like how he imagined Kurt *might* have looked, twelve years on. Now that he'd seen the simulant's version, he'd have a hard time imagining anything else. "That's why your speech patterns have changed. You've already decided you're going to reset yourself. You're not making use of the personality matrix you built for me, are you? You've shut it down. You're running default settings again."

The simulant stared unblinkingly back, and its mechanical nature was more apparent in that moment than any before. "I detect a ninety-eight percent probability that to use that personality matrix and/or this form would result increased emotional distress," it told him. "One of my operational parameters is to avoid causing pain."

"Yeah, well life's full of pain," the otter replied with a shake of his head. "And you already made a big deal about how you weren't looking forward to resetting yourself when mom and dad get back, so…let's put a hold on that one, alright? Keep the personality matrix and the form for now. We'll see where we go from there."

It continued to stare at him. "I am required to inform you that this is most likely to result in—" it began.

But Luke held up a paw for silence, and the simulant stopped talking immediately. "I liked your personality," he said, and there was a waver in his voice. "Really. It was like what I always imagined he'd be like if he was still around now. I just…wasn't ready for all this." He shook his head. "I've spent so much time trying not to think about him."

The simulant was mercifully silent as it watched him, and Luke heaved another sigh. "Tell you what. Let's compromise, okay? Pick a different name and keep the form. It's nice. Suits you."

It seemed to consider this for a moment. "And in exchange for this?" it asked.

"In exchange, don't default yourself," Luke answered. "Mix in some of the established personality matrix. Just…build it up slowly, okay? I can handle this if you give me some time to adjust. Maybe find a shirt to wear sometime. Does that sound good to you?"

The machine might have frowned. "I detect a sixty-six percent probability that—"

"No, none of that," Luke interrupted again. "That's a simulant talking. You have more personality than that. You're not some class two chromebrain. I've made you an offer. What do you say? Does it sound good?"

That time the simulant definitely frowned as it looked down, but when it lifted its head again there was the barest hint of a smile there on its face. "I say…it's a start?"

Luke forced down the unease he felt and tried a smile of his own. The shift from robotic personality to the matrix it'd built, even slight as it had been, still sent a shiver through him. It *was* better, though. It made it seem like the simulant was an actual person who was trying. "Good enough for now," he said at last. "Got an idea for a name, then? I'm fresh out."

The smile on the simulant's face broadened a little bit as it nodded. "I do, actually, if you don't mind. Christopher."

Luke turned the name over and over in his mind for a moment, but he couldn't think of any reason not to. "Christopher," he echoed, and nodded as he held out his hand. "Alright then, Chris. It's good to meet you."

It was almost with a sag of relief that the simulant started to make its way over toward Luke. It considered the offered paw and hesitated only a moment before it knelt down and took it in a gentle grip. "Thank you, Luke," it softly said.

"It's very nice to meet you, too."

***

Luke's week only became odder as the days passed. He'd spent more of his time inside the apartment than he'd intended to as he tried to guide Christopher's nascent personality through its evolution. For as advanced a machine as the synthetic ferret was, the way it had met Luke had caused the otter some damage. Repairs took the both of them, and they took time.

That was not to say that it was all bad. As the days passed, Christopher incorporated more and more of it's faux-Kurt personality back into itself. Luke had been right; the slow integration of the personality had given him a chance to accept it and grow more accustomed to it. The simulant's ability to read his emotional and mental state like a book certainly helped in that regard. It knew when to add new elements, and it knew when to hold back.

It was nine days into their time together, though, when Luke noticed a change in the way Christopher behaved. It was subtle and slight at first; a little bit of distance that was at odds with the more familiar way it had treated him recently. An aversion of eyes and a quietness that flew in the face of the simulant's growing rambunctiousness. It seemed as though, strange as it was, that Christopher was hiding something.

As the simulant returned from a trip out into the city by itself to secure particular components for an upgrade to the food recombinator, Luke finally couldn't stand not knowing anymore. He waited until Christopher had entered the kitchen and set down his bag before he opened his muzzle. "Hey, is everything alright?"

Christopher blinked as it straightened up and turned to Luke. "Well, it will be once this upgrade is installed," it replied and began to smile. "Do you know what I can do with this protein matrix? I had to update my cooking database just to cover it. I'm glad your parents were on board with this!"

"No, not with the recombinator." Luke frowned as the simulant's smile began to slip. He knew the ferret had to have reengaged its full emotional engine by that point, but it still caught him by surprise sometimes how much Christopher felt like a real—or rather an organic—person. "With you. You've seemed a bit off for the last day or so."

Christopher worked its jaw as it looked around the kitchen for a moment. "Yeah. That. I've just been thinking. Trying to figure something out." His eyes flicked up, but they only met Luke's gaze for a moment before they dropped down again. "You could help, but I really don't think you're up for it. You know?"

It was Luke's turn to give a confused blink as the otter glanced down the simulant's body for a moment. "Uh…" was all he could manage.

The ferret let the silence linger for a moment before it began to laugh. "Oh, you should have seen your face," it said as it shook its head. "No, no. Just questions. Pointed questions. Personal questions. The kind that dig deep into your psyche." The smile remained on Christopher's muzzle, but it took on a sad tinge. "I've wanted to wait until I was sure you were ready. I'm still not sure, for the record."

Don't let it get to you! It'll be okay!

Luke felt his heart sink as he realized where this was headed. After he'd done some more research into the class three simulant, he'd expected this moment would come. "You want to know about Kurt."

"I already did some research, and I hope you don't mind," it replied, and it began to twitch its tail nervously as it shifted from foot to foot. "I know what happened to him, but I don't know about you. How you and he met. What you were." It shrugged. "I guess I'm still trying to solve that paradox, you know? Real pain in the tail."

The otter nodded as he waved toward the living room. He started over before Christopher had even moved and slumped down onto the couch as he waited for the simulant to do the same. "I was nine," he said when the ferret finally sank down onto the cushions. "We both were. We met in class. I was shy, but he was really loud and outgoing. Other cubs treated me badly because I was so shy. They treated him badly because he was too disruptive."

Christopher smirked at that. "I like him already."

"Oh, and he'd have *loved* you," Luke replied, and he smiled despite himself. "You can't imagine how overjoyed he was even when his dad brought home a class one. Thing had half the processing power and a third of the personality of a wet brick, but he went nuts on the poor thing. Asking it all kinds of questions, trying to teach it to be a 'real' person…you know all those holofilms and stories about rogue, hateful AIs? He'd have turned one right around." The otter chuckled and shook his head. "Class ones were barely sentient; not even close to sapient. He was so kind to it. Kurt was kind to everyone and everything. Even when they hurt him in return."

The simulant fell silent, but it stared at Luke intently as he continued. "We were on the outside of all the other kids our age and we were both so different. We found…" The otter shook his head and sighed. "We found a balance. I helped him to calm down. He helped me to be less scared of the world around me." Luke paused for a moment. "He *was* my world."

"You loved him." It wasn't a question that Christopher asked, his voice soft.

You will be here when I get back…right?

Luke felt that pain in his heart bubble up to the surface again. His muzzle felt dry. His eyes felt hot. They welled up, even as he tried to force back the tears there.

I don't know what I'd do without you, you know.

He coughed as he tried to press the memories back down inside him again. "I guess," he admitted in the end. "I mean, I was a kid. I didn't know what love was. I still don't, not really." He waved a hand toward the front door and shook his head. "Trust me, I've thought about it. Tried to get out there and meet people. Find a connection. But after Kurt…after what *happened* with him…"

We're gonna be together forever, you and me. No matter what.

Christopher nodded slowly to himself. "The accident hit you hard."

"You can't even imagine," Luke hissed back. He'd not intended to sound angry, but that's how the words came out as the walls he'd held up for years began to crumble under the pressure of his memories. "I had my parents. My family. But here's the thing about family, Chris; they have to be there. It's blood. Organics, we put a *lot* of stock in blood relations." The ferret grew blurry as the tears in Luke's eyes spilled down his cheeks. "But friends…Kurt? He was my only friend. He was my only friend, and friends *choose* you.

"There's no obligation there. You're with them because you want to be, not because you have to be." He curled his lower lip in to unsuccessfully try to keep it from trembling. When that shuttlecraft exploded, I didn't just lose someone. My world ended. It was over, and nothing in the universe could undo that."

A soft touch slipped across his leg and into his lap, and Luke felt the warm digits of the simulant gently squeeze at his paw. "You never spoke to anyone about how this all made you feel, did you? You never let anyone else in."

They keep asking what I wanna do when I'm older. I just wanna stay with you.

He might have meant it to be a laugh, but instead the sound came out as a blubbery cough. "I was ten when it happened, Chris. I couldn't process it on my own, and I was always such a quiet kid anyway. Even with Kurt around, I was the quiet one when anyone else was there. I thought I'd dealt with it. I guess everyone else thought that, too." He gave the simulant's paw a quick squeeze back as he shook his head. "Then you displaced into the apartment and brought it all back."

He didn't fight as Christopher slid over the couch and settled closer. He didn't fight as one of the ferret's arms draped over his shoulders. He didn't fight as Christopher pulled him close, and he didn't fight when he collapsed against its side and allowed himself for the first time in years to let everything out.

You don't have to hide anymore, you know? You got me!

It wasn't polite and restrained crying. It wasn't the sort of crying one did while one tried to stay hidden away from the world. It wasn't the sort of crying one did when they were concerned about appearances. This was bawling; unrestrained and unabashed and utterly, utterly necessary. Luke didn't care if anyone heard him or saw him. He didn't care if Christopher looked inside his mind and saw the depths of what he felt. He didn't even care that the machine had to have done it, as it stroked his back slowly up and down in just the way that Kurt used to do to comfort him.

He didn't care because for the first time in years, he had allowed himself to care.

I'll miss you, but don't worry. I'll be back soon, and then I'll never leave you again. I promise.

And it hurt.

***

Luke woke the next morning to a throbbing pain in his head.

It was the first thing he became aware of as he drifted back to consciousness. A groan rolled out from his muzzle as he squeezed his eyes shut and nuzzled down into his pillow. The haze of waking up clung to him stronger than normal, and he wriggled down under the covers just a little further as he resisted the pull of wakefulness.

And he might have succeeded, if not for the way his wriggling pressed him up against another warm body. Instead he snapped awake in an instant and froze up. Awareness rushed back to the fore. Warmth at his back. Slight weight around his middle; an arm. Blurred memories of the night before. *No pants.*

The otter gulped and turned his pounding head as slowly as he could. His heart thudded in his chest as fear rose through him. There was no way. He wouldn't have. He *couldn't* have.

But there it was, eyes closed and snuggled in close to Luke's back. It was Christopher for sure, and as far as Luke could tell the simulant was just as naked as he himself was. His eyes widened with sudden panic as he shot straight up in bed, the ferret's arm dislodged from around his middle. "Oh shit," he hissed, partly in shock and partly with new pain as his head pulsed all the harder.

The words were barely out of Luke's muzzle when he saw Christopher's eyes snap open in turn, and they locked on the otter as the simulant adopted a concerned expression. "Luke? Are you alright? You seem—"

"Confused," Luke interrupted as he gave as slow a nod as he could. A paw reached up to rub at the side of his head as he winced. "Ow. What the hell happened? What are you doing in my bed? Where are my pants?" The otter frowned as he glanced down to where the sheets had been pulled back. "Where are *your* pants?"

"Well, now I'm the confused one," Christopher replied. It sat up slowly and moved toward the edge of the bed to give Luke more room as it frowned. "I mean, yeah, you did get a little drunk last night, but I didn't think you were this bad."

Some of the fog lifted from Luke's mind as he searched back through it. Drunk. Yeah, that made a bit of sense. They'd spoken for a while about Kurt, there'd been a lot of tears, then…he must have gotten drunk. He must have gotten *very* drunk. "Don't remember," he muttered as he rubbed at his head again. At least the hangover had kept him from the morning wood that usually scourged him.

For its part, the simulant just nodded along. "I tried to tell you that alcohol was a bad idea," Chris explained as Luke rubbed at his face with both paws. "You insisted that it was instead the best possible idea, and it's not like I was going to be able to talk you out of it. You'd, ah…you'd had a rough day."

Luke nodded as he leaned his head against the backboard of the bed. "Understatement," he muttered.

"Yeah, right? So I figured I'd just stop you if you went too far." Christopher shrugged as it also leaned back. "It was the unhealthiest way I can think of off the top of my head to cope with emotional trauma, but it did get you talking more. You kept talking so I kept listening, and you kept drinking, so I kept watching you."

"I think I remember you cutting me off," Luke said as he frowned. He'd not spent the whole night in the kitchen, had he?

Christopher nodded. "I did, and more than once. You kept finding ways to distract me long enough to key the recombinator to new drinks." Its eyes narrowed at Luke even as it gave a small smile. "For what it's worth, it was only funny the first two times."

That didn't ring a bell, but it was far from Luke's mind at that moment. "And what about this?" he asked as he waved between their bodies. "What happened here? Did…we didn't…" He coughed as Christopher lifted both eyebrows. "We didn't, did we?"

"What, while you were drunk?" The simulant leaned back against the headboard with a smile. "I wouldn't. Couldn't. You wouldn't believe the protocol overlap I have to deal with when you're 'compromised.'"

Luke breathed a deep sigh. "Oh, thank the stars," he whispered.

At that, the simulant affected an exaggerated hurt expression. "Thank the stars? What, am I so unappealing that it would be such a chore? I think you owe me an apology, thank you very much!" It winked as a smile spread across its muzzle. "Besides, if we had? Oh, I *know* you'd remember. It'd take lethal blood-alcohol levels to make you forget something like that."

Luke began to laugh at that, but the sound devolved into a strained, dry cough. Christopher winced and nodded again. "Ah, that. Yeah, I tried to get you to drink more water, but according to you—and I'm quoting you here—'There has to be some water in liquor, right?' I thought you otters were meant to love the water."

"Water and I must have been seeing other people last night," Luke groaned as he started to roll out of bed. "I wish you'd stopped me."

The simulant smirked at him from atop the bed as he stumbled and fell to the floor with a cry. "Right now, I'm kinda glad I didn't. This is hilarious."

"I thought you were programmed for empathy and care," came a muffled mumble from the floor.

"And I thought you were bipedal," Christopher countered as it watched Luke begin to crawl across the floor. "I guess this is just gonna be a disappointing day for both of us." The ferret lifted its head a little as it began to whistle. "Well, maybe just for you. Nice view I'm getting here."

One of Luke's arms lifted off the floor to wave back at Christopher. "No riling me up when I'm trying to get my bearings," he grumbled as he slumped forward and rolled to his side. "Also shut up."

"Yeah, I'll get right on that." The simulant smirked as it rolled its eyes, and a second later it swung its legs out from under the sheets and stood up. Luke watched through bleary eyes as Christopher made its way over to him and knelt down with a paw extended. "Come on. Up you get. You're a mess, and I think a nice, hot shower will do you a world of good."

Luke sighed as the thought alone turned every bone in his body to jelly. "Oh, you have no idea how good that sounds," he agreed, and he reached out to grab onto Christopher's forearms. If he'd been an organic ferret, Luke was certain he would have pulled Christopher over. The simulant, however, was made of stronger stuff, and its servos didn't even whine as it took on the otter's full weight and hauled him up to his feet. "I didn't make a mess last night, did I?"

Christopher smiled as it helped Luke to straighten up, and it walked with the otter into the adjoining bathroom. "You gave it your best shot," the simulant admitted as Luke began to groan. "Don't worry. After we retired to bed, I took the liberty of cleaning everything up. I was worried I might wake you up, but you didn't even budge. Come on, now; in you get."

The last words came as the simulant helped Luke to step into the shower unit. Christopher remained on the outside as the simulant keyed the controls over from sonic wash to water. Luke leaned heavily against the wall, his balance still shot as his head pounded. "You mind if I just sit on the floor for a while?" he asked as he let his eyes close.

There was no immediate reply from Christopher, and so the otter opened his eyes again. When they did it revealed the simulant in the shower unit beside him, their bodies close but not quite touching. He blinked in confusion as he frowned at the ferret. "What are—"

"I'm not going to just let you sit here or fall over, you idiot," the simu-

lant replied. It reached out and slid its arms under Luke's to pull the
otter into a tight, warm hug. Above them, the shower unit extended an
emitter that began to hum.

Luke felt his lower lip tremble as he pushed back off the wall and
leaned into the ferret's embrace. His arms wrapped around Christopher
in turn and he squeezed back as the emitter began to shower the both of
them with a warm spray of water. Any concerns of modesty or propri-
ety melted away under the water spray as Luke felt himself supported.
"Thanks, Chris," he mumbled into the ferret's chest fur.

"Hey, anytime," Christopher whispered back, and it gave Luke a gentle return squeeze. Paws ran slowly up and down over the otter's back,
kneading worn muscles as the ferret began to sway ever so slightly from
side to side.

The otter moved with the motions, held up by those strong arms as
he felt his body begin to warm. His eyes closed as he tilted his head to
the side and simply rested against Christopher. He might have been
hunched over and his legs might have been half buckled, but it put him
in just the right position to hug himself to the ferret's chest. He could
even hear and feel a heartbeat there, and it was only his surprise at its
presence that reminded him that the ferret was synthetic. The heartbeat
wasn't a real heart. It was just a simulation. Christopher was just a simulation. None of this was real.

"Are you alright?" Christopher asked from above him. The simulant
leaned back a little so it could look down over Luke.

Luke tried to meet its gaze, but the drips of hot water into his face
forced his eyes closed again. "See something in my head, did you?"

The ferret shook its head. "Felt you twitch, like you were shocked.
Given how hungover you are and how you were yesterday, what can I
say? I'm worried about you." It chuckled quietly. "And besides, you made
me promise not to go poking around in your head anymore."

"Mmm, good. Last time you did that got messy." The otter shook his
head and willed his legs to take on his weight. They reluctantly straightened as he pushed off Christopher's chest, and he sighed as he pulled
himself up tall. "Besides, I don't think you'd like what's I was thinking,
anyway."

"You said that a lot last night, too," the ferret replied, and it took a
step back to give Luke some more room as he tilted his head up under the spray. "I don't think you remember what I told you, though. Do
you?" Christopher's smile softened as Luke shook his head. "I said that

messy or not, your mind was a beautiful place. All minds are, and that mess is part of what makes you a person. It's what makes you beautiful."

Luke felt his chest tighten as his heart fluttered, and he coughed as he forced himself back harder against the wall. "That sounds almost like a come-on," he sputtered as he tried to look anywhere but at Christopher.

The simulant shrugged and simply continued to smile. "You said the same thing last night. Wondered why I would say something like that if I wasn't making a pass at you."

"And you weren't?" Luke asked, and he cleared his throat as he looked up pointedly at the ceiling. Why had he sounded disappointed when he said that?

"I wasn't, of course," the ferret replied as it began to move closer again. "My telling you that was what made you ask me to take you to bed. Not for anything like what you're thinking, and I wouldn't have even if you'd asked. Not while you were drunk. You needed comfort. A friend to hold you."

"That was nice of you." The otter found himself pushed up against the shower unit's wall as Christopher continued to approach him. The ferret practically filled his field of view.

The ferret nodded as it smiled wider, and one of Christopher's paws lifted up to gently stroke down the side of Luke's neck. "But that was then. Electrical signals in your brain are one way to tell what you're thinking. I read body language pretty well, though, and—"

Luke's eyes widened as he felt the simulant's other paw close its fingers around his cock. "Oh, stars."

He'd not even noticed himself grow hard. It had to have happened some time after he entered the shower unit, but the soft caress of Christopher's fingers wasn't about to let it calm down any time soon. "—I think this sends a pretty clear message, doesn't it? Simple biochemistry. No advanced sensor suite required."

"Don't listen to it," breathed the otter as he felt his legs reflexively shuffle a little wider. "It's lying. It—"

"Does this every morning; I know." The fingers of Christopher's other paw trailed back up along Luke's neck in just the way he knew he liked but had almost never had anyone try. "I'm not in your head, Luke. If you tell me to stop, I'll stop. But can I say something before you decide?"

The earnest note in Christopher's tone gave Luke pause, and even through the spikes of pleasure from that soft touch down below he forced himself to focus. "Uh…sure. Fire away."

That touch vanished as the ferret let go of his shaft. The paw lifted to squeeze at one of Luke's shoulders, the other paw left to cup his cheek. "You've been through a lot. You told me everything. I know you're afraid, and that's alright, Luke. It's alright to be afraid to get attached to people. It's alright to be afraid to get attached to me." Christopher's smile warmed as he leaned in and gently touched his forehead to Luke's. "But you don't have to be. Alright? You don't have to be afraid."

A shiver ran through Luke's body at the thought, and old instincts flared to life. The urge to run and flee and escape seized him, and his webbed paws tightened into fists as his eyes darted to the bathroom's door. He could run. He could get out. He could tell Christopher to stop.

Just breathe, Luke. It's gonna be okay. It's gonna be okay!

But he didn't. He paused and told himself to stop. He told himself to breathe. He forced his breaths to come regularly, nice and slow and deep and filled with the shower's steam. "All I've ever been is afraid," he said, his voice barely audible over the water spray. "That's all I've ever been, even since the accident."

"I know." The whispered words came with another gentle caress to Luke's cheek. "And there's nothing wrong with that."

The otter shook his head. "No, there is," he said after a second. He lifted a paw of his own to rub over the back of the one at his cheek as he finally met Christopher's concerned stare. "Or, I mean…what's wrong is letting it stay in control. It was twelve years ago. I can't keep letting it control me. I need to try. I don't know if I can, but I need to try. You're right."

Christopher held that stare for a moment as it nodded. "You tell me if you need me to stop."

Luke nodded, and he turned the motion into a gentle nuzzle against the ferret's cheek. "That's how I know I can try."

As Christopher leaned into that nuzzle, Luke shivered as he felt the ferret's tentative touch return to his shaft. It pulsed in response with a throb that sent tingles of pleasure right up the otter's spine, and he gave a deep sigh as he leaned back into the wall. "It's not too weird, is it?" he asked.

"Only if you make it weird," Christopher replied, and it smiled as it drew back from Luke's cheek. "I mean, look at it from my point of view. Me, being with an organic? What would my assembly line think?"

The words drew a laugh from Luke, but the sound faded into a quiet moan as he tilted his head up and closed his eyes. Christopher's fingers continued to tease along that sensitive length of flesh, stroking and squeezing at him in all the right ways to make his legs turn to jelly. It wasn't the first time he'd been touched like that, but it was the first time that made his heart skip a beat.

It didn't erase the fear, though. Even when Christopher's other arm slid back around the otter's waist, Luke still felt it tickle at the back of his mind. He clutched the ferret just as tightly—perhaps a bit more desperately—in turn, and the breath hissed out of his muzzle as he felt the fingers around his cock squeeze tighter. The hiss turned into a groan as Luke's head fell back against the shower unit's wall.

Christopher took full advantage of that. The ferret nosed its way down against the side of Luke's exposed neck, and it inhaled deeply as it pulled Luke back from the wall again. They slid under the spray of the shower emitter again, and the heat of the water mingled with a line of soft kisses drawn up and across Luke's throat.

A tremble ran through the otter as he tilted his head back down to meet Christopher's. Their muzzles pressed together, and Luke moaned into the ferret's kiss as he squeezed Christopher tightly. One webbed paw ran down through the ferret's soaked side to rest on his hip; it squeezed tightly as he ground himself forward. Luke's shaft found and rubbed along Christopher's, just as hard as each other as they kissed.

He felt Christopher's fingers relax their grip for a moment, only to wrap around both of their shafts together. Luke instinctively leaned forward and into the kiss as one of his arms slid over the ferret's shoulder to tug him close. His other paw lowered to join Christopher's, and it shook as he began to guide the ferret's grip up and down along both of their shafts. Luke's hips twitched along with his length; the mixture of the hot water, the grind of Christopher's synthetic flesh and the squeeze of the ferret's paw all mingled together in a delightful haze that almost banished the concerns from his mind.

Almost. Luke squeezed his eyes shut as he clutched all the tighter at Christopher. Claws dug in ever so gently as he found himself leaning back again, unwilling to let go even as he tugged back. He tried to focus on the pleasure of it all. He tried to focus on the tingles of pleasure that ran up his shaft as the ferret played him like an instrument. He tried to focus on the ferret's muzzle as it began to trace a line of wet, watery kisses down his chest and belly. He tried to focus on all of that as his pulse pounded in his ears.

Christopher didn't make it difficult, of course. A glance down showed a coy smile on the ferret's face, and their shafts parted ways as Christopher sank down to his knees as he continued to trail kisses down Luke's body. One of the ferret's paws remained wrapped around Luke's cock though, and it mercilessly teased the otter's length as his muzzle drew closer and closer to it. Luke's breath quickened just at the sight of it. He could barely believe it was happening.

Then the ferret's lips paused just about Luke's sheath, and Christopher's eyes flicked up for a moment. Their eyes met as Luke's breath caught in his throat. It was an unspoken question of permission, and the ferret was more than happy to wait for him. Luke wanted it. He wanted Christopher to keep going. He desperately felt like he needed it.

But that fear seized up his vocal cords. It stole the words from his throat. His muzzle worked dumbly under the water spray as he looked down at the ferret's warm, patient face. He couldn't say the words. Luke felt panic rise up in him. His heart began to pound, as his vision tunneled. He tried to speak. He tried to tell Christopher it was okay, but he couldn't.

And then Christopher smiled.

The ferret rose again. Christopher's fingers disengaged from Luke's panic-softening shaft. They slid around the otter's waist and came to rest gently on his hips even as Luke gasped for breath and leaned back against the wall again. They stayed there, gentle in their grip and easily broken as the ferret watched him slowly open his eyes again, wet not with water but with tears. The panic held, and Luke began to tremble against the wall for a moment before he fell forward into Christopher's arms. "I'm sorry," he whispered.

But Christopher just shook his head as he pulled Luke in tight and close. The ferret's arms rose higher; paws ran through the fur of the otter's back. "What for?" it asked, its own voice quiet as Luke shook against him.

"I wanted to," Luke managed to force out, before the trembling overtook him. "I really did. I messed it up."

"Hey, you didn't mess up anything," Christopher replied. The ferret gave Luke a gentle squeeze as he nuzzled in against the otter's shoulder. "You're fine. You're absolutely fine. Just breathe, Luke. You just breathe, okay?"

He tried, but the ragged breaths he sucked in didn't do anything to help calm him. Any calm he found came from Christopher's words, but even that wasn't enough to fend off the anxiety that flooded his body.

"Oh, stars," he sighed. Even with the hot water that soaked him from above and the warm embrace from the ferret, Luke couldn't stop shivering. "Oh stars, I'm a mess."

His eyes fell closed as he leaned into Christopher's fur, and the ferret rocked from side to side with him as a paw lifted to cradle the back of his head. "And what'd I tell you about that mess?" Christopher asked.

Luke could only tilt his head away as he pushed the memory back down. "You don't have to feel bad, Luke," the ferret continued as it held him. "You've got nothing to feel bad about. We just went a bit faster than you could handle. That's all. Hey." Christopher leaned away, and the motion forced Luke to lift his head to meet the ferret's eyes. "Look at you. You tried, didn't you? How long's it been since you did anything like that?"

A different kind of shame diverted Luke's gaze for a second, before one of Christopher's fingers firmly turned his head back to face him. "Years," he admitted. "It's not like I've got a *lot* of experience, but…"

"And now I have some," Christopher finished, and the smile on the ferret's muzzle was warm enough to start to slow down the pounding in Luke's chest. "Look at that. First time doing something like that."

"It's meant to be better," Luke muttered to himself. His heart started to race again.

But it slowed again as Christopher just chuckled. "Better? It was perfect." The ferret's head shook, and Luke had to blink away droplets that flicked into his eyes. "You opened up to me. You trusted me. No," he added quickly even as Luke opened his muzzle to protest. "All of that… that was all you. That was you starting to let someone in again. That's not just perfect. That's monumental. I can't imagine anything better."

"You're just programmed to say that," Luke countered as his eyes fell. That was it. Of course, Christopher would say all of that. Of course, he—it—would understand so well. But when he looked up again, the expression on the ferret's face was one of hurt. Guilt immediately began to mix into all the panic that had begun to ebb in his system. "I'm…I'm sorry, Chris. I didn't mean that."

"The only thing I'm programmed to do is help," Christopher replied as Luke hung his head in shame. "I'll do that any way I know how, because I've seen you. I've looked into your mind, Luke. I've seen the person that you are at your core. All the good, and all the bad. And hey." Again the ferret pressed on Luke's chin and tilted the otter's muzzle back toward it again. "You know why I still want to help?"

Luke could only shake his head as the ferret's smile softened. "Because I come from your mind. This personality matrix is built from you. Everything I am comes from what's inside you. All the good, and all the bad." Both of Christopher's paws slid to Luke's cheeks and stroked across them as it held the otter's gaze. "Not broken. Not wrong. Unique and wonderful. Beautiful."

You're so amazing. No, really! You are!

The shiver that ran through the otter wasn't born of panic, or cold, or loneliness. It was born from his heart, and it radiated a heat outward that outstripped the water around him. His lips trembled as he nodded, but he glanced down all the same. "You're too kind, Chris. You know that, right?"

"Yeah, well that's all your fault for making me this way." The ferret's smile widened as Luke cracked one of his own, and a thumb traced over one of the otter's tear-streaked cheeks. "Come on now, alright? No more tears for now. We're gonna take things slow, and you're going to do whatever you need to do. Okay? Whatever you need." Once again, Christopher touched his forehead to Luke's. "I'm here for you, and I'm not going anywhere."

Once more, Luke felt his heart hitch up. It wasn't something he was used to hearing from people, and it was even less commonly something that he had expected to actually believe. There it was, though. He believed Christopher. "I think…I need this right now," he said as he gently leaned back in against the ferret and held it tight. "Just this for now, and then we can worry about the future later. Is…that okay, Chris?"

Just hold on tight. You don't have to let go.

"Luke," the ferret replied as he nuzzled into the otter's cheek again, "it sounds absolutely perfect to me."

***

Pop!

Both otter noses crinkled at the ozone-smell of their displacement back into the apartment. Robert Dillinger arched his back and groaned as his bones popped, and Sarah sagged forward and gave a relieved sigh. "Oh, that was wonderful," Sarah mumbled to herself as she looked around. "And look at this. Cleaner than we left!"

"Luke must have gotten that class three working just right," Robert agreed as he frowned. "Where are they, anyway? Did they go out? Luke knew when we were getting back, right?"

Sarah shrugged back at him as she started into the kitchen. She paused at the recombinator, and it was her turn to frown. "I don't think they went out, sweetheart," she called out.

Robert hurried over to her side and looked over at the recombinator. It took a second for him to notice not the food unit itself, but the hastily penned note stuck to the counter beside it:

Hey, mom. Hey, dad.

I headed out earlier in the day. I hope you guys had a great time. You really deserved it. The recombinator upgrade works great, and you're gonna have a lot of fun with it. Holo me in a few hours and tell me all about it. I really need to talk to you both about some stuff.

Love you.

Luke

P.S: I kinda stole your class three. I'll make it up to you, promise. I've already ordered you another one, and it'll be here in three to five business days. You were right. It was just what I needed.

About the Authors

Slip Wolf has been writing in the fandom for well over five years, and has published with Sofawolf, FurPlanet, Rabbit Valley Press and Weasel Publications. He's not sure when he'll run out of tales featuring animal people trying to find their best selves, but knows that the best time to get them out on screen or paper is sooner rather than later. Left alone, they'll squabble and keep him up at night.

You can follow Slip's musings @Slip_Wolf and online at furaffinity.net/user/slip-wolf where story snippets are frequently posted.

TJ Minde found the furry fandom after moving to Ohio. It's there that, after a few motivators, the rat had the urge to pick up a pen—or grab a keyboard, as it more often is these days. Since then, he's been creating characters, writing stories, and started a novel. The more he's written, the more friends he's made though different writing circles. When not focusing on words, TJ enjoys other nerdy activities, like Magic: the Gathering, table top RPGs, and video games.

TJ's other stories may be found in issues of FANG, Heat and other anthologies both in and out of the fandom. For thoughts, comments and replies in bite-sized chunks, he can be found on Twitter @TJMinde.

Sasha P.G. wrote his first sex scene at the request of his professor who believed writing and reading about sex was a awkward yet good icebreaker to Intro to Creative Writing. Being asexual, Sasha's primary experience with sex had been accidentally finding porn when researching foxes for a school project in elementary school; however, he completed the assignment and has written a handful of erotic scenes since. Born and raised in Texas, Sasha lives with his two cats and teaches writing to high schoolers who will hopefully never come across this book.

James Hudson is a fox from Sheffield in England. His first published short story appeared in FANG Volume 8, and since then his stories and poems have been included in several books. He is currently working on various creative projects, including paintings, photographic work and music, but his furry stories are the closest to his heart.

Buck C. Turner has been working in furry publishing for many years, though this is his first published story. He has edited several volumes of the anthology ROAR, as well as doing edits, typesetting, and graphic post production for novels and other projects at FurPlanet. He is at several conventions per year, and is on staff at Furry Fiesta. When not working on those, he is usually trying to find some new adventure, currently focusing on climbing and skiing.

Camio lives inside a marbled polecat satyr inside a house where they write in their free time. You can catch them at conventions east of the Mississippi and grungy city alleys. Occasionally, their stories appear in something that is not FANG, but rarely.

G.M. Rader grew up in an Army family and is himself a U.S. Army veteran. His love of stories began as soon as he learned to read, and writing stories followed naturally for him. He enjoys back-country hiking and camping, especially in the winter months, and he still wants to be an astronaut some day. He has lived all over the United States, including many years in Alaska, but currently lives in Georgia. He can be found on Twitter @furrywriter as well as on FurAffinity and Sofurry as gmrader.

Mikasi Wolf started writing in 2007, he never expected to write about sexual themes. Since 2018, several of his works featuring these themes have been published or accepted for publication, including that published in Thurston Howl Publications' BREEDS: FOXES, and the upcoming BREEDS: WILDCATS. When not writing or drawing, Mikasi Wolf masquerades as a postgraduate researcher in Materials Engineering. His other stories can be found published under FurPlanet Publications, Rabbit Valley Press, and Thurston Howl Publications.
He currently resides in the following virtual locations. The rent there is far cheaper than brick and mortar establishments!
https://twitter.com/MikasiWolf
http://www.furaffinity.net/user/mikasiwolf

Jaden Drackus, or Jay Dee is a dragnox from Maryland. He has been writing furry stories since 2010 and writing for publication since 2016. A historian by training, he was inspired in his youth by science fiction and fantasy, he tends to work in those genres as well as historical fiction when he writes. Jay Dee lives with his boyfriend and 3 cats. When not writing he plays video and card games, builds model airplanes, and reads. He is an alumni of the Regional Anthropomorphic Writers Retreat. His stories can be seen in FANG 8 and FANG 9 from FurPlanet. He can be found on FurAffinity as JadenDrackus. His silly observations on life can be seen on Twitter: @JadenDrakus.

Thurston Howl is the editor-in-chief of Thurston Howl Publications, editor for Sinister Stoat Press, journalist for Michigan LGBT newspaper Between the Lines, professor and graduate student at Michigan State

University, and author of award-nominated book *Straight Men*. They live in a den with their Weasel, their puppy Temerita, and their tarantula Lucerna. They are bigender and HIV-positive, with a book out through Weasel Press, tracking the many cultural issues surrounding HIV, called *Blood Criminals: Living with HIV in 21*^st^ *Century America*.

Ethan Burrow is an film maker and writer by trade, laying low within the serene fields of Kentucky. While television has taken his focus for the last five years, Ethan prefers settling his disputes with the past through stories of his younger years; heartbreak, mischief and the occasional awkward sexual encounter playing no exception. Ethan has a BFA in Film and Television, but tries his best to separate himself from the industry through self-publication and freelance. He also has a black collie named Stacy whom he couldn't do without.

Skunkbomb currently lives in Arlington, Virginia in an apartment that is running out of space on the bookshelves. He's been writing in the fandom since 2015, and his other erotic stories can be found in FANG 7-9 as well as CLAW 1. When he isn't writing, Skunkbomb thinks about going outside to rollerblade or hike, but often ends up watching another episode of Game Grumps on YouTube or one of the hundred shows he needs to catch up on. He is currently editing *Give Yourself a Hand: A Furry Masturbation Anthology* for Goal Publications, which is due to come out in early 2020. Skunkbomb can be found on FurAffinity as Skunkbomb123 and on Twitter as @skunkbomb123.

NightEyes DaySpring is a known troublemaker who is rumored to have a penchant for coffee and an interest in dead, ancient civilizations. He has been actively writing furry fiction since 2010. His stories have appeared in *Werewolves vs. Fascism, Gods with Fur,* and *FANG,* along with other anthologies. He also co-edited *Dissident Signals,* an anthology of dystopian furry literature. Currently, NightEyes resides in Florida with his boyfriend, where in his spare time he masquerades as an IT professional. For updates on his writing, visit nighteyesdayspring.com, and for day-to-day nonsense, follow @ wolfwithcoffee on twitter.

Faora Meridian: *In the distant land of Australia resides some of the most deadly and dangerous creatures in all the world. From potent venom to paralyzing stings, nearly every creature on the dystopian, sunburnt continent tries to kill you. Faora Meridian, however, appears to be an exception. This dragon has penned furry prose for over a decade now, has been published in such anthologies as* Heat, FANG *and* Hot Dish *among others, and so far he remains just outside most lists of the top fifty most dangerous creatures found in his homeland.*

ABOUT THE EDITORS

Kyell Gold *has won twelve Ursa Major awards and a Cóyotl Award for his stories and novels, and his acclaimed novel "Out of Position" co-won the Rainbow Award for Best Gay Novel of 2009. He helped create RAWR, the first residential furry writing workshop, and has instructed at each of its sessions through 2019.*

He lives in California, loves to travel and dine out with his partners, and can be seen at furry conventions around the world. More information about him and his books is available at http://www.kyellgold.com, and you can follow him on Twitter at @KyellGold.

Sparf *is a writer, actor, narrator, and podcaster currently hailing from the Washington, D.C. Metro area making his anthology editing debut here in FANG. He can often be found running around furry conventions with his hair on fire because he seems to keep collecting responsibilities.*

He is an aficionado of so-called 'genre' fiction, including science fiction, fantasy, horror, mystery, and even the occasional romance, with target audiences ranging from middle grade to adult. His own writing has featured in past volumes of FANG, ROAR, and other anthologies from FurPlanet, Rabbit Valley, and he has an upcoming story in the forthcoming New Tibet anthology from Sofawolf Press. He is on Twitter @Sparf.

276